MYSTERY LOVER

Michael reached out and captured her wrist. Slowly pulling Kate to his chest, he used his other hand to remove her wineglass and set it on the table next to his own. Tilting her face up to his, he whispered, "You have the most beautiful eyes I've ever seen," just before he brought his mouth down on hers.

His lips grazed hers with an unbelievable tenderness, searching, exploring, and Kate felt a small moan escape from the back of her throat. Unconsciously, she pressed into him, for her legs felt too weak to support her. As if sensing her unsteadiness, Michael brought both his arms around her, crushing her to his chest. His lips became more demanding, seeking the same response from her.

Kate gave it. Instinct drove her, and she was overwhelmed by the most primitive of feelings. Freeing her arms, she raised them to his shoulders and weaved her fingers through the blond silk of his hair. At her touch, the kiss deepened, driving them both to an unforgettable spiral of passion . . .

TIME-KISSED DESTINY

CONSTANCE O'DAY-FLANNERY

ZEBRA BOOKS
KENSINGTON PUBLISHING CORP.

ZEBRA BOOKS

are published by

Kensington Publishing Corp.
475 Park Avenue South
New York, NY 10016

Fourth printing: August, 1990

Printed in the United States of America

TO MY MOTHER, Ann O'Day—who taught me to love the written word.

ACKNOWLEDGMENT
AND SPECIAL THANKS

Hilari Cohen and Leslie Gelbman—for turning a Cajun lunch into inspiration.

and

THE LADIES OF THE CLUB: Colleen Quinn Bosler, Barbara Bretton, Linda Cajio, and Luanne Walden—who willingly ransom their royalties to Ma Bell, and keep me laughing. And always, Dale Fountain, my dearest friend—who provides me with a balance.

Chapter 1

Bermuda, 1987

It was supposed to be her time. *Her time,* her friends and relatives had proclaimed—to live, to enjoy life. She deserved it, they had murmured comfortingly. She had been a good daughter.

Looking about the lovely room, Kate Walker shook her head. They hadn't known her mother, not really, she thought as she made her way to the balcony overlooking Bermuda's Hamilton Harbour. Leslie Walker had been one hell of a woman, before her stroke, and even after. Gazing out to the lush scenery before her, Kate couldn't help experiencing a rush of relief. She was out of it . . . all of it . . . for two glorious weeks. In the three months since her mother's funeral, she'd listened to consolation, advice, and had even had to put up with her ex-husband's frequent calls. But not now . . . not now.

Her well-meaning friends had been right about one thing though—this *was* going to be her time.

Taking a deep breath, she watched a sleek sailboat join the scores moored in the remarkably blue water and thought of her mother. Unconsciously, a smile played at her lips. It hadn't been easy, juggling a full-time job and caring for an invalid, but Kate had managed, somehow, for over a year and a half. Nor had it been unusual for her to arrive home from work, relieve her aunt, and spend the rest of the evening listening to her mother's halting voice telling her of her past. More often than not, she would berate Kate for staying by her side.

"You should get out more, Katie. Live," she had once whispered. The memory of that conversation came back with a sharp clarity, for it was something she'd played back in her mind many times. Still staring at the harbor, the expensive boats blurred as she once again heard her mother's slow quiet voice . . . "Do you remember when you would spend two weeks, every summer, with Grandmom? Do you know what I did? It was my time, Kate. You were too young to remember when your father walked out, but I did—for years. There was a loneliness, a sort of vacuum, and I had to find a way to fill it. So every summer, I took two weeks off from the accounting department, two weeks off from being your mother, and I lived. A fling, you'd probably call it. I just remember those times as being so special. Every year—two weeks I could call my own, and answer to no one, but myself. Promise me, Kathleen Anne Walker," she had haltingly whispered, "when this is all over . . . promise me you'll have your time. *Live,* Katie. Do it for me. Do it for yourself."

Refocusing her eyes on the boats, Kate blinked several times and automatically brought her fingers up to brush away the tears from her cheeks. She was determined. Walking back into the room she had rented in the old manor house, Kathleen Anne Walker made up her mind that three months of preparation for this trip would not be wasted.

"I'm going to do it, Mom," she whispered aloud. "Just you watch . . ."

Charleston, South Carolina, 1868

Michael Sheridan leaned up against the stout tree trunk and stared at his brother kneeling in the garden. "Just what the hell do you mean? *Go in your place?*" Jerking his head back toward the three-storied home behind him, he demanded, "And what of the old man? You're finally prepared to go up against him?"

Kevin Sheridan, older by fifteen months, packed the rich earth around the base of the rosebush and looked up at his younger brother. "No, Michael," he said quietly. "That's why I'm asking you to go in my place." Wiping his hands on a nearby rag, Kevin stood up and gazed at his brother. It was no wonder so many women ignored Michael's brusque attitude. How many times had Kevin been forced to entertain one of Charleston's young maidens, and watched as their eyes left his and slid to Michael's rugged form? Kevin knew he himself was considered a proper catch. Yet all he wanted was to be left alone. There were too many impoverished women since the war who only thought of him as a means of surviving. He didn't blame them. He just didn't need them, or want the intrusion. Unlike Michael, something had died in him and he just didn't

11

know if he wanted it rekindled. He was a coward when it came to women . . . in truth, when it came to life. It was clear women found Michael to be more intriguing. How many dreamed of changing his roguish ways? Michael *was* life. He never gave up.

A gentle smile softened the face that, since the war, always seemed to hold a look of sadness. "We've had this conversation before, Michael. All I'm asking is that you go to this island and pretend to go through with the marriage our uncle is so intent on arranging. From what I've heard, the girl is as much against this as I am. Take her back to England—wherever she wants to go. I understand she has relatives there." He came closer to his younger brother. "Look, I know you think I'm spineless. The truth is, I just don't care anymore."

Michael cursed as he kicked at the ground with his polished boot. "Damn it all, Kevin! I can't keep fighting him alone."

"Martin doesn't even know you're fighting him now."

"Kevin, our dear uncle knows more than you think . . ."

Kevin held up his hand to stop the torrent of words he knew was coming. "Please . . . don't start again. I've listened to your arguments. I don't know if I believe you, but I've given you all the money I can spare."

"It's not enough," Michael quickly added.

Kevin shook his head. "You've gone through your inheritance; I've given you just about all of mine. What more can we do?" He watched as Michael's blue-gray eyes became a deeper blue. He took notice of the way his brother's tanned skin tone became tinged with red. Shorter by three inches, Kevin looked from his brother's sandy blond hair to his clenched fists. Poor Michael, he thought, he still has fight left in him. Why couldn't he accept defeat? Taking a deep breath, he asked the question: "How much more do you need?"

Michael squared his broad shoulders. "Sixty thousand, maybe seventy."

"What?" Kevin threw the rag to the ground and shook his head. "It's impossible. Why don't you just give it up? Surely you must realize this path of revenge is doomed."

Quickly Michael grabbed his older brother's shoulder, unconsciously digging his fingers into the white cotton shirt. "You know why. Because our father's dead! Because that bastard in there killed him. And I won't be satisfied until we regain control of Sheridan Shipping . . . and the truth comes out."

Realizing that he was hurting his brother, Michael Thomas Sheridan slowly removed his hand and stared at the man he had always looked up to, had always admired. What had happened to him? He'd asked himself that question more times than he could count over the last year. As he watched Kevin return to his precious garden, Michael tried to ignore the tight knot of anger in his chest and remember that, like all southerners, Kevin had had a bad time of it. Too many memories ran together, and Michael was tired of trying to sort them out. Only the important ones mattered.

They had both served in the War Between the States—Kevin in the infantry and Michael running the blockades. Both came home heroes, honored for their efforts. While most southerners suffered, the Sheridans seemed to come out of the war richer . . . thanks to their uncle Martin's investments. It wasn't until a few

13

months after Appomattox that the newspaper had started running the stories about the deplorable way the funds for suppliers were misused. Their father, chief supply officer for the Confederate Army, was appalled by the reports of spoiled foodstuffs, threadbare clothing, defective artillery. Soon the newspaper had started making insinuations about their father, and the public outcry was loud and clear. Never an admirer of his mother's older brother, Michael's dislike turned into full-blown hatred when Martin Masterson pointed an accusing finger at his brother-in-law and joined the opposition.

Staring at Kevin's back, Michael almost pleaded, "How can you forget? Kevin, he called our father a traitor! Helped build a case against him! Now he sits in father's study and controls our company—*our* company—with an iron fist."

Keeping his attention on the plants in front of him, Kevin whispered sadly, "It was a court order, Michael. He didn't seize control."

His patience nearing its end, Michael ground out between his teeth, "A court order issued by a judge he owns. Hell, he owns half of the Yankee politicians in Charleston." Not getting the response he had hoped for, he switched tactics. "Do you have any idea, Kevin, who this woman is he wants you to marry?"

Without looking up, his brother said, "She's the daughter of Winston Barnett, a business acquaintance in Bermuda."

"Winston Barnett," Michael said slowly, "is Martin's silent partner."

Kevin turned around. "How do you know that?" he asked suspiciously. "How do I know anything you've

14

been telling me is based on fact, and not just part of this crazy scheme to ruin Martin?"

A deadly gleam came into Michael's eyes. "If you, my dear brother, would take your hands out of the goddamned dirt and pay more attention to what's going on around you, you wouldn't have asked that!"

The two men stared at each other, their eyes locked in anger. Kevin watched his brother's deep, uneven breathing and his anger quickly dissipated. Michael hadn't changed since boyhood. He was still the bandy rooster, ready to take on anyone who challenged him. Hadn't the war taught him anything?

Seeing the anger swiftly die in his brother's eyes, Michael's shoulders sagged slightly in defeat. For a moment, just a moment, he'd thought the old Kevin might be back. *What the hell did I ever admire in him?* he wondered. Quickly, Michael knew the answer. Kevin Sheridan had the ability to adjust, to conform. He was the perfect eldest son—obedient, intelligent, ready to do his duty to family and country. Michael, on the other hand, knew from childhood he was born to rebel. Nothing came easy to him, not obedience, not his schooling, and especially not his participation in the war. However, being a blockade runner had taught him two very important things: discipline and patience. Both of those virtues were factors that would pay off now, if he were very careful. Only one more block of shares to acquire and he and Kevin would be the majority stockholders in Sheridan Shipping. Then he would go in, kick his uncle out, and gain access to the books he knew Martin had hidden.

"I want those shares, Kevin, and I'll marry this girl to get them if I have to," Michael stated forcefully. "But I intend to let everyone think I'm you. I doubt Barnett would welcome 'Michael' Sheridan into his family. Besides, once it's discovered who I am, the marriage wouldn't be legal."

"Do whatever you want, Michael," Kevin stated wearily. "You always have. I've given up trying to reason with you over the business. Just don't marry the girl in my name."

Michael stared at his brother as he returned to the extensive garden outside their home. Was there a word to define what he secretly hungered to do? How many times had he relished the daydream of killing his mother's brother? How many times had he seen in his mind's eye his uncle's face when he finally destroyed him? It was what kept him going. It was what kept him from kneeling down next to Kevin and burying his own ugly memories in the earth.

Bermuda, 1987

"We'll all dive together. Wait till you see the difference between here and South Jersey."

Kate looked up at the attractive scuba instructor and gave him a friendly smile as she zippered up her short wet suit. Keeping her balance in the small boat, she reached for her weight belt while glancing at the five other divers. This is it, she thought. This was what she had spent six weeks preparing for. Thinking about all the hours of lectures, pool training, and open-water instruction she had enjoyed in New Jersey, Kate had to control her smile. The last thing she wanted was to let on that she was a novice. And she wasn't . . . not really.

She had worked damn hard, pushing her physical and mental limits to become a certified scuba diver . . . and had a card to prove she had endured.

Trying to look as casual as possible, Kate prepared her mask, fixed the knife to her lower leg, stowed her snorkel in a safe place, and put on her fins. Looking up, her eyes met those of the instructor for this dive. Returning his smile with a little more warmth, she stood up and accepted his unspoken assistance with her breathing set. Lifting her dark brown hair up from her shoulders with one hand, she shifted her back to adjust to the weight. Once the cylinder was in place and the straps tightened, she turned around and thanked him.

She could tell by his eyes and by his smile that he was being more than polite. And that was okay by her. She had every intention of enjoying these two weeks. Holding her breathing regulator in one hand, she grasped the side of the boat with the other as it came to a slow stop.

"Are there really shipwrecks down there?" she asked, peering into the clear water that reminded her more of a pool than a cove off open sea.

He laughed. "That's what we like to publicize. In truth, you'll probably only see portions of one. After so many years, the wrecks have broken up and shifted." He watched her nod and wished she would look up at him again. She wasn't beautiful, not really. Nor was she young. He'd guess her age to be twenty-six, twenty-eight, somewhere around there. Dark brown, almost black hair framed a face that was already starting to burn in the tropical sun. It was her smile and her eyes that were startling. Her lips could form into a sensual greeting that became an invitation for more . . . but it

17

was those eyes . . . They were such a pale blue, they reminded him of two beautiful aquamarine jewels, and he'd never seen anything quite like them before. He decided that liking her hadn't had so much to do with her outward appearance, though the sight of her in her black French-cut maillot, before she'd put on the wet suit, was enough to drive his thoughts elsewhere. It was her attitude. One could almost sense her excitement, her craving for adventure. Making up his mind to get to know her better when they went back to shore, he again thought that moving from the States to Bermuda to open his own diving shop had been one of the best decisions of his life. The women were gorgeous . . . and plentiful.

It was as if she had descended into another world, filled with a quiet, serene beauty. Tiny red, blue, and yellow fish swam in schools of color, darting away from her every slow-motioned movement. She caught sight of the cute instructor, swimming about fifteen feet away from her and put her thumb and index finger together in the okay signal.

Watching him return the sign, Kate turned away to explore the reef. He was right, she thought. This was nothing like diving in the gray Atlantic. Branches of coral weaved a brilliant pattern of colors that dazzled the eye. It was a watery oasis of swarming life, and she had to remind herself to breathe normally—she was that overwhelmed by the world she had just entered. Within minutes, a slightly larger, cream-and-black-striped fish decided to explore her. Trying not to move, she patiently waited until it grew confident and approached her. Watching its mouth open and close, as if in speech, she giggled, releasing a surge of bubbles that scared it away. Following it with her eyes, Kate started to move on when she caught sight of a quick glint of something shining near the base of the reef.

Checking her depth gauge, for she didn't want to descend farther than thirty feet, she pushed off and slowly swam downward. Her fascination continued as she watched colors change. Acting as a selective filter, the water progressively absorbed the sunlight. Red was the first color to disappear, then orange. Staying close to the reef, Kate let the crystal water carry her toward the spot where she'd seen the shining object. As if on a quest, she stopped only long enough to touch the pieces of encrusted cargo laid out among the coral heads, almost as if they'd been placed there for inspection.

Her excitement grew as she discovered pieces of wood, fragments of tortiseshell, broken pottery. Quickly, she glanced around to see where the other divers were. Realizing they were too far away to signal, she had a moment of hesitation as the words of her instructor in New Jersey came back to her . . . "Never, never dive alone. Only a foolish diver goes on by himself."

Turning back, she waited a few seconds and surveyed the area. There! Again, the sunlight caught the metal of the object. Without further thought, she decided to go the few feet more and discover what exactly it was that teased her with its recurring flashes.

It lay nestled, half in and out of the sand, and Kate merely stared at the gold medallion. She blinked several times, hoping her contact lenses hadn't slipped. It had to be fake! Through the bubbles of her sharply exhaled breath, she looked into a wide crevice of the reef and saw a partially buried skeleton, with only a rib cage and arm above the sand. Wrapped around its encrusted bones was a heavy chain. Fascinated, she wondered if it might also be gold.

Shaking her head in wonder, Kate smiled inwardly. Out of all the scuba shops in Bermuda she was lucky enough to pick one that, unbeknownst to her, offered treasure hunting along with boat trips. They must have planted all this bogus treasure for the tourists, and she supposed you got some sort of prize for discovering it. Well, she might not be a seasoned diver, but she was certainly lucky. Perhaps it shouldn't be disturbed, she thought, while reaching out her hand. The entire scene looked so authentic.

Unable to stop herself, she picked up the medallion and wrapped its chain around her weight belt. Immediately her ears started to ring . . . the pressure on her lungs increased, as if she were at a greater depth . . . Trying not to panic, she again looked to the others, this time for help. But they were gone . . .

Instead, a huge, dark shadow hovered at the surface of the water. Instinctively, Kate knew it was the hull of a large ship . . . and it hadn't been there moments ago!

"'Tis a fool's mission, Michael Sheridan, and well you know it. Why, your old father'd be turning over in his grave to see you do this!"

Stripping off his shirt, Michael handed it to his first mate and grimaced. "My father is already turning over in his grave, Denny. I'm doing this to let him rest in peace."

Denny Moran crumpled the white cotton into a ball and threw it on top of Michael's discarded boots.

"Peace? What kind of peace would the man have to know you're about to throw yourself overboard, I ask?"

Eyeing the clear blue water, Michael muttered, "You know why I'm doing it."

From behind him, he heard a muffled curse. "Aye. 'Cause you fell for a fool's tale. Everybody knowed old Tom was half crazy, carryin' that ratty leather map of his all them years. Even you used to laugh at him."

"I never laughed at him," Michael threw over his shoulder. What was that thing he'd just seen? That glimpse of black and white? It was too large to be a fish.

"Ah, you never came right out and laughed," Denny persisted. "But even when he willed it to you, I can remember you shakin' your head at the fool."

Blinking a few times, Michael dragged his eyes away from the water. "Maybe Tom was a fool to believe there was treasure down there. I don't know. I just know I have to find out for myself."

"Why now?"

Looking beyond the cove where they were anchored, Michael took a deep, steadying breath as he viewed the island of Bermuda. "Why not? I'm here to take Kevin's place at this marriage." He shrugged his shoulders. "Might as well put old Tom and his legends to rest, too. But what if there is something down there, Denny? I'm desperate. I've got to find money someplace."

The first mate's bushy gray eyebrows came together as he scowled at the younger, stronger man. "I served under your daddy, and I fought the war with you, Michael Sheridan. Waited for you to grow up, too, and turn into the man me and your daddy could be proud of . . . What you're plannin' to do to that young girl, waitin' over there for a husband, is wrong. And you know it. This here," and he jerked his head toward the blue water of the sheltered cove, "is plain stupid. There ain't nothing down there but an old man's dreams."

Looking back to the sea, Michael squinted as again he made out the movement of something, its image distorted by the water. Checking for the knife at his waistband, he looked back at Denny. Smiling, he handed him the faded treasure map that a trusted seaman, more than that, a friend, had placed in his hand with his last dying breath.

"Keep it, Denny," he said, forcing the old man's gnarled fingers around the leather. Patting one of the still strong shoulders, Michael smiled, yet the first mate refused pacification. Still seeing the mixture of anger and confusion on Denny's face, he turned to once more face the sea.

He knew it was foolish, an act of desperation, yet he also knew time and opportunity were quickly running out.

Climbing up on the cap rail, he shouted back over his shoulder, "Think of it, Denny, as washing up for my bride . . . !" just before he pushed off, executing a clean dive into the crystal-blue water.

Chapter 2

Kate had to remind herself to exhale. In her panic, she desperately tried to remember everything her instructor had drilled into her, in case of an emergency. Her breathing was too fast, too irregular, and she consciously made an effort to slow down. It wasn't unusual to get disoriented underwater, she knew that, yet how could she have wandered so far from the others? Where was the safety boat? And when had that huge ship come?

Just as she decided to surface, she saw someone, a man, break through the water. Kate watched his powerful arms propel him downward toward her. What was wrong with him? Was he crazy? Diving at this depth without so much as a snorkel? Dear God, she had only made a few emergency ascents sharing the same regulator . . . and that had been practice! This man was coming right at her! She blinked quickly. He wasn't even wearing a bathing suit—he had on *pants!*

Fighting her panic, she raised her arm straight up, her open palm facing him in the "Stop! Stay where you are!" signal. She watched in amazement as he ignored her and came within a few feet.

They stared at each other for no more than a few seconds before Kate could see he was as frightened as she. As she made a move toward her regulator to indicate they could share the breathing apparatus, he jerked a knife out from his waistband and held it out before him, as if to protect himself from her.

She quickly moved backward, into the crevice of the reef, hovering over the fake treasure. Panicking, feeling she was trapped and about to die, Kate made a desperate effort to swim past him and felt her fin slap his body as she made her escape.

She never looked back, had no idea where she was going, and had barely enough sense to make sure she swam parallel to the surface, and not into a greater depth. Her first instinct was to get out, to reach the surface as quickly as possible, yet from somewhere within her jumbled, frightened thoughts came the message that to do so could prove fatal. Slowly, slowly, she ascended—her mind screaming at her to exhale, not to hold her breath in fear and overextend her lungs.

Michael Sheridan's arms hooked between the rope ladder, his head resting on them while he desperately tried to regain his breath. What the hell was it?

What was that *thing* down there? It was female. At least he thought it was female—its long black hair matching its half-black skin. It had a woman's legs, yet black fins like a fish!

He slowly shook his head, his breath coming a little more easily. Letting himself relax next to his ship, he heard Denny's shout from overhead.

"Well, Michael. All clean now, are we? Where's your

booty? Don't tell me them Spaniards didn't leave you nothin'."

He heard the laughter of his men and brought his head up to face them. Immediately, the laughter ceased. Using his strained muscles, Michael started to climb up the ladder and, upon reaching the top, he didn't object to the help he received to be brought aboard.

Bent at the waist, he grabbed hold of the cap rail and stared back into the water. It was down there . . . the woman-fish . . . his . . . his mermaid.

Standing next to him, Denny leaned against the side and asked quietly, "Are you through, Michael? Have we seen an end to this foolishness?"

Slowly turning his head, Michael swept his wet hair back from his face and looked directly into old Denny's brown eyes. "An end? Nay, Denny, this is just the beginning!"

Again he searched the water for her. She was down there. Somewhere . . .

Kathleen Anne Walker knew her life was in danger, and not just from the maniac who'd attacked her at the reef. She was near exhaustion and still had a distance to go to the shore. After she had surfaced and seen the old masted ship, she'd decided that snorkling was the safest way to reach land. Since she was swimming on the opposite side of the ship, she could only pray no one would notice the tip of her snorkel as it broke through the water.

Drawing on all her reserves, she continued her swim to safety. It couldn't have taken more than fifteen minutes, yet to Kate it felt as though she'd been alternately swimming and treading water for hours. When her fins finally touched the sandy bottom of the cove, she raised her mask and let the tears come. Panting with exhaustion and fear, she paused in the surf and glanced over her shoulder to the ship. In the distance, it stood like an eerie reminder of days gone by.

Kneeling in the shallow waves, she removed her breathing set and fins. As she gathered her scuba equipment, Kate moved very slowly out of the water. Not wanting to attract any attention from the ship, she made sure to exit closest to the tree line. Feeling the warm sand beneath her feet, her movements quickened and, mercifully, she finally entered the shelter of the trees. Crouching in the undergrowth, Kate tried to catch her breath as she watched the ship pull up anchor and raise a few small white sails.

The man must belong to the ship, she reasoned. Yet why had he attacked her? She'd been trying to help, damn it! Angry with him for scaring her half to death and for ruining the beginning of her vacation, she squinted her eyes to see if there was a name to identify the ship. When she got back to her room, she was going to make sure that man paid for his dangerous behavior. Too far away to read its name, Kate stood up and walked toward where she'd seen a road, her arms already straining with the heavy equipment.

She wasn't lost. She knew she wasn't. This was the same coast road she'd come over two days ago from the airport. It was paved then, though, not a mixture of dirt and crushed shells. She shook her head, as if to clear it. What was she thinking? How could a road change? Of course it must have been unpaved . . . *wasn't it?*

Staying to the side of the narrow lane, for her bare feet could not endure the crushed shells, Kate walked up the hill that led to her hotel. Vaguely, her mind registered that the other hotels were no longer visible from the road. Yet, in the distance, she could see the old manor house that had been turned into small studio apartments. Just a little while longer, she told herself, and then she would be able to call the dive shop and have them pick up her equipment, for she had lugged it far enough, and then, after filing a complaint with somebody, she had every intention of crawling into bed and sleeping until tomorrow morning.

Kate had a definite feeling of unease as she approached the large white-bricked building. It looked different . . . the shrubbery was less formal, the comfortable lightweight patio furniture that had been on the wide veranda was replaced by a wicker sofa and chairs with deep green cushions. Come to think of it, she thought, even the shutters surrounding the windows and doors were painted green. This morning she could have sworn there were no shutters!

Carefully making her way to the side entrance, Kate opened the door that should have led to a long hallway. The hallway was there, but in each room she passed the door was open and the furnishings were different . . . more formal . . . less casual.

How could everyone have left? When she'd made the reservation, the travel agent had told her she was lucky to have gotten the last vacancy. Where was everyone?

Quietly, Kate tried to maneuver the stairs that led up to the second-floor apartments. From below her she heard the voices of two men and moved faster. Once more the rooms on this floor were also open for inspection, only this time it was obvious they were bedrooms. All doors wide open . . . except hers.

Standing silently in the hallway, she counted the rooms from the stairs. Third one. Why had the lock been changed on her door? *Lock?* There wasn't any— just a highly polished brass doorknob.

Placing the heavy cylinder on the also new Oriental runner that reached from one end of the hallway to the other, Kate took a deep breath and turned the knob.

She was in the wrong room, that was it! Immediately, she was aware of the sound of someone weeping. Slowly, she looked toward the bed. With her face in the pillow, a young blond-haired girl was thrown across a postered bed. Kate's heart started thumping against her rib cage and she tried to back out as quietly as possible. Dear God, what was happening?

Almost to the door, Kate's bare foot stepped on something sharp and she automatically hissed in sudden pain.

The girl jerked up from the bed and stared at her as if in shock.

"Who are you?" Kate asked in a quiet voice, while trying to stay calm.

"Who are *you?*" the girl whispered, quickly standing behind the paneled poster, as if the pale-blue velvet might shield her from the intruder.

Swallowing several times, Kate glanced down and picked the broken shell away from the soft pad of her foot. Raising her head, she tried to smile. "I'm Kate Walker. Why are you here in my room?" she asked. Looking at the strange furnishings, she added, "At least I *think* it's my room."

The girl's eyes followed hers until they came to rest on Kate. "What are you?" she asked in a timid, alarmed voice.

Despite the hair rising at her neck, Kate giggled nervously. "I'm a woman, of course. Just like you." Not liking the strange feeling she was getting, Kate once again questioned the young woman dressed in a very old-fashioned white gown. "Who *are* you? And why were you crying?" she asked, her forehead creasing with puzzlement.

The girl raised her delicate chin. "I'm Helene Barnett . . . and I was crying because of that hateful man who calls himself my father!"

Before Kate could answer her, Helene Barnett wiped her eyes and dropped the portion of drape from her hand. Coming around the bed, she stood in front of Kate and looked her over. When her eyes met Kate's, they were filled with wonder. "Who are you?" she whispered.

Nervous with the girl's inspection, Kate stammered, "I . . . I told you." Looking over Helene's beautiful lace gown, she couldn't help but comment, "That's a lovely dress."

Helene looked down and fingered the delicate material. Kate could see her chin trembling. "It's for my wedding," she said softly.

"Your wedding!" Picking up her breathing set, Kate started to back out of the room. "Look, I'm really sorry." And shaking her head, she tried to explain, "I don't know how it could have happened. I thought this was my hotel. EdgeHill Manor. I can see now it's a private home . . ."

"But this *is* EdgeHill Manor!" Helene Barnett quickly walked toward her. "Please! Please don't go."

Kate stopped backing up and stared into the girl's frightened eyes. "What do you mean? This is . . . this is a private home. This isn't the hotel I left this morning!" Looking about the strange bedroom, she again shook her head as her heart started beating heavily. "What's happening here?"

Bravely stepping closer, Helene touched Kate's wet suit. "Why are *you* dressed that way?"

Kate took a step backward, now frightened herself. "I was diving. Haven't you ever seen a wet suit before?"

Eyes wide, Helene brought a hand up to cover her gasp. "You were in the water? Like that?" Bringing her fingers away from her mouth, she stated quietly, "Your suit didn't feel wet, but your hair is damp."

Kate felt completely disoriented. What was wrong with the girl? Was she backward? How could her parents marry her off when she wasn't completely normal? Backing even closer to the door, she took a steadying breath. "Look, Helene, I'm sorry, but I'd better get out of here before someone . . ."

"Shh . . . !"

The two women stared at each other as they heard heavy footsteps in the hallway.

"Come," Helene whispered, the frightened look back on her face. "My father! Hide in my wardrobe closet. He would never understand you!"

For such a small woman, Helene possessed great strength as she pulled Kate's arm and led her to a narrow doorway. Confused and also frightened, Kate let herself be gently shoved in between two rows of long gowns. Just as she put the heavy cylinder on the floor and Helene shut the door, she heard a loud knock.

"Helene! I wish to speak with you!"

Trying to control her breathing, Kate pushed the satin sleeve of one gown away from her mouth and quietly listened. She could hear the bedroom door open.

"You will stop that mewling and listen to me, young lady! You are going to go through with this marriage, as I have arranged."

"But, Father . . ."

"That's right, I am your father and you'll do as I say . . . not as you think. I will not listen to any more of your nonsense. Nor will you ruin five years of planning. I'll not hear of it, do you understand?"

Without seeing him, Kate didn't like him. His English-accented voice and words held an unmistakable note of cruelty. She could hear Helene's quivering answer.

"I don't know him. How can I marry . . ."

"You *will* marry. I've just had word Kevin Sheridan's ship is in the harbor. He's probably on his way here now. Everything is in motion, young woman, and you will give me no further trouble. Do you understand?"

"Father, *please* listen! I'm not part of some cargo that you can sell to the highest bidder. I want a marriage, a man I can . . ."

Kate heard a slap and Helene's cry and her own body stiffened in outrage. Just as she was about to open the wooden door and confront the man, she was startled by his words.

"You have always been a disappointment—just as your mother was. Why do you think you were kept at boarding schools since her death? If you were male, I

31

could have withstood it all. But no! Now you hear me out . . ." His voice sounded even more menacing. "The minister is downstairs. The papers are in my study waiting for the signatures. *You,* missy, will present yourself when you're called! If you should disobey, I'll drag you down by your hair. This wedding is going through!"

Kate heard the slamming of a door and ventured to peek out of the wardrobe. He was gone. Immediately, she went to Helene and touched her arm. "I'm so sorry," she whispered to the young girl's back. She couldn't control a gasp as Helene slowly turned around and Kate saw her swollen cheek.

"My God! The man ought to be locked up!"

Helene startled her by issuing forth a small bitter laugh. "Believe me, people have tried. I told you. He's a beast . . . I hate him."

"Isn't there anyone that could help you?"

Helene shook her head and brushed a blond curl back off her face. "Not really. My aunt moved here after my mother died in 1865, but lately Father refuses to let Aunt Madeline even visit. When I left my school in England, I also left any family that could help me out of . . ."

Kate felt her ears again ring and her breath was coming in shallow gasps as she fought to ask the question. "What did you say? What year?"

"When my mother died? Eighteen sixty-five. Kate, what's wrong? You look sick!" Puzzled by the older woman's reaction, Helene helped her to the edge of the bed. Seating her on the pale-blue spread, she again asked, "Is something wrong?"

Once more, Kate looked about the room and took

notice of the antique furniture. Refusing to believe what her mind was screaming, she raced toward the window that no longer had a balcony. Grasping the painted sill, she gazed out at Hamilton Harbour.

It was different . . . yet strangely the same. It was the same body of water, the same view, but the landscape had changed. Spinning back toward the room, her voice actually squeaked as she pleaded with the girl who was looking at her with a confused expression. "Helene, what year is it? Tell me!"

"You can't be serious!" When she saw Kate's look had not changed, she answered in a small voice. "Eighteen sixty-eight. Don't you know that?"

Kate's eyes widened with shock. "No! It can't be!" She shook her head, as if the gesture might negate the possibility that she'd wandered into something crazy.

"I don't understand," Helene whispered.

"Look, I'm from New Jersey, in America," Kate said, feeling desperate. "And I just want to go home." Whatever was happening to her was taking place in Bermuda. If she could only get back to Jersey, to reality, everything would be normal. Wouldn't it?

Before Helene could make a comment, a light knock on the door was heard.

"Miss Helene. I have your veil."

Helene motioned for Kate to be silent as she answered the maid's call. Kate watched as the girl opened the door and accepted a large white hat with a heavy veil attached to its brim.

When Helene turned back to the room, she shrugged to Kate. "It's for the wedding," she said, despair again entering her voice.

Kate stared at the hat for the longest time. "Did I

33

hear your father say this man you're supposed to marry has a ship?"

Helene nodded. "I'm to marry him in less than fifteen minutes and then he's taking me to his home in Charlestown, South Carolina." Fear showed in her eyes. "I don't even know him! How can my father expect me to leave everything familiar and . . ."

"This is ridiculous! No one can force you to marry, even your father."

Helene slowly placed the veiled hat on the bed, as if fighting for her control. "You don't understand. It's been arranged."

Sensing defeat in the young girl, every feminist instinct surged up within Kate. "Understand? No one, not even your father, has the right to subjugate you like this. You don't *have* to marry this man, Helene."

Blond curls shook in denial. "What can I do? You heard my father. If I don't go downstairs of my own free will, he plans to drag me down. It's hopeless."

Pushing her hair off her forehead, Kate said, "It isn't. It's only hopeless if you let that man control your life. Why don't you just go to your aunt's? Leave now."

"I . . . I can't. If I don't go downstairs, he'd know I ran away."

"Then you can say no to the wedding vows. Surely whoever is officiating would stop the ceremony."

Helene's eyes widened in horror. "I could never do that! Then I would be dealing not only with the wrath of my father, but also Mr. Sheridan." The muscles in her face quivered and tears ran down her cheeks. "I'm not as strong as you are, Kate. I don't know how to stand up to them."

Breathing deeply with indignation, Kate stared at

the girl as she picked up the hat from the bed. It was insanity! She was standing in her hotel room talking to a young woman from the last century! Surely it was the strain of the last year that had brought about this hallucination . . . her mother's illness and death, the reappearance of her ex-husband in her life . . . Abruptly turning her head, she fought for her own control, her own sanity, as she looked out the window. Helene was real. She wasn't a figment of the imagination, and the cruelty in her father's voice was also indisputable. *Something* had happened to her on that reef, something so frightening, so terrifying in its possibilities, that she immediately pushed it to the back of her mind rather than deal with it. There would be time to examine it later, when she was calm and rational . . . but not now. Now she needed to act quickly.

"I'm going home," she stated in a strong voice. "And you don't have to marry anyone today."

Helene's mouth dropped open, and a look of puzzlement transformed her features as the veiled hat slipped from her fingers. "How? What are you talking about, Kate?"

Coming back to Helene, Kate picked up the hat and said, "I'm determined to get back, and your Mr. Sheridan is going to help me . . . help us both."

Helene continued to stare at her as if she'd lost her mind. "I don't understand," she muttered. "Why would he ever help us?"

Kate looked down at her body and compared her black wet suit with Helene's elegant white gown. Raising her chin, she grinned at the young, frightened girl.

"What size do you wear?" she asked, plans already starting to form in her head.

Michael Sheridan eyed the dowry displayed so enticingly on Barnett's desk. Twenty thousand shares of Barnett Importing, endorsed to Kevin Sheridan. Assuming his brother's role in this marriage, Michael had to control his impulses. First, he would have liked to connect his fist with Winston Barnett's jaw for being his uncle's accomplice in defrauding the Confederacy. Even though his fingers itched to snap up the sheaf of papers before him and make a hasty exit, Michael knew he had to go through with his plans.

Smiling back at Barnett, he then looked to the fidgeting minister who waited to perform the ceremony. With any luck, Michael thought, there wouldn't be a ceremony. If only he could get his hands on the dowry before Barnett's daughter appeared. All he wanted was the money the girl could provide—one way or another . . .

Clearing his throat, Winston Barnett gathered the stocks together and reinserted them into a leather folder. "Such a shame Martin couldn't be here today," he pronounced. "We've waited many years to join our two families together."

Michael had to choke back a truthful response. Instead, he pulled at the snowy white cuff of his shirt and brushed an imaginary speck of lint from the arm of his black, formal suit. Never taking his eyes off Barnett's hands as they clasped the folder, Michael said smoothly, "Yes, I'm sure Uncle Martin will deeply regret not being here to witness this marriage."

36

Barnett looked to the doorway, his face lined with irritation. "I told the girl you were pressed for time. Perhaps *you* can teach her some discipline. Those schools she attended . . ."

He never finished his sentence. Instead of a bride, a highly agitated servant quickly rounded the doorway and stared at Winston.

"Well?" Barnett demanded. "What is it?"

The dark-skinned man rubbed nervous palms on the front of his cotton breeches. "Mista Barnett, it's your stable, suh. She's burning! The horses is all over the place!"

Just as the words came out of his mouth, the servant looked to the window as a huge dark flash thundered before it.

"What?" Barnett ran to the window in time to see one of his prize Thoroughbreds disappearing into the heavy junglelike brush that surrounded his estate. "God damn it!" he bellowed, ignorant of the minister's shocked expression. "I want those horses back!"

Without a word to the young man at his side, he thrust the portfolio into his jacket and ran out of the study.

Michael repeated Barnett's curse, only in silence. When he had instructed Denny and his men to create a diversion, he hadn't counted on Barnett pocketing the dowry and taking it with him! Knowing his first plan had just been rendered useless, Michael turned at the sound of rustled silk and concentrated on his second strategy. The bride.

He couldn't see her face, yet even behind all the expensive silk and the heavy lace veil, he could tell she was frightened. As well she should be, Michael thought, as he straightened up to his full height. She was his means of revenge. If he couldn't take possession of the dowry, he planned to hold her for ransom. It seemed to him the height of irony that his uncle's accomplice should provide the money to destroy Martin. And Michael planned to get it, one way or another.

Turning back to the minister, he asked abruptly, "Are you ready, Reverend?"

The older man pulled at the starched white collar that marked him as a man of God. "I . . . ah . . . Shouldn't we wait for Mr. Barnett?"

Reaching for the girl's elbow, Michael brought her closer to the desk and looked directly into the minister's confused eyes. It was imperative that he go through with this ridiculous marriage before Barnett came back into the room. "Mr. Barnett expressed his desire for a quick wedding and told you that I must be sailing back to America this afternoon. I wish to leave Bermuda while it is still light."

Reverend Hailey looked from the tall man's determined expression to the hidden face of the young girl he had never met. "Wouldn't you rather wait until your father returns?" he asked gently.

Both he and Michael were surprised to see her shake her head. The first to recover, Michael moved next to her and faced the man across the desk. "There! Miss Barnett and I both wish to be married as quickly as possible. Will you *please* begin, sir?"

They made the proper responses, though the girl's were barely audible, and, before either party expected, Kevin Sheridan was officially married to Helene Barnett. All that was left was the signing of the marriage documents. It wasn't until the bride's heavy luggage was lifted into Mr. Sheridan's carriage and the couple had departed that Reverend Hailey nervously looked down at the signatures.

In bold script was the name *Michael* Sheridan. In a much plainer style was the strange name of *Kathleen Anne Walker*. Slumping into the leather chair behind the desk, the man of God issued a whispered curse of his own. Wiping his forehead, the Reverend Leonard Hailey immediately offered up a small prayer of forgiveness, and another, stronger, one for deliverance from Winston Barnett's impending wrath.

Chapter 3

"Madam, it will take a separate trip to transport your luggage. I trust you did not bring your entire household with you?"

From behind the heavy veil that covered her face, Kate looked to the strangely dressed men who were struggling to lift the trunk containing her scuba equipment. Waiting until they had placed it on the powdery pink sand in front of the carriage, she turned to the handsome man with the sarcastic voice.

Over six feet tall, he stared down at her with piercing eyes that now looked to be more blue than gray. The light breeze coming from the water gently lifted his dark blond hair from his tanned forehead—enough to show the lines of impatience as he waited for her answer.

"I only brought what was necessary," she said quietly, wondering how this stranger could possibly look familiar. Dear God, if she were to believe Helene, and everything around her, the man was living in the last century!

"Necessary? Well, if nothing else, we'll use it for ballast on the way back to the States," he muttered, more to himself than anyone else, as he handed her into the small rowboat that was to take them to the ship.

That's it! Kate thought, as she looked across the blue water to the masted ship. *He* was the diver! That's where she had seen him before. He looked different now, without the contortions of holding his breath, and with dry hair, but now that she really looked, she could see it was him all right.

Keeping her eyes fastened on the man, Kate allowed herself to think back as to how she had gotten into this predicament. It seemed impossible that her and Helene's crazy idea of switching places was actually going to work!

Seated next to her, Michael could feel her staring at his profile and turned his head slightly to see beyond the lace that fell from her large hat. Although he couldn't distinguish her features, he could tell her eyes were wide open as they continued to stare back at him. It was annoying that her voice was so low and whispery—that her dress was obviously too tight—and that he wanted to rip the veil away from her face so he could see the girl, no woman, that he'd just married.

Abruptly, he turned to gaze at the *Rebel* anchored beyond the reef. He now considered it to be his home, far more than the stately brick house in Charleston that he'd grown up in. It further annoyed him that he should now have to bring the Barnett woman aboard—at least until he negotiated her ransom. Once it was discovered that he, Michael, had married the girl instead of Kevin, thereby invalidating the contract, all hell would break loose both here and in Charleston. He planned to be safely hidden away in the cove, waiting out both Barnett and his uncle. And while there, he had every intention of investigating the ridiculous apparition of a mermaid guarding treasure.

Standing precariously in the rowboat, with both hands gripping the rope ladder, Kate glanced up at the old man waiting patiently at the ship's railing and once more gulped down her fear. It really was an insane, desperate idea, one pounced upon by Helene, that the two women switch places. Kate, realizing that this was the first ship leaving for the United States, agreed to take Helene's place. All she wanted was to get back to the United States, to go home and hope this insane nightmare would cease. Whatever circumstance had placed her in the nineteenth century, she had believed it would be safer to deal with it on more familiar ground. Now, hearing the old man encouraging her to climb the rope ladder, she truly doubted the wisdom of her decision.

"Madam, be assured the ladder will hold you. We have no time to dally over childish fears," Michael added, while standing at her side. Glancing at the distant shoreline, he silently cursed. They *had* to set sail and be well gone before Barnett discovered his daughter's abduction.

Kate wanted to shriek at him that it wasn't childish to be frightened of climbing thirty feet of rope attached to a bobbing ship, but she bit back the scream. She was into it now, this stupid deception, and would follow through until she reached America. Looking down at Sheridan's booted foot that held the bottom of the ladder taut, she hiked up the voluminous white skirt with one hand and ripped off the veiling covering her face with the other.

Throwing the hat and veil back into the rowboat, she shook out her hair and looked up to the tall, arrogant man at her side. He appeared to be startled as he stared into her eyes, and Kate took advantage of his speechless state. "See you at the top," she challenged quietly, and defiantly pulled herself up another rung. Keep looking up, her mind screamed. Whatever happens, don't look back down! The muscles in her arms were strained, yet Kate refused to give in to the pain. Concentrating on the rope, she slowly continued her ascent. Sooner than she thought possible, strong arms covered in white downy fuzz grabbed ahold of her, lifting her onto the ship's deck.

Breathing deeply, she nervously laughed as she straightened. "I *did* it! Didn't I?" she asked the old man, the exhilaration of accomplishment rushing through her veins. Denny looked at the small, fragile beauty whose eyes and coloring were infused with life and felt his own heart quicken with nostalgia and remorse. It weren't right, he thought again. They had no right to do this to the poor girl . . . even if she were that devil Barnett's own.

"Aye, missy," he said with a smile of admiration, "you sure enough did!"

They both turned as Michael climbed over onto the deck. When he stood before Kate, she unconsciously held her breath as deep blue eyes locked with hers. It was the swaying of the ship. That must be it, Kate thought, as the butterflies in her stomach began another assault.

"I'll show you to your cabin," Sheridan muttered before turning away. Shrugging her shoulders, she

43

smiled at the old man and followed the one whose eyes held a mixed look of anger and seduction.

They passed an open hearth, the galley house and two cargo hatches before Sheridan led her down a narrow set of stairs. Holding on to the rope railing and maneuvering the steps took a certain amount of skill, considering the way she was dressed, yet as Kate's slippered feet finally connected with the dowled wooden floor, she smoothed the white material of her gown and lifted her chin—just to show him she was capable of being independent. In that instant, she made up her mind never again to whine and listen to his sarcastic replies.

Following him to the back of the ship, Kate watched as he opened the door to a cabin and walked inside. Coming in behind him, she stopped short as he turned around to face her.

"You'll be staying here. It's my cabin. You should be comfortable."

"Your cabin?" she asked, alarmed at the thought of sharing this room with the man.

He nodded.

Before she could manage to formulate some sort of question to clear up the arrangements, Sheridan walked toward the door. Holding the brass latch, he turned once more and looked at her with that questioning gaze. "You're older than I thought," he murmured.

Kate broke the hot stare and lifted her chin. "I'm not that old," she stated defensively. Lord, the way he said it—like she was teetering on the brink of senility.

"Just how old are you?"

Unconsciously, Kate sucked in her already flat stomach. "I'm twenty-seven . . . and proud of it."

He almost grinned, while shifting his weight against the door molding. "Twenty-seven, and you've never been married. I find that hard to believe."

Kate couldn't tell if he was teasing her or giving her a compliment. It was on the tip of her tongue to tell him she had been married, and just what she thought of that institution, when she remembered that she was supposed to be Helene. Helene would probably lower her eyes and blush. Well, she might have to impersonate the young girl, but she was too old to blush. And anyway, Sheridan was just too damn sure of himself. Far too sure.

"Believe whatever you wish, Mr. Sheridan. And may I ask: Just how old are you?"

His grin widened. "Thirty-one. Listen, your trunk should be brought to you soon. In the meantime, why don't you relax until we get under way." He started to close the door, then hesitated and peeked his head around it. Still grinning, he said, "Oh, and by the way, I'm proud of it, too."

Kate stared at the closed door and groaned. Why did he have to be nice? She preferred him the other way—arrogant, overbearing. She could handle him that way. But this—this way he pulled at something deep within her. And in truth, when he smiled like that . . . he was gorgeous.

Shaking her head, she walked to the window at the rear of the cabin and leaned her arms across the wooden molding. As she looked out to the beautiful blue water, Kate again groaned. It was going to be a very long trip.

She was left alone as the ship began to move. She listened to the creaking of the wood, felt the surge of power as the wind caught the sails. Determined not to lose her control, Kate looked about the cabin. How had it happened? How could she have been tossed back in time? She felt immobilized by her fear, and powerless against whatever force had brought her to this century. It was as if she were a unwilling player, a puppet, with some unseen power pulling the strings and rearranging her life. Why her? And why now, after she had fought so hard since her divorce to regain her self-esteem? It had finally been starting to work out. Her job. Her life. A new beginning. She had a right to that. She'd worked so hard toward it.

Standing up, she crossed her arms and clutched her shoulders while gazing at Sheridan's personal belongings: the enameled shaving cup and brush secured on a recessed shelf, the brown leather boot lying on the floor that took the shape of his foot. Her eyes were drawn to the rolled maps that were neatly stacked by his small desk. She'd been right to take Helene's place, for traveling on this ship was the first step in getting home to New Jersey, to the life she had left behind. And she was determined to find a way back.

Looking over her shoulder to Sheridan's bunk, she pictured the handsome, arrogant man with his surprising smile. It would be foolish to dwell on him, yet nestled in the recesses of her mind was the terrifying thought that she might never get back, that she might

46

be forced to make her way in this foreign time . . . alone. A shiver of panic began at the back of her neck and spread to her scalp. What would she do if her mother's home in New Jersey didn't exist? If her friends, everything familiar, were erased? A small voice inside her said she would do whatever was necessary. Hadn't she already proved she was a survivor? The answer provided her with only a small measure of confidence.

Too confused to dwell on what she might find when they reached the United States, Kate opened Helene's trunk and tried to take her mind off the frightening possibilities as she began to unpack. Hidden by layers of gowns, Kate viewed her diving equipment. Carelessly thrown on top was her black Ralph Lauren bathing suit. She wished she had the nerve to put it on, for it definitely was more comfortable than the layers of clothing she now wore. Without thought, her fingers moved to the tiny covered buttons at her throat and, just as she opened the material at her neck, she unconsciously felt the movement of the ship slow down.

Confused, she stood for a moment, trying to judge whether the vessel had lost the wind or was actually stopping. Not an experienced sailor, she was about to walk over to the window when she heard a firm knock at the door. Instinctively, she slammed the lid of the trunk down and sat on top, as if her body could protect her scuba gear. Taking a deep breath, she tried to sound calm as she called out with an expectant, "Yes?"

She knew it was Sheridan, even before his tall muscular body filled the doorway. He seemed almost uncomfortable as he entered the cabin. With his hands jammed into the pockets of his pants, he paced the length of the room.

"We've . . . ah, we've stopped," he pronounced, ceasing his pacing and staring into her expectant face.

Kate was taken aback by his look of almost hostility. She was glad now that young Helene was not joined to him for life. He was domineering and arrogant, and for some reason he disliked her. Gathering up her courage, she lifted her chin and stated, "I thought so. Why *have* we stopped, Kevin?"

He was thrown when she called him by his brother's name, yet hoped that he concealed his confusion with his next words. "We've developed a problem with one of our windlasses. Without it, we can't up the mainsail. It should be fixed in a few days."

Kate stared at him. "You mean we're stuck here? We're not going to America?"

Michael took a deep breath and continued the lie. "Madam, this is an emergency stop. Thank God it didn't happen when we were out at sea."

Not knowing anything about the working of a ship, Kate merely nodded as she continued to stare at him. Thick, dark blond hair was brushed back off his forehead, allowing her to once again see the lines of annoyance as he returned her gaze. Blue-gray eyes held hers, as if daring her to argue with him. She broke his stare and allowed her eyes to travel down his body. She could see the muscles under the thin cotton of his white shirt and the gray material of his pants. She mentally shook herself. Of course he would look as though he lived in a health spa—he was a sailor. Didn't he spend most of his day outdoors, climbing rigging and such? Forcing her eyes to once again meet his, Kate took a steadying breath and asked, "Where are we? We can't have traveled very far."

Michael cursed the betrayal of his body that her bold eyes had caused and turned to the window. Pushing open the square-paned glass, he looked out. "We're anchored in a small cove on the other side of the island. I'll send word to your father," he added. Another lie. It was becoming easier and easier, but then so far he had refused to allow his conscience any freedom.

Kate tried to keep the quiver out of her voice. "You don't . . . that is . . . My father would only be worried. Why don't you wait and see how long it takes to fix the—whatever it is that's broke." God, she sounded like an idiot! She never was good at deceptions and lies. Hadn't she *always* been caught at it in the past?

Michael turned away from the window and almost smiled. The little beauty was playing right into his hands. In fact, ever since she had walked into Barnett's study, she'd seemed almost as anxious as he was to be away from her father. And looking at her, he inwardly admitted she was a beauty. Too old to be called pretty, she was exotically beautiful, and he was fascinated by the contrasts of her features. Straight dark hair framed a delicate face. A full, sensuous smile held promises that teased the imagination. Freckles dotted her nose and high cheekbones, giving her an earthiness that was refreshing when compared to the pale, pampered complexions of the women he had known. But it was those eyes . . . They were almost scary. He had never seen eyes that were such a startlingly pale blue. They reminded him of the water surrounding the island. It was as if she were a part of it . . .

Suddenly he remembered who she was and he

scowled. Brushing past her, he hesitated at the door. "Try and make yourself comfortable. We'll be here for a few days," he muttered, without looking at her. And not giving her a chance to reply, he closed the door behind him.

Kate listened to his determined footsteps as he walked away. What had just happened? Never had a man looked at her in such a way. She'd felt almost caressed by his eyes, stroked by the unconscious soft smile at his lips. It was as though he had actually touched her! Shivering in response to the memory of his intent gaze, Kate once more walked over to the window for a breath of fresh air.

As she gulped in the salty breeze, her fingers tightened on the wooden molding, her eyes became narrow slits as they took in the scenery before her.

"Why that sneaky son of a b—!" She never finished the forceful curse as she identified the sheltered cove where they'd *both* been diving earlier. So! It was some wind-something that needed to be fixed! How convenient that it would break right above the treasure. And realizing that it was real treasure down there, not some phony junk planted by the scuba shop, Kate looked back at her trunk and smiled.

Mr. Sheridan was going to have company.

"Michael, I've been thinking on this . . ."

"Always dangerous, Denny. Do me a favor and don't think, just help me out."

Denny Moran watched as Michael shucked off his trousers and stood in his underdrawers. His conscience was bothering him more and more. This whole plan was foolhardy. "She never done nothin' to you, Michael Sheridan. Don't make the child pay for the father."

Leaning over the rail to look down at the sea, Michael muttered, "She's no child. We're only going to keep her until Barnett comes up with the ransom." Not seeing the strange woman-fish, he looked back at his mate. "The note is there, isn't it?"

Denny ran a hand through his wiry gray hair. "Aye. It's there all right. Had a hell of a time gettin' back into the house after those horses started runnin' crazy. Funny thing, Michael. It weren't us that started that fire."

Lowering his head in surprise, Michael whispered the question. "Who then?"

Denny shrugged. "Can't say. We all saw a young yellow-haired girl riding like hell into the forest, but nobody can say who started it. Could'a been her, I 'spect. A man like Barnett probably's got lots of enemies."

"But who was she?"

Again, Denny shrugged. "Just be glad she seems to hate Barnett as much as you do. If it was her, then there's two of you against him. It might give us some extra time."

Suddenly, Michael smiled. "Why, Denny. It almost sounds as if you approve of this after all."

The old man scowled. "You know how I feel. It's all crazy. Just like what you plannin' to do now," he said, jerking his head toward the water. "You're hell-bent on killin' yourself, one way or another."

Michael grinned. "I have no intentions of killing myself. Besides, who would you nag if I weren't here?"

"It ain't naggin' to tell you you're a fool. Just don't wear yourself out down there . . . you got a weddin' night comin' up, Captain Sheridan."

Looking at the frozen expression on Michael's face, it was Denny's turn to chuckle.

Actually, it was easier than Kate had imagined. The hardest part was getting out the window with her tanks. Standing on the wooden rudder below the two square rear windows of her cabin, she realized that she would have to store the scuba equipment somewhere outside the ship. She decided that the heavy chain attached to the rudder would probably be the safest place. It would also be easier for her to get to, if another dive was necessary.

Preparing her mask, she had to stifle a laugh as she brought the regulator to her mouth. She couldn't wait to meet the lying Mr. Sheridan again! And thinking of that imminent meeting, she quietly, slowly, lowered herself into the water.

Surprisingly, she was calm. Here she felt she had the upper hand. She could stay under for a longer period, while he would only be granted seconds with the treasure. It was easy to spot the reef, since the ship was anchored so close by, and Kate swam toward it with smooth gliding strokes of her fins. All she had to do was find that treasure and wait.

Concealed in the small crevice of the reef, Kate saw him before he caught sight of her. It was the bubbles of her exhaled breath that gave her away.

Michael thought his eyes were again playing tricks on him. The mermaid was here! He forgot the treasure—he forgot everything as he tried to touch her to make sure she was real.

Kate saw his extended hand and instinctively reached out with her own. Immediately her eyes widened behind the tinted diving mask as she saw the wedding ring on her finger. Quickly, she switched hands and ran the fingers of her right hand over his open palm. Sheridan pulled back, looked at her with a frightened expression, and pushed off the reef to the surface.

Kate watched his ascent, knowing he was only catching his breath before he returned. Hurriedly, she reached down and attempted to pick up the small casket nestled in the sand by the skeleton. It was too heavy and this time she tried using both hands. Straining, she managed to lift it a few inches when she felt a movement by her shoulder.

Turning her head, she saw Sheridan. The small box slipped from her fingers and she moved away. Almost in slow motion, Sheridan reached out his hand and touched her hair.

Although he had filled his lungs to capacity, Michael fought the burning in his chest. The maid's long black hair swirled around her head as the water lifted it in a sensuous dance. He was no longer afraid of her. She had touched him, and it was a gentle caress. He wanted to touch her, to feel the strands through his fingers, and he almost smiled as she allowed him. Suddenly, he felt a panic, as his body rebelled from the lack of air.

It was as if the maid recognized his danger and she placed both her hands on his waist. With unbelievable strength, she pushed him upward, toward the surface. Desperate to reach air, Michael propelled himself toward it.

Kate watched as Sheridan clawed his way to the surface. From below she could see the thrashing of his legs and she was about to swim up and support him when she realized he was only treading water. Grateful that he was all right, she turned back to the reef. It had dawned on her, while she was waiting for Sheridan, that—if she actually was transported back in time—she had no income. No money at all.

The treasure didn't belong to anyone, at least not yet, and she intended to make sure that a good portion of it came her way. She had, after all, found it first. Once again struggling with the casket, Kate almost flipped the regulator out of her mouth as she glanced up. He was *back!*

Michael was fascinated with her. Half of her had the body a goddess would envy, even if her torso was covered in a slick black skin. The black skin stopped at her shoulders, revealing slender human arms. She also had a woman's legs, a woman's shapely legs. Yet they ended in long black webs, instead of feet. The other half of her was unnatural, almost ugly. Her face was a distortion, her eyes almost hidden by a thick masklike protrusion that entered her mouth and came out again to cover her nose and eyes. It had long tubes, or arteries, that were attached to her back. There, it seemed, was a separate apparatus fastened to her by belts.

He watched as she dropped the small trunk and came closer to him. Almost as if she knew the power she held over him, the maid reached for his hand. Holding it firmly in hers, she started to swim toward the surface. This time he had only been under for seconds, and he had no trouble holding the air in his lungs. He felt transported to an almost mystical place as she brought him with her. He was surrounded by tiny bubbles that tickled his skin, bubbles that came from her. Again, he touched her, this time running his free hand up her thigh to her waist. She was a figure of contrasts. Slippery smooth skin gave way to a tough, spongelike covering.

Realizing his touch had startled her, Michael found himself shaken as the maid let go of his hand and allowed him to pass in front of her body. As he moved upward, her breasts brushed at his chest, her fingers traced the outline of his waist and thighs—until reaching his ankles, when her hands tightened and forcefully propelled him up and away from her.

Again, Michael was surrounded by bubbles. But this time they quickly vanished, as his mermaid swam away from the reef . . . and away from him.

Chapter 4

It had been too close, and Kate found herself shaking as she tried to fasten her scuba gear to the heavy chain. Successful, she struggled out of her wet suit and prepared to hoist herself back up through the square window. Balancing on the rudder, she first threw her mask inside, then her diving suit. By the time she stood inside the cabin, she was breathing far more heavily than the exertion warranted.

"My God!" she whispered aloud, as a shaking took over her body. "What just happened?"

With an unsteady hand, she grabbed for the towel lying on one of the built-in shelves and wrapped it around her wet hair. As she stood, staring at volumes of nautical books, Kate unconsciously fingered the gold medallion that hung from her neck.

He wasn't frightened . . . and he should have been, she thought with conviction. She should have appeared more menacing, like the first time. Yet, when she had seen him struggling for breath, her instincts had taken over. She never should have touched him. That was

56

what had broken his barrier of fear. And now, he had touched her . . .

Thinking of his hand as it slid up her body, Kate closed her eyes and again shivered. She was honest enough to admit that the involuntary shaking wasn't from the temperature—for it was seasonably warm. It was because Sheridan had touched her . . . And he was gentle, totally unlike his nature above water.

As she opened the trunk to find Helene's robe, Kate mentally warned herself to watch Sheridan, both above and below the water—and she'd better keep a watch on her own feelings, too. It was better to remember that Mr. Sheridan had lied to her, bullied her, and intended to take her share of the treasure. It was what her mind told her to remember . . . her body told her something else entirely different.

Two hours later, she sat across the table from Sheridan. Ravenous, she devoured the meal set before her. It was nerves. She always ate too much when she was nervous. And Sheridan didn't make it easier, she thought, as she deliberately put down her fork and sipped her third glass of wine. He kept glancing at her, as if expecting something, while she desperately tried to avoid his eyes. It had been easier to concentrate on the food, rather than the man.

"I'm glad you have a healthy appetite."

His voice ran down the back of her spine, like the soft brush of a feather, causing her to straighten her shoulders. Kate replaced the glass onto the table. "It's . . . ah, the sea air, I guess," she mumbled.

God, why did she always sound like a blithering idiot

around him? Wanting to make a better impression, Kate tried to center her thoughts on something intelligent. "How is the windlass coming? Do you think we'll be here long?" There, not exactly profound, but it sounded reasonably knowledgeable.

Sheridan smiled and picked up his own glass of wine. "As I said earlier, the windlass will take a few days to repair. Are you bored already?"

Kate sat up straighter. Unable to help it, she smiled back. "Bored? Oh, no, Kevin, I'm hardly bored. Are you?"

The glass was forcibly replaced on the table. Michael hated it when she said his brother's name, especially when she said it like an endearment. He silently admitted that he wasn't exactly comfortable with her abduction. Maybe Denny was right. Maybe she shouldn't have to pay for her father's sins. He supposed the least he could do was make her time with them as easy as possible.

"No, I'm not bored, Helene." He said her name as softly as she had spoken his brother's. "A sailor devises ways to pass the time."

Kate couldn't help the giggle that escaped her lips. It was only when she stood up, glass in hand, to cross the room that she felt slightly dizzy. Liking the way the gauzy white gown felt against her body, and fascinated by the way the material moved with her, she widely swung back in his direction. "Ah . . . Kevin . . . and what *do* you do to pass the time now?"

Michael's eyebrows came together. Was she drunk? Whatever, it grated on his nerves to hear her call him Kevin, especially when her voice sounded like a caress. "There's always constant work on a ship," he replied roughly. "By the way," he added, as if an afterthought, "I am addressed by my middle name—Michael." There! No longer would he have to listen to her use his brother's name like it was . . .

"I like Kevin better," she interrupted his thoughts. "You look like a Kevin."

"I answer to Michael," he stated firmly, and stood up. Walking over to her, he almost smiled as he watched her back away from him. Using another cabin, he had dressed formally for this dinner, and he now removed his heavy jacket. He kept his eyes on her as he tossed it onto the wide bunk. "Why don't you sit back down," he offered, and had to suppress a laugh when he read the relief on her face.

With the ease of a dancer she gracefully slid away from him to refill her glass. "I'm fine," she murmured, with a mysterious smile. "You see, I haven't had the chance to stretch my legs . . . like you. What did you do this afternoon, Kev—Michael?" she amended.

He appeared confused for a moment. "Why, nothing interesting—just chores."

Kate nodded as she now came in *his* direction. She stopped directly in front of him. Gazing up into his face, she could feel the wine mixing with her blood, making her warm and languid. Okay, her mind admitted, he was great looking—all blond and bronzed. And when he looked at her, like he was doing now, the memory of their underwater meeting seemed all the more sensuous. Holding the long-stemmed glass in her left hand, her right moved upward to his tie. Very slowly, she pulled at the strand of dark satin. As the material easily slid from the knot, Kate raised her head and stared back at him.

Keeping her eyes locked with his, she felt the exciting tension between them build. Concentrating all her efforts, she brought the wine to her lips and delicately sipped. Still probing the depths of deep blue, Kate whispered, "You must be careful, Michael. Local legend has it that this cove is the home for a powerful mermaid. It's been said that once she took a man for husband and, Michael . . ." Her eyes widened. "He was never heard from again!"

Backing away from her, he was momentarily speechless. He wasn't sure what affected him more—her words, or her actions. Recovering, Michael stated, "I don't believe in legends."

Kate smiled. It was so easy. "Normally, I don't, either. But, you see, the story goes that there's a treasure and the mermaid guards it for her husband . . ."

"No, that isn't how it goes at all," Michael interrupted, his earlier look of superiority back on his face. "The treasure belongs to Malinalli, Doña Marina the Spaniards called her. She was said to be very beautiful and served as Cortez's translator with the Maya and Aztecs."

Kate's mouth dropped open. "Really?" she asked in amazement, while forgetting her own story. "What else?"

She watched as he took his drink to the window and looked out to the cove. "Supposedly, she became Cortez's confidante, both as his translator and mistress. It's also said she bore him a son."

Fascinated, Kate asked, "How do you know all this?"

Michael looked back at her for a brief moment, then

returned his gaze to the water. "It's probably only sailors' talk. We can be a very superstitious lot. One old salt wouldn't stop rambling on about this particular legend. He used to say that Moctezuma was haunted by the prophecy that a god—ruler named Quetzalcoatl would someday come and claim all the Aztec land. He thought Cortez was that god. Old Tom said that Moctezuma paid tribute to Cortez with priceless gold objects, studded with precious stones. When Cortez went back to Spain, he left Doña Marina and his son. The legend goes that when Doña Marina was old and she longed for the Spaniard, she sent him her own tribute, a gift from her heart, begging him to return. The ship bound for Spain was wrecked during a hurricane and Cortez never knew of her desire. He died in Spain, without ever seeing her again, but stated that his bones be buried in Mexico."

Almost reluctantly, Michael tore his eyes away from the scene outside the window. Looking at the beautiful woman before him, he said quietly, "It's said the treasure will bring you not only your fortune, but your heart's desire."

Kate exhaled heavily. "It's a beautiful story," she whispered. "Do you believe it, Michael?"

He left the window and came back to the table. Refilling his own glass with wine, he brought it to his lips and emptied the goblet. Turning his head to look at her, he then smiled. "If there's really treasure down there, I believe it will bring me my fortune. And yes, Helene, I need the fortune to accomplish my heart's desire."

Kate moved closer to him. "I don't understand. How can money give you your heart's desire? Most people

61

desire happiness, love, something . . . What is your heart's desire, Michael?"

She didn't mean it as an invitation. In fact, she was merely curious to know what such a man would want above all else. He was looking intently into her eyes, studying her, and Kate felt a warm rush of emotions run through her veins. She blamed the wine for making her speak. "You didn't answer. What does your heart desire?" she asked hesitantly.

He reached out and captured her wrist. Slowly pulling her to his chest, he used his other hand to remove her wineglass and set it on the table next to his own. Tilting her face up to his, he whispered, "You have the most beautiful eyes I've ever seen," just before he brought his mouth down on hers.

His lips grazed hers with unbelievable tenderness, searching, exploring, and Kate felt a small moan escape from the back of her throat. Unconsciously, she pressed into him for her legs felt too weak to support her. As if sensing her unsteadiness, Michael brought both his arms around her, crushing her to his chest. His lips became more demanding, seeking the same response from her.

Kate gave it. Instinct drove her, and she was overwhelmed by a primitive sexuality. Freeing her arms, she raised them to his shoulders and weaved her fingers through the blond silk of his hair. At her touch, his kiss deepened.

Michael felt lost in the sweetness of her. It had been so long since he had come close to feeling this way, and he had thought it was lost to him forever. Yet, just as his joy was renewed, there also came the creeping thought that this was Winston Barnett's daughter. This

62

was the woman that his uncle planned to use to create a dynasty . . . and, furious with himself, more than her, his lips became angry instruments.

Kate sensed the change immediately. She opened her eyes just as Michael broke the kiss and set her away from him.

Breathing heavily, he spoke, "You want to know my heart's desire, Helene?" Not waiting for her answer, he said the word with bitterness. "Revenge!"

Immediately, her hand reached for the table. Using it to support herself, she merely stared at him.

Michael caught the almost hurt expression on her face and he was tempted to tell her the truth—that he, too, was using her—but something held him back. Probably sanity, he thought. He'd already told her too much.

Kate watched him turn away from her and face the door. Before he could react, she quickly closed the few feet that separated them and placed her hand on his shoulder. She'd just remembered what her mother had said to her, what she had promised . . . and, in truth, what she herself wanted. She wanted to live. She wanted to enjoy life. And damn it, she hadn't asked for this craziness, this transportation of time, but she had spent too many years since her divorce terrified of relationships, and the agonizing hurt that came when they ended. She didn't expect anything from Michael, so her heart was safe.

Not responding to her, he had merely stopped when he'd felt her touch on his shoulder. Gently, Kate ran her fingers down his back and smiled when she felt his muscles tighten.

"Why, Michael," she whispered softly. "I think you

really do believe in legends." She didn't expect an answer and none was given, at least not verbally, yet as she came closer to him and used her other hand to brush back the hair at his temples she heard his quick intake of breath.

Smiling, Kate continued, "Who is it you want to revenge? I've been there, Michael. It's a hollow emotion. Be careful you're not destroyed along with it."

Watching her, Michael told himself that he must dismiss her beauty, her playful sensuality, but he couldn't stop the grin from creeping up the corners of his mouth. She was a minx, and fully aware of the power she held over him . . . almost like the mermaid. Dismissing the maid from his mind, Michael looked at the woman before him and couldn't suppress the laugh. "I think you're going to be trouble, Helene."

Kate placed her hands on her hips and laughed with him. Still grinning, she said, "You might be right. And by the way, no one calls me Helene." She winked. "Like you, I go by my middle name. It's Kate."

"Kate?"

She nodded.

"Should I say that you don't look like a Kate? After all, you said I don't look like a Michael."

Kate giggled again. "I'll tell you what—why not let Helene and Kevin work out the confusion. You'll be Michael and I'll be Kate."

Liking the sound of her laughter, Michael joined her. When he reached for the door, he checked himself and shook his head. Glancing in her direction, he said, "I almost forgot. This is our wedding night. I have some chores to do, but I'll be back."

Kate couldn't answer him. Her throat felt paralyzed, her mouth as dry as a desert. *Wedding night?* She hadn't thought of *that!*

She couldn't stop staring at the closed door, and finally managed to swallow only when she heard Michael's renewed chuckling in the hallway.

He hadn't come back. Kate sat at the table, staring at the door until her eyes watered from the strain. Closing her lids, she leaned her arms against the tabletop and rested her head. The eyes would soon feel better. It was the emotional strain that was almost unbearable.

She admitted that, in spite of everything, she found herself liking Michael—and she shouldn't. She also found herself attracted to Michael—and that could prove disastrous. Although she'd had three glasses of wine, she couldn't blame the drink for her actions. She'd wanted to flirt with him, to see if she could evoke the same reactions he had inspired within her. God, it had been so long . . .

The wine made it easier to allow forbidden thoughts to reenter her mind. She had refused to dwell on her past, yet now, faced with a wedding night, of all things, perhaps it was time to understand that it was her past that had made her the woman she was today. Flashes of her first wedding night filtered across her mind. She'd been so young, maybe not in years, but in naive expectations. She should have known something wasn't right, but then, at that time of her life, she'd been the eternal optimist. And why not, she'd married the man she loved—a handsome, sensitive young actor who had just landed his first TV series. They had quickly become part of southern California's beautiful people, and at the time she'd thought life couldn't get any better.

Bringing her head up, Kate opened her eyes and loudly sighed as she eyed the ship's cabin. Living with Jon in California had been like a drug, and just as difficult to break away from. But she'd done it. It had taken desperation to put behind her the outwardly beautiful husband, the lovely home, the days of leisurely pampering for the wild, sometimes frightening, nights. She'd lost her identity . . . A small-town girl not able to cope with life in the fast lane. When she had returned home to her mother's after five years, her relatives had thought she'd gotten religion. No one, except her mother, knew that she'd been fighting for her sanity . . . and to regain her self-respect.

The journey back to finding herself had taken almost two years. It was a long time to remain alone—an even longer time not to feel the comfort of a man's arms. At least she could look in the mirror now and recognize the woman who stared back at her. Most of the time she even liked her.

Kate stood up and walked to the oval mirror hanging on the cabin wall. What of the life she had left behind, the life she had painstakingly rebuilt? What would happen when she failed to return from her vacation? Her aunt Natalie would contact the authorities and she would be reported missing. How long would they hold her job, before giving it to another? Unanswerable questions ran through her mind as she thought about her relatives, her friends, even her ex-husband. Knowing Jon, he'd probably turn her disappearance into publicity for his career, she speculated, and unwillingly pictured the man who'd had a profound effect on her life. How could she have been so naive?

Gazing into the glass, she brought her fingers up to her lips. They still felt sensitive from Michael's kiss, a kiss that had shaken her, awakening a dormant longing. Michael Sheridan was the most intriguing man she had ever come across—and the most confident. Intently staring into her own eyes, she could almost hear her mother whispering to her: "*Live,* Katy. It's your time . . ."

Her time? Shaking her head, she turned away from the mirror. This wasn't her time. It was Michael's. All she had wanted was a vacation, a two-week respite from the almost hermitlike existence she'd been living. Since discovering Jon's unfaithfulness, and since her mother's stroke, she'd gone from one extreme to another—from a young woman who fiercely needed to prove her femininity to an older woman who fearfully denied it. What she needed was a balance—to find her place.

Pacing the cabin, she crossed her arms over her chest. "This is definitely *not* my place," she muttered aloud. She had merely wanted to regain some of her confidence, and the scuba lessons had been a start. She'd exhaustively planned this escape to Bermuda to get away from all reminders of her past. Now, it seemed, she had no past at all. Jon didn't exist; her mother's split level home had yet to be built.

It came to her suddenly, and chills broke out over her skin. She had no past. She was *free!* If she weren't having a nervous breakdown, if her mind hadn't snapped, then she had nothing to escape from—no ugly scenes of her husband in the arms of another, no degrading reminders of her attempts at revenge—absolutely nothing!

Revenge. It was what Michael had said he most desired. Who had caused such anger and pain in him? She wondered if it was a woman who had broken his heart and taken away his joy for life. Maybe that was why he pulled at something inside her, because she recognized his emptiness. Now, if she believed everything taking place around her, she'd just been given the greatest gift of all—a new beginning, a clean slate. Here, while she was held captive in this time, she could begin a new life.

Kate stood in front of the table and lifted the half-empty bottle of red wine. Picking up the cork, she jammed it inside the neck of the container.

That was it! Life. Michael had forgotten the joy of living, just as she had done . . . just as her mother had reminded her. Smiling, she held the bottle in one hand and picked up two stemmed glasses in the other. Wedding night, huh? Well, she wasn't about to wait for him to return. Shifting the wine under her arm, she managed to open the door and close it behind her. Now that she was free, Michael Sheridan was going to learn the emptiness of revenge . . . and the joy of living. She wasn't going to wait, either, to start his lessons.

For a moment he thought the maid had grown feet and was coming to him. Before a background of pink and deep purple sky, she came toward him as the dusk held on to its beauty before giving way to night. It lasted for only a few seconds, until he realized it was Kate, and his disappointment was mild. He watched as she came closer, noticing the bottle of wine and glasses that she held. Delicately, she picked her way over the coils of rope and Michael was again reminded of her innate grace of movement.

"You shouldn't be up here," he gently reproached her, ridiculously glad that she was standing beside him.

Turning her head, she looked over the length of the ship. "Why?" she asked. "It seems everyone is below. I'm not bothering anyone." She offered him a glass. "Am I bothering you, Michael?"

He studied her face for a moment, before coming to a decision. Taking the bottle of wine from her, he uncorked it and poured the red liquid into both glasses. After placing the bottle on the deck, he took one of the glasses from her hand. "I don't suppose it would hurt to let you get some fresh air," he commented. "Though I doubt the wisdom of your having another glass of wine."

Kate gave a short laugh. "You aren't accusing me of being drunk, are you?"

He smiled. "That was quite a performance you put on earlier. You know, Kate, you're nothing at all like I'd imagined."

She lifted her eyebrows in question. "I hope you aren't going to start in again about me being too old."

"I never said you were too old. I said you were older than I thought you'd be."

"Twenty-eight is not old! I'll have you know, Kevin Michael Sheridan, that I am just now approaching my prime."

He laughed out loud, and Kate couldn't help chuckling along with him. He had a great laugh. She'd have to make sure she heard it more often.

Holding up his hand, he said, "Please! Just Michael, remember? You sound like a schoolmaster. Anyway, I wasn't talking about your age, though it still puzzles me."

Looking out through the darkness to the outline of the island, Kate asked, "What then?"

He studied the perfection of her profile and felt the renewal of stirrings he had experienced earlier. "You're nothing at all like your father," he stated abruptly.

Kate quickly turned her head to look at him. It was on the tip of her tongue to tell him she didn't even remember her father, until she realized he was talking about Winston Barnett. "My father and I don't agree on very much," she truthfully announced, as she remembered Helene's confrontation with the man.

Attempting to change the subject, Kate asked, "And what about you, Michael? Are you like your father?"

Immediately, she could see the change in him. His eyes narrowed slightly, causing tiny lines to appear at the corners. His mouth lost its relaxed softness as his lips tightened. "My father is no longer alive."

Breathing deeply with embarrassment, Kate looked away. "I'm sorry," she murmured. "I didn't know."

From beside her, she heard his voice, "I'm surprised. I'd have thought your father would have filled you in on our family history."

"We . . . we didn't talk very often," she mumbled, still looking out to the water.

"He never mentioned our home in Charleston, the family members, not even my uncle Martin?"

Kate heard the difference in his voice, the deeper inflection when he'd said his uncle's name. Realizing an answer was necessary, she decided to stick to the truth

70

as much as possible.

"The name doesn't sound familiar to me." Turning to face him, she smiled brightly. "Honestly, Michael, you must have guessed I wasn't too enthusiastic about being married off to a man I'd never even met." She touched the edge of his sleeve. "Be truthful. Isn't that how you felt?"

He stared at her fingers until she returned them to her glass. Slowly, his gaze moved up from her waist to settle on her face. It wasn't supposed to have been like this, he thought in confusion. She should have been a young, spoiled brat. It would have been much easier that way, and his conscience wouldn't have been activated by her seemingly genuine warmth. Looking directly into her gorgeous eyes, he said quietly, "I'll be truthful, Kate. I didn't expect to like you. I'm not even sure why I do now."

Again she laughed. This time throwing back her hair, as she lifted her face to the moonlight. "Why, Mr. Sheridan, was that almost a compliment?"

"Take it any way you want," he muttered, just before bringing the glass of wine up to his lips.

Sipping her own wine, Kate looked back to the water as it quietly slapped against the hull of the ship. Coming to a decision, she swallowed down her apprehension and bravely spoke. "Listen, Michael. About tonight . . . ?"

She heard an expectant, "Yes . . . ?"

"Well," she began slowly, "don't you think . . . I mean, we really don't know each other, do we?"

Again he sipped his wine. Looking beyond the water to the darkened outline of the cove, he said, "No, Kate. I don't suppose we do." Emptying the glass, he turned

71

to her. "I'll walk you back to the cabin. You've had a long day. You should rest."

It was, perhaps, the most polite dismissal or the most gallant gesture she had experienced in some time. Either way, she smiled into his eyes and said, "You're right. Why don't you stay here, though. Finish the wine. I know the way."

He didn't say anything, just continued to stare back at her. Feeling the beginnings of a lazy warmth entering her belly, Kate quickly widened her smile and whispered a hasty, "Good night, Michael."

Making her way down the companionway, she rushed to her cabin. Once the door was shut behind her, Kate leaned against it and grinned. He might be a stubborn student, she silently admitted, but he'd passed his initial lesson. He probably didn't even realize it yet, but Michael had just started a friendship. The first step was accomplished.

He didn't even bother with the glass. Bringing the bottle to his lips, Michael took a long swallow of the wine. He used the back of his hand to wipe away the droplets that clung to the corner of his mouth as he gazed out into the darkness.

It wasn't going as planned, he thought. Nothing was going was planned. Ever since he'd come to this island everything was confusing. It had begun with en-countering the maid. It seemed incredible to him that such a creature could really exist. Perhaps that was the reason he had kept her a secret, not telling any of his crew. But she was real, she existed under the water . . . protecting his treasure.

His problems above the water were even more troubling—all centering on one person—Winston Barnett's daughter. There was no marriage, not when he had signed his own name instead of Kevin's. His grip tightened on the cap rail. *Was there?* He shook his head. Of course there was no marriage. Barnett had probably ripped up the marriage certificate as soon as he'd seen the wrong Sheridan's name.

But what of Kate? Did the end result of revenge justify using her? In less than a day, she'd worked her way under his skin and he admitted that the thought of returning her to her father also didn't sit well with him. She'd made it clear tonight there was no love lost between the two, and for some strange reason, he was glad. The best solution, he decided, was to get that treasure up as quickly as possible.

Which meant tomorrow he'd have to deal with the maid. It was strange that meeting with the mermaid brought its own rare feeling of expectancy. Again he shook his head in dismay. All those years, ever since he'd realized the futility of the war, he hadn't seriously thought of a female. All his encounters had been casual, a means of fulfillment, for his mind had been centered on revenging his father. Now, when the end was so near, he was driven to exasperation by two females: the sensuous, gentle mermaid, and the beautiful, flirtatious Kate—the first woman in two years to make him laugh.

Thinking of her, he chuckled and wished he hadn't volunteered for the night watch. It was a hell of a way to spend one's wedding night!

Chapter 5

Kate was reluctant to open her eyes. The gentle swaying motion lulled her to continue sleeping. It was only the persistent soft knocking that made her stretch with irritation, yawn, and lift her eyelids. What was revealed was a confusing blur.

Squinting, she rose up on her elbow and clutched the sheet in her fist. Dear God! It hadn't been a nightmare! She was in Michael's cabin, which meant he was real, too . . . yet for some strange reason, that didn't bring the panic she'd expected.

"Miss! You awake? I got your breakfast."

Kate scrambled out of the bunk and grabbed the white robe she'd used yesterday. Still squinting, she made her way to the door.

Denny viewed her appearance and knew he'd gotten her out of bed. She was a vision, a real beauty, and he thought both Michael and Kevin were fools if neither one of them wanted her. Embarrassed for staring, Denny cleared his throat and motioned to the tray in his hands. "Brought you somethin' to eat, here," he said in a gruff voice.

Kate smiled and held the door open wider. She watched as he placed the tray on the table, replacing the dishes from last night with the ones he'd just brought. Satisfied, he lifted the tray and faced her. "Eat hearty, miss. The cap'n said to tell you he won't be seein' you till lunch."

Again Kate smiled and came closer. Making a controlled effort not to squint, she asked, "I met you yesterday, didn't I?" At his nod, she laughed self-consciously. "It wasn't much of a meeting, though, was it?"

"The name's Denny Moran. You did real good, miss," he remarked of her rope-climbing.

She laughed. "Thanks. Why don't you call me Kate?"

The gray-haired man looked confused and she was quick to add, "It's my nickname. Everyone calls me Kate. You know, just like Michael goes by his middle name, rather than Kevin."

This time the older man coughed so loud, Kate was tempted to come to his aid. "Are you all right?" she asked out of concern as Denny's face turned a deep red.

He bobbed his head. "Fine," Denny answered hoarsely, wanting to get out of the cabin. He motioned with his head to the table. "You sit and eat. I'll be back later to clean up."

As Denny Moran closed the door behind him, he shook his head. Michael was gonna have a hell of a lot of explaining to do before this mess was over, he thought in disgust!

Kate didn't dwell on Denny. As soon as the door was shut, she hurried over to the built-in shelves and peeked

75

into two tiny crystal glasses. Part of a set of six, Kate had appropriated the two for her contacts. Careful not to mix them up, she brought the glasses down and peered inside. It had seemed logical last night to place them in salt water, for it was the closest thing she could think of to the bottled saline solution she used once a month. Unfortunately, extended wear only extended until last night. Actually she was three days late in taking them out. Hoping her homemade solution would work, she dipped her index finger into the glass and brought out her right lens. Using the fresh water Denny had brought, she rinsed the clear, flexible plastic between her fingers and inserted it into her eye. Blinking a few times, she shut her left eyelid and looked about the cabin. A wide grin appeared at her mouth. As long as she could see, she would survive Kevin Michael Sheridan's tricks . . . and, hopefully, the nineteenth century.

She'd quickly finished the breakfast of fruit, thick bread, and tea with leaves staining the bottom of the cup, in order to straighten the cabin. Satisfied with her work, she'd brought the tray back to Denny in the galley and had met three other seamen. Content to have established herself as an able woman, Kate had hurried back to the cabin, eager to execute the plan she had formed last night. While rummaging through Helene's trunk for suitable clothing, she'd come upon the girl's jewelry. Most was too ornate for Kate's taste, but she had found a use for it. It was while holding a large brooch that the idea came to her. What if she switched whatever was in the treasure box for a few of

Helene's things? As long as she got to the treasure first, Michael would never know.

Grinning, she picked up her black bathing suit.

Kate worked quickly. Using the handle of her knife, she was able to chip away centuries of encrustation around the lock. Taking a deep breath, she placed the tip of the blade inside and gave it a hard yank. She blinked several times as she watched it fall next to the skeleton in the sand. By God, she'd done it!

It had been years since she had felt such expectation, and Kate tried to keep her breathing even as she lifted the small lid. It was impossible to remain calm as she viewed the contents, and tiny bubbles clouded her vision as she quickly expelled her breath. Dodging the little bursts of air, Kate brought her head closer to the treasure.

Unbelievably, she stretched out a hand and touched a large gold cross studded with emeralds. Her fingers grazed over a golden, hollowed out rock, brimming with chunks of stones. Immediately, she thought of Doña Marina and wondered if this really might be the tribute she'd sent to Cortez. Quickly following that was thoughts of Michael, and Kate hastened to pick up the cross. Taking one of Helene's drawstring bags off her wrist, she placed the cross inside it. Hastily, her hand returned to the treasure and one by one she removed the colored stones. She knew the heavy ingot would weigh her down and decided to leave it while she brought up the cross and stones.

It took only minutes to tie the one purse onto the rope she had used for her equipment and resubmerge.

Plunging back into the water, Kate swam under the hull of the ship and far enough away so as not to attract attention. Coming back to the casket, she kept telling herself to contain her excitement until her task was complete. Picking up the weighty chunk of gold, she replaced it with Helene's jewelry. The few pieces she put inside looked pathetic compared with what she had taken, and Kate wished she had left one of the colorful stones for Michael. Mentally shrugging, she closed the lid and fitted the lock back into place. It was done. She gave one last look at the partially buried skeleton. Who had it been? A Spanish soldier, entrusted with bringing the tribute to Cortez? Had the heavy chain around him weighed him down, so that he couldn't possibly have survived the hurricane? Or, had he been so committed to the beautiful Mayan woman that he'd refused to give up her tribute?

Shaking her head, Kate gently patted one of the exposed ribs and pushed upward. The treasure was in her care now . . .

"Holy—!" Quickly, Kate's hand clamped over her mouth to suppress the startled exclamation. Her vision flew to the door and, satisfied that no one had heard her, her eyes returned to the treasure. Seated on the floor, Kate viewed the priceless objects before her. Cradled in the hollowed ingot were chunks of large emeralds and amethysts and stones that she believed to be unpolished diamonds. It must be worth a fortune! she thought, as she picked up the gold cross. Touching the emeralds that adorned it, she slowly and quietly whistled. Approximately three inches by six inches, it contained ornate scrollwork and she couldn't even begin to estimate its worth.

Gazing lovingly at her booty, Kate started to giggle with excitement. Who'd believe this? she wondered. For that matter, who'd believe *any* of it?

From the open window of the cabin, she heard a man's shout. Quickly gathering up her treasure, Kate hid it in the trunk and ran to the square window at the rear of the cabin. Peeking her head out, she was able to see Michael as he swam toward the side of the ship.

"Bring the boat, Denny. I've found it!" he yelled. Although she could no longer see him, from his voice she could tell he was climbing the rope ladder.

Holding on to the window molding, Kate near collapsed in uncontrolled giggles. Poor Michael! Wait until he opened the treasure box . . .

She listened as Denny issued the order to lower the rowboat and shouted back at Michael about fool's treasure. Again, she laughed. Denny didn't know how true that was. No longer able to hear any conversation, Kate considered going on up on deck to watch Michael retrieve his "fortune," when something even more wicked entered her mind.

Why not meet with him one last time? As much as she hated to admit it, there was something extremely pleasing about Michael underwater. Below the sea, she was free to be as playful as she desired. And thinking of his strong hands gently touching her legs made her eye her wet suit with anticipation. Just one more time . . .

She had come to him with a sensuous grace, a voluptuous beauty from the sea. The heavy strands of

79

her dark hair floated about her head as she beckoned to him with her human hand. And in the silence of the ocean, he could almost hear her voice inside him calling out his name: Michael . . . come. I have waited so very long for you . . .

He held on to the reef, afraid to let go, afraid to give in to her power. As if she could read his thoughts, her voice carried through the water and whispered to his mind: Do not fear. You'll be safe. Come, Michael . . . I promise you an astonishing journey. He hesitated, yet her words pulled at him and set off an amazing need throughout his body. Reaching out his hand to hers, he felt her fingers clasp his own as she pulled him away with her.

She took him deeper, deeper . . . and he was amazed that the air in his lungs could last so long. Following her, he extended his free hand to touch the human skin of her leg and she turned to him as they floated together in the arms of the sea. No longer did he find her repulsive, for she continued to talk to him with her mind. His excitement grew as he listened to her telling him of her own need, how she had waited centuries for him to appear . . . Her fingers caressed his bare chest; her legs entwined with his as she allowed her body to slide against him, creating a wild friction. He wanted her. His mouth kissed the flesh of her arm, the rough texture of her shoulder where the black skin began. As if sensing a deeper need for contact between them, the maid turned her face toward him. He worried where to kiss her, for the mask and tubes distorted her mouth. As if sensing his confusion, the maid lowered her head, causing her long hair to wrap itself around her face. To his shock and utter amazement, when she slowly raised

80

her head it was Kate's face that emerged from the waving tendrils of hair! Gone was the deformity of the tubes and mask. Replacing them was Kate—with the sensuous smile, the laughing eyes . . . Afraid the maid would quickly change back, he clasped her to him and crushed her lips with his own.

As the pressure of his mouth increased, he felt exhilarated to once again experience the passion of Kate's kiss. Unable to comprehend how the maid had transformed into the woman in his cabin, his mind concentrated on the thrill, the excitement, the pain—

The pain?

A white-hot stab of pain shot through his toes and ran up his foot. Blinking a few times, his vision cleared to reveal the tip of Denny's boot applying pressure to his bare extremity.

Standing at the cap rail of his ship, Michael looked out to the water then quickly turned to his first mate as he began to speak.

"I worry for ye, Michael," Denny noted sorrowfully, as he removed his boot from the younger man's toes. "You've been standin' here for no less than five minutes staring down at that water. Didn't hear a word I said. What were you thinking? I tell you lad, this treasure has become an obsession with you."

Suddenly aware of the telltale bulge in his trousers, Michael kept the front of his body close to the ship to hide his embarrassment. How could he tell Denny that he'd been reliving his dream of last night? The same dream that had awakened him with an adolescent humiliation. At the time he had blamed it on Denny's ridiculous remarks about a wedding night. Now he didn't know. Maybe Denny was right. Maybe he was becoming obsessed with the treasure, for thoughts of it were tightly connected to his vision of the mermaid . . . and that part of it had to be a hallucination. Didn't it? But the treasure was real. Hadn't he just found it, before ordering Denny to lower the rowboat? And the maid . . . she, too, had to be real. The alternative was that he was losing his mind.

Desperate to regain control, Michael looked down to the small boat bobbing next to his ship. "You're worse than a nanny with your nagging," he said with a forced smile. "Instead of standing here arguing, why don't we get started?" he asked while motioning to the waiting boat. "When you see what I've found, you'll understand my obsession."

Denny gave forth a sarcastic snort as he lowered himself over the side. Following him down the rope ladder, Michael only hoped someday he might understand it all.

This time Kate came up behind him and strongly exhaled through her regulator, causing tiny clouds of bubbles to surround his head. Startled, Michael quickly turned around. She almost smiled at his reaction. He had already opened the small chest and, upon seeing her, had dropped Helene's large brooch. They both watched as it slowly sank to the sand.

The first to respond, Kate felt his eyes on her as she bent to pick it up. Taking his hand, she placed it on his palm, then closed his fingers over it. With her own hand, she pointed to the surface—indicating that he should take it up.

She watched as Michael nodded and pushed upward

toward the rowboat. Unable to control it, she inwardly laughed as she waited for him to return. She was certainly having fun, playing this dual role, and, since this might be the last time she encountered Michael under these circumstances, she decided to really enjoy herself.

When he came back, she had the rest of the "treasure" out of the chest. One by one, she handed them to him, running her fingers over his hands and forearms—as if trying to discover what type of creature he was. She never let him stay under too long, always gently pushing him toward the surface after each piece was placed in his palm.

She knew he would come back after he had received the last. There was something about his eyes and the distorted smile on his face that reassured her. She felt almost melancholy that she no longer had any excuse to continue her charade. When he resubmerged and swam in her direction, she again marveled at the perfect symmetry of his body, the way each muscle was defined with every powerful stroke of his arms. Something deep inside her made her yearn to feel those arms around the woman, and not the mermaid.

He swam to her and pointed to the skeleton. Confused, Kate watched as he tried to remove the chain from around its ribs. He struggled, for at least half of it was buried under the sand. Lending her strength, she, too, pulled on the encrusted chain.

The combined effort caused the whitened keeper of the treasure to leave its centuries-old home and flip upward. Frightened when the arm of the skeleton arose like a specter from a horror movie, Kate fell backward into the sand and lost her regulator. Panic set in as she grasped for the floating mouthpiece, and it was only when she had it tightly clasped between her teeth that she saw Michael was in trouble.

Trapped under the weight of the chain, he struggled to free himself. Immediately, she reacted. Grabbing ahold of the back of his hair, she kept his head firmly in place and jammed the breathing regulator into his mouth. He was forced to breathe. He had no other alternative. She pushed on his diaphragm to make him exhale through his nose, and nodded as she watched the bubbles released into the water. Letting him take another deep breath, she removed the regulator and brought it to her own mouth. Deeply inhaling, she held her breath as she returned it to his mouth. She then fought with the chain and the skeleton, dislodging both, until Michael could pull his legs free.

They were attached by the tube of air, and it was Michael who brought the regulator to her mouth so she could breathe. They alternated for less than half a minute, his hand clasped over hers as they directed the apparatus from one mouth to the other. Kate had time to be grateful for the darkened glass of her mask, for if it had been clear, even the distortion of being underwater wouldn't have hid her features.

His empty hand reached out for hers. While the regulator was in her mouth, he brought the fingers of her right hand up to his lips and placed a kiss upon them. Tiny bubbles of air escaped from his mouth when he smiled. Kate felt shaken by the gesture. Almost of their own volition, her fingers traced the outline of his lips. Michael took another breath and reached down to the chain. Finding its end, he slipped a link off and pressed it into her hand.

Kate was afraid of the emotions that surged through her body. She was touched by his actions and ashamed by her own. Here Michael was free to be himself, and the man he revealed to the mermaid was someone the woman wanted to know better.

Holding on to his shoulder to keep him submerged, she moved closer to him, wanting to feel his body against hers. He slid an arm around her waist, pressing her breasts against his chest. Their mouths were so close, only separated by the regulator, and it was almost an intimate kiss as they passed it between their lips.

They both sensed the disturbance at the surface at the same time. Looking upward, they could see Denny slapping the water with his oar. Michael looked once more at her, then pushed off the reef toward the rowboat.

Kate clutched the encrusted link of chain into her palm. Dear God, she wanted him to come back . . . She wanted to feel his arm around her waist, his mouth so close to her own. She waited. Looking upward, she could see Michael climbing into the rowboat. Whatever was happening above the surface, it must be serious, for she was sure Michael would have returned.

Deciding she had better get back to the cabin, Kate looked one last time at the spot where she had first met Michael and then swam away. Watching a school of brightly colored fish dart from her path, she realized that she was tired of playing this dual role of innocent bride and not so innocent mermaid. Her whole life had been turned upside down, and Kevin Michael Sheridan was now at its center. That admission created an uneasy tightness in her chest.

Surfacing right behind the ship, Kate could hear shouts from the deck. "I don't care what you found down there! Charlie says Barnett's got men combing this island and two of his ships took off in different directions. I say we clear out now—while we still can!"

Kate clung to the rudder, waiting to hear Michael's reply. When it came, her whole body tensed.

"Let's do it . . . *Set sail!*"

Amid the creaking of the timber, Kate forced her shocked body to move. She had to get her scuba gear into the cabin. Damn! She had to get *herself* into the cabin!

She cursed the wet suit as she shimmied out of it and tossed it through the window. Her mask followed; her snorkel caught on the corner of the molding, but ricocheted in anyway. Desperately trying to keep her balance, she hurried to lift her tank up to the window. It would be difficult, but she realized that either she somehow managed or she'd have to leave it behind. At any moment, the ship was going to take off and the rudder would certainly be in use. Straining, Kate hoisted the tank to her shoulder and attempted to pull herself into the window.

Suddenly, the heavy weight was removed and Kate watched in disbelief as it disappeared into the cabin. Slowly, dreading what she would find, she brought her head up and peeked inside.

Her breath caught in the back of her throat; her heart skipped a beat then started thudding at an alarming rate. Automatically gulping down the choking coil of fear lodged in her mouth, Kate slowly brought her head down and hid for a moment.

Realizing she couldn't remain on the rudder, she

tried to get moisture back into her mouth, attempted to restore movement to her limbs as she gripped the molding of the window and clumsily climbed inside.

Standing in her bathing suit, she blinked a few times and tried an unsuccessful smile as she viewed the scene before her.

Poised a few feet away, in a tiny puddle of water from his own dripping clothes, Michael held her wet suit over his arm, her mask in his hand, and the tank of compressed air in both.

His eyes seemed ready to leave his head as he stared back at her. His mouth appeared incapable of speech as he muttered something unintelligible. When the color returned to his face, it deepened until it became a threatening purple-red.

Working his lips, he finally emitted a strangled sound. It was only one word, whispered with a mixture of disbelief and anger:

"You!"

Chapter 6

Michael was stunned. His mind refused to accept what his eyes revealed. *It couldn't be!*

Breathing heavily, his fingers gripped the canister in his hands—the very same apparatus the maid had worn on her back. *His maid!* The gentle, seductive creature who had saved his life by giving him her own air; the same one who had given him the treasure . . .

"Michael! You're needed on deck. You got in this here cove, now navigate us out!"

Both Kate and Michael glanced at the door as Denny's voice came through the other side. Quickly, their eyes returned to each other's face.

"Michael," she whispered. "Let me explain . . ."

"You!" he repeated in a shocked, disbelieving voice. Slowly, he lowered the canister to the floor of the cabin and touched the damp *whatever* that was draped across his forearm. It was the mermaid's skin—the black covering he had thought was skin. Quickly, he threw everything onto the table.

"Please, Michael," Kate again whispered as she

pushed the wet strands of hair away from her eyes, "if you'll just listen."

"Michael!" Denny's voice was louder.

Michael jerked his head toward the door. Denny was right. As captain, he was needed on deck to get them the hell out of here! Turning back toward the practically naked woman, he slowly advanced in her direction. She was wise to back away from him, he thought. The rage that swiftly coursed through his body was almost blinding. He managed to walk to the window, check the rudder for damage, and, finding none, close the square porthole.

"You, madam," he rumbled in a barely controlled voice while pointing a shaking finger at Kate, "you will not move until I return! Do you understand?"

Kate stood opposite him, her arms crossed over her chest. She was shivering, though not from the damp bathing suit that clung to her like a second skin. She was shaking from fear. Never had she seen a look of such anger. His face was intensely red, the veins in his neck looked magnified as they clearly stood out. She had the distinct impression he would explode, if he didn't soon vent his wrath, and was extremely grateful that Denny was calling him. The once large cabin now seemed far too small for both Michael and herself.

"I asked you a question . . . and I expect an answer!" he gritted out between clenched teeth. His eyes narrowed and the corner of his upper lip lifted in a sneer. "Or would you be more comfortable shaking a fin?" he asked, looking down at her feet.

Kate followed his gaze with her own eyes and hastily removed the black rubber flippers from her feet. Glancing back up at him, she merely nodded her understanding that she was to remain in the cabin, and winced as she listened to his explosive curse and the slamming of the door. Both were done simultaneously, and with such force Kate was sure the entire island of Bermuda must have looked to the sky for signs of lightning. She herself had no doubt as to the severity of the coming storm.

Several hours later, as she gripped the edge of the bunk to keep her balance, she told herself that she'd only been making a pathetic joke about the storm. When the rain had started, she'd blessed it—hoping nature had created a diversion for Michael's attention, for anything would be better than having him return. She had changed out of her bathing suit, restored her scuba gear to Helene's trunk, and had dressed in the girl's most proper outfit—a white embroidered cotton shirtwaist with a high neck and a plain brown skirt. Yet now, even the layers of underwear and slips couldn't keep her warm. She'd even donned heavy black stockings that ended at her thighs and clumsy shoes that reminded her of a pair her grandmother had worn. Nothing helped.

Wrapping the blanket from the bunk around her shoulders, she firmly told herself not to watch the swinging lantern that hung from the ceiling. Some time ago, she'd found herself unconsciously moving her head in unison with its sickening swaying motion. Yet, because it was forbidden, her eyes would sneakily return to the damn thing. It had become her own barometer. The wider its arc, the more the ship pitched, and the tighter her grip on the bunk became.

God! It was the pounding rain, the rolling of the ship, the frightening creaking of wood, and the muffled shouts she could hear from on deck that had Kate on the brink of screaming. Whatever was happening, it couldn't be worse than her imagination. Even though she'd never been on a ship before, especially a sailing vessel, she had seen *The Poseidon Adventure,* movies about the *Titanic,* and both of those disasters had been brought about by nature. And there's no engine on this thing, she thought in a panic!

The scream bubbling up in her throat was finally let loose as the door slammed open and hit against the wall.

"Sorry, ma'am," the young sailor she recognized from this morning apologized. "Denny thought you'd want somethin'. Only tea and a tin of biscuits here. No time to cook proper. 'Fraid that's it, until we ride this one out."

Kate marveled at the young man's ability to move with the crazy swaying motion of the ship. Anxious to know what was going on, she managed to rise and make her way to the table by holding on to fixed pieces of furniture.

"Tom," she remembered his name. "Are we all right? I mean, this is just a regular rainstorm. Isn't it?"

Trying not to look serious, Tom opened the tin for her. "Can't say myself. Never been in these here waters, ma'am, but heard the cap'n say we're riding ahead of a hurricane. You best eat while you can. I 'spect it's going to be one long night."

"A hurricane!"

Tom took one look at the frightened woman and immediately regretted his words. Hoping he could make up for his hasty remark, he added, "Not to worry, though. Cap'n Sheridan's the best. He'll get us through." He smiled nervously. "I'd better get back up on deck. You're safe down here."

The ship pitched at an alarming angle and Kate was thrown back onto the bed. When she looked about the cabin, Tom was gone and, closing her eyes, she began to pray.

She'd lost count of time, and days. She had no idea whether it was day or night—everything ran together. Nor had she seen Michael. For a period, she hadn't seen anything at all when the oil in her lantern had burned out. Denny had come, refilled it when he'd brought her more tea, and, after making a feeble attempt at reassurance, had quickly left. She'd already lost the contents of her stomach, and felt as though she'd been in bed for days, wrapped in the scratchy wool blanket. There was no reality anymore. Her world was filled with fear and sickness. As the storm intensified, her feeling of isolation and abandonment grew with it. She tried prayer, but the last time she had prayed to God it was to end her mother's misery. Now it seemed hypocritical to beg for her own life. She would die here, she thought as she opened her eyes— here, in this time where no one knew or cared about her. This cabin had become her prison, a place where she was haunted by memories of her past and those she'd left behind. The faces of her friends and relatives swam before her eyes like pages from a scrapbook of her life. She didn't deserve this . . . this separation from reality. Now she didn't know what was real anymore. Was reality this wretched cabin? Dear God, how could she hope to survive this?

She closed her eyes tightly to shut out the room, yet the sickening motion of the ship forced her to reluctantly open her lids. She avoided looking at the window. Hours ago, she had watched as water seeped in when the window dipped under sea level. Deep inside her, she had a feeling that they were doomed, for surely the ship could not withstand much more of nature's fury.

As if reacting on her thoughts, the wooden hull groaned eerily, just before the glass windowpanes shattered and torrents of sea water entered the cabin.

"My God!" The words were screamed from her numb lips. The ship was sinking! And she'd go with it, unless she got out of here! Panic overcame illness and Kate dragged herself off the bunk. As the ship violently swayed, it brought water to her feet, making it more difficult to proceed to the door. Chairs moved of their own accord. Books and papers flew off shelves and tables, reacting to the ship's motion. She felt as if she were in an absurd carnival fun house as she fought with the door, slammed into the walls of the companionway, and bucked the rope-lined stairway—all the while fighting to keep her balance. When she reached the top of the stairs, she unlocked the wooden covering and strained to open it. Succeeding, she was drenched with a fresh deluge of water.

Soaking wet, Kate gasped as the wind robbed her breath from her throat. She held on fast as another wave crashed over the side of the ship, taking her to the deck. The water receded for seconds and she attempted to stand, only to be thrown back down as it returned.

The sea was almost a living creature—angry, punishing those who thought to tame it—yet, Kate wasn't ready to give in. She grasped a rope that held barrels together and clung to it. Able to breathe only by holding her mouth wide open, Kate tried to see through the blinding rain. Even Michael's shout in her direction didn't have the power to frighten her. She was beyond that—she was fighting to survive!

"Get back to the cabin!"

She tried to keep her eyes open long enough to see him and had a brief glimpse of Michael in a black slicker, his hair plastered to his head, his face a wet mask of exhaustion.

"I . . . I can't!" she screamed over the wind. "The window's gone! Water's coming in!" She was thrown into the barrels, yet held on for dear life—waiting for the water to briefly recede.

Michael grasped her upper arm and helped her stand. Over her head, she heard his shout, "Tom! Cabin window's out! Take . . . take Andy with you!" Again the waves crashed over the ship and both of them lost their footing. Michael was the first to rise. "Go below," he shouted down to her before he was knocked back to the deck.

Still holding the rope that secured the barrels, Kate managed to stand up. Just as she was about to help him, the line suddenly snapped! Everything happened so fast, she only had the strange sensation of riding a wave that never seemed to end . . . right before she was swept overboard into the angry ocean.

"*Kate!*" Her name tore out of his throat as he was hit by one of the free barrels. Scrambling to his feet, Michael only heard Denny's frantic shout as he grabbed hold of the free line and took the next wave over the side of the ship.

He could catch glimpses of her white blouse as she rode the crest of a wave. Clutching the rope in one hand, he prayed there was enough slack to reach her as he swam in her direction.

She tried to swim toward Michael, knew it was her only chance, yet she was fighting an insurmountable battle—the fury of nature at sea. Attempting to shout to him only made her swallow great amounts of salt water . . . and she was already tired. Despite the buoyancy of water, she felt too heavy to remain afloat . . . Everything felt so heavy. She couldn't even see him any longer. Dear God! Not like this, she prayed. Don't let it end like this!

The pain at her scalp exploded inside her brain as her head was jerked upward, her chin pointing to the blackened sky.

"I've got you, Kate! Move your legs! Move, damn it!"

Suddenly on her back, she felt herself being pulled by Michael. She reached up and gripped his hand at her hair while her legs moved furiously, tangling with the sodden woolen skirt.

He shouted over the wind. "Kate! Grab hold of my arm!"

She tried, but the slicker proved too slippery for her rooting fingers. Attempting to turn around, she pulled Michael under with her. When they resurfaced, she never even saw the floating barrel as she was hit in the shoulder and knocked away from him.

In a fraction of a second, he made his decision. Letting go of the taut rope, Michael immediately swam to her. He clawed at the material of her blouse, clutching the high neck. With his other hand, he made a quick grab for the barrel. If he'd had the strength, he would have cried out his triumph as he clasped one arm around the large wooden barrel and the other around Kate. Maybe, he thought, as he fought the waves to keep both close to him, just maybe they had a chance of surviving. Bringing his head up, Michael caught one last brief look at the *Rebel* as she disappeared behind a sheet of driving rain . . . and then she was gone.

Time and again he had to tell her to keep her head up. They'd been in the water for hours and conversation had ceased along with the driving wind. What remained was a fine drizzle that lulled them into relaxing their guard. Michael had grabbed another barrel before it floated away from his reach and their small measure of luck had been the three feet of rope hanging from it. Tying the two barrels together, he'd managed to create a makeshift floating preserver. It was the only thing keeping them above water.

Kate's wrist was loosely tied to one and it would quickly tighten when she'd let go. She tried so hard not to, for she felt guilty that Michael was now going to die along with her. Poor Michael, she thought with pity. It had been suicide to come after her. It was hopeless, and only a matter of time before one of them floated away to a chilly grave. Leaning her head against the barrel, she fought the sleep that beckoned to her. It would be so easy, she thought, to close her eyes and let the peacefulness take over. What was the point, anyway? Neither one of them . . .

"Kate!"

She jerked her body and snapped open her eyes. "I'm not sleeping," she lied through cold, numb lips.

He slapped her back. "No! Kate . . . look!"

She turned her head and tried to see above the curve of rough wood. Michael reached down and slipped his arm around her waist. Bringing her up higher, he repeated, "Look, Kate—*land!*"

She clawed at the barrel and hoisted herself halfway up onto it. Through a gray mist, she saw it in the distance. It was the most beautiful sight she had ever seen in her entire life! Turning back to Michael, she slid down the barrel and wrapped her free arm around his shoulder. "Oh, Michael," she breathed, her wide smile making it difficult to speak. Leaning over to him, she kissed his chilled lips. "We're going to make it, aren't we?"

His smile matched hers. "Damned right, Kate!" His laughter sounded like a little boy's. It was triumphant . . . once more he'd beaten the sea. "Let's do it," he shouted in a hoarse voice while taking her hand and placing it on the rope.

She watched as he started kicking with his legs and quickly added her own strength to his. She didn't even marvel that either one of them had any reserves at all. They were riding on euphoria.

Untying her wrist, she started crying the second her foot touched sand. It didn't matter that she was thrown around in the surf. She let it carry her, knock her to her knees. Nothing mattered anymore, as long as she could touch down on something solid. Michael made it out first and she slowly crawled toward him. Collapsing next to him, she closed her eyes and dug her cheek into the wet sand, almost in a caress. They were both breathing hard, letting their aching muscles relax for the first time in countless hours. She wanted to stay there forever . . .

"Come," he whispered in an exhausted voice, while brushing her shoulder with his hand. "Get out of the water."

Kate opened her eyes and looked at him. He was crouched on all fours next to her, his sand-covered hair hanging in his eyes, his face white as a sheet, his lips a strange purple-blue. Half in, half out of the water, Kate felt the foamy tide rise to her hips before it would gently recede down her legs. She made a valiant effort to move. Her limbs rebelled, yet she ignored the screaming muscles and clung to Michael's arm as he helped them both to stand.

Supporting each other, clinging to the other's shoulder and waist, Michael and Kate stumbled, fell, pulled at each other until the Atlantic Ocean was behind them.

"Michael," Kate whispered his name. "It's stopped raining," she announced, her hoarse voice filled with reverence.

Looking up at the sky, his legs buckled under him and they both fell to the sand, finally giving way to oblivion—before either could see the sun peeking out from behind gray, retreating clouds.

Kate awoke to a soft tickling sensation on her hand. She didn't want to open her eyes. The sun felt so good against her skin, its warmth entering her pores and melting away the memory of the hours in the chilly ocean. It was bliss, and she wanted it to go on indefinitely, yet the annoying tickling on her hand spread upward over her wrist and onto her forearm.

Reluctantly, her eyelids lifted and she searched for the cause of her harassment. Seeing the prehistoric creature crawling up the arm of her blouse, she let loose a shriek and jerked backward into Michael's hard body.

"Wha—?" His voice was confused as he attempted to rise on an elbow.

Looking into his sand-covered face, she pointed to where she had thrown the thing. "It was crawling over me!" Kate exclaimed. "You should have seen it!"

Michael squinted in the bright sunlight and looked in the direction where she was pointing. Abruptly his eyes closed and his head sunk back into the sand. "It's a crab, Kate," he said in a tired voice.

She looked around and watched it bury itself into the sand. Breathing easier, she blinked a few times. Well, close up it looked different, and it was one hell of a way to wake up. But now that she was awake, she looked around. Beyond the sand was a treeline . . . and nothing else. No houses, no signs of life. Nothing.

"Michael," she whispered. "Where are we?"

He didn't raise his head. "I don't know," he muttered, keeping his eyes closed. "Before you woke me, I thought it must be heaven." He brushed sand away from his mouth. "Now, I'm not so sure."

Resigned to being awake, he rolled over onto his back. Shielding his eyes, he looked at her. A slow smile spread across his lips. "You look like hell," he pronounced in a dry voice.

"You ought to see yourself, Captain," she said while

99

pushing back sandy, stringy hair off her face.

"Half of your face is sunburned."

"So's yours."

They both touched the sides of their cheeks that were exposed to the sun. Kate was the first to speak again. Swallowing was difficult, yet she couldn't stop the words. "God! I'm thirsty. I feel like I've swallowed half the Atlantic."

Michael slowly sat up and removed the black slicker. Letting it fall to the sand, he remarked, "You practically did. Do you know how lucky we are, Kate?"

She looked into his eyes. Without thinking, her fingers reached up and brushed particles of sand that clung to his lashes. "I know," she said quietly, gratefully. "You saved my life, Michael."

Staring at her, he said, "I owed you that."

Quickly, she looked away. She didn't want to deal with the mermaid charade yet. There was enough right here on the beach to contend with—like fresh water, and food.

Michael sighed and looked across the beach. He was too tired to demand explanations now. Suddenly his eyes narrowed and he attempted to stand up. Groaning from the aches in his body, he slowly placed one foot in front of the other. The barrels had washed up onto the sand.

Kate watched as he walked away from her. When she saw where he was going, she gathered up her heavy skirt and followed. Coming to stand behind him, she looked as he slid his pant leg up and removed a knife from the inside of his boot. Using the tip, he pried away at the fat round cork in the side of a barrel.

When it was removed, he whispered, "Say a prayer,

Kate," and tipped the wooden barrel forward. As he cupped his hand at the hole, Kate held her breath—then squealed in delight as water overflowed his palms. Immediately, Michael brought the water to his mouth. Kate waited anxiously until he opened his eyes. Gazing up at her, he laughed. "It's fresh, Katie! It's *fresh!*"

She sunk to her knees and held out her hands. Still laughing, Michael poured out the water and watched as Kate devoured it.

"More," she pleaded, and he obliged. Giggling like a child, she waited as he took a second drink. When he looked up at her, she reacted instinctively and brushed a droplet of water from his bottom lip. "Thank you, Michael," she said sincerely. "Thank you for everything."

His grin froze. Slowly he brought his thumb to her mouth and wiped at her lips and chin. They knelt in the sun, staring at each other for endless seconds—each inexplicably moved by the emotions that ran through them. From that moment on, each knew the other was bound to them. They could keep the knowledge secret, never utter it aloud, yet the binding was permanent. They owed each other their lives. Together they had fought death, and won. They were survivors.

"We'd better get out of the sun," Michael whispered in confusion, tearing his eyes away from hers.

Kate nodded and reluctantly stood up. Lending her strength to his, she helped him drag the barrels to the treeline. It was only when they sat in the shade that Michael used his knife to work on the sealed rim of the other barrel.

As if luck were trying to make up to them for its absence, Michael and Kate discovered long lengths of

101

canvas and, hidden in between its white folds, a large tin of tea biscuits.

"Denny!" Michael announced. "He was always complaining that at the end of every voyage, he never had a tin to take home to his sister. One of the deckhands always pilfered it before we made port."

Kate rubbed her hands together in anticipation of the food. "God bless Denny," she said reverently, adding as an afterthought, "And God bless his sister. Let's open it, Michael!"

Chapter 7

"Aren't you tired?"

Kate glanced over at Michael as he fashioned a makeshift tent. Using the canvas and branches from scrub pines, he had succeeded in making them a shelter of sorts.

"Of course I'm tired," he admitted, never stopping his work. "As soon as I'm finished, you can rest."

"What about you?" Kate asked, lending him a hand.

He gave her the knife as he tied off a knot. "We'll have to take turns. One of us must keep an eye out for Denny."

Kate wiped her forehead on her sleeve and grimaced as the sand scratched her skin. "Do you really believe he'll find us? How do you even know the ship survived the hurricane?"

"The *Rebel* survived," he stated with authority. "I know it. There . . . !" Standing back, he surveyed his finished tent. Nodding, he said with pride, "You can use it now to sleep out of the sun."

Kate looked over the lengths of canvas, the black

103

slicker that served as a flooring. "You know, Michael, if you would have built it back by the trees, you . . ."

"I told you. That's too far away. I want one of us on this beach at all times so we can spot Denny."

Kate sighed in exasperation. She was tired, sunburned, and covered in sand. "Fine," she said in a strained voice while unbuttoning her skirt. Pulling off the heavy wool, she threw it on top of a barrel and reached for the waistband of her slip.

"What the hell do you think you're doing?" Michael demanded, his hands on his hips.

"What does it look like I'm doing?" she asked in a tired voice.

"It looks like you're undressing."

Keeping her head down, Kate stepped out of her slip. "Very good, Michael," she said, pulling off the old-fashioned shoes and rolling down the black hose.

"May I ask why you feel the need to do so now?"

Kate picked up a shoe and held it out to him. Before he could take it, she turned it over and let the sand fall out in a steady stream. "You see that?" she asked. Without waiting for an answer, she continued. "Well, that's what it's like all over me! There's sand in my hair, in my clothes . . . everywhere!" She poked at his chest with her finger. "I am not sleeping until I get it off me," she pronounced, enunciating each word with a jab.

Letting the shoe join its match on the beach, Kate reached up and unbuttoned her blouse. Defiance was written on her face.

Unconsciously, Michael rubbed his chest after her sharp assault and looked up the wide, flat beach. "Really, Kate!"

Standing in the thin cotton chemise and knee-high

pantaloons, she laughed sarcastically. "I didn't realize you were such a prude. After all, you've seen me in less!"

She was tired, beyond exhaustion, and her emotions were too close to the surface. She was also weary of waiting for Michael to ask about the mermaid. She wanted to get it over with.

His jaw hardened. "Look, I know you're tired and hungry. Just don't push me, all right?"

She shrugged her shoulders and turned away. Slowly walking toward the surf, Kate mumbled, "It didn't seem to bother you when you thought I was a mermaid."

Immediately, Michael was at her side. Grabbing her arm, he asked in an irritated voice, "What did you say?"

She pulled away from his grip and kept on walking. Michael kept pace. "What did you say, Kate? Surely I couldn't have heard correctly."

Leaving him on the beach, she ran into the cold waves. She wouldn't answer him. Not now. He'd worked her like a convict—ordering her to search the scrub for branches, making her strip the poles of all twigs, hoarding the water and biscuits. Standing waist-high, she held her breath and braced herself for the water. Ducking under it, she scrubbed her hair, hoping to dislodge most of the sand. Bursting into the sunlight, Kate held her head back so that her hair fell straight on her shoulders. From the corner of her eye, she saw Michael walking back to the shelter, and she watched as he picked up her shoe and threw it against a barrel.

Taking a deep breath, Kate slowly walked out of the surf. One of them had to bring it out in the open. She'd had the distinct feeling that Michael was making her pay silently. It was after they had discovered the canvas and Denny's tea biscuits that she had noticed the change in Michael. It was as if he'd wanted to shut her out. When he'd started talking about building a shelter, as tired as she was, she'd offered to help. In a curt voice, he'd sent her over the sand dunes and into the palmettos and pine trees. Time and again, he'd sent her back, stating that her branches were too thin, or too wide, not tall enough, or too tall. She'd suffered his moodiness with patience—after all, he had saved her life, and possibly lost his ship. But enough was enough!

Walking over to her shoe, she picked it up and slowly removed the long slip. She could feel his eyes on her as she shook out the black lace. Putting it over the slicker, she sat down and proceeded to braid her wet hair.

"Have you no shame at all?" He towered over her, hands on his hips. Dear God, the sight of her when she'd walked up to the tent was enough to drive him mad. The thin wet cotton of her underwear hid nothing from his eyes.

Hastily tying a knot at the end of her long braid, she glared up at him. "Don't talk to me about shame! It didn't bother you one bit on the reef. In fact, the truth is . . ."

"*Truth?* You, madam, wouldn't know the truth if it hit you right in the face. Your father would be proud of you, Helene."

She crossed her arms over her knees. Taking a deep, steadying breath, she narrowed her eyes and said it. "That man isn't my father . . . and I'm not Helene Barnett."

He looked at her as if she'd lost her mind. "What do you mean he's not your father? Of course he is. He

106

arranged with my uncle for the wed—"

"I repeat," Kate interrupted, not frightened of his anger any longer, "Winston Barnett is not my father. I don't even remember what my own father looked like. My name is Kathleen Anne Walker. I was in Bermuda on holiday—not to marry you."

She remained calm, despite the incredulous look on Michael's face. Since he seemed incapable of speech, she continued. "Helene didn't want to marry you. I'm sorry, but she didn't. I needed to get back to the United States and your ship was the first to leave. Whatever Barnett and your uncle tried to arrange between you and Helene just wasn't meant to . . ." Her hands quickly rolled into fists. "Michael, what are you laughing at?"

He shook his head and held up his hand to stop her words. Frightened, Kate rose to her feet and stared at him. "I don't see what's so funny."

He tried to catch his breath. Wiping away the tears at the corners of his eyes, he again laughed then asked, "You're really not Helene Barnett?"

When she shook her head, he looked at her again and once more burst into self-deprecating laughter. Falling to the sand, he sat back against a barrel and stared out across the ocean. Abruptly, he raised his head and gazed into her turquoise eyes. "I'm holding Kathleen Anne Walker for ransom," he whispered, as much to himself as to her.

"*What?*" Kate sunk down beside him, staring at Michael as if he had lost his mind.

He nodded. "I'm supposed to be holding you for ransom—holding Helene Barnett for ransom. Jesus! Why the hell was Barnett after me, if his daughter's safe

107

at home?"

"Why were you supposed to hold Helene for ransom?" Kate pushed drying tendrils of hair off her forehead. He's unbalanced, she thought in a panic.

Michael looked into her eyes, and Kate swore she saw sanity. That frightened her even more.

"I was marrying her for her dowry, shares of Barnett Importing. When that didn't work out, my second plan was to hold her for ransom." He shook his head in bewilderment. "I can't believe I've gone through all this for nothing!"

She could feel her jaw hardening as she clenched her back teeth. "Michael, *why* did you want to kidnap Helene?"

He glanced at her, then looked back to the ocean. "It's a long story. I needed the money to get my father's company back from my uncle—Barnett's partner."

"So you were going to use an innocent girl?! My God, Michael, even for you this is too much!"

He dismissed her anger. Instead, he quietly asked a question, dreading her answer before it was given. "Kate, what name did you sign on the marriage certificate?"

She brought her chin up. "My own. I wasn't about to sign Helene's."

Michael leaned his head back against the barrel and closed his eyes. Slowly, he let out his breath. "I think, Kathleen Walker, very possibly you and I are legally married."

"*What?*" Kate gave a nervous laugh. "You've been in the sun too long. That marriage, Michael, was between you and Helene. Since I signed my name, instead of hers, it isn't binding."

Keeping his eyes closed, he said, "That marriage was supposed to be between my brother, Kevin, and Helene Barnett. I didn't want him legally married to her, so I signed my own name instead of his." Opening his eyes, he looked directly at her. "My name is Michael Thomas Sheridan. Kevin is my older brother."

Kate couldn't answer him. Her mouth had gone completely dry. Desperately, she wanted water. "This is a joke, right?" she finally asked, hoping to God Michael would soon laugh.

He shook his head. "The Reverend Hailey only asked, 'Do you take this man? Do you take this woman?' He never used names, Kate. Do you realize what we've done by protecting the others?"

Kate stood up and backed away from him. "This is ridiculous! I am not married to anyone . . . and that includes you. *Whoever* you are!"

Quickly, Michael came to his feet. "Whoever *I* am? I hope that's not a superior tone I hear in your voice, Kathleen Anne Walker! I wouldn't be too quick to condemn my actions, if I were you. I would say you're the master of deception here!"

Kate placed her fists on her hips, her anger matching his. "So! We're finally getting to it, aren't we? Let's try honesty for a change, shall we? You, Michael Thomas Sheridan, can't stand the fact that you were falling in love with a mermaid!"

He looked as if she had slapped him. Raking his fingers through his blond hair, his eyes narrowed dangerously—making him look like a lion staking out its prey. "Obviously, you're the one who can't take the sun," he stated in a falsely calm voice. "Let's talk about the mermaid . . . shall we, Kate?"

She crossed her arms over her chest and raised her chin. "Why not? We've both been waiting days for this conversation, so let's have it."

"For starters: Where did you ever get that equipment? And who taught you how to use it? Who the hell are you?"

She gave a false laugh and sat inside the shelter. As much as she hated to admit it, the sun was too hot for her fair skin. Surprisingly, she wasn't afraid of Michael's anger. She had nothing to lose anymore. Her scuba gear *and* the treasure were probably lying at the bottom of the ocean by now.

"You'll want to sit down, Michael," Kate stated calmly while crossing her legs, Indian-style, and brushing the sand off the soles of her feet.

He hunched down before her, resting his elbows on his thighs. Sighing, for despite everything he made a devastating picture with the ocean in the background, Kate tried to collect her thoughts. "First of all, I was scuba diving when you found me. All that equipment you were talking about is called scuba gear. And it's not unusual where I'm from."

"And where is that, may I ask?"

She took a deep breath and said it plainly. "From the future. Nineteen eighty-seven."

Michael just stared at her, his mouth open. Finally, he seemed able to muster his ability to speak. "You really have been in the sun too long. I think you'd better get some sleep. Perhaps, then, you might be capable of the truth."

"I'm telling you the truth, Michael. I'm not from this time. I know it seems crazy to you," she admitted. "It seems crazy to me, too. Have you ever seen equipment

110

like I was using before? Have you? You used it, too. Remember?"

He sat down on the sand so he could see her better. "Kate, what you're saying is insane."

"Don't you think I know that?" she demanded in a frustrated voice. "I don't know how it happened. One minute I was diving with a group, and in the next your ship appears at the surface and you're there." She shook her head. "Maybe it has something to do with the treasure. I don't know."

"The treasure?"

She nodded. "First I found the medallion. As soon as I picked it up, my ears started to ring, breathing was difficult. I was . . ."

Michael's head snapped up and he stared intently into her eyes. "What medallion?" he interrupted. "I didn't see any."

"I told you," Kate said patiently, "I have it. I picked it up before you came."

"Where is it, then?"

She sat up straighter, her back tensing. "It's . . . it's on the ship. I put it in one of the drawers of the trunk."

Michael looked down to the sand that separated them. "The *Messenger* was supposed to have been wearing a golden medallion given to him by Doña Marina."

"Michael, what the hell are you talking about? What Messenger?"

He looked back up at her. "In the legend. The Messenger who was bringing Cortez her tribute. It's said the Messenger would bring you both your fortune, and your heart's desire."

Kate's eyes narrowed. "Well, he certainly wasn't very

lucky. Was he? I mean, look what happened to him. He's down there wrapped in a rusty old chain."

"According to legend, you're now the Messenger. You found the medallion, and the treasure."

She squinted her eyes and screwed up her mouth. "Huh? Look, Michael, I'm no messenger. Nor are we married. All I want is to get back to the United States. None of this matters anyway. The treasure's gone, along with my scuba gear." The last she murmured under her breath.

"So, you really do have it! I knew those pieces you gave me weren't the real things. There had to be more!"

Kate raised her hand to stop any further words. "Hold it right there and listen to me. That's *my* treasure. I found it first."

He looked serious. "No, Kate. I think you have it wrong. You're the Messenger. You're to bring good fortune to another."

She nearly screamed at him in frustration. *"I am not the Messenger!* That is my damned treasure. Find somebody else to bring you your good fortune, Michael. I've found mine. *If* the *Rebel* didn't go down in the storm, then that treasure belongs to me."

His expression was that of annoyance. "You're a strange woman, Kate. You've lied to me, deceived me, cursed . . ."

"Hah! Talk about liars, Sheridan! You're as bad as I am. At least I had a good excuse . . ."

Even his sunburn couldn't hide that his face was becoming a deeper angry red. "Just one moment, madam! I had a very good reason for my actions. Whereas your main motive was greed. Admit it, you used that equipment of yours to switch whatever was in the casket for those pieces of jewelry."

Kate flicked sand away from her knee. "You don't know that," she nervously commented, and looked back up at him. "Why don't we both admit that we've been using each other? And it's over."

"What was in the box, Kate?"

"I'm going to sleep," she stated, while lying down on her slip. "If you want to sit and stare at the ocean, go ahead. Call me if Denny suddenly appears."

"Kate, what was in the box? I don't believe you've told me the truth about anything. You're working with somebody, aren't you? Somebody who made all that scuba gear, as you call it? Kate . . . ?"

She closed her eyes and smiled. "Go to sleep, Michael," she advised. "Maybe when you wake up, you'll be able to think clearly." She shook her head and refrained from giggling aloud. "That's my big message, Michael—get some rest. The sun is frying your brains."

Almost shaking with anger, Michael turned away from her and faced the ocean. Getting to his feet he started walking toward the water. He had to get away from her. She had ruined his life, completely ruined it! There was a very good chance that he was married to a greedy, lying, crazy woman. Searching the horizon, he vowed that the first thing he was going to do, if he ever got off this lousy island, was find the Reverend Leonard Hailey and burn that damn marriage certificate!

Denny Moran stood at the helm as the *Rebel* limped into Charleston's harbor. Within twenty minutes of docking, he watched as Martin Masterson's carriage pulled up and Michael's uncle stepped out. Behind him was Kevin. As both men came on board, Denny steeled himself for the meeting.

Tall, thin, with age leaving its mark on his pale skin, Martin Masterson, known for his cold control, was barely able to find his voice as he glared at the *Rebel*'s first mate.

"I'll speak with you below, Mr. Moran," he finally snapped out through clenched teeth.

Denny squared his tired shoulders and nodded, without once looking at Kevin. Leading them down the companionway, he dreaded telling Michael's brother what had happened. When they were inside Michael's cabin, Denny turned and watched as Masterson closed the door behind them. As the man turned around, it took every ounce of willpower for Denny to remain still.

Eyes blazing his inner fury, Masterson cracked his cane down on a trunk. "Where is that bastard? What has he done with Helene Barnett?"

Denny looked at Kevin, who seemed shocked by his uncle's behavior. "Kevin, lad," he began slowly, "I don't know how to tell you this . . . Michael's gone. We were caught in a hurricane and the girl was washed overboard. Michael went in after her. There was no stopping him. The last I saw was the two of them in the water."

Kevin sank onto a chair. Staring around the cabin, he said in a disbelieving voice, "No! It can't be!"

Denny placed a hand on his shoulder. "Aye. We searched the coast until we came to port. The *Rebel*'s taken a beatin', lad. We did what we could."

"You saw him go over?" Masterson's voice sounded

114

strangled with rage.

Denny nodded without looking up.

"Son of a bitch! The girl? You're certain?"

Raising his head, Denny looked into the evil eyes of his sworn enemy. "She didn't deserve what she got, no matter whose daughter she was."

Masterson held his gnarled fist out to the old man. "The sea has denied me the pleasure of killing that bastard, but I'm still capable of shutting your stupid mouth . . . permanently!"

"Martin!" Kevin jumped between the two old warriors. "Have you no respect? My brother, your nephew, is dead!"

Breathing heavily, Martin looked into Kevin's face. Seeming to calm down, he broke away and tapped the trunk more lightly this time. "Is this the girl's?" he asked in a cold, breathless voice.

Kevin looked at Denny. Reluctantly, the first mate nodded.

"It's hers," Kevin acknowledged to his uncle. Never had he seen Martin lose control like that!

"Mr. Moran," Martin said in a much calmer voice, while straightening the jacket of his well-tailored suit. "I want this trunk taken to my home. I'll ship it back to her father with my condolences." Walking to the door, he addressed Kevin. "You, sir, shall have the pleasure of disposing of your brother's belongings. Were it up to me, I'd torch this whole damn ship!"

Kevin and Denny stared at the slammed door. As he turned back to Denny, Kevin could still hear Martin calling the three-storied brick home that had been in the Sheridan family for well over a hundred years *his* home.

115

Looking at the tired old man across from him, he placed a hand on his rounded shoulder and whispered, "Okay, Denny, what really happened?"

Kevin watched as Denny slowly raised his head. A smile played at the corners of his mouth, a twinkle shone in the old eyes. "Aye, Kevin boy, you know me too well. Thank God that old goat Masterson doesn't."

Kevin's grip tightened. "Are you telling me Michael is alive?"

Denny raised his shoulders and Kevin removed his hand. "I have to ask ya— Are you with your brother on this, Kevin? Or do you believe that bastard you call an uncle?"

Kevin straightened to his full height, insulted that his allegiance was being questioned. "My brother has always had my loyalty. Up until now, I'd thought his problems with Martin were because the two of them never got along. Martin says he's received a letter from Winston Barnett saying Michael had kidnapped the girl! That was never to be a part of it. Michael had this consuming hatred for Martin, wanting to ruin him for what he's done to Sheridan Shipping. He made all these accusations against him, with nothing to back them up. And you, Denny, you and Martin have always been at each other's throats from as far back as I can remember. But just now I saw hatred in my uncle's eyes . . . and fear. I think now, maybe Michael was right about a few things. Answer me, is my brother alive?"

Denny smiled. "Michael's too stubborn to die. I was tellin' the truth about the two of them goin' over in the storm. There was barrels floatin' all around 'em, though. Michael'd use his head and get 'em both to

116

land. I figure only a couple of hours in the water before they'd be washed up on the coast."

He ran his hand over the girl's trunk. "You work with me, Kevin, and in less than a week we can have the *Rebel* fit to sail again. I'm plannin' on takin' her out to look for them." He stared at the younger man. "Are you with me?"

Kevin looked at his father's good friend, at Michael's first mate, and had the eerie sensation of being taken back to another time when the same question was asked of him. It had been at a social gathering, a small lawn party. It had been at a time when his world was intact, and life was simple. Everyone had thought it would only take a few weeks to show the stiff-necked Yankees the obvious superiority of the South. When his friends declared their intentions of joining the cavalry, they had turned to him and said those words . . . *Are you with us?*

Counting himself lucky to be alive after the war, he knew since that time he'd lost something of himself, something vital. Maybe, just maybe, this was his chance to get it back. He had something to prove to Michael, the brother he'd let down, but more important, he had something to prove to himself.

Kevin Sheridan raised his chin and smiled at the old man across from him. "Aye, Denny," he stated in a strong voice, "I'm with you!"

Chapter 8

The cold woke her. Kate shivered and rolled her body into a ball in an attempt to gain warmth. Not finding any, she reluctantly opened her eyes. It was almost dark. As she sat up, her muscles ached from lying on the ground and she rubbed her arms and legs to remove the stiffness. Leaning forward, she saw Michael's legs outside the tent and, slowly, she crawled toward its opening.

He was asleep. Leaning against a barrel, with his chin resting on his chest, and his arms crossed at his waist, he snored lightly. Kate couldn't help smiling. He looked so innocent. Making herself more comfortable, she studied him. He must have taken a dip while she was sleeping, for the sand was removed from his hair and from most of his clothes. Even though he infuriated her a good deal of the time, she could no longer deny that she found him devastating. It had been a long time since she admitted something like that to herself—that she could be this attracted to a man again.

118

Sighing, she fought the urge to touch the stubble of beard that was now growing on his sunburned chin. Awake, he had a very strong face. It spoke of authority, demanding respect with just a look of his ever-changing eyes. His mouth was now soft in sleep, yet most of the time there was a tightness at its corners that told of a man with unresolved problems. Quickly, a mental picture of Michael laughing flashed through her mind. She liked the sound of his laughter, the way his eyes softened, the way it erased the tension around his mouth . . . She had a feeling it was something he didn't do very often.

God! He touched at something deep inside her, something that brought both excitement and fear. Shivering, Kate rubbed her upper arms. Had she only imagined the hungry look in his eyes the first night on the ship? When they had discovered the barrel containing the water and had wiped each other's mouths, was it only gratitude for being alive that had made her think he was going to kiss her? Was he so embarrassed to admit his attraction to the mermaid now because it would be an admittance of his attraction to her? She briefly closed her eyes in denial. Be honest with yourself, she thought. Michael cannot stand the sight of you. We just rub each other the wrong way.

Opening her eyes, she sighed, shivering as the sun slowly receded from the sky. They should build a fire, she thought. Wanting to show Michael that she could be useful, Kate put on her slip and her blouse. Tying the white cotton into a knot at her waist, she again looked at the sleeping man. She hunched down in front of him and inched his pant leg up. Placing her hand on the hilt of his knife, she very slowly pulled it out of his boot. Her heart lurched when he moaned and turned his legs to the side, yet that very action helped to quickly remove the knife. Leaving his pant leg up, Kate picked up her shoes and straightened. She hadn't been a Girl Scout for nothing, she thought with a smile, as she headed for the trees.

When she returned to the campsite, less than a half hour later, Michael was awake . . . and waiting for her. Even though she was scratched and her arms ached from carrying the load of dead branches, Kate took one look at Michael and straightened her shoulders. Through the last rays of daylight she could see the anger on his face.

"Don't ever take off like that again without telling me!"

Kate dropped the wood at his feet and looked up at him. "You were asleep," she stated patiently. "I thought we should build a fire."

He clenched his jaw. "You took my knife. I want it back."

Reaching to the waistband of her slip, she withdrew it and handed it over. "I only wanted to let you rest. I was hoping when you woke up, your disposition would be better." She brushed her hands together to remove the tiny pieces of bark that had stuck to them. "I can see now that was wishful thinking."

"*I'm* in charge here . . . and I have every intention of building a fire," he proclaimed, kneeling down to pick over her wood.

Kate's eyes narrowed, the anger she had been trying

to squash quickly rising to the surface. "Who put *you* in charge? And leave my wood alone! *I'm* building the fire."

Throwing a piece of twisted dried bark back onto the pile, he glanced up at her and smirked. "You?" he asked in disbelief.

Unconsciously, her fingers rolled into her palms and became fists. "Move out of my way," she ordered. Brushing past him, Kate knelt in the sand and began digging a small depression. Satisfied with the neat hole, she reached into her blouse pocket for the thin, flat piece of wood she'd found. "I'll need to borrow your knife again," she stated, while holding out her hand.

Looking very amused, he handed it over.

Kate used the knife's tip to make a small hollow in the center of the wood. Several times, she compared a thin, straight stick to the hole until she was satisfied with the way both fit. Handing the knife back to Michael, Kate ignored his look of superiority and reached for the dried grass that she'd earlier cut from the sand dunes. First she inserted the stick into its matching hole in the flat wood, then gently placed the dried grass around it. Holding the stick between her palms, Kate quickly started rolling it between them.

Crouched over the hole, she could feel Michael's eyes on her. Neither spoke as she worked. At each interval, when her palms hurt from the constant friction, Kate silently prayed for success—for there was more to prove here than just her ability to make a fire. Again, she bent over her work, creating pressure and heat, and was rewarded by a tiny curl of smoke.

"I'll be damned," Michael whispered.

Kate didn't answer him as she ever so gently blew

121

down into the hole. Even when a spark lit the curling, dried leaves, she ignored the burning sensation in her hands and didn't stop. It wasn't until she could actually see the small flame that she took a deep breath and quickly put more dead grass on her fire. Placing broken twigs and larger pieces of dried wood on top, she waited until it all caught before she looked up.

Smiling with satisfaction, she tried to take the triumph out of her voice as she said, "Now it's your turn. While there's still some light, you should find us enough wood to last the night."

Michael stared at the fire, then back at her. "Who taught you that?" he asked in amazement.

Kate smiled. "Another woman," she answered, emphasizing the last word while mentally blessing her old Girl Scout leader. Rubbing her hands together over the flame, she said, "The wood, Michael. I believe you were going to get more wood."

It wasn't said as an order, yet she could tell he didn't like her words. Without commenting, he walked away from her and Kate grinned as she watched him take off for the trees. She stood up and threw another branch onto the fire. Hands on her hips, she admired her work. She was proud of herself. A few more pieces of wood and she'd have a veritable inferno going!

She spent the time while Michael was away by gathering up and washing out large shells. Spreading a narrow piece of canvas in front of the fire, Kate used the shells to hold their biscuits, and deeper ones to hold their water. It was the best she could do, she thought, as she piled four precious tea biscuits onto a shell.

Just then, Michael came out of the trees. She had to admit he'd been more successful than she in securing

122

wood. His muscled arms were strained with thicker, more lasting pieces. She tried smiling as he dropped his wood on top of hers, yet he ignored her friendliness and looked at the shells.

"That's too many biscuits," he said in a brusque voice. "We're going to have to ration them."

"Oh, come on, Michael. We have something to celebrate! We're alive. We have fresh water. We have a shelter . . . and now we have a fire. Besides," she said, sitting down by the food, "tomorrow I'm going to see if I can catch some fish."

He snorted. "You? Now you're going to tell me that you're a better fisherman, I suppose."

Kate bit into a biscuit. Chewing several times, for she wanted to savor each bite, she carefully picked up the shell containing her water and delicately sipped. Shrugging, she returned it to the ground just as Michael sat next to her. "I really don't know who's better. I just know I have more patience."

Reluctantly, he reached for his food. "Have you ever caught a fish before?"

Kate heard the sarcasm in his voice, but refused to let him anger her. "No," she admitted, "but it can't be too hard."

He gave a harsh laugh. "You forget, madam, that *I'm* the sailor here. *I'll* catch the fish!"

She returned his look with a sweet smile. "Just because you can sail a boat doesn't mean you're a fisherman . . ."

"I sail a *ship,* not a boat!" he interrupted. "And I'll catch the damned fish! All right?"

Kate again smiled sweetly. "Fine, Michael," she said in a soft, calm voice. "I don't know why you're so upset.

123

I mean, it isn't as though we're in competition with each other, is it?" She patted his arm. "I'm just glad to see you agree that the only way to survive this island is with team work. You and I are partners until we get out of this." Her grin was wide. "I hope you catch Jaws . . . I'm starved!"

"I beg your pardon?" he asked, his mouth full.

Kate laughed. "Jaws. It's a gigantic shark, about thirty feet long, and it terrorizes a New England town."

He swallowed the biscuit and stared at her. "There are no sharks that big. I wouldn't believe everything you hear."

She picked up another of Denny's little treasures. Right before she popped it into her mouth, she grinned and said, "I didn't hear about it. I saw it."

"You saw it? I don't believe you—you're lying again."

She shook her head. "No I'm not. It's not real, Michael. It's a mechanical shark . . . and I saw it at a movie studio."

She didn't mind his laughter. It was better than his sarcasm and resentment.

He wiped at his mouth with his sleeve. "A *mechanical* shark? Surely, you're not serious! Why would anybody want a mechanical shark?"

She found herself enjoying the turn of the conversation. "Now, Michael, where would they find a thirty-foot shark? You yourself said they aren't that large. And they needed one for the movie—so they built it. It was very realistic . . . you should have seen it."

He nearly choked. "Kate, what in the hell are you talking about?"

She took one look at his face and collapsed back

onto the sand in laughter. Lying on the canvas, she continued to giggle—much to Michael's annoyance. Finally, she recovered enough to speak. "In the twentieth century there are movies . . . Look, think of pictures, photographs, that are strung together to show continual movement. In fact, they were first called moving pictures. They're a form of entertainment, like a play. Only instead of seeing them performed live on a stage you see them on a huge screen. And they can be shown over and over again, all over the country." She started to laugh at her own simplified explanation, when she turned her head and looked directly at Michael. Something about his eyes made her swallow down her laughter. Her voice sounded slow, and thick. "They aren't invented until the turn of the century."

Michael merely stared at her, unable to speak. Although he had heard her explanation, he didn't believe a word of it. It was her light, breathy laughter that wound its way around his soul. The way the firelight highlighted the long column of her throat as she flung her head back and stared at the darkened sky created a longing deep inside him. And he was fascinated by the beauty of a female, not bound by convention but living with an earthy freedom.

"Where do you come from, Kate?" he asked slowly, quietly.

She raised herself up on her elbow and wound a strand of hair between her fingers. "I told you. From the future. When I left my time, it was 1987."

He closed his eyes briefly as if her words produced an actual pain inside his head. "*Please!*" Staring at her, he said with exasperation, "No more of this talk of being from the future. You insult me with it."

Kate's mouth hung open. "Insult you? Look, you asked me where I was from, and I told you. It isn't my fault if you can't accept the truth."

"And the truth is that you're from a time one hundred and nineteen years from now? I'm expected to accept *that?*"

Knowing how ridiculous it sounded, she shrugged her shoulders. "All I can tell you is that before I encountered you on that reef, I was living in the twentieth century, well into the twentieth century."

He issued a sarcastic snort and shook his head. "Do I appear as if I've suffered a head injury at birth? Only a simpleminded dolt would swallow that story you've thrown at me."

Holding her palms out to the fire, she tilted her chin and studied him. "You know, Michael, in this light, the left side of your hair does look fuller than the other. I'm not saying you were dropped at birth, mind you. It could be caused by your overinflated ego. I'm not sure which side of the brain controls that process."

He merely stared at her, the muscles in his cheek moving as he clenched his back teeth.

She couldn't help it; she began to giggle. "Well, you started it," Kate laughingly accused, relieved to see that the muscles in his face were beginning to relax.

"I only asked where you were from," he muttered.

"And I told you."

He shook his head. "It wasn't the answer I was expecting. You're an American. Where do you live? Where is your family?"

She pushed the hair back off her forehead, and her laughter vanished while thinking of her response. "I live . . . I used to live in New Jersey. Since my mother

126

died, I don't suppose I have any close family."

"No one's waiting for you?" Even as he asked the question, he couldn't help wondering why he was so fascinated with her. Besides being an accomplished liar, she was the most unconventional woman he had ever come across.

She shook her head.

"No one?"

The way he said it made her think he was talking about someone other than a parent. Again, she shook her head. "I told you . . . there's no one waiting, Michael. There isn't a person in this world right now who's even concerned about my whereabouts." She returned his hot stare.

That was stupid, she thought! What if he plans to do away with me in order to keep the treasure for himself? Wanting to correct her blunder, she quickly added, "Except Helene, of course. She's waiting to hear from me."

He blinked a few times in confusion. "Helene Barnett?"

Nonchalantly, she nodded while gathering the shells that had contained their ration of tea biscuits.

"Where is she?"

Kate took a deep breath and looked up at him. "I don't suppose you can do anything to her now, so I might as well tell you. When we heard you'd arrived, Helene let all the horses loose and started a small fire in the stables. She went to her aunt's, and from there I believe she intended to hide out in a convent."

Michael smiled. "Is she blonde?"

Kate nodded, not sure why he was smiling. "Yes. And she's young. More like what you were expecting.

Does that please you?"

He shrugged his shoulders. "Why would that information please me?"

"I don't know. You're sitting there grinning, and you did think I was too old when we first met."

His smile increased. "Now, Kate. Just because you're a spinster, doesn't mean you haven't time yet. Gathering from your performance while playing mermaid, I would say you might still catch a husband. I'd play down your streak of independence, though, and definitely drop the story of being from the future. A man doesn't want a crazy woman for a wife."

By the time he finished, she was kneeling in front of him, her fingers itching to slap his face. *"A spinster! What would make you think I'd even want a husband? I'll have you know, Mr. Sheridan, that I have been very happy not being married!"*

He seemed amused. "Have you, Kate? What a shame then that you've spoiled your happiness."

Her eyes narrowed. "What are you talking about?"

He threw a few more pieces of wood onto the fire. Turning to her, he shook his head and laughed. "Until it can be annulled, you're married to me!"

She felt as though the wind were knocked out of her. Sitting back on her heels, she stared at his satisfied expression. "I am not!" she insisted. "I'm not married to anyone!"

"Yes you are, Kate," he calmly stated. "I am your husband, and you're my wife. It's all legal." Lying back, he leaned on his elbows and studied the stars. "Now, as your husband, all your possessions become mine—and mine become yours, of course. When Denny finds us, I think I'd like to start with your trunk."

128

"You're crazy!" she nearly screamed.

"No, dear Kate, that's where you excel."

Stay calm, she told herself, even though she wanted to punch him senseless. "If what you say is true, then your ship must now belong to me. If Denny comes, I think I'll order him to leave you here!"

He laughed. Still star-watching, Michael shook his head. "Oh, Kate . . . if you want to be independent so much, you should learn the law. The *Rebel* was mine before we married, therefore I retain ownership. You, my sweet wife, took possession of the treasure *after* our marriage." He drew in a deep satisfying breath. "I'm afraid that means joint ownership. And a husband is always in control of his wife's holdings."

She rushed to her feet. Glaring down at him, she only managed to say through clenched teeth, "Go to hell, Michael! I'm not buying any of this!"

His mouth lost its smile, his eyes became hard as he turned his head up to her. "There's always another way, Kate," he said in a harsh voice. "I'll give you an annulment, in exchange for a more fair distribution of the treasure."

"You'd blackmail me?" she asked, not believing he'd stoop so low.

He shrugged. "Why not? I'm sure by now I've been accused of kidnapping. What's one more offense? You see, Kate, I'm determined to get my father's company back."

She was breathing heavily from a mixture of anger and hopelessness. "How much?" she asked in a tight voice, knowing if they ever were rescued, Michael would take charge and she might lose the entire thing.

His face relaxed. "I think a seventy percent share

would do it. I want to be fair and leave you enough to live on."

Her mouth dropped open. *"That's* fair? I'd call it thievery! Forget it, Sheridan," she snapped, walking the few steps to the tent. Taking her wool skirt, she wrapped it around her shoulders and sat inside. Just before lying down, she said in an exceptionally clear, calm voice, "I believe you've overlooked something very important. I've got the treasure. You don't . . . and possession is nine tenths of the law." She fell back onto the slicker and closed her eyes. *"That's* a percentage I can live with!"

The next morning Kate found herself alone. Immediately upon waking, a faint memory crept into her consciousness of strong, warm arms around her during the night. She vaguely remembered pressing against a broad chest and feeling muscled legs against the back of her own. Kate shook her head. Surely it had been a dream. It couldn't have been Michael. He'd been too angry last night to share even his body warmth. Then again, maybe he'd only wanted to share the wool skirt that she'd been using as a blanket. Thinking of him, she stuck her head out of the tent and looked around. Squinting from the bright sunlight, Kate looked up and down the deserted beach.

"Now what's he up to?" she muttered aloud. She stretched her arms upward and took a deep breath of sea air, feeling the kinks in her muscles relax. Slipping her bare feet into the uncomfortable shoes, Kate grimaced when she felt sand beneath her toes. *Sand!* It was in everything. Opening the tin, she took two biscuits and walked toward the treeline in hopes of finding some privacy. Dear Lord, she hated roughing it!

Ten minutes later, as she made her way back to the camp, a sudden noise in the underbrush stopped her dead in her tracks. She didn't move, she barely breathed as she slowly turned her head. Peering through thick pine branches, Kate heard the warbled sound again. Looking in the direction where it had come, she stretched her neck down and was able to make out a large bird.

Her mouth started watering . . . Food! Very quietly, she bent down, prepared to lunge for it. Every latent primitive instinct took over. It was survival, and she was the huntress. Only seconds before she made her move, the bird must have sensed her and it attempted to escape. When Kate saw it was a duck, and noticed its bleeding leg and foot, her heart melted and primitive became humane. Making a soothing noise with her mouth, she crept closer. Kate hesitated when it made frightened noises and, slowly, she reached into her blouse pocket. Taking out the second biscuit, she broke off a small piece and threw it the short distance to its mouth. Three times she fed the gray and white bird before she moved closer. Knowing it wouldn't be able to travel far with such an injury, Kate held the remaining biscuit in her hand and sat down.

"It's okay, fella," she whispered. "I can wait until you trust me."

Michael bent over the flames, a very satisfied expression on his face. Not only had he used Kate's method to restart the fire, but this morning he'd caught a fish. It hadn't been easy, either.

Last night he'd stayed awake trying to figure out a technique for fishing, for he'd be damned if Kate was going to show her superiority again! It had finally come to him that he could use a bent nail for a hook. Rolling the barrel away from the tent, he'd used his knife to work one of the long nails out of it. This morning he had secured a sturdy wooden pole and had tied a thin strip of canvas to it. Finding bait had been no problem once high tide was over. Among shells and sand dollars, he'd found several large clams. After prying one open, he'd tried eating it raw, but it was too big and nearly gagged him as he'd attempted to swallow it. It had made terrific bait, though.

When he had come back to the tent, he'd been disappointed that Kate was already awake and gone. He'd wanted to show her his catch. Quickly he'd devised a second plan and had scouted the treeline for rocks.

Now, at least three quarters of an hour later, he had a makeshift fire pit, a fish cooking, and no one but himself to admire it. Where the hell was she? He would give her a few minutes more, and then he was going to eat the damned fish himself!

Once more admiring his accomplishment, Michael heard her call his name from behind as she came out of the trees. His chest swelled with pride and self-satisfaction as he rose from his knees. Smiling, he turned around to see her expression.

His smile froze. Under her arm, she carried a duck, its leg bandaged with the missing bottom ruffle from her slip.

"Guess what, Michael?" she asked in an excited voice, while carefully making it over a sand dune. "Look who I found!"

He couldn't answer her. Frustration had rendered him speechless! He'd labored all morning to catch a single fish, and *she'd* caught a bloody duck in less than an hour!

"Isn't he cute?" she asked, running a finger down the back of its head.

He could feel the blood rushing from his heart to gather at his neck. Feeling almost strangled with indignation, he stormed toward the ocean. As he faced the water, he clenched his fists by his side and yelled his fury across the currents.

Kate jumped at the primeval scream and had to struggle to control the duck from bolting out of her arms. Moving closer to Michael, she continued to soothe the bird while watching Michael's shoulders rise and fall with each deep breath.

"God, Michael! What's wrong with you? I nearly jumped out of my skin."

He gave her a withering look and walked back to the camp. Following him, Kate noticed the fire. As she moved closer, she saw the small fish cooking on hot rocks. Thinking he was angry because she hadn't immediately remarked on it, she smiled and said brightly, "How about that! You really did it . . . you caught us a fish. Congratulations."

He slowly turned around and faced her. "It's not the thirty-foot shark you spoke of last night, is it?" he asked in a harsh voice. "Nor will it provide us with a feast . . . like your friend will."

Kate's eyes widened in shock while she tigthened her

grip on the duck. "You can't *eat* him!" She held the squirming duck closer to her stomach. "I saved him. How could you even think of killing him?"

If it were possible, Michael looked even more angry. He ran a hand through his hair, pushing it out of his eyes. "Why in hell are you talking about it like it's human? It's *food,* Kate—something you and I haven't had too much of in several days!"

She sat down opposite him and kept her hold on the duck. "You caught a fish. You can do it again. I won't let you kill him, Michael."

He closed his eyes in frustration. Opening them, he glared at her before taking out his knife. When she saw it, Kate gave a frightened yelp. She attempted to move away until she saw him reach for the cooked fish and use the sharp blade to pull it off the rocks.

Feeling a bit foolish, she sat back down and waited as Michael handed her a shell containing a piece of fish and a biscuit. Forced to put the duck down on the sand, she thanked Michael for breakfast and broke off a large crumb of biscuit for her new friend.

Just as she was handing it to the bird, Michael's voice boomed across the fire. "You will not feed that thing with our provisions!"

The duck flapped its wings and hobbled a few feet away. "Now look what you've done!" Kate reprimanded. "You've scared poor Donald!"

Michael put his own shell down in the sand. "You've named it?" he asked in a disgusted voice. "You've named a duck?"

She couldn't help the giggle as she tasted the fish. In between bites, she said, "You wouldn't understand, Michael, but it fits him. It really does!"

134

Chapter 9

Sitting under the canvas, Kate watched Michael walk in the surf. He was barefoot, with the legs of his pants rolled up to his calves, and he kept looking out to the horizon, as if waiting for his ship to miraculously appear. She shook her head in confusion.

It was the craziest damned thing! In her wildest imaginings, even when she'd thought life could no longer hold any surprises, never would she have believed someone actually could be transported back in time! Michael was right to think she'd lost her mind. In the last few days, she'd questioned it herself. Taking the braid out of her hair, she wound the dark shoelace tie around her finger. Michael must be right, she thought. It must have something to do with the medallion.

But she was no Messenger! She was the Finder . . . and she was going to make sure the treasure stayed in her possession. It was greed, pure and simple—and she wasn't very proud of that revelation. She needed money to survive, yet it was sheer stupidity to have taken the entire treasure. She should have left something for Michael. Maybe then he would have been satisfied, and not have become suspicious.

Petting the duck that, since this morning, had stayed by her side, Kate thought about the legend. Maybe the medallion was cursed. Maybe anyone who wore it was doomed. The first person who had worn it had spent centuries at the bottom of the ocean . . . and look what had happened to her when she'd touched it!

Kate quickly shook her head to stop her train of thought. Dear God, she was actually starting to believe this legend stuff!

She looked to the contented bird at her side. "What do you think, Donald? Am I going nuts here?"

The bird flicked at the sand with its bill. "I'm actually talking to a duck," Kate said in disbelief. "Is there any question as to my sanity?"

It was the silent treatment Michael had been giving her since this morning that was driving her crazy. Since breakfast, he'd been about as verbal as her feathered friend. She wondered, for at least the tenth time, what she'd done to have caused his glacial stares and isolating silence. She'd praised him on building his tent, complimented him on his fish. Was she being punished for being able to build a fire? For saving a duck? The last thing he had said to her was that if she insisted upon feeding the bird to take him down to where he'd cleaned the fish. There, she'd found the head and entrails. Although Kate hadn't been able to watch, Donald had made quick work of the gruesome sight. It was when she'd returned to camp that Michael had refused to speak with her.

Again, she looked out to him. Bending down, he

picked up a handful of shells and started throwing them back to the ocean. He reminded her of a bored young boy. But he certainly isn't a boy, she thought as she watched him fling another shell across the water. Most definitely, he's a man . . . a very attractive man, she again admitted.

Kate laughed at herself. She couldn't help thinking of the age-old question: If you were stranded on an island, who would you want to be with?

Her first answer had always been the current gorgeous hunk of the day. Then she would be sensible and say any gorgeous hunk who also happened to know carpentry. Now she knew the correct answer. It was Woody Allen.

Feeling she was an expert on the stranded island business, Kate nodded approval of her choice. Physically, Michael was as good-looking as any man she'd seen—and she'd seen a lot of good-looking men in California. He'd also proved his survival skills with the tent and this morning's breakfast. What he lacked was the ability to laugh at himself . . . and right now, she wouldn't exactly call him a great conversationalist.

Kate stared at Michael for a full minute before making up her mind. Coming out of the tent, she stood up and took off her blouse. Clad only in her old-fashioned underwear, she walked in his direction. About ten feet from Michael, Kate broke out into a run and playfully slapped his back as she passed by. "Last one in's a rotten egg!"

She knew he wouldn't follow her immediately, so she continued through the surf. Bracing herself for the water, she was pleasantly surprised by its warmth. The broiling sun of the last two days had burned away the storm's chill. Wading out until she was chest-high, Kate turned around to look at Michael. He was examining the shells in his hand. Smiling, she started to swim in line with the shore.

"Look, Michael," she shouted, turning onto her back. "Water ballet!" Knowing he had never heard of it, she giggled as she raised her leg, while pointing her toes and bringing her one arm up in a graceful arch. Slowly, she let herself submerge, concentrating on keeping a balanced, statuesque position.

He turned his head away so she couldn't see him laugh, and had to bite the inside of his cheek when he looked back. He almost lost control as he watched her make a comical bow, as if he'd applauded her effort. Watching her twirl around in circles, her face turned up toward her outstretched, posed arms, Michael wondered, not for the first time, what manner of woman she was. Even in the war, he'd never met a female who lived with more abandon, who had such a vivid imagination, who took more risks. She stood up for herself, refusing to be subdued, and he couldn't imagine her accepting defeat in any circumstance.

She was a rebel. And in a far different way, he admitted she was as beautiful as the ship bearing that name. Yet whereas the *Rebel* brought images of contentment, Kate tended to infuriate him. Watching her frolic in the ocean, Michael took a deep breath and silently confessed a grudging regard for her. He didn't want to care about Kate, knew it was dangerous to do so, yet conceded he'd been fighting his own feelings since he'd met her. God . . . it had been so long since he'd laughed.

Kate—with the astonishingly beautiful eyes, the

quick easy smile, the soft inviting lips, and the lush, firm body had crept into his thoughts and captured his mind.

And she spelled danger.

He watched her ride a wave and come closer to shore. Fighting the undertow, she almost fell. No more than eight feet away, she pushed the long, dark strands of hair away from her face and smiled at him.

"C'mon, Michael. Stop brooding. You're not going to make the *Rebel* appear any sooner by standing there and staring. Why don't you come for a swim?"

The thin white cotton of her underwear was almost transparent against her skin, revealing every luscious curve, every hollow, every soft swell of her body. He could feel the tightening in his groin as he continued to stare.

She startled him by reaching down and splashing. "C'mon. The water's wonderful!"

"Stop it, Kate . . ." Her playfulness created an ache within his heart. Part of him wanted to join her, to forget the many problems that faced him, and just enjoy the moment. Yet, a stronger part was telling him it was dangerous—that he must keep his distance.

She splashed him once more then returned to deeper water, and he felt confused by a mixture of regret and relief as he watched her swim away. She was so graceful. He remembered her as the mermaid and, yes, he admitted he'd been strangely attracted to her. After she'd saved his life and had shown him how to use her equipment, he'd experienced emotions completely foreign to him. She had bewitched him while they were under water—teased him with her mermaid masquerade, enchanted him with her innate playfulness and curiosity. In short, he was fascinated with her.

Watching her come back to shore, he reminded himself it was a dangerous fascination. She was stubborn, greedy . . .

"Kate! Watch out . . . !" Michael's warning was yelled right before a huge wave rose up in back of Kate and crashed into her head and shoulders. He reacted instinctively, rushing into the surf to help her. He tried to reach her as she fought the undertow, yet lost sight of her until she was thrown onto shore. Rushing to Kate's side, he reached under her waist and helped her to stand.

Trying to maintain his balance, he half carried, half dragged her out of the water. "Are you all right?" He sat her on the sand and shooed away the duck who was loudly making its concern known.

Keeping her head down, Kate took great gulps of air and nodded.

"You've scratched yourself," he announced, kneeling next to her and holding up her bleeding calf. "Don't move."

Without another word, he peeled off his white shirt and wrapped it around her leg. When she protested his use of the shirt, Michael dismissed her objection and helped her stand. Leading Kate back to the tent, he gently reprimanded her. "You have to be more careful, Kate; there's a strong undertow. You never think of the consequences, do you?"

She didn't answer him as she limped back to the canvas. Upon reaching it, she collapsed in an exhausted mass. Michael left her and rolled the water barrel closer. Untying his shirt, he pulled the plug out of the barrel and tilted it toward her injured leg.

When Kate felt the water she jerked her head up. "No! Michael, don't waste it!"

"I don't consider it a waste," he said while gently picking granules of sand away from her scratches.

Her bottom lip trembled. There was a tightness in her chest and a rawness in her throat that had nothing to do with the salt water she had swallowed. Tears freely ran down her cheeks, stinging the scratches on her face.

Satisfied that he had done everything he could with her leg, Michael carefully placed her heel back onto the sand and looked up at her.

"Kate! What's wrong? It isn't serious . . . just a few scratches."

She sniffled and wiped at her nose with the back of her hand. In an unsteady voice, she whimpered, "That's the first nice thing you've said to me in days . . . ! I've tried to get along with you, Michael. I really have! But you always put a distance between us. All I wanted to do was make you laugh . . . so you'd stop brooding about everything . . ."

He bit his bottom lip, but it wasn't enough to stop the grin from spreading. Kate looked nothing like the independent woman she had always tried so hard to be. Instead, she reminded him of a disheveled little girl. Her hair was hanging over her face in tight, wet strands; sand was sticking to the scratches at her cheekbone where her tears had not touched. Her lovely mouth was screwed up in a hurtful pout.

Chuckling, he wet a clean spot on his shirt and sat next to her. When he attempted to wipe at the scratch on her cheek, she hissed in pain and pulled away.

Pushing the hair out of her face, he held her head and

141

again brought the cloth closer.

"I laughed, Kate," he quietly admitted while softly brushing the sand away from her cuts.

"Really?" she asked, looking up into his eyes.

He briefly gazed down at her before saying in a stern voice, "Yes, really! Now, will you sit still?"

A slow, satisfied grin spread across her mouth and she tilted her head, offering him her cheekbone. Her injuries were minor. Any child who had played at the beach would have incurred the same at one time or another. It was a small price to pay, she thought, for breaking through Michael's tough outer shell.

Thinking of his concern for her, she turned her vision toward him. His bare chest was so close. Her eyes leisurely traveled across it, noticing the crisp mat of dark blond curls between his breasts, the sharp definition of his stomach muscles, his lean, tapering waist. She could feel her body growing warm as she inhaled the clean masculine scent of him mixed with the sea.

Slowly, very slowly, she lifted her eyes to his. He'd been watching her. A sudden awareness, an undeniable attraction, linked pale blue and gray. Neither could pull away from the magnetism. Neither one really wanted to.

A small voice in the back of his brain was sending out danger signals: She's stubborn, independent, argumentative. She lies, connives fantastic stories . . .

His hand almost shook as he pushed a damp lock of hair behind her ear. Listening to a stronger, more compelling voice, his fingers wrapped themselves behind her neck and brought her face closer to his. Never breaking the hot current that ran between them, he continued to stare into her eyes, waiting for her to raise her mouth to his. He only nudged her soft lips with his own, teasing, waiting . . .

Kate was astonished by the thrilling sensations coursing through her body. A tight coil was building in her lower abdomen, spreading a delicious heat to her limbs. A tiny voice inside kept telling her it was all right to feel this way. The time for repression was over. She was finally free to start anew, yet it was like being with a man for the first time again.

Her searching lips grazed his, tasting the salt that clung to them with the tip of her tongue. Twice he allowed her to tease him thus, before his mouth became hungry, demanding more.

"Kate . . ." Her name sounded almost like a plea just as his lips crushed her own in a breathtaking kiss.

Her breasts melted into his chest, her arms wrapped themselves around his neck as she pulled him even closer. She relished each awakened yearning that Michael brought alive. There had been so many lonely, empty years . . .

There was no sanity, no logical thinking, as he ground his mouth against hers. He wanted more of her. Too long had he fought the attraction, denied himself this pleasure. For over a week she had driven him to the brink of sanity with glimpses of her body, and now he wanted to discover every inch of it. Holding her tightly, he lowered her to the sand. Again and again he kissed her, drinking in the sweetness of her mouth, letting the wild tension build to a pleasurable pain. Her hands were everywhere—down his back, in his hair, on his face—and knowing she was an avid participant, Michael broke away from her mouth. His starving lips

143

roamed over her chin, down the graceful column of her neck, to the inviting swells of her breasts that were exposed above her chemise.

Tiny moans of pleasure escaped from the back of Kate's throat, as her fingers twined through his hair. She felt transported to a magical place, a place where nothing mattered, nothing was important except the overwhelming sensations she was experiencing. Her senses were so acute that she could feel the sun adding its warmth to her already inflamed body. She could hear the ocean combine the crashing of its waves with the roaring in her ears. Years of denial made her more sensitive to each delight.

Michael couldn't remember wanting a woman more. Needing to feel the length of her body next to his, he half lay over her. His mouth hungered to fully taste her breast, and he slowly untied the damp ribbon that held her chemise together. Impatient, he pushed the thin material away so it lay at her sides. Watching her chest rise and fall with each expectant breath, Michael inhaled deeply with his own pleasure at her beautiful offering.

He looked into her face, read the passion written upon it, and returned his hot gaze to her breasts. He adored them with his eyes. The moment was so intense that they reacted and grew without the slightest touch. An involuntary moan escaped his lips. Lowering his head, his tongue flicked against her nipples like the wings of a butterfly—and it seemed an exquisite eternity until one was enveloped in his mouth, gently pulling, suckling.

Kate felt the stirrings of his arousal against her thigh and her fingers impatiently moved to the buttons of his pants, eager to feel him against her skin. Wanting the same, Michael sat up and quickly shucked his trousers at the same time that Kate threw her pantaloons into the sand.

Naked, they stared at each other. There was no awkwardness, no embarrassment.

"I knew you were beautiful, Kate," Michael whispered in a husky voice. "I just didn't know how much."

Her hands reached out and cupped his face. Drawing him closer, her mouth trembled as she murmured, "I have wanted you, Michael. For so long . . ."

His mouth crushed hers as he pressed her back into the sand. His lips found her ear and gave it fervent attention. Strong white teeth nibbled her lobe, while a hot burning breath sent ripples of fiery torture throughout her body. Kate's hands explored him, learning the slopes and planes of his muscled back, the firmness of his buttocks, the masculine strength that was a counterpoint to her own softness. She could feel the hard pulsing of his heart against her chest, and it was an echo of the frantic throbbing in her femininity.

Grabbing ahold of his hair, she pulled his head back so she could look into his face. "Please, Michael . . ." Her plea needed no further words. He understood.

By mutual consent, by common need, they were joined quickly . . . their bodies meeting in an age-old ritual. A sharp cry escaped Michael's lips as she seared him with her tight, inflamed body. Kate dug her head back into the sand, lifting her face to the hot sun and Michael's feverish kisses.

So much that had happened between them had been governed by nature. It was only fitting that nature, in a force as old as time, would drive them both to seek fulfillment on a deserted beach—blessing them with its basic elements of water, wind, and sun.

It was astonishing, overwhelming, and they loved with a passion kept too long under control. In its final moments, Kate cried out her wild need, her joy at finding renewal. With her voice, with her small body, she begged Michael to travel with her, to discover the wonder and awe of their union. Listening to her, feeling her surrender, Michael sensed something tight in his chest explode, releasing the hard shell around his soul. With a sense of almost reverence, he flung his head back—his body taut with intense pleasure. In that sweet moment, that fraction of time, he willingly allowed Kate to softly enter and take complete possession of his heart.

They continued to lay joined, their labored breaths the only sign of their exertion. Kate basked in the warmth inside her body and the strong rays of the sun on her face. Michael's forehead rested at the base of her throat, his hot breath feeling like a gentle caress against her damp skin. Lazily, she ran her fingertips up and down his back, and, when she felt him raise his head, she merely smiled, unwilling to open her eyes and break the spell.

Once a slight measure of sanity had returned, Michael had the eerie feeling of another's presence. When he had raised his head to look, he couldn't stop the chuckling that rippled through his body.

Confused by his laughter, Kate quickly opened her eyes. Following Michael's line of vision with her own, her body convulsed with giggles. Not two feet away, contentedly nesting on the sand, was the duck—looking very bored by their performance.

Michael gazed down at her and Kate gasped at the happy, carefree expression on his face. Her heart filled with tenderness at glimpsing the real man behind the mask of responsibility.

Tightening his hold on her, he smiled. "He doesn't seem very impressed, does he? You gave him the wrong name, Kate. He should be called Casanova. He makes one hell of a jaded voyeur!"

He joined her laughter and Kate clasped him tighter to her chest, reveling in happiness.

"You made a joke, Michael!" she exclaimed between giggles. "You actually have a sense of humor!"

For a moment he looked embarrassed, then quickly laughed at himself. "I also have a sense of discomfort." He brushed sand away from her shoulder. "Come . . ." he invited, while standing up and extending his hand. "Let's get this sand off us."

Kate's eyes met his and she smiled while placing her fingers inside his palm. "So I finally got you to go swimming," she proclaimed with satisfaction as she rose to her feet.

Pulling her toward the water, Michael leisurely looked over her exquisite body and smiled. "You, madam, have always been dangerous in the water. I plan to be on guard!"

Kate laughed as they started running toward the surf. Within minutes, they were washing each other, rediscovering each other with slippery, sensuous movements.

Attracted by their shouts of laughter, Casanova stood at the shoreline looking much more interested.

Chapter 10

Like dozens of fireflies, the air lifted tiny sparks from their campfire into the night. Beyond it, the Atlantic Ocean provided a rhythmic base to the natural symphony of the insects and night birds that inhabited the island. Sitting in front of the fire next to Michael Kate stared into the flames, as though hypnotized. It was difficult to remember when she had felt more contented. Thanks to Michael's skill in catching two fish, her stomach was full. Taking a deep, satisfied breath, she couldn't help smiling. And thanks to Michael's skill in another area . . . her heart was full.

"That was a mysterious smile if I've ever seen one."

Kate looked to her side and her grin widened. "You think so?" she asked, gazing at Michael's handsome face. The firelight emphasized his cheekbones, giving the short stubble of beard on his face a reddish gold hue . . .

Michael returned her smile and nodded. "Most definitely. Yesterday, I would have worried about what you were planning."

"And now?" she asked expectantly.

"Now," he said softly as he pushed a strand of hair behind her ear, "I'm just wondering what caused you to smile."

"I'm happy," she whispered.

He stared at her for a few moments before putting his arm around her and bringing her head to his chest. Even through the cotton of his shirt, he could feel her soft breath, and his heart ached with the beauty of her answer. She was so open, so willing to live and enjoy life. He now knew she'd been trying to teach him how to regain that joy. Holding her close, he ran his hand up and down her arm and lowered his face to kiss the top of her head. "You know, as crazy as it seems—we have to ration our water and I don't know how long I can provide us with food—yet, I'm . . ."

She immediately straightened. "You weren't looking at Casanova when you said that, were you?"

He gave a short laugh and brushed biscuit crumbs from the corner of her mouth. "No, I was not looking at your duck. Though when my stomach grumbles, I will admit to fantasies of roasting Casanova . . ."

"Michael!"

"Listen," he continued. "I was going to say that, despite everything, for the first time in many years I'm . . . well, happy I guess."

Her expression softened. "Really?"

Embarrassed by his admission, Michael threw another log onto the fire. "Yes. Really. Though why you persist in making that bird your pet, when we're practically on the verge of starving, I'll never know."

Kate smiled and ran her fingers through the hair on the side of his head. "Yes you do, Michael. You couldn't eat him now, either."

He snorted. "Oh, yes I could! But don't worry. As long as the fishing holds out, Casanova is safe." He shook his head. "I don't believe I'm talking about a duck like this! Why, during the war . . ."

His voice drifted off and he stared at the flames as though regretting his words.

Kate felt the change in him immediately. His whole posture was reminiscent of the Michael she had first met—guarded, closed off to outsiders. Hoping today had changed her status to an insider, someone to share experiences, Kate picked up a handful of sand and let it slowly sift through her fingers. "Do you realize I know almost nothing about you?" she asked quietly. "The only thing I do know is that you have a brother named Kevin, and an uncle you aren't too fond of. Do you have any other family?"

He nodded. "My mother. My father used to say that Lydia Masterson captured his heart in the month of April, and it was springtime ever since."

Kate noticed his slight smile as he remembered. "They sound as if they had a wonderful marriage."

"They did," he agreed, yet his voice held a note of sadness. "After he died, she was sick for a long time." He shrugged. "She's never been the same, even after she recovered."

Kate stared into the flames. "Illness changes people. I know. My mother knew she was dying and yet she opened up to me. It was almost as if she wanted me to really know her. I think she thought that if I understood her, I might begin to understand myself. I'll always be grateful for the time we had together."

Kate's throat felt constricted with emotion. How she wished she could tell her mother about Michael. How she wished the two of them could have somehow met. Instinctively, she knew each would have approved of the other. "What of your father?" she asked, wanting to prolong the feeling of closeness. "Tell me about him."

Michael glanced at her, and Kate had the feeling he was judging whether or not to continue. When Kate saw him inhale deeply and begin to speak, she let out her own breath, grateful that he still seemed to trust her.

"My father's family go back to when Charleston was known as Charles Town. He was very proud of his heritage, of being a southerner. He was a man who took his responsibilities very seriously, yet he had the ability to appreciate the lighter side of life." He looked at her and smiled. "You would have liked him, Kate. The man loved a good joke."

She laughed. "Sounds like my kind of person."

He nodded and looked back to the fire. "I've always seemed to frustrate my mother, though, never fitting into her mold of the perfect son . . . that's where Kevin shined. But my father was different. I don't think he objected that I had a mind of my own, my own way of doing things. Right before the war, he'd taken me into the business. I think he shared my surprise at my sudden command for figures." He looked down to her hands and shook his head. "I never really applied myself when I was younger," he admitted. "Then it seemed like a waste of time. It wasn't until I became curious about the Stock Exchange that I took a real interest. I guess my father realized my fascination, and left the investing to me."

"And were you successful, Michael?" she asked shyly.

"In 1860, Sheridan Shipping was worth over three million dollars." Instead of pride, his voice rang with sadness.

Remembering what she had heard about the South's reconstruction, Kate asked softly, almost apologetically, "Did you lose everything in the war?"

His laugh was sarcastic, angry. "Kevin and I lost everything to my *uncle* . . . not the war!"

She was frightened by the vehemence in his voice. "I . . . I don't understand. Your uncle?"

"My mother's brother—Martin Masterson. During the war, he managed the family's business while my father, Kevin, and I served in different branches of the Confederacy."

Kate was fascinated, hearing firsthand about history, and she motioned with her eyes for him to continue.

Michael took a deep breath. "Anyway, when the war was over and my father died, my mother turned to her brother for support. I can remember thinking at the time that it was natural. She was ill. She needed someone of her own generation to confide in. But soon it became obvious that Martin was abusing that trust. Once he had my mother under his control, he started to take over our home, the shipping company . . . he was into everything . . . and Kevin and I were slowly shut out."

His breathing was uneven and Kate could sense his anger building. "I'm an adult, Kate . . . a grown man, yet because of my uncle I'm forbidden to even return to my own home. I have to meet my brother outside. I don't understand how she could turn away from her son . . . how she could believe every lie that bastard has told her, and refuse to even listen to me!"

He closed his eyes, as if the pain of remembering were too much. Kate smiled sadly and rested her head against his shoulder, wanting to comfort him. "That first night on the *Rebel,* when we talked about revenge . . . He's the one, isn't he?"

Michael didn't answer. He didn't need to—Kate knew she was right. For whatever reason, Martin Masterson sounded like he intended to ruin Michael's life and, as a great wave of possessiveness swept over her, Kate's eyes hardened as she thought about the faceless stranger.

"What about you, Kate? Are you ready now to tell me the truth?"

It was said gently, without a hint of reproach, and she blinked a few times before raising her head. "But I have told you the truth. I don't know what I can say that would make you believe me."

There was a fleeting look of near hurt in his eyes before he turned them toward the fire, and Kate knew he was feeling foolish for opening up to her. She couldn't give him what he asked. He wanted a sane, pat explanation for her actions. There wasn't any, and she felt a surge of frustration that she had nothing with her to prove her transportation of time.

Suddenly, she smiled. "I'm going to do something, Michael. Promise me you won't look away."

"Kate . . ."

She heard the hesitation in his voice, but still persisted. "Promise me."

He looked toward the darkened sky in exasperation. "All right! I promise."

Her grin widened. "Now look at me," she ordered.

Slowly, her hands came up to her eyes. With the fingers of her left hand, she pulled down her lower right eyelid and raised her upper. Gently, ever so gently, she used the index finger of her right hand to slide her contact lens off her cornea. Once it was on the white of her eye, it was a simple matter of using her thumb with her first finger to lift the lens off. Holding it in the palm of her hand, she smiled triumphantly and said, "There! Have you ever seen anything like *that* before?"

His openmouthed expression was comical as he stared at her hand, back at her eye, and then again looked at the contact lens.

"How . . . ? Jesus! How long have you had that in your eye?" he demanded in a disbelieving voice, yet continued to stare at the tiny, fragile, glasslike object in her palm.

Kate giggled. "Longer than I should. Trust me, Michael. It's called a contact lens, and it helps me to see better."

"It looks like glass, or maybe a drop of water. How could you keep it in your eye like that?"

"You don't even know it's there, unless it gets dirty. Which is why you'd better look quickly, because I'm already running on borrowed time with these things. I have to put it back in before it dries out!"

Michael took deeper breaths. "Doesn't it hurt?" he asked in a skeptical voice.

"No, it's flexible. See?" Kate pinched the lens with her fingers.

"How does it stay in?"

"Michael, I'll answer your questions once I reinsert it. Okay?" Balancing the small lens on her index finger, Kate brought it in contact with her eye. Blinking a few times, she smiled and lifted her head. "Well?" she asked with a wide grin. "Now what do you think?"

He was looking closely into her right eye. "Hold your head still," he quietly ordered. "There! I can still see it!"

Kate let her breath out in a frustrated rush. "Of course you can see it. It doesn't disappear. But you never noticed it before, did you?"

He brought his head back so he could see her face. "No. I never did," he admitted. "But then I wasn't looking for strange objects in your eyes. Do you have it in both?"

Kate nodded. "What were you thinking when you looked into my eyes just then?"

"What?"

"When you were looking for the lens . . . what were you thinking?"

He gazed at her lips, then slowly let his vision return to her eyes. "Are you searching for a compliment? I'm sure I wouldn't be the first man to tell you that you have beautiful eyes, quite remarkable."

Kate smiled. "Thank you, but that wasn't what I meant. Didn't it cross your mind that you've never seen anything like a contact lens? Just like you've never seen anything like my scuba equipment?"

"You're going to tell me this is from the future, aren't you?" He sighed when she nodded. "Kate, what you're asking me to accept is beyond reason. Your explanations sound like a child's fairy tale."

"There's only one explanation, Michael. I don't belong in this time. Where I come from, contact lenses and scuba equipment are commonplace . . . and boats that still use sails are only used for recreation." She hoped that bringing their discussion to something he could relate to might help him understand.

Michael's eyes narrowed. "The *Rebel* might be small, but she can outrun a ship twice her size—and has done so on many occasions," he stated defensively.

Kate shook her head, wondering how she could explain something she knew very little about. "That isn't what I meant. Ships in my time use fuel, instead of the wind."

"You're talking about steam. It isn't new, Kate."

"No, I'm not. I'm talking about a different fuel: oil . . . gasoline. Huge tankers, maybe twenty times larger than the *Rebel,* are powered by it . . ."

"No ship that size could stay afloat," he interrupted.

"I'm telling you it's true—in the twentieth century. Look, what do you use to get from one place to the other? Maps? The irregularity of the wind? Maybe a compass?"

His look was condescending. "You've oversimplified it, but yes—all of those."

"In 1987," she began earnestly, "a ship is independent of the wind. The captain would determine how far its destination is, and bring enough fuel—gasoline—to get there and back. Its crew might use charts, but those maps are on a lighted screen and radar would tell them how far they are from land, or if any other ships are in the area."

"Radar?"

Kate screwed up her mouth. "I was afraid you were going to ask about that," she dismally noted. "Look, I'm not going to explain it very well, but it's a device

156

that throws a frequency, a . . . an invisible wave of . . . of energy," she stumbled to explain, "out from the ship. This . . . this energy, this sound, bounces off any object and then returns back to the ship, telling the person who's looking at the screen the distance between them and the object by . . . ah, by measuring the time that it took between sending out and receiving the energy." She was nearly out of breath by the time she'd finished, and had to inhale deeply. Her voice sounded triumphant when she exclaimed, "If my uncle George were here right now, he'd kiss me for remembering!"

Michael didn't move an inch, but she could mentally feel him pulling away from her in astonishment. She hurried to explain. "My mother's oldest brother George served in the Navy during World War II. He never had any children of his own, so he loved to recount his submarine days with me."

She could see the confusion in his eyes. "I did it again, didn't I? God, every time I try and explain something, it gets more complicated." She took a deep breath and slowly exhaled. "You're going to find this one *really* hard to believe!"

Breaking off a small twig from the stack of firewood, Kate began drawing in the sand. "A submarine sort of looks like this. It's an enclosed ship that travels underwater."

She heard his short, astounded laugh, but didn't bother to look up as she drew a wavy line above the cylinder ship. "This is the water. Now, see this thing? It's called a periscope, and the person below the water, in the submarine, can look above and see if it's safe to surface, or if there are enemy ships in the area."

"We had one during the war," he interrupted. "The *Hunley* carried an explosive attached to a long pole on its bow. In '64, it rammed the Union's *Housatonic* in the Charleston Harbour. Oh, it sank the *Housatonic,* but went to the bottom along with it." He shook his head. "So much for your submarines. I wouldn't want to captain one— Man was made to travel on the water, not below it."

"You're wrong, Michael. The submarine has become a very important invention, not only during wartime. They also explore the sea, going to the bottom of the ocean, traveling under the Polar Cap to the North Pole, discovering all sorts of . . ."

"You have a wonderful imagination, Kate," he pronounced, while trying to hold back his laughter. "You must have inherited it from your uncle George. World War II?"

She'd been so patient, wracking her brain for explanations to his questions, and her patience was at its end. "Don't you dare say one word about my uncle! He was the closest thing to a father that I knew. And it wasn't only my uncle's stories. I saw them myself, and read about them."

"These submarines? You read about them?"

She could feel the hot blush of anger creeping up her neck. "Does that surprise you, Michael? That a woman can read? I'm probably better educated than most of the people you know!"

She could see the muscle in his cheek move as he ground his back teeth together. "I'm not in the least bit surprised that you can read. No matter what I've told you about my younger days, I believe in education . . . even for women, if they should desire it. All I asked you

158

for, Kate, was the truth—not some crazy, insane story about ships with energy bouncing all over them, and diving ships that go under the water. The next thing you'll tell me is that they can fly!"

Her smile was condescending, and he thought her whole attitude smacked of superiority. "They're called airplanes, Michael," she said in a low, patronizing voice. "But don't worry, I'm not going to attempt to explain them. In fact, you've just heard my last explanation. I am not going to waste my breath trying to make you understand."

Her anger increased. "When I think about how patient I've been with you . . . !" She shook her head. "You have no idea, Michael Sheridan, how appalling my life has been since I met you on that damn reef! You have no conception of what I've left behind . . ."

"That's what I'd originally asked you!" he interrupted. He was as angry as Kate. Ever since this afternoon, when they'd made love, there was a tightness in his stomach that had been growing. It was a feeling he was unfamiliar with, an emotion that was difficult to define. He realized now it was jealousy, a burning need to know who else she had given herself to, for he wasn't the first. "What I want to know, Kate, is—besides your uncle is there any other man I should know about?"

Her head jerked up in surprise. Immediately, she thought of Jon, her ex-husband, but dismissed him as being in her past, having nothing to do with her present. "No," she whispered in a shaky voice. "No one."

He should have been happy, but the tightness in his stomach increased until it was almost painful. He'd

159

seen the indecision in her eyes, heard the hesitancy in her voice . . . She was lying. The pain in his middle started spreading upward to his chest, wrapping itself around his heart. The familiar isolation was all the more piercing because of one beautiful afternoon, a time when he'd laughed, loved . . . and trusted. Damn it! What, or who, was she hiding?

He looked back to the fire and tried to bring his breathing under control. "You might as well go on to sleep," he said in a hard voice. "I'm going to stay up a while longer."

Kate stared at him, not wanting to believe he was shutting her out again. God, she hadn't meant to push him this far! She closed her eyes and briefly shook her head in silent denial. "Michael . . . ?"

He continued to look into the flames, ignoring her. Finally he said, "Every time we start out talking, we end up arguing."

"Then let's not talk." It took every ounce of courage she possessed to say those words. When he didn't answer, Kate looked at his profile and felt a tremendous sense of loss for what they had created only hours before—something so beautiful, so special.

She couldn't even bring herself to say good night as she turned toward the tent. Her throat was incapable of speech. There was a burning rawness to it from unshed tears, but she wouldn't make her humiliation complete. She waited until she was lying on the canvas. Alone, Kate brought her clenched fist to her mouth and bit down. It was over two years since she'd been with a man—a long, lonely time to get over rejection, to rebuild her life and self-esteem.

Michael's rejection was different from Jon's, per-

160

haps even more hurtful, for she had never felt such joy with her ex-husband as she did when making love with Michael. Why did she always make the wrong choices when it came to men? Would she never be able to trust herself, or her judgments? As the tears slid off her face and onto the canvas, Kate prayed that she was strong enough to again survive . . . for this time, there was no safe place to run.

When she was a young girl, her mother would try and comfort her by saying, "Everything always looks better in the morning." As a child, upset over something minor, she'd wanted to believe that adage. As an adult, she knew the old saying wasn't dependable . . . and this morning was a perfect example.

Not knowing exactly where Michael had spent the night, Kate bent down and picked up another sand dollar. Brushing the sand off the flat white shell, she looked in his direction and sighed. Down the beach, he continued to ignore her as he surf-fished for their breakfast.

Kate placed the shell into her skirt pocket and continued her morning walk. When she'd awoke earlier, Michael had been prying another nail out of the barrel to use as a hook. He'd been polite, wishing her good morning, but it had been a formal greeting that maintained last night's distance. Nothing had changed in the light of day. Looking down at Casanova, she smiled sadly. "What did I do?" she whispered.

Last night she had gone over everything in her mind. Granted, she'd lost her temper, but so had Michael. What did he want from her? He refused to accept the truth, and that was all she had to offer. In her heart, she couldn't really blame him. If the situation were reversed, she wouldn't believe in time travel either. Letting out her breath in a rush of frustration, Kate pushed her hair back off her forehead and looked out to the ocean. There must be something to convince him she was telling the truth. She wanted him to trust her, and God knows she needed to trust somebody . . .

Her eyes narrowed as she stared at the horizon. Her lips parted as her heart started beating more quickly. Squinting, hoping it wasn't a film over her contacts, Kate watched as the image took shape.

"Michael!" Not sure if she'd said his name aloud, she started running back toward him.

"Michael!" This time she screamed with excitement. As he turned around to her, she stopped running and pointed out to the water.

"A ship! Is it the *Rebel?"*

Shielding his eyes with his hand, Michael dropped the makeshift fishing rod into the surf. Only seconds passed before he threw back his head and laughed, letting out a joyous yell.

"We're going home, Kate! We're going home . . . !"

Chapter 11

They stared at each other, their faces glowing with the happiness of being rescued. Instinctively, Kate wanted to throw herself into Michael's arms and hug him, but something held her back. Perhaps it was the same awkwardness Michael felt, yet their eyes revealed volumes of emotions. Grinning once more, he turned back to the ship and waved. The moment of silent communication was lost.

Kate watched the horizon as the *Rebel* grew larger, then slowly turned away as Michael said, "Come, we'd better pack up."

Again, she acted as his assistant—only this time it was to dismantle their tent. Watching their shelter quickly disappear, Kate couldn't help feeling a bit nostalgic. She was thrilled that they were finally getting off the island, yet something deep inside her was sorry to leave.

As she and Michael folded a long length of canvas, he again laughed. "I told you Denny would find us! I knew he'd come."

Nodding, Kate handed him her half of the canvas and he continued to fold it. "Yes you did, Michael," she admitted. "I'm sorry I doubted you."

He shrugged his shoulders, dismissing her need to apologize. They packed everything into the one barrel and, as Kate picked up the tin of biscuits and opened it up, she held it out to Michael.

Offering him the last remaining one, Kate smiled. "Poor Denny—again, he'll have nothing to give to his sister. Why don't you finish it, Michael? You haven't had breakfast."

He shook his head and looked out to his ship. Although still a good distance away, the *Rebel* was anchored and a rowboat had been lowered. "You eat it," he said absently, starting to walk toward the surf.

She felt dismissed, unimportant, yet knew his reaction was only normal. Of course he'd want to meet Denny and whoever was in the rowboat. Closing the tin, she placed it in the barrel and picked up her shoes. As the small boat came closer to shore, Kate took a deep, steadying breath and walked down to Michael. Might as well get it over with, she thought in resignation. It was time to make amends . . . for, after today she might never see Michael again.

Feeling thoroughly depressed and suddenly realizing that now that she was rescued she had nowhere to go, Kate stopped at Michael's shoulder.

Looking to his side, he grinned and turned back to the boat. "Good old Denny!" he exclaimed. "He's got Kevin with him!"

Immediately, Kate searched the approaching rowboat and spotted Michael's brother as he waved. She had no time to form an opinion as Michael started wading out to meet him. Soon, the two brothers were hugging each other, slapping each other's back, while standing in water up to their knees.

Feeling like an outsider, as she watched Michael greet Denny and another sailor in the same manner, Kate tried to smile as the four men came up to her.

With an arm around his brother's shoulder, Michael smiled and said, "Kevin, I'd like you to meet Kathleen Anne Walker."

He was shorter than Michael, and his hair was a light brown instead of dark blond, yet Kate would have had to have been blind not to know that they were related to each other. Unlike her first meeting with Michael, however, this man before her appeared open and friendly. She realized what she must look like, not having had the benefit of a comb or a bath in days. Overcoming her embarrassment, she dug her toes into the sand, took a deep breath, and held out her hand.

"It's nice to meet you, Kevin," she said in what she hoped passed for a calm voice.

Looking at her offered hand, Kevin smiled before taking it. "I'm very happy to finally meet you, Kath—" Suddenly his expression became confused. Releasing her hand, he turned to his brother. "Kathleen Anne Walker? I thought . . ." He cut his words off and looked over Kate's shoulder to the deserted beach. "What happened to Helene Barnett?"

Kate and Michael's eyes met and held for a few tense moments before Michael again slapped his brother's shoulder. "I'll explain it all later, Kevin. The only thing I want to do now is feel the deck of the *Rebel* under my feet. How did Denny convince you to come with him?"

After saying hello to Kate and inquiring about her

health, Denny turned to the brothers. "The *Rebel* took a beatin' in that storm. We were lucky to make it into Charleston. Masterson was there not a half hour after we reached port. I told him you and the girl was washed overboard." He grinned at Kate and Michael. "The old goat thinks you both are dead!"

Seeing their shocked expressions, Denny continued. "Told Kevin here you was too stubborn to die. I never doubted you'd make land somewheres."

Michael's features hardened. "Martin was on the *Rebel?*" he asked in a tight voice.

It was Kevin who answered. "He'd already received a letter from Barnett telling him you'd kidnapped his daughter." He looked at Kate, still confused over who she was. Turning his attention back to his brother, he continued. "He was furious and he'd had men watching the docks for you. When he heard the *Rebel* was in, I went with him to intervene between you two. Of course when Denny told us you'd both been washed overboard, I said I'd come with him to search for you."

Michael nodded. "I just hate to think that man was on my ship!" he stated in a hard voice.

Kevin shook his head as everyone started walking toward the dismantled camp. "He only stayed a few minutes and took Helene's belongings to send back to her father." Again, he shook his head. "This is damned confusing! Martin is sending condolences to a man whose daughter is still alive . . . she is alive, isn't she?"

Michael and Kate had stopped walking. "Where is that trunk?" Michael demanded, before Kate could open her mouth.

Kevin looked at Denny and then back to the couple. "Martin said he's returning it to Winston Barnett with a letter explaining what happened."

"Son of a bitch!" Michael's jaw became rigid with anger; his eyes turned a cold gray. Without explaining his change of mood, he walked up to the barrel and started rolling it toward the surf. "Let's go," he ordered over his shoulder. "That bastard is about to be visited by his nephew's ghost!"

The remaining three men were quickly mobilized into action, and within minutes all that was left of their camp was the residue from the fire. Even Casanova had disappeared with the appearance of the crew. Kate stared at the darkened circle in the sand for a few seconds. Although her eyes were burning and her stomach churning, she refused to cry. If she ever had any hopes that Michael was a decent human being, they had been wiped away by his words.

All he had ever wanted from her was the treasure. He'd used her, played with her emotions to gain control over it. That's why he'd wanted to know about her life, demanding to know if there was anyone in her past. He'd only wanted to know whether she had an accomplice, someone else he'd have to mislead before he could get his hands on what rightfully belonged to her.

Sitting in the rowboat, Kate smiled at Kevin and Denny and the young sailor who'd accompanied them, yet refused to look at Michael. Was it only yesterday, she thought, that she'd been so happy? That after hearing how his uncle had nearly destroyed him, she had made up her mind to share the treasure with Michael? Thank God she hadn't opened her mouth, she reflected, as she listened to the shouts from the *Rebel*'s crew. Even though she was homeless, penniless, and

167

humiliated, her one consolation was that Michael Sheridan wouldn't benefit from the treasure, either. It seemed fate had decided to punish them both for their greed.

It felt strange to be sitting at a table again—even stranger to be in Michael's cabin, with him and his brother seated across from her. Kate had fantasized about this moment—when real food was placed in front of her. Instead of devouring each morsel, she pushed the fried eggs and thick ham slices around on her plate. She knew if she tried to swallow, she would choke, for surely nothing could pass by the huge lump lodged in her throat. She felt like such a fool . . .

"I say you're asking for disaster if you confront Martin now," Kevin warned his brother.

Taking another drink of coffee, Michael glared at Kevin. "He's not getting away with this! I told you what's in that trunk. Do you actually think he won't open it first?"

Kevin looked at Kate, silently imploring her help. Knowing she wouldn't have any influence with Michael, Kate merely shrugged. The conversation, however, had captured her attention.

"Listen, Michael," Kevin appealed, "why don't you stay at Haphazard, and let *me* find out what's going on? Do me a favor and stay dead a little while longer. It'll buy us some time."

Michael put his cup back on the table. Shaking his head, he laughed. "That's one hell of a favor, Kevin!"

Clean-shaven, dressed in fresh clothes, Michael appeared so handsome that it angered Kate. He had no right to look so good, when she still resembled a witch. Self-consciously straightening the collar of her worn blouse, Kate sat up in her chair and looked at the men.

Her action had drawn their attention, and both looked in her direction. Seeing Kate's miserable expression, Michael felt a twinge of remorse. It wouldn't be easy to say good-bye to her, yet he knew the time was coming when he must. Wanting to be as fair as possible, he said, "Tell me, Kate, where do you want us to take you? Are you going back to New Jersey?"

Kevin seemed embarrassed. "Please forgive us, Miss Walker, for dragging you into our family's problems. Neither Michael nor I intended to ignore you."

Kate was staring at Michael, unwilling to accept what he'd just said. He actually thought he could drop her off somewhere, like a bag of old garbage! Did he really think she was going to let him walk off with the treasure? Without even a fight? He might have hurt her, he might even know how much he'd hurt her, but she wasn't defeated. What Michael didn't possess was the knowledge that, once a challenge was made, Kate didn't know how to back down.

Keeping her eyes riveted on Michael, she addressed his brother. "There's no need to apologize, Kevin. Feel free to discuss any family problems that might arise. You see, whatever affects my husband also affects me."

The coffee in Michael's mouth shot out and flew across the table, staining Kevin's shirt-sleeve.

Kevin looked at his arm, then at Kate. "I beg your pardon?" he asked in a shocked voice.

She smiled at Kevin, then slowly gazed back at Michael. He was gaping at her, a horrified expression on his face. "Ask Michael," she sweetly instructed.

Kevin looked to his brother. "Well?"

It did her heart good to hear Michael stumbling for an explanation. "Well, I . . . What happened was . . . That is, we were . . ."

"We were married in Bermuda," Kate said in a strong voice, since Michael didn't seem capable of continuing. "I took Helene's place at the marriage, and of course you know Michael took yours. What we didn't realize at the time was that both Michael and I signed our real names on the marriage certificate . . . to protect you and Helene. Michael insists we're legally married—and now I agree."

Both men were staring at her, their faces etched with disbelief. Taking advantage of their silence, Kate picked up her knife and fork and cut off a small piece of ham. Smiling at them, as though they'd just had the most delightful conversation, she said, "Tell me about this place we're going to. Haphazard? What a strange name." Popping the ham into her mouth, she chewed the delicious meat and raised her eyebrows in question as she waited for an answer.

So good was her acting that Kevin made an attempt to collect himself. "It's . . . it's our family's retreat. We've used it as a hunting lodge in the past, but nobody's been there for . . ." He stopped and looked at Michael. "Is this true?" he demanded. "Are you and Kathleen married?"

Michael was glaring at Kate, as if by sheer willpower he could send her through the window and back into the ocean.

"Michael, is what Kathleen said true?" Kevin again asked, this time his voice tinged with anger.

170

Tearing his eyes away from the woman across from him, he said through clenched teeth, "It's a fairly accurate description of what took place. We'll have to see whether it's really legal or not."

Kate picked up her napkin and delicately dabbed at the corner of her mouth. Looking properly bewildered, she addressed the older brother. "Excuse me, Kevin, I don't mean to embarrass you, but I think you should be aware that all the requirements for a marriage have been met."

Seeing his look of confusion, she squared her shoulders and said it. "The marriage has been consummated."

At her words, Kevin pushed his chair back from the table and glared at his brother. Trying very hard not to laugh at Michael's expression, she gave him a look of pity before digging into her eggs.

Feeling their eyes on her, Kate looked up from her plate. Astonishment would accurately describe their expressions, she thought. Sensing she had to say something, she murmured, "I'm sorry, but using your words, Kevin, this really is *damned* complicated, isn't it?"

Not really expecting an answer, she reached for a piece of bread and gracefully dipped an edge into her egg yolk. Closing her eyes in bliss, she swore she'd never tasted better food in her life!

Haphazard. There was an obvious reason the house was given that name. As Kate stood in front of the cottage, her shoulders sagged in disappointment. If she used her imagination, she could envision what the

171

place must have looked like at a time when someone had taken care of it. Now, after years of neglect, its stone walls were covered with growth, vines that climbed up to the slate roof and chimney. It appeared to her as though the nearby forest had laid claim to the house.

Putting her hands on her hips, Kate continued to stare at the house in disbelief. As the men from the ship brought supplies, she turned her attention to Kevin as he stopped at her side.

"I know it doesn't look too welcoming," he said in an apologetic voice, "but it's quite comfortable inside." He indicated the growing mound of supplies. "I'll be coming back at least once a week and you can let me know if you need anything else."

Kate looked back at the house. "I think a machete, to start with, would be in order . . . followed by a broom."

Kevin stared at her a few seconds, then threw back his head and laughed. His actions reminded her so much of Michael, that she couldn't help but smile. "I'm afraid to see what it's like inside."

"Don't worry," Kevin shouted, while returning to help the men. "We'll cut away most of the overgrowth and get you two settled!"

Settled. It was definitely the wrong word to describe what would happen when Kevin, Denny, and the crew left her and Michael alone, Kate thought as she came closer to the house. In the three hours it had taken them to get from the coast of North Carolina, where she and Michael had been stranded, to this hunting lodge somewhere outside of Charleston, neither of them had actually spoken to the other. All conversation, it seemed, had passed through Kevin. Kate sensed an impending explosion within Michael, and, peering into the house through a dirty window, she couldn't help but wonder if the structure was going to be strong enough to withstand it.

There was one large room used for a kitchen, a living area and sleeping quarters. The furniture was covered in sheets and Kate had insisted that they not be removed until she'd swept the wooden floor. When first entering the room, she'd felt defeated by the amount of work that needed to be done. It would take days, she realized, to make it livable . . . if she had to do it herself. Then had come the brilliant idea of using the men, and, within twenty minutes, she had organized a seven-man work crew. Although reluctant at first, even Michael had been enlisted to fix the water pump in the kitchen area.

It was near dusk when Kevin and the men prepared to leave. Kate looked around the large room and smiled with satisfaction. Although there was still a great deal to be done, the basic housework had been accomplished: visiting animals and designer cobwebs removed, rugs taken outside and beaten, the floor swept and washed. And after hours of listening to Michael's cursing and beating on the iron plumbing, they even had running water. It was almost habitable.

"Kate, is there anything else we can bring next week—besides what's on the list?"

Leaning on her broom, she smiled at Kevin. He was so friendly, so helpful . . . so different from his brother. Placing the broom against the wall, she wiped the dirt off the front of her blouse and walked up to him. "If it wouldn't be too much trouble, could you possibly find me a change of clothes? With the trunk gone, I have nothing to wear."

"Why, certainly," Kevin said, a little embarrassed. "I'm sure I could find someone to shop . . ."

Picturing Kevin purchasing women's clothes was almost laughable and Kate turned toward Tom, the young sailor who'd brought food to her cabin during the storm. Eyeing his youthful body, Kate's smile was wicked.

"Do you have another pair of pants, Tom?" she asked.

The poor boy's eyes nearly popped out of his head. With everyone looking at him, he managed to mumble, "On the *Rebel* . . . Yes, ma'am."

"Now hold on there!" Michael quickly entered the conversation and, for the first time since arriving at Haphazard, addressed Kate. "This is too much! You will not wear Tom's pants! I have gone along with everything up until now, however nothing was said about a member of my crew sharing his clothing!"

Facing him with her hands firmly placed on her hips, she said, "Your clothes are too big, or, believe me, I would use them. Tom here is closer to my size."

Kevin looked at the disheveled yet beautiful woman and saw her anger was quickly rising to the same level as Michael's. Wanting to avoid another argument, Kevin hastened to interrupt. "I can see her point, Michael. Her clothing is soiled and she really does have nothing else to wear." With his head, he motioned for Tom to get the clothing.

As the door closed behind the young man, Michael glared at his brother. The room was filled with an uncomfortable silence until Tom returned. In his absence, several other members of the crew nodded to Kate and Michael and made a hasty exit back to the ship.

When the black trousers were placed in her hands, Kate smiled her thanks to Tom and turned to Denny. Kissing the old man's whiskered cheek, she said, "If it wasn't for you, I don't know how I would have managed to get through all this. You and the men were such a help."

Embarrassed, Denny avoided looking at Michael and mumbled, "Couldn't just leave you with that mess now, could I? You take care, Miss Kate. We'll find you some proper clothes."

Shaking Michael's hand, he said, "Me'n Kevin'll snoop around and find out what Masterson's up to. You listen to your brother and stay put. Ain't nothin' to be gained by makin' trouble yet."

Michael reluctantly nodded and patted Denny's shoulder. Turning to Kevin, he looked into his brother's eyes and quickly hugged him. "Take care of the *Rebel* for me," he said quietly.

"I will," Kevin promised, and pulled back so he could see Michael's face. "I'm glad you're alive," he said in an emotion-filled voice, "but give me your word you'll stay dead a while longer."

Both men laughed and Kate waved good-bye to Kevin as he went through the door. When it was shut, she and Michael stared at the wooden door for a few tense moments, neither willing to be the first to speak. It was going to be a very, very long night, she thought, and a shiver of apprehension ran up her arms as Michael slowly turned around.

Chapter 12

Michael's eyes blazed with righteous indignation, and, unconsciously, Kate took a step back into the room.

She pushed tendrils of hair off her forehead in a nervous gesture. "You know, I really like your brother." Realizing her voice sounded like a high-strung squeak, she added, "Everyone certainly pitched in, didn't they?"

He didn't answer, just continued to breathe deeply and stare at her, his complexion mottled with a barely contained anger. Placing Tom's pants onto a nearby chair, Kate took a deep breath and said, "I know you're angry, but . . ."

"I'm past anger," he interrupted in a deadly quiet voice. "I am enraged, incensed," his voice grew in volume, "by what you've done! You are the most infuriating woman I have ever had the misfortune to meet!"

"I think you're blowing this all out of proportion," she said in her defense. Deciding distance was needed,

Kate turned away and walked into the kitchen area. "Would you like some coffee?" she asked, searching through the cabinets. "I swear I saw a coffeepot here earlier!"

"You, madam, are a manipulator!"

Finding the coffeepot, Kate dropped it into the sink when she heard Michael's explosive shout. He was directly behind her.

Spinning around, she felt the edge of the sink at the small of her back as she pressed against it. He was towering over her, his eyes wide with unsuppressed fury, his angry complexion a startling contrast to his light hair. Bringing her chin up and squaring her shoulders, Kate forced herself to meet his eyes. "I wouldn't start calling anyone names, Michael. Didn't you ever hear that people in glass houses shouldn't throw stones?"

She could actually see his nostrils flare and was barely able to control the urge to bolt for the door.

"I have no idea what you are talking about," he nearly growled, his eyes slits of anger. "We will stay with the issue at hand: How dare you manipulate my life to fit in with your greedy plans? I once asked if you had any shame. You never really answered. Now I know why—you have none!"

Reacting instinctively, Kate brought her hands up and shoved Michael backward. "How dare you talk to me like that?" she demanded, her fear forgotten. "You have the audacity to call *me* a manipulator? Well, what about you, Mr. Sheridan? Who was it that was ready to drop me off in New Jersey? Did you really think I would just let you walk off with *my* treasure?"

Michael felt insulted . . . and furious. "If you had

177

given me the chance, I would have explained that I was willing to share it with you."

"Share?" Kate was shocked, yet she hadn't lost her sense of humor. Looking up at the ceiling of the cottage, she gave a sarcastic laugh. "How very generous of you, Michael. You were going to share my treasure with me!"

Michael shook his head. "That has nothing to do with your actions. Why, may I ask, did you suddenly find it convenient to claim me for a husband? I seem to recall a conversation where you vehemently denied such a possibility!"

"I didn't know then that you were planning to dump me and steal everything!" Kate picked up the coffeepot and began pumping water into it. "And it has everything to do with my actions. You're just mad because I've made it my business to watch every move you make." Finding the coffee beans in a small sack, she looked around in confusion.

Taking the cloth sack away from her, Michael opened a cupboard and brought out a mill. Pouring the beans inside, he began grinding. "The trouble in my family is none of your business," he said in a gruff voice as he poured the ground beans into the container.

Kate snatched the pot away from him and replied, "If your uncle has what belongs to me, then I'm making it my business." She slammed the coffeepot down onto the cast iron stove and fooled with its many doors and lids. Completely baffled, she stood back with her hands on her hips.

"I suppose you're going to tell me you've never used a stove before?"

Her eyes narrowed with impatience. "Not like this I

178

haven't. Give me a microwave, or gas, or electric . . . I know you don't want to hear this, but I'll have you know that I was able to program my coffeemaker and it would automatically be ready when I woke up in the morning." Taking a deep breath, she sighed while thinking of the fresh aroma of coffee that had greeted her the moment she'd opened her eyes.

"You're right . . . I don't want to hear it," Michael grumbled and gave her a look that said he hadn't understood, or believed, what she'd said.

Frustrated, Kate looked back at the antique stove. "I don't even remember my grandmother having one this old. What do you use in it? Wood?"

"Very good, Kate," he said while opening the larger door on the bottom and placing several pieces of wood inside. "At this rate, you might have your coffee tomorrow morning at breakfast. I take it," he asked when he finally had the stove lit, "you aren't much of a cook?"

"I happen to be a spectacular cook. Why, in California, I gave dinner parties that . . ." Kate's mouth clamped shut.

Leaning against the wooden counter, Michael crossed his arms over his chest. "Please continue," he urged in a caustic voice. "Am I actually about to hear some truth concerning your past?"

Kate ignored him as she searched the cabinets for cups and saucers. Finding both, she rinsed them out and placed them on the counter to wait for the coffee to brew.

"You certainly are well traveled for a young woman, Kate. Bermuda, New Jersey, and now California. Why, even I've never been to California."

179

"It doesn't surprise me," Kate said in an undertone as she opened a sack of raw sugar. She didn't like where the conversation was leading. Her past was her own business and it had taken her too long to put it behind her. She had no intention of dragging it out for this man to examine.

"I'd be interested in knowing how you traveled clear across the country. Did you go by wagon train? By ship?" He was determined not to let her escape this time. What bothered him, more than anything, was that she had deceived him. It had been many years since he'd trusted another, man or woman, and he was as angry with himself for misjudging her as he was with Kate's constant lying. "How did you get to California?" he repeated.

She turned around and faced him. "You wouldn't believe me if I told you," she stated.

Michael shrugged his shoulders.

"I flew," she said simply and watched as the anger returned to his eyes.

"You . . . You're ridiculous, Kate! Do you know how ludicrous that sounds?" He started to pace the small kitchen area. Abruptly, he stopped and glared at her. "Have you no conception of reality, at all?"

Pushing back the hair on her forehead with one hand, Kate pointed her finger at his chest. "You don't want reality! You want something that's none of your business. How about this story then, Michael? I went by wagon train to California. It was a long, hard journey," she said dramatically. "We were attacked by Indians. They were dragging me away to be their captive when . . ." Her hands were clutched at her chest and she spread them in the air. "When John Wayne, the

180

Lone Ranger, and Tonto came riding over the horizon!" She looked out to the darkened sitting room of the cottage. "The Duke was wonderful, as always," she said in an awe-filled voice. "And the Lone Ranger?" She lifted her head as if recalling a miracle. "Let me tell you, before the day was over, those Indians who hadn't been shot to death by silver bullets were shaking their heads wondering, 'Who was that masked man?' Tonto, his faithful Indian companion who always was on the side of right and the downtrodden, left them dazzled as he rode off with his *kemosabe*." She looked at the startled man across from her and smiled sweetly. "It was a hell of a trip, Michael. I decided to take a ship back to New Jersey."

He was speechless, and continued to stare at her as if she'd lost her mind. Venturing closer, Kate couldn't help chuckling. "Well? Did you like that story any better?"

He was furious. First she lies, he thought, then she laughs at me! Well, he'd put an end to that. "You must be hiding something very important to make up such elaborate stories. Not that you don't do it well, mind you," he said while checking the coffeepot. "You're very imaginative. Unfortunately, you're also laughable. Your story is preposterous and the men in it sound like tabloid heroes. However, your comical expressions added a nice touch to the farce."

He turned back to her and stared into her wide eyes. "You're such a liar, Kate," he said with a disdainful sneer.

She felt as if he'd slapped her. Knowing if she stayed in the room much longer, she'd give in to the urge to hit his face, Kate tightened the muscles around her eyes and refused to cry. She would not give him that satisfaction.

"And you're such a bastard, Michael!" she replied in an angry, hurt voice. "You refuse to see any farther than what's in front of your nose . . ." Kate calmly stepped to the door and opened it. She had every intention of closing it gently behind her, to show him she had control of her anger. Instead, she slammed it with all her force. It wasn't much, but it certainly felt good.

Kate walked about twelve feet from the cottage while mentally applying to Michael every barnyard curse she had ever heard. How long must she endure the man's hostility? Abruptly, she halted her hike and looked around in the darkness. As she folded her arms over her chest, Kate realized she had no idea of where to go. Feeling the night's chill and hearing the noises of the nearby forest carried on the wind, she admitted it was foolish to have left. From the corner of her eye, she peered back at the cottage. Even if Michael were inside it, it was warm . . . and safe. Now, how in the world was she going to get back in?!

Pride. It was a curse, a wicked emotion, and it had gotten her into more trouble over the years than she cared to remember. Hugging herself to ward off the cold, Kate meandered through the yard, and closer to the house. Why did she have to walk out? Michael should have been the one to leave, she thought with conviction. Now, she'd have to swallow her damn pride to get back inside. What was she supposed to do? she anguished. Produce signed affidavits from the future to prove she belonged there?

Without thinking, she kicked a small pile of wood

that was stacked in the yard. Her frustration turned into pain as a sharp ache traveled up from her foot to settle in her brain.

"Damn it!"

Hobbling around in circles, Kate winced as she tried to bring feeling back into her toes. About to issue another forceful expletive, she immediately straightened when she heard the front door open.

He was silhouetted with the light from the room behind him. Unable to see his face, Kate could only make out the rigidity of his body. Neither of them said a word. It was only when Michael turned back to the interior of the house that Kate released her breath in relief.

He'd left the door open.

She continued to stare at the welcoming sight. She'd still have to swallow her pride to walk back in, but she'd do it. Kate Walker might be occasionally foolish, but she wasn't stupid. And it would be sheer stupidity to remain outside, she decided. Taking a deep breath, she squared her shoulders and tried not to limp as she crossed the distance between the night's cold and sheltered warmth.

Shutting the door behind her, Kate could feel her cheeks burning with humiliation and prayed Michael would leave her alone to work her way through it.

"Your coffee's ready," he announced, his voice tinged with amusement.

Closing her eyes briefly in exasperation, she turned around and faced him. He was casually leaning against the wall, sipping coffee while holding out a cup to her. Swallowing down a sharp reply, she crossed the room and accepted his offering.

Michael waited until she had tasted the hot liquid before looking down at her foot and smiling. "I should have told you to bring in more wood for the night. It would have saved me a trip outside."

As Kate felt the coffee spread a warmth through her limbs, she decided not to rise to his baiting. It was what he expected and, whether he was aware of it or not, Michael Sheridan was fascinated by the unexpected. Realizing she had a way to diffuse their confrontation, she glanced up at him and laughed.

Shaking her head, she said, "Michael, it's your house and I'm the guest. I'm sorry I argued with you."

His smile froze and his eyes narrowed suspiciously. "*You're* apologizing?" he asked in disbelief.

Kate nodded while sipping her coffee. Walking over to a dark green sofa, she sat down and looked at him. "It isn't going to be easy for either one of us. You know that, don't you? It'll be at least a week before Kevin and Denny come back and, meanwhile, you and I have to share this room."

She watched as Michael came farther into the living area. Waiting until he sat down in one of the chairs opposite her, Kate forced herself to appear humble. "Neither one of us is used to confinement," she explained. "If we continue to argue about everything, it'll only make it seem that much worse. I think we should make an attempt to get along . . . call a truce until this whole thing is over."

She let the words hang in the air and waited for him to answer. Warming her hands on the hot cup, Kate watched him as he considered her words. Michael propped his booted feet up on a small table separating them and, as he studied the ceiling, she studied him.

Michael Thomas Sheridan was too good-looking to be called merely handsome, and spending three days on an island had done nothing to detract from his appeal, Kate thought sullenly, as she pushed back dirty strands of hair off her forehead. What infuriated her was that after everything, all the lies, all the deceits, he still had the power to make her body respond to his nearness. It was almost shameful that she could barely control the intense longing when she viewed his half-buttoned shirt, his rolled-up sleeves . . . the way the material of his trousers fit snugly across his muscled thighs. Shutting her eyes briefly, as the dulled memory of them on the beach suddenly burst sharply across her brain, Kate sighed in frustration.

"I agree," Michael abruptly announced, in answer to her sigh.

Her eyes snapped open. "You do?" Kate asked, afraid he had read her mind and seen the passionate picture she had conjured up from their lovemaking.

"Yes. I think you're right," he answered, while watching her eyes widen in surprise. "It makes no sense to continually be at each other's throat. As you've reminded me, you're a guest and I've been very inhospitable. I agree to a truce . . . but only until we regain possession of the treasure. Then, we'll each be free to lead our own lives."

It was exactly what she wanted. Yet, if that were so, why did she have to force a smile? Why did the thought of making her way in this time without Michael seem unsatisfactory? And especially, why did the fact that she couldn't forget their lovemaking, while he had obviously dismissed it, have the power to hurt her so deeply?

The age-old sentiment of feminine vanity quickly surfaced. Something deep inside her, an emotion she didn't wish to identify, made her want to force an admission from him.

Standing up, Kate again smiled and brought her cup back into the kitchen. "I'm going to take a bath," she proclaimed over her shoulder. "Now might be a good time to bring in more wood!"

Twenty minutes later, she had three huge pots boiling with water on the stove. Michael had reluctantly brought out an old-fashioned tub and it was almost half full with now warm water. Perspiration dripped off her as she worked, but she was determined. It had occurred to her that, of course, Michael wouldn't remember their beautiful afternoon on the beach while she looked like such a drudge. Using a thick towel to protect her hands, Kate picked up the handle of a pot and brought it over to the tub. Pouring the steaming water into it, she heard his voice behind her.

"I still don't see why you couldn't have waited until morning for this. Do you realize how late it is?"

Kate smiled sweetly as she turned back to the stove. "I told you," she said patiently, "that I can't wait until morning. You forget, Michael, you had the opportunity to get cleaned up on the *Rebel*. I can't even remember the last time I used soap. Don't worry," she said while placing the last two pots on a towel next to the tub, "you don't have to stay up."

Satisfied that everything was ready, Kate straightened as she pulled out the bottom of her blouse from her skirt. "I'll be fine, Michael. Go on to bed if you're tired."

186

She had to bite the inside of her lip to keep from smiling at Michael's expression. His eyes seemed glued to the waistband of her skirt as her fingers hovered over its buttons. As if catching himself, he coughed, murmured a quick good night, and turned away from the kitchen area . . . all the while avoiding her eyes.

It was bliss—absolute heaven—to lay back against the tub and feel the steam entering and cleansing her pores. Reveling in the hot, relaxing water, Kate slowly slid down the tub's length and held her breath as she dunked her head. Sitting up, she pushed her hair back from her face and looked around. A sudden feeling of despair came over her when she spied the large bar of soap, not in the tub as she had thought, but resting by the sink.

"Oh, God!" she whispered in desperation and looked out to the now darkened living room. Maybe if she was fast, she could make it across the room and back without him seeing her. Just as she was about to rise, she suddenly sat back down and smiled. It was wicked, she thought, and not really worthy of her. But at that moment, she couldn't think of a better way to get the soap, nor a better way to get to Michael.

He could hear her bathing, and the pictures he conjured up in his mind were nothing less than torture. He wondered if she was aware of the effect she had on him . . . how he had watched her all afternoon playfully ordering his men? He had been amazed by how easily his hardened seamen had taken to housework. It was almost as if they had enjoyed it, each trying to outdo the other in an attempt to please Kate. In his life, he'd never seen so many grown men acting so foolish in one place.

Shaking his head, Michael shifted in his chair before the fireplace. From this side of the room he couldn't see into the kitchen, yet his imagination was quickly activated. Because of the wide L shape to the cottage, Kate was hidden from his view, and Michael had to grasp the upholstered arms of his chair in an effort to control his instincts. He must, of course, he quickly told himself. Kate had offered a mature temporary solution to their problems and he had agreed. But that was before he knew she was going to bathe. Just knowing she was beyond the wall, nude, bringing a cloth over her wet breasts, down a long, shapely leg . . .

"Michael—could you come here a moment, please?"

His eyes watered from staring at the dancing flames and he blinked a few times, not quite sure he had actually heard her voice. Did she really call to him? Or was his mind so besotted with mental images of Kate as she had been on the beach that his ears were playing tricks on him?

"Michael? Did you hear me? Are you asleep?"

Slowly he rose from the chair to answer her siren's song. His heart beat loudly inside his chest and echoed in his ears. His palms began to perspire. His knees felt too weak to support him for the short walk. It was ridiculous, he scolded himself, to feel like a young, inexperienced boy . . . yet that was exactly how he felt. In that moment of honesty, Michael Sheridan also admitted a strong, sometimes strange, attraction to the woman beyond the wall. In a short period of time, she had become an important part of him, and despite her lies and crazy stories, he didn't want to lose her . . . or scare her away.

Rounding the corner into the kitchen, Michael

automatically stopped and stared at Kate as she sat in the steaming tub. Holding a wet towel over her breasts, she shyly smiled at him.

"I'm really sorry, Michael, but would you hand me the soap?" She looked toward the sink.

He had to swallow several times before there was enough moisture in his mouth to speak. "Soap?" he asked hoarsely, unable to tear his eyes away from her. Her long, black hair was slicked back from her face and lay heavily on her shoulders and back. The wet cotton towel clung to her chest, outlining each luscious mound beneath, and his imagination went wild as he instinctively tried to see below the water. Slowly, ever so slowly, he allowed his eyes to devour each exposed part of her body before returning to her face. She stared at him with an innocent expression.

"I . . . ah, I forgot the soap," she explained and shrugged her shoulders. "I'd have gotten it myself except I'd have hated to have ruined the floor after everyone worked so hard. Do you mind?"

Mind? His feet felt rooted to the floor and he had to force them to move. Picking up the large cake of soap, he clasped it tightly in his hand as he slowly walked up to the tub. She looked wet and seductive, her lovely skin glistening with moisture, and his eyes locked with her light-blue ones, afraid to look anywhere else.

She appeared innocent, and her unusual eyes asked a question as she held out her hand. Instinct was telling him to kneel next to the tub, to take her hand and kiss it, to remove the towel that hid her beauty, enfold her wet body in his arms and make love to her. Sanity told him that to do so would again make him vulnerable— and, besides, Kate trusted him to adhere to their truce.

If he did dare to touch her, he would again be lost ... and that was something he couldn't afford right now.

Gently placing the soap in her hand, he smiled and whispered, "Enjoy your bath, Kate," before turning away.

Bringing the soap into the water, Kate watched him walk back into the living room. As she lathered her shoulders, she thought about Michael and a smile slowly appeared at her lips.

Michael Thomas Sheridan hadn't forgotten one moment they had spent on that beach, not one moment ... it was written all over his face.

Her grin widened.

Chapter 13

Wrapped in a long, fleecy towel, Kate shivered as she wrung out her underwear and blouse. Just as she wondered where to hang them up to dry, she heard Michael's voice coming from the other side of the room.

"Kate . . . are you decent?"

Smiling before answering, she said, "I think so. Why?"

She turned around at his footsteps. "I was . . . Well, I was giving some thought about what you had said concerning your wardrobe." He seemed startled at finding her in the towel and it looked as if he was extremely uncomfortable. "And it occurred to me," he continued, after clearing his throat, "that you were without night clothes.

"Here." Holding out a white shirt, he remarked, "You can roll the sleeves up."

Accepting the shirt, Kate was touched by his thoughtfulness and smiled warmly. "It'll be great, Michael. Thank you."

He nodded, and nervously ran a hand over his stomach. "I'll leave you to finish in here," he said quietly, while slowly backing out of the room.

At his words, her expression changed and she took a step in his direction. "Michael, how do I get rid of the water in the tub?" she asked with a grin on her face.

He looked at the tub, then back at her. "I'll do it," he volunteered.

"No, I'll do it," she insisted. "Just tell me how."

For a moment, he questioned her lack of knowledge. She had a brilliant imagination and somewhere in her life had acquired some sort of engineering background. He shook his head in bemusement. She could operate her complex scuba equipment, but couldn't empty a tub? Kate was unlike any other woman he had ever met. "You're shivering," he observed. "Go on into the other room and dress before the fire. I'll take care of this. I insist."

Kate was again going to protest, but seeing he was determined, she murmured, "Okay, Michael. Thanks," before gathering up his shirt and her wet clothes. She really was freezing!

Ten minutes later, he found her sitting in front of the fire. She'd turned around two high-backed wooden chairs and had draped her underwear across the tops. He stared at the lovely picture she presented, and wondered if she had any idea what she was doing to him?

Sensing him, Kate slowly turned her head and smiled. "It's so nice and cozy in here, isn't it?"

Not answering, Michael walked farther into the room and sat down opposite her. It didn't help matters that her underwear was separating them. He concentrated on the flames, not daring to look at the flimsy garments.

"I think we have a problem," Kate whispered.

Startled, Michael's head snapped toward her. "What?" he asked in a ragged voice.

"There's only one bed."

The words were left hanging in the air while they continued to stare at each other. Finally Kate said, "I'll take the couch."

Mentally shaking himself, Michael spoke up. "No, you take the bed," he offered. "I'll take the couch."

Kate smiled and shook her head. "Don't be silly. This is your home. I don't mind sleeping on the couch."

"Kate, it's all right. You're the guest here. You've been deprived of a proper bed long enough."

"Well, so were you," she persisted. "You were on that island with me. And, besides, I'm smaller than you, so I should take the couch."

"You will sleep in the bed," he muttered, his voice sounding deeper. "I insist."

Kate wasn't sure whether the heat from the fire was making his face look so red, or whether the firelight was just causing shadows. Not wanting to take the chance that anger might be the cause of his changed complexion, she stood up and said, "Fine. But we'll take turns. Tomorrow you'll sleep in the bed."

"Just get in the damn thing and go to sleep!"

He hadn't meant to lose his temper with her, but she was driving him to exasperation with her bantering, and he was on the edge of losing his self-control. When she'd stood up, his shirt had barely reached her knees, and he'd found himself jealous that the material, and not his hands, was touching her. Watching her storm over to the bed, he finally released his breath as he observed her climbing onto the mattress.

He probably should apologize, he thought sullenly, as he stared back at the flames, but was afraid to trust his voice. Michael slowly shook his head. How his life had changed since he had met Kate on that reef. In less than two weeks, he'd located a treasure and lost it, without ever laying eyes on it; had probably been charged with kidnapping Helene Barnett, and never even met her; had been declared dead, and obviously was very much alive . . . and, worse, had deceptively married a veiled woman, and now found he might very possibly have a wife! Even his years in the war seemed easier by comparison than the last two weeks of his life.

Again shaking his head, he stood up and threw a few more logs onto the fire. Satisfied that it would continue to provide warmth until they both fell asleep, Michael walked over to the couch. Surprised, he stared down at it. While he'd been emptying the tub, Kate had obviously prepared the couch with pillow, sheets, and a blanket. He suppressed a sigh as he sat down and removed his boots. Taking off his belt, he hung it over the arm of the couch and lay down. As he pulled the blanket up to his chest, Michael attempted to get comfortable by punching the pillow, shifting to his side, and, finally, staring across the room into the fireplace—in hopes that the dancing flames might entice him into sleep.

Instead, his vision slowly shifted to Kate's damp underwear. Abruptly, he closed his eyes and mentally cursed the tantalizing sight. He'd never make it through the week until Kevin came back . . . never! They hadn't spent one entire day together in the house

194

and he was ready to forget everything and walk across the room to Kate's bed. Groaning, Michael knew without a shadow of a doubt that it was going to be a hellishly long night!

With her back to Michael, Kate brought the blanket over her shoulder. As she inhaled, she smelled the scent of cedar that clung to everything she had brought out of the large chest. It wasn't overwhelming, just reminded her that whoever had stocked this cottage had done a good job. Which brought her to another point. It *was* Michael's home, and she should be grateful that she was inside of it. Even if she'd had to do some fancy maneuvering to get here, she was warm and dry . . . and clean. And she wasn't fending for herself. The world outside the front door might as well lead into a foreign land. She had no idea how to survive out there, and in the honesty that comes at night, Kate admitted she wanted to stay close to Michael. He was the one constant in an otherwise confusing existence. It was Michael who had found her . . . Michael who had saved her life . . . and it was Michael who had loved her on that beach with such an intensity that just thinking about it could bring tears to her eyes.

How strange, she thought, to share this room and sleep apart. Together, they had found something so special, and yet, now it seemed like a dream, something only to fantasize about. Isolated in the large bed, Kate wondered how Michael could sleep. He remembered. She knew he remembered. Maybe it just didn't mean as much to him . . .

Shifting to her side, she stared across the room. She couldn't make out his face, but he appeared to be sleeping without a care in the world. Kate smiled sadly in the darkness. Michael had his cares, they'd just been postponed for a while. Soon, he'd have to deal with them.

Acknowledging her own problems, she admitted that she was frightened. Unlike Michael, here she had no past to settle—but she also had no future. Closing her eyes, she hugged the pillow for security. She had battled her demons once before, and had come out victorious. But then she'd had her mother's help and guidance, and the futility of revenge had been a tough lesson to learn.

Opening her eyelids, she looked toward the couch and felt a surge of tenderness, a need to protect, for deep inside her she knew that Michael's turn was quickly coming . . .

The delicious aroma of fried ham entered her nostrils and awakened her taste buds. Quickly, her mouth was filled with moisture as she attempted to swallow. Grimacing with pain, Kate opened her eyes and stared about the room. Taking in the rustic furnishings, she heard, for the first time, the sound of rain as it pounded against the windows and roof. Because of the lack of sunlight it was difficult to tell what time it was, and, looking toward the lighted kitchen, she could only assume Michael was cooking breakfast.

Not yet ready to give up the warm comfort of the bed, Kate closed her eyes and languidly stretched her arms and legs. Enjoying the pulling sensation as it traveled through her limbs, she snuggled deeper into the pillow. It had felt wonderful to sleep in a bed again, she thought lazily. Maybe she could just stay put and listen to the rain. It was a childhood luxury she hadn't indulged in many, many years. But her throat was so dry—

Hearing the sounds of pots and pans, curiosity got the better of her and she opened her eyes. Michael was cooking breakfast?

Deciding to rise, she wrapped the blanket around her shoulders and left the warmth of the bed. Her toes curled under when her feet hit the cold floor. Moving quickly, Kate brushed the hair back off her forehead and entered the kitchen.

"Hi." Her voice sounded hoarse, and she rubbed her throat while squinting.

Turning around from the stove, Michael took in her appearance and smiled. "I thought I'd let you sleep in. Hungry?"

Kate looked at the thick slices of ham sizzling in the frying pan. "Sure," she answered. "But I think I'd like some water first."

"What's wrong with you?" He sounded concerned. Walking up to her, Michael placed his hand on her forehead and looked into her eyes. "You have a cold, don't you? Your voice is raw. I knew you never should have taken a bath last night."

He brought his palm away and tilted her chin up toward his face. "You don't have a fever," he stated while staring into her eyes. "Maybe it's from the fire. I should have boiled water to put the moisture back into the air."

Although moved by his interest in her welfare, Kate took a step backward. She had to fight the urge to rest her head on his chest.

"Look at you," he observed in a disapproving voice.

"Why didn't you put something on your feet? If you don't have a cold now, walking around without shoes and socks will surely give you one." Not waiting for her reply, Michael wrapped a towel around the frying pan's handle and took it off the heat. Without speaking, he walked into the living area, only to return moments later and hand her a pair of gray woolen socks.

"Put them on," he ordered. "Neither one of us can afford to get sick."

Accepting them, Kate sat in a kitchen chair and slid her feet into Michael's socks. They felt wonderfully warm, far warmer than her own thin, ripped hose. She smiled her thanks and looked toward the window above the sink. "Has it been raining long?" she asked, while loosening the blanket from her shoulders.

Watching the woolen blanket slide down to her waist, Michael inwardly groaned and turned back to his cast iron skillet. As he returned it to the stove, he muttered, "It started last night. Somewhere around two or three in the morning."

"You were awake? I knew you should have slept in the bed!"

He looked over his shoulder at her. "I was fine, Kate. I had a lot to think about, that's all."

She nodded and stood up. Not wanting to question what he might have been thinking about in the middle of the night, she left the blanket on the chair and moved next to him. Pointing to the coffeepot warming at the center of the stove, she asked, "Could I have a cup?" while picking up an empty mug.

Michael looked down at her attire. She was still wearing his shirt and, now, his socks. "You should have tea, with honey, for your throat," he said gruffly, yet shifted slightly so she could pick up the coffeepot.

Pouring the strong brew, Kate inhaled its aroma while wondering when Michael had become such a mother hen. "The coffee's just fine, Michael," she said, deciding that since he had gone through the trouble of making a nice breakfast she wouldn't argue with him.

"What can I do to help?" she asked, sipping the hot coffee while waiting for his answer.

Michael lifted a lid off a smaller pot and stirred. "You can set the table, I guess."

Putting down her coffee, Kate quickly reached for the plates Michael had set aside. Finding utensils and napkins, she set the table with care. When finished, Kate smiled and glanced up at her handsome cook. He had a towel tucked into the top of his pants. His sleeves were rolled up, and she could tell he was hot by the way he kept wiping his forehead on his shoulder.

"Do you know that you're very liberated, Michael? Considering the . . ."

"Liberated?" he interrupted, while bringing the pots and pans over to the table. "I don't understand."

Waiting until they were both seated, Kate placed a napkin on her lap and smiled across the table at him. "All of this," she observed, and indicated the food with her hand. "You don't seem to have any hang-ups about cooking."

He took the lids off the pots and glanced up at her. "What are hang-ups?" he asked, more interested in the food than her answer.

Kate still tried to make conversation. "What I mean is, you don't seem to object to cooking for a woman."

Placing three slices of ham on his plate, he asked, "Why would I object to cooking for you? You were

199

asleep, and I was hungry. Besides, you'd said you couldn't cook."

"I never said I couldn't cook! I said . . ." She shook her head and bit her bottom lip to stop the sharp reply. She refused to be the one to break their truce. "All I wanted to say was thank you for making breakfast."

"Then why didn't you just say that? Do you realize you have the most confusing way of speaking?" Seeing she wasn't going to answer, Michael pushed the smaller pot in front of her. "You'd better eat while it's hot," he commented. "There's nothing worse than cold oatmeal."

Kate stretched her neck to look into the pot. Bringing her head back, she reached for the platter containing the ham. "I'll just have some of this," she stated quietly, while putting a piece on her plate.

Michael placed his knife and fork down on the table. "You mean you're not going to eat the oatmeal?" he asked in a hurt voice.

Kate tried to smile. "I wish you would have asked me first. You see, I hate hot cereal. I always have. My own mother couldn't get me to eat it."

"You're not going to eat the oatmeal?" he again asked, a slow anger replacing the wounded tone of his voice. "Do you have any idea how much trouble that was to make?"

Looking at his injured expression, Kate stifled a laugh. "Look, Michael, I can't help it if I hate it. I told you—you should have asked first."

He pulled the pot across the table. "I *couldn't* ask!" he proclaimed as he scooped a large mound of the oatmeal onto his plate. "You were asleep. Remember? And how do you manage to eat cereal cold?"

Kate had to avert her eyes from the congealed gray mass on his plate. Even the sight of it could turn her stomach. Reaching for the loaf of bread that had been brought from the *Rebel,* she tore off a piece. "I'll tell you what," she offered, "tomorrow, I'll cook breakfast . . . and tonight, I'll ask you what you want. If we take turns and consult each other, a lot of this arguing can be avoided."

Reminded of their fragile truce, and how often he'd come close to breaking it, Michael merely grunted, while bringing another spoonful of hearty oatmeal to his mouth. She didn't know what she was missing, he thought righteously.

By noontime, Kate's patience was at its limit. Because of the rain, they were forced to stay indoors, and Michael was like a caged animal—pacing back and forth, only stopping long enough to look over her shoulder as she attempted to finish her chores. She knew if he didn't soon find something to occupy his time, she was going to strangle him. And smile while doing it!

Dusting the fireplace's mantel, she felt blessed by heaven when she discovered the deck of cards. "Look what I found!" she exclaimed, removing the kitchen towel from the waist of her pants.

Staring out the window to the rain-soaked forest, Michael turned around at the sound of her voice. There was a quick tightening in his groin as he again viewed the young man's trousers hugging her hips and outlining every curve that was already burned into his memory. Had she any idea of what she was doing to him?

"Cards! Do you want to play?" she asked, feeling like an adult trying to entertain a child.

Slowly, he walked toward her. "Where did you find them?"

Kate looked back at the fireplace. "On the mantel. Do you want to play?" she again asked.

He looked surprised. "You know how?"

She brought her chin up. "Of course I know how," she stated while placing them in his hand.

Michael shrugged his shoulders. "I suppose we might as well," he said while walking into the kitchen. "If you really want to."

Kate's mouth dropped open and her eyes shot imaginary daggers into his broad back. If *she* really wanted to? Forcing herself to follow him, Kate squared her shoulders and her smile could only be described as sly. Michael Thomas Sheridan was about to be taught a badly needed lesson.

Although eager, Kate held back. She thought she was being very sedate as she sat down opposite him at the kitchen table. Folding her hands in front of her, she smiled pleasantly. "What would you like to play?"

"What do you know how to play?" he asked while shuffling the cards.

Kate watched his hands. He was adequate. He didn't fumble, like some unprofessionals. Her assessment made, she looked up to his face. "Let's see . . . I've played a little poker from time to time. My mother and I used to play gin rummy. And, oh yes, some blackjack." She held her breath as she waited for his reply.

He looked astounded. "Poker? You've played blackjack?"

She nodded. "Have you?"

"Well, yes. Of course I have . . ."

"I don't mind playing blackjack," she interrupted before he could change his mind. "Why don't you deal?"

He looked as if he had a few more questions for her, so Kate quickly stood. "Do you want anything?" she asked. "Since it's close to lunchtime, I'm going to set out some bread and cheese."

It had worked, she thought, as she placed the food on the table. Whatever Michael had been about to ask had been forgotten as she'd successfully turned the conversation away from her ability to play cards.

"Now, before I sit back down, what can I get you to drink? Coffee, water . . . or coffee?"

"I suppose I'll take coffee," he said dryly.

"Good choice," Kate remarked while returning to the warm stove.

She beat him five times in a row . . . and she wasn't even trying. In the back of her brain, she had a strange feeling Michael was letting her win. That wasn't her plan. She had wanted him to win, to lull him into a false sense of security. Realizing she would have to come up with something to change his attitude, Kate announced after another easy score, "This is getting boring, Michael. Why don't we make it more interesting?"

He smiled at her. "What do you mean?"

"Why don't we bet something. It doesn't have to be money, since neither one of us has any to speak of."

He looked around the kitchen. "What about

203

matches? It's the only thing I can think of."

Kate smoothly returned his smile. "Sure. Why not?" Her smile widened as she watched him walk over to the stove. Matches . . . it was a start.

Kate's pile of wooden sticks slowly dwindled down to a few. It seemed once Michael had something to play for, he played for real. He wasn't bad, Kate observed . . . nor was he reckless. She'd watched him hold on thirteen, and still win. At times, she'd had to take five cards to lose. She didn't lose steadily, just systematically. It was enough to make Michael think luck had deserted her and embraced him.

Finally, when she had only two matchsticks left and the bet was three, she made her move.

"Well, Michael, it looks as though you've just about wiped me out. I don't have anything left to cover your bet."

He leaned back in his chair, very pleased with himself. Shrugging his shoulders, he grinned. "It was only a game, Kate. I guess I've played longer than you, that's all."

As Michael gathered his large stack of matches, Kate's hand shot out across the table. "It's not over, Michael," she said softly.

He seemed surprised as he stared at her hand atop his, and looked up into her face. "You have nothing to bet. It's over," he said with a finality.

Kate tried to suppress a grin as she anticipated his reaction to her next words. "But I do. It's not here, not in this house. But I most definitely have something of value. I'll bet part of my treasure."

She let her words sink in.

At least ten seconds lapsed before Michael was able

to speak. "You're willing to wager part of the treasure on a card game?" he asked with disbelief. "We weren't even playing seriously!"

"You were," Kate remarked. "You like winning. It shows on your face." She took a deep breath. "I hate losing, Michael. I'm surprised you didn't see it on mine."

"Are you serious?" he asked in a rough voice. "What part of the treasure are you willing to wager?"

Kate forced herself not to smile. "There's a large uncut emerald," she said, watching his eyes widen. "It's about the size of a hen's egg."

"It really exists?" he demanded, amazement showing on his handsome face. "What else did you find?"

Kate threw back her head and laughed. "Ah, Michael . . ." She said his name like an endearment as she stared into his excited eyes. "The only way you'll find that out is if you win."

In the real world, the one where she belonged, Kathleen Anne Walker had discovered how to put her natural talent to work for her. Three years ago, when she had left her husband in California, she'd started working as a blackjack dealer in Atlantic City. In less than a year, she'd been promoted to pit boss . . . overseeing her area of the casino, comping the high rollers and steady betters, and most importantly, spotting the card counters. For Kate, it wasn't difficult to do. She was one herself.

Some people achieved their potential by transferring to canvas the vivid pictures inside their heads. Others could evoke strong emotions by producing beautiful music. Kate could remember every single card played in a deck. It wasn't until she was an adult that she had even considered what a useful talent it actually was.

While living on the West Coast, she'd made a few profitable forays in Las Vegas, and had left with everyone thinking it was merely luck. Needing money until her divorce was final, Kate had returned to her mother's home in New Jersey and had made infrequent visits to the state's gambling community. They had been like missions to her: Get in and get out fast; never play at the same casino twice. She didn't consider it gambling, for luck had nothing to do with her considerable winnings. Card counting was, however, illegal and she had known it was only a matter of time before she was found out.

Since she was too sensible to be a real gambler, Kate had decided not to play the odds. Before she was spotted and blacklisted from the casinos, she went legal. With her winnings invested in real estate, she'd applied for her dealer's license.

No longer had she been plagued by wondering what she wanted to do when she grew up. Working her way through the pain of a broken marriage, she had at last managed to accept life as an adult. And because she had been using her talent, for the first time in her life she'd been happy and successful. Nothing had excited her more than spotting a counter and beating them at their own game. She had liked the glamour, had enjoyed being wooed by other casinos to join their management. Kate Walker had a reputation for honesty, and she'd treasured that. After all the confusion, all the false paths, she'd thought she had finally found her place.

*　　　*　　　*

Looking across the kitchen table, Kate noticed the hardening of Michael's jaw as his pile of matchsticks slowly found themselves in front of her. He was distracted by her string of winning hands, and vented his frustration by unconsciously eating the bread and cheese. Kate hadn't touched the food. She'd watched Michael, studying his face and counting the cards already played.

"How can anyone be that lucky?" he demanded, baffled by her good fortune.

Kate smiled and shrugged. Soon. He'd know soon enough. "It's uncanny, isn't it? Do you realize you're in exactly the same situation I was? Michael, you don't have enough to bet."

She knew his masculinity had taken quite a beating, and wasn't surprised to see the determination in his face. He wasn't playing for fun anymore—or for matchsticks. He was serious. He wanted the emerald . . . and he wanted to beat her.

Kate inhaled deeply with satisfaction as she waited for his solution. She had patiently brought him to this point, and if she'd judged him correctly, Michael was about to play right into her hands.

She could see he was wracking his brain trying to come up with something. "My money's in Charleston. When we . . ."

She interrupted him by shaking her head. "I don't want your money," she said in an emotionless voice. "Find something else."

His eyes narrowed suspiciously. "What do you mean, you don't want my money? Whatever the emerald is worth, if I should lose, I'll sign a promissory note of equal value."

207

Again, she shook her head. "I repeat, I don't want your money, Michael. I have money in New Jersey. You forget, you're supposed to be dead. You can't get to your bank today, and neither can I."

"Well, what do *you* suggest?" he demanded. His face showed his exasperation, his voice told of his growing anger. "What the hell do I have, Kate, that you could possibly want?"

Her vision never wavering, she sat back in her chair and whispered, "You've overlooked something, Michael. You have the *Rebel*."

Chapter 14

"The *Rebel?*"

His mouth hung open in shock. His eyes seemed to have grown larger as they stared at her in outrage. "The *Rebel?*" he repeated, obviously appalled by her suggestion.

Kate told herself to think of him as any other player she had sat across from in the past. She reminded herself not to show any emotion, not to react to the knot in her stomach, the instinctive urge to flee the room.

Instead, she forced her hands to remain relaxed and said softly, "It's the one thing of value I know you have." She lifted her chin in a challenge. "Of course, we can always call the whole thing off. I keep all the matchsticks . . . and the emerald."

"You would actually have me put up my ship in a card game? What kind of woman are you?"

Ignoring his last question, Kate smiled. "Not the whole ship, Michael. Just a portion of it. I would think my emerald would be worth—say, a fifth share in the *Rebel.*"

His blond hair looked lighter in contrast with his red face. A muscle worked furiously in his cheek as he ground his back teeth together, and his eyes—his eyes turned a deep angry blue.

"Actually, the stone is probably worth more," Kate stated calmly despite her screaming nerves. "But I'm not greedy, Michael. I'll settle for a fifth of the *Rebel*."

He leaned across the table. "You're . . . not . . . greedy?!" His words were like fists into her stomach.

Flinching at the anger in his voice, Kate pushed her chair back from the table. "Look, don't take your anger out on me because you're afraid I might win. I said we didn't have to play."

His hand shot out and captured her arm. "I'm not afraid of you, Kate," he said in a hard voice while staring into her eyes. "Sit down."

Slowly she lowered herself back onto her chair. Not caring for the look in his eyes, she murmured, "Let's forget this. I didn't mean for it to get out of . . ."

"Deal the cards," he interrupted in a deadly quiet whisper. "Or is it that you're afraid I just might win?"

Kate closed her eyes briefly. She'd led him to this point. She'd planned for this to happen. Yet, why didn't she feel triumphant? Why was there an empty, hollow feeling spreading inside her?

Her mouth grim, Kate opened her eyes and said, "You deal."

Neither spoke as Michael quickly dealt the cards. Using her thumb, Kate turned up the edge of the card in front of her. A ten. She watched Michael's face as he did the same. Despite the churning of her stomach, she had to admire Michael's poise. His face never revealed a thing. His hands were steady and sure as they dealt

210

the next round faceup.

Kate drew a king of diamonds, Michael, an ace of hearts. Their eyes met over the cards, and held. The small kitchen was filled with a thick tension and the only sound was that of the driving rain outside.

Keeping her eyes on Michael, Kate took tiny, shallow breaths. She had him beaten. There was no need for Michael to turn his card over, for Kate had drawn the last face card. The most he could get was twenty, or go over twenty-one. With an impassive shake of her head, she indicated that she would stay. To his credit, Michael merely blinked a few times while deciding how to play his cards. Finally, he began drawing from the deck.

Kate's shoulders sagged slightly when she saw Michael was planning to use his ace as a one. He didn't stand a chance either way, but this strategy was going to be more painful to swallow. Patiently, she waited as Michael's cards accumulated to a total of seventeen showing. Knowing there were no more fours in the deck, Kate's mind screamed at him to stop. Michael's mind, however, was not in tune with hers. He turned over an eight.

Her eyes flew to his face, yet Michael was staring at the last card he'd drawn. She thought she detected a slight crumbling of his expression, a minute cracking of his hard exterior. If it had been so, it had been only fleeting, for he'd recovered quickly. He sat back in his chair, raised his eyebrows in finality, and let out his breath.

Kate looked into his shocked face. He was still staring at the eight of clubs as if stunned, and it was his expression that made her change her mind.

"Look, Michael, it was only a friendly game of cards. Nothing more . . ."

Her words trailed off as he slowly raised his head. Looking across the table at her, he said in a bitter voice, "You won, Kate. It's what you wanted, isn't it?"

She felt as if he'd slapped her. Bringing her head up, she met his harsh gaze. "Keep your precious boat. But I'd like to know, if the tables were turned, if you'd won—would you have returned the emerald to me?"

His eyes never blinked as he asked, "Why don't we find out?"

"I beg your pardon?" Kate wanted to be sure she'd heard him correctly.

"I said, why don't we find out?"

Kate tried to control the rush of pleasure at his words. She'd tried to stop him, she'd really tried. Not exactly proud of where she'd been leading him, Kate attempted once more to dissuade him—for the sake of her conscience. "Michael, it's over. I told you I don't want part of your ship."

He leaned his elbows on the edge of the table. "A gentleman would allow me the opportunity to recoup my losses."

"I'm not a gentleman."

He looked deep into her eyes. "But you are a lady?"

She sat up straighter, swept the hair back off her shoulders, and met his vision. "I'll deal."

Gathering the cards in front of her, she made a point of not shuffling with her customary flourish. "Just what is it you're going to bet?" she inquired politely.

"Since you already own part of my ship, I wouldn't think you'd object to owning more. I'll wager another fifth of a share."

Kate studied his face. Although his bet sounded desperate, his expression didn't show it. In fact, he looked supremely confident. As well he should, she thought, and sighed inwardly. She had no intention of winning.

"Another share of the *Rebel* against the emerald? Be careful, Michael," she forced herself to say lightly, "or I may wind up owning the entire thing."

His smile was bold; his eyes fearless. "The emerald? I would have thought you'd keep the treasure all to yourself and wager what you'd just won."

It was Kate's turn to show self-confidence. "You seem to forget why you wanted to play this hand. If you should win, we're going to see whether you'd offer to return it. That is what you said we'd find out, isn't it?"

It was the damndest thing Michael had ever experienced. Once he'd gotten over the initial shock of losing part of the *Rebel* to her, he'd actually admitted a certain admiration for Kate. Never in his life had he seen a woman play cards so well. She had the uncanny knack of knowing just when to hold, or ask for a hit. It wasn't easy to concede that a woman had beaten him, especially when he'd been foolish enough to wager part of his ship. Since he'd been the one dealing, he had to grant that Kate had won fairly, and now he also had to acknowledge that his pride was involved.

"Deal the cards, Kate. You'll soon find out the answer."

Less than three minutes later, Kate proved to be a gracious loser. "You win, Michael. I didn't think you were holding a face card." She turned over her cards, totaling seventeen, and said, "The emerald is yours."

Michael's delight over owning the stone was short-lived. The joy in his eyes turned to suspicion and he asked, "Why did you ever hold on seventeen? For someone who has played exceptionally well, it was a very poor move."

Resting her elbows on the table, Kate sighed audibly. "I told you, I didn't think you had a face card. I took a chance, and it didn't pay off." She rubbed her forehead to remove part of the tension that had been building. "I don't know—I guess I'm just tired."

"Are you saying you don't want to play any longer?" His voice was quiet, his words spoken in disbelief.

Without looking at him, Kate nodded and stood up. Walking over to the tall upright cabinet, she said, "That's right. I have a headache and I'm hungry. I think I'll begin din—"

"You have to continue!" he interrupted. "You still own part of the *Rebel*."

Bringing out a sack of flour, she looked at his handsome face and smiled. "I do, don't I? But then you own part of my treasure." Taking the sack over to the small counter, she uncovered the partially finished ham. "I don't know about you," she remarked, "but I'm getting tired of ham. Didn't Denny leave a smoked roast of beef?"

Michael rose to his feet. "It's in the spring house," he absently answered. "What did you mean by that last statement? You aren't even going to give me a chance to get back that share of the *Rebel?*"

He was standing directly behind her, and Kate turned to face him. The grin that spread over her mouth was slow and confident. She shook her head. "No, I'm not. Are you going to give back the stone?"

She watched the indecision cross his face. When he

didn't answer immediately, she spoke up. "Why don't we try for a little honesty here? You want your ship *and* the stone. I don't blame you. I want the treasure . . . and your ship."

"Why?" Michael's eyes widened in surprise, but Kate could read no anger, just intense curiosity.

"Because," she began slowly, "your uncle is holding what belongs to me. And if part of the treasure is rightfully yours, you'll make more of an effort to get it back. Because if I own a portion of the *Rebel*, then I have every right to go with you when you find that trunk. I want to be a partner, Michael. I'm a real woman, not some mermaid with strange powers. I have no one in this time I can depend on, so I have to look after myself."

He appeared offended. "I've taken care of you, haven't I? You aren't stranded on an island. You aren't making your way penniless and afraid . . ."

Kate instinctively touched his shirt collar. "I'm talking about the future. I'm talking about being able to take care of myself." Her fingers softly traveled down the white cotton material. Resting her hand on his hard chest, she could feel the steady beating of his heart beneath her palm. "The *Rebel* was all you could call your own. The treasure was all I had. I want the right to go with you when you get it."

She could feel his lungs expand as he took a deep breath. "Partners should trust each other. It doesn't sound as if you trust me."

Her hand quickly flew away from his chest and she turned back to the counter. Grabbing its edge with her hands, she whispered, "I don't know how to trust . . . not anymore."

In the brief moment before she'd turned around, Michael had seen and recognized the pain in her eyes. Intuitively, he'd raised his hand to her shoulder, but had stopped inches from her shining dark hair. He wanted to comfort her, to say, I know how you feel. I, too, have lost the ability to trust another. I, too, have been hurt.

Instead, he slowly lowered his hand to his side and murmured, "I'll go out and get that roast."

Hearing him take the black slicker off the wall and open the door, Kate's shoulders sagged in a strange mixture of relief and sorrow. She was thankful Michael didn't question her further about her statement, and at the same time she was near overwhelmed by the sudden insight that after all these years, all her work, the scars that Jon had caused were merely healed on the surface. Deep down inside her, she knew she wasn't free of him.

As Michael held her chair out for her, Kate flushed with pleasure as she sat at the kitchen table and viewed their work. Dinner looked delicious, though how it tasted might be another matter entirely. She quickly dismissed the thought as she inhaled the tantalizing aroma of the food. Watching Michael take his seat, she thought how different he was acting. When he'd come back from the spring house, he'd stayed in the kitchen and had offered his help. Together they had prepared this meal. It was simple fare—roast beef—yet because they had cooked it together, Kate thought of it as a feast.

Almost simultaneously, they placed their napkins on their laps and looked at each other.

"Would you like me to carve?" Michael asked politely.

Noticing that he had combed his hair and rolled down the sleeves of his shirt, Kate self-consciously pushed a strand of hair behind her ear and nodded. This Michael wasn't hard to get along with, at all. Since he'd come back into the house, he'd been courteous, easygoing, and helpful. It was Michael who had showed her how to use the stove, who had made several diplomatic suggestions on the preparation of the beef. He'd even told her a couple of jokes while she'd pared the potatoes and carrots. The entire time, though, he'd never said a word about their discussion. He never brought up her offer of a partnership, or her emotional remark and, afraid that one might lead to the other, neither had she.

When they had served themselves, Kate and Michael each took a bite of the beef. Kate found the taste to be a little too smoky for her, but Michael grinned as he chewed.

"I take back everything I ever said about your cooking," he remarked, while cutting a browned potato in half. "It's delicious, Kate."

Since it was one of the few times Michael had ever complimented her, Kate couldn't suppress a giggle. "I'd have burned it five times over, if it hadn't been for your help. Give me a little time and I'll learn how to master that iron monster of a stove," she vowed, before tasting a carrot.

"You did fine, Kate. Just fine."

She stopped chewing and looked at him. Nodding, he winked his approval, then turned his attention back to his food. Kate almost choked. What was he up to?

What did he mean by that wink? It was as if he was trying to be flirtatious, and Michael was never flirtatious. Forcing herself to swallow, she reached for her glass of water and mumbled a shy, "Thank you."

"Who taught you how to play cards?" he casually asked, while placing a second helping of beef on his plate.

She wiped her mouth with her napkin and said carefully, "My mother, and my grandmother."

"Really? What an extraordinary family of women you come from. You're quite good."

She didn't know how to answer him. He couldn't know about her. She knew she hadn't told him anything about her past, not even what her job was. He was either merely curious, or suspicious. Hoping it was curiosity that had made her ask, she said, "Actually, that was how I learned my numbers. My earliest memories are sitting next to my grandmother and reciting the numbers on cards."

He seemed very interested. "Were you close to your grandmother?"

Kate smiled. "Oh, yes. Gran took care of me while my mother worked and I spent two weeks every summer with her. She had a wonderful sense of humor."

"That must be where you get it from," he said with a smile. "How was your mother employed?"

Kate stared at him, wondering why the discussion was centering on her past. He seemed friendly and interested, and he wasn't prying, not yet. "She worked as an accountant for Proctor and G—ah, a company that makes soap. She was a terrific lady. I'm glad I realized that before it was too late." Feeling it was time to turn the discussion around, she asked, "What about your mother? Kevin's told her you're alive, hasn't he?"

He shook his head.

"Michael! How could you do that?" Kate was shocked. "I know you said the two of you hadn't gotten along lately, but to let her think you're still dead . . ." She couldn't continue speaking, all Kate could envision was her own mother's sorrow if the news had been about her.

It was as if a totally unfamiliar Michael was sitting across from her. He slowly placed his knife and fork down, and wiped his mouth with a refined ease. Kate thought his body language spoke of formality, of good breeding and distance.

"Kevin and I agreed, for the time being, that it was best for my mother not to know I'm alive."

"Why? She's your mother."

"Stop scolding me, Kate," he said in a slightly less reserved voice. "I believe I told you that our relationship was never good. Since my father's death, it's deteriorated further. Don't compare my mother with yours. I doubt whether the news of my passing caused irreparable damage."

Kate didn't want to believe he could talk of his mother with so little emotion. "Don't you love her?" she demanded.

He didn't answer immediately. After picking up his utensils and cutting his beef, he said slowly, quietly, "Yes, I love her. I just can't . . . I can't seem to please her."

Kate had a vision of a small lonely boy yearning for his mother's love. The scene was so heart-wrenching that she wanted to reach across the table and enfold

Michael into her arms. She wanted to tell him that it shouldn't matter to him any longer, but she knew it did. She wanted to make him believe that it was also his mother's loss, but she knew he wouldn't. She was also positive Michael would never want her pity. And so she said nothing.

The silence hung heavy in the air until Kate cleared her throat. "Do you think your uncle has the treasure?" she asked, wanting to change the subject. "Or do you think he just shipped the trunk back unopened?"

He gave a short laugh. "Martin opened the trunk," he said derisively. "He's too curious, and too selfish. Besides, he'll be looking for that dowry."

Kate lost her appetite. "Do you mean he's going to think the treasure is Helene's dowry?"

Shaking his head, Michael leaned back in his seat. "The dowry was shares in Barnett Importing. My uncle and Winston Barnett are partners. They made a fortune during the war by defrauding the Confederacy." He looked down at his tightly held hands and made a deliberate effort to relax them. Reaching for his water, Michael added, "Martin's too devious, though. He wants his heel on Barnett's neck; that's why he insisted that the dowry be shares in Barnett Importing."

He took a sip of his water and placed the glass back on the table. "Personally, I think Martin's setting him up. And Kevin, too. Sooner or later there's bound to be an investigation. This time coming from Washington. Since Kevin carries the Sheridan name and, if the marriage had gone through, married into Barnett's family and held stock in Barnett Importing, the Federal Government would suspect Kevin and Winston . . . not Martin, who's been playing the role of beleaguered brother-in-law and uncle—just trying to keep the Sheridan business together for his sister's family."

Kate's mouth hung open in shock. "What a sneaky bast—" She bit her bottom lip to stop herself.

Michael smiled and laughed inwardly. "Your characterization is absolutely correct. He is a bastard. He's got the treasure, all right. If he'd sent it back, Kevin would know and Denny would have intercepted it."

Kate pushed her plate aside and crossed her arms on the table. "What are your plans? Do you think it's in your home?"

Michael stood up and brought the coffeepot to the table. Without asking, he poured them both a cup. Watching him sit back down, Kate thought how natural his actions seemed and realized they were falling into a routine, getting to know each other's likes and dislikes, becoming more comfortable and accepting each other. She also found herself studying his profile, the way his golden hair curled at the nape of his neck, the tiny freckle behind his earlobe. She could get used to this, she thought dreamily, as she continued to watch him. There was definitely something to be said for this type of domesticity.

"I believe it's in the house. Martin would never keep anything that valuable at the shipping office." He offered her the sugar. "Just how valuable is it, Kate? What does Martin have?"

She stopped stirring her coffee. Glancing up at him, she noticed that his smile held a look of seduction and promise. It instantly reminded her of that day on the

221

island when they had made love. His mouth had formed that same smile while they had played in the water afterward, when his hands had washed her body, his eyes almost devouring her with renewed hunger. She blinked several times to clear her mind. Now was not the time to recall those special moments. Now she needed a clear head, for her response was important.

"*Are* we partners?" she quietly asked. "You never did answer that."

Taking a sip from his cup, Michael returned her gaze. "If there's going to be a partnership, then there should be some rules. I agree to help you recover the treasure, and you can decide what my services are worth. In exchange, I can keep the emerald and you'll give me the opportunity to buy back your share of the *Rebel*. What do you think?"

Kate couldn't help grinning. His offer was better than what she had planned when she'd manipulated the card game. "I think it sounds fair—very fair. And I promise to be generous when we get the treasure back." She held out her hand.

Placing his larger hand in her smaller one, he firmly shook it. "Now . . . what did you find? What was in that box?"

Excited, Kate sat up straight and ran her fingers through the front of her hair. Leaning closer to him, she said in a conspiratorial voice, "It's *fabulous,* Michael! Laying on top of everything was a gold cross, studded with emeralds, about six inches high." Seeing his eyes widen, she couldn't help but laugh. "The best was underneath! There was a thick gold ingot with a hollowed-out center and cradled inside were chunks of uncut stones . . . more emeralds, amethysts, and diamonds. The diamonds were unpolished, but, Michael, everything was more the size of rocks than stones." She shook her head. "It's unbelievable!"

Michael suddenly pushed back his chair. Looking up to the kitchen ceiling, he started laughing. "Good old Tom! We should build a monument to him!"

Laughing with him, Kate stopped abruptly and asked, "Who's Tom?"

"He was a crazy old sea dog who carried a map with him for as long as I knew him. When he was dying and gave it to me, the leather was cracking, the drawings were fading, but I kept it because it was so important to Tom." He shook his head, as if trying to absorb everything she had told him. "I was starting to think I was as crazy as old Tom when I met you."

Kate's smile was genuinely warm. "I never thought I'd say this, but—I'm glad you did. I don't even want to think about where I'd be if I had to . . ." Embarrassed, she stopped speaking. "Anyway, I'm glad we met, Michael."

The room was filled with emotion as Michael saw on her face what her admission had cost. Kate's mouth held a shy smile, her cheeks were flushed, and her eyes took on even more beauty as they filled with a sheen of clear liquid. Swallowing through the tightness in his own throat, he answered hoarsely, "So am I, Kate. So am I."

It was a new beginning, a time to put aside old hurts and resentments and, as their eyes met and held, both Michael and Kate silently admitted it was also the beginning of something deeper, something so frightening, so foreign, that neither one was ready to acknowledge it.

Not knowing how to handle the situation, Kate asked, "If the treasure's in your home, how do we get in? Do you think Kevin will help us?"

Michael had to blink several times in order to stop staring at her. His heart was beating at an unnatural rate, his limbs felt heavy with a desire that was completely out of place. His mind seemed to explode with a fierce surge of possessiveness, and he wanted to know who had hurt her, who had caused the pain he had seen in her eyes that afternoon. He also wanted to protect her from ever experiencing it again. Trying to control the rush of emotions that he was feeling, Michael picked up his cup and sipped the warm coffee. "My house?" he asked, fervently hoping she'd repeat her question.

Kate nodded. "Do you think Kevin will help us get in? Where do you think Martin has the treasure?"

He couldn't believe how beautiful her eyes were. "Ah, probably hidden in his bedroom. I don't think he'd trust the wall safe, since Kevin knows the combination."

Her eyes lit with excitement. "When do we start?"

"Start what? What are you talking about?" Michael couldn't understand why he had ever thought the freckles across the bridge of her nose were merely exotic. They were also endearing.

"Michael! Pay attention!" Kate demanded. "When do we break into your house?"

Chapter 15

He couldn't have possibly understood her. "Break into my house?"

Kate gave him a patient look. "Well, of course, Michael. You don't think Martin's going to let us in through the front door, do you?" Giggling at the thought, she shrugged her shoulders. "Anyway, it wouldn't really be breaking and entering. It's your house, too."

"I'm not going to burglarize my own home! Have you given any thought to what might happen if we're caught?" Michael could well imagine Martin using his influence and having them carted off to jail.

Dejected by his attitude, she sat back in her chair. "Geez, Michael, you're supposed to be dead. They'd probably think they were seeing a ghost."

Suddenly her head snapped up; her eyes sparkled with excitement. Pushing the dishes to one side, she knelt on her chair and leaned across the table. With her face a mere foot away from his, she looked him straight in the eyes and said, "What if the old coot really did see

225

ghosts? What if Denny spreads the rumor about the legend to old Marty?"

Taken aback, Michael could only stare at her. Recovering, he laughed uproariously. "Kate . . ." He shook his head and held up his hand to stop her.

Kate took his hand and placed it back on the table. "Now, wait a minute," she insisted, liking the idea more with each second. "Poor dead Michael shows up in his uncle's bedroom with . . . with Doña Marina! Think about it! He's taken away your family's business, ruined your father, and wanted to ruin you. And he's taken my treasure. This is not a nice man. But somewhere, somewhere deep in his subconscious, he knows he's wrong. You and I could bring that right to the surface by appearing in his bedroom and demanding our treasure back. We'd scare the hell out of him."

Although he continued to laugh, Michael kept shaking his head during her impassioned speech. When she finished, he chuckled once more and said, "It would never work. He has no conscience. And what would we do when he refuses to give the treasure to ghosts? Disappear?"

Kate sat back in her chair. "Well, I haven't thought it all out yet. But I will! Maybe we could make a few appearances, really haunt him, and then . . ."

"I have other plans for my uncle," Michael interrupted.

She crossed her arms over her chest in disappointment. She'd really liked the ghost idea. "What?"

"I plan to harass him, to throw him off guard. Martin likes a structured life, everything in its place, nothing taking him by surprise . . ."

"That's why my plan would work! Can't you just

picture him if we . . ."

"Kate, *will* you let me finish?" Despite her interruptions, Michael smiled. "I plan to rob him."

Kate's lower jaw dropped. "Rob him?" She immediately grinned, and delight shined in her eyes. "How? How are we going to do it?"

Michael let out his breath in a rush of exasperation. Running his fingers through his hair, he said sternly, "Not we . . . *me!* I don't want you to have anything to do with this."

Her pleasure in Michael's plan turned to disappointment. "I thought we were partners. I thought we had agreed to get the treasure back together."

"We are partners," he said softly. "But not in crime." Again, he slowly shook his head. "Kate, have you no fear? If not for yourself, then for what could happen to you if you're caught? My uncle is a powerful man with the authorities in Charleston. Doesn't it bother you to contemplate something illegal?"

"Does it bother you?" she countered.

"Not where my uncle is concerned. Besides, there are extenuating circumstances. Ever since the war ended, he's set out to destroy me."

Her chin lifted in determination. "Well, from everything I've heard, I don't like him, either. I'm going with you."

"No, you're not," he insisted.

She cocked her head to one side and narrowed her eyes. "How are you going to stop me? Tie me up? I don't care what you say or do, I'm going with you."

"Kate, think! You could get hurt!" Where was her fear? Never had he met a woman so bold, who took such chances with her life. Ever since he had met her on

227

that reef, Kathleen Anne Walker had proved herself to be a worthy adversary. First, with her incredible scuba equipment that she'd used to trick him and bring up the treasure, then on the island, when she had affirmed her determination and mettle by building a primitive fire and testing his resourcefulness at every turn. And now, here at Haphazard, she had again beat him—this time at the male pastime of cards. Having Kate around was a blow to one's ego, for she was self-reliant, head-strong, and fearless. Surely she was part of that new movement of suffragettes that had started up North. It was frightening to think that today's woman was so . . . so modern. What was a man to do with one, when he'd been brought up believing that a gentleman should be protective? How the hell do you protect a woman that has proved herself a match for any man? Confused by the obstinance of the beautiful woman across from him, he cleared his throat and tried again. "Even if you have no fear of injury, you could be put in jail. Think about that."

Having watched the concern and confusion in his eyes, her expression softened. "Michael, listen to me . . . I have nothing to lose. If you left me here, I'd probably die from worry anyway. You said we're partners. I'm willing to take the risk. And besides, I refuse to let you go alone."

He saw the stubborn tilt of her chin, the determination in her eyes, and sighed in defeat—knowing the only way she'd stay behind was if he really did tie her to the chair she was sitting in. All he could do was try to protect her—even if all she wanted was a partnership over the treasure. It surprised him to realize he wanted something more.

"All right," he said finally. "But if you go, I'm in charge. You listen to everything I say and obey without any argument. Do you understand?"

Kate's grin widened. She wanted to lean across the table and kiss the concern from his mouth. Instead, bringing her hand up to her forehead, she executed a smart salute. "Aye, aye, Captain Sheridan. When do we start?"

"We start," he said firmly, "tomorrow."

"Tomorrow? What about Kevin? Didn't he say to stay put until he comes back?"

Michael got up from the table and brought his plate to the sink. "I can't sit around here and wait while others fight my battles." He turned around and faced her. "Every Friday night, Martin has dinner at the Braddock Hotel. From there he goes to Dunnemores. I told you, he's a creature of habit. He leaves precisely at eight-fifteen for the hotel. Anywhere from an hour to an hour and a half later, he'll leave the hotel and take his carriage to Dunnemores."

"What's Dunnemores?" Kate asked, while clearing the table.

Michael coughed. "It's . . . actually, it's a very re spectable gaming house, where a gentleman might also find . . . That is, one might find . . ."

Standing next to him, Kate looked up at his face and read the hesitation she could also hear in his voice. "Might find companionship?" she offered mischievously.

He cleared his throat. "Well, yes. But it's very respectable. It . . ."

Kate laughed. "I'll just bet it's respectable," she teased, while pumping water into a pot. "Every Friday night, huh? Why that old devil! When are we going to rob him?"

Taking the filled pot to the stove, he lit a fire underneath it. Not caring for the teasing quality in her voice, he straightened and wiped his hands on a towel. "Listen, Kate, Dunnemores is owned by a good friend of mine. He really does run a respectable place. Whatever 'companionship' that takes place is done away from the gaming rooms, and it's also very discreet. I don't want you to get the wrong idea."

She pursed her lips to stop from laughing. "Oh, I think I have a very good idea what kind of place Dunnemores is. It sounds as if you know it *intimately*."

"I told you, the owner is a friend of mine. That's why we'll stop Martin before he gets there. I don't want anyone saying it isn't safe to leave Dunnemores."

She tied the long, thin towel around her waist and started stacking the dishes to be washed. Without thinking, she handed another towel to Michael and asked, "Okay, now exactly how are we going to do it?"

Laying on the couch, with only the light from the fireplace to illuminate the room, Kate looked over at the bed. She should try to sleep, she thought as she closed her eyes. Tomorrow was going to be a long day, beginning with a seven-mile walk to Charleston. Hearing a long, drawn-out sigh coming from the bed, she opened her eyes and stared across the dimly lit room.

"Michael?" She said his name in a whisper, in case he actually was asleep.

"Hmm?" His voice sounded tired.

"Did you come here often when you were young? I mean with your family?"

It took him a full half minute before he answered. "Kevin and I spent most of our summers here. Haphazard was a boy's paradise. We learned how to fish, how to hunt and ride out here."

"Who taught you?" she whispered, for some reason intensely interested in his childhood.

"My father," he answered in a quiet voice. "And Wiley. We would stay here with Wiley—he's practically a member of the family—and my father would come on weekends."

"Sounds great," she commented. "Your own cabin in the woods."

"It was."

Kate turned on her side. Even though she couldn't see his face, she could make out his shadowed form. "What about your mother?" she asked gently. "Did she come, too?"

Immediately the pleasant mental picture from his childhood vanished and Michael brought his arm up to cover his eyes. Breathing deeply, he said slowly, "No. She never came. She preferred to stay in Charleston."

Please, Kate, he silently begged, no more. In a solemn voice, he whispered, "Go to sleep now. We have a long day ahead of us."

He barely heard her soft "good night" as he tried to banish the picture of his mother from his mind. What had he ever done, he wondered for the thousandth time, to make her soft beauty turn cold and polite whenever he walked into a room? Why did he always feel so lacking, so inadequate, when she looked at him? Pressing his fingers to the bridge of his nose, he tightly shut his eyes. He couldn't allow himself to think about it now. He must only concentrate on Martin . . . and on tomorrow.

He couldn't resist them, for they drew him like a moth to a flame. Completely fascinated, Martin Masterson picked up one of the large uncut stones and held it up to the lamp. Grinning, as the light enhanced the color of the amethyst, he brought it back to join the others laying on his bed.

It was a fortune, and it was his! Who would have thought the Barnett brat would have been carrying a king's ransom? Surely Winston didn't send it, and it mattered little if he did. As far as Barnett knew, his little Helene and her "dowry" were at the bottom of the Atlantic. Too bad about the shares, though, he thought as he gathered the stones and placed them inside the huge, hollowed gold ingot. They would have provided just the right . . .

"Martin. May I speak with you?"

At the sound of his sister's voice coming from the other side of the door, Masterson quickly picked up the jewels and placed them behind a pillow just as Lydia entered the room.

"Honestly!" he exclaimed in an irritated voice. "I would think a man might be allowed some privacy!"

With a grace that had been inherited from generations of carefully bred women, Lydia Sheridan closed the door behind her and walked up to her brother's bed. Brushing an imaginary speck from the cuff of her black watered-silk gown, she smiled carefully.

"For the last five days you've spent every evening in

this room. One can only wonder what you find so alluring. I trust you're well?"

Not wanting to attract attention to the bed, Martin slowly stood up and walked to the window. "Such concern, Lydia, is touching. Rest easy, I've never felt better."

"How assuring," she said in a low voice, "that you're in such robust health. I'm afraid that when Winston gets here it will be put to the test."

Martin spun around and faced her. "You've had word? Nothing was sent to me!"

Coming to the window, she raised her fingers to the heavy drapery and pushed it to one side. Idly looking out to the rain-washed deserted street, she slowly let out her breath. "Winston Barnett will be coming to Charleston," she stated with a certainty. "My son kidnapped his daughter and she died while in his care. Barnett will come, Martin, to extract justice. One way or another."

"God damned Michael! If he were alive, I'd kill him myself! All those years of planning for this marriage!"

Lydia slowly let the drape return to its proper position and turned around. "Keep your voice down," she said sternly. "Only a handful of people know what he did. Michael was a hero during the war . . . and you forget I'm a grieving mother."

Martin sneered. "Yes, you're such a tragic figure. First your husband, and now your son."

Suddenly Lydia's face came alive with anger. "Be careful, Martin. For a man of such intelligence, you have a foolish mouth." Breathing deeply, she regained control of her emotions and sat down on a handsomely cushioned chair. She ran her fingers across the material in appreciation and glanced up at her brother. "I had forgotten how attractive this room is," she stated. "Joseph would always drop his clothes onto this chair, and Wiley . . ."

Martin snorted in disgust. "Please, the night is no longer young," he interrupted. "Why don't we reminisce about your husband another time?"

Lydia's face hardened. "Then why don't we talk about how you're going to deal with Barnett? And how we're going to protect Kevin?"

"Protect Kevin? Why would Barnett harm Kevin? My letter explained Kevin had nothing to do with what happened."

Lydia sat up straighter and lifted her chin. "I will not jeopardize my son. In the last week, he seems to be acting like his old self."

Martin smiled evilly. "Since Michael's death, you mean. Perhaps, they weren't as close as everyone thought? In which case, he truly is your son, Lydia. A consummate actor."

She stared at the man whose blood ran through her veins and felt a shudder of distaste. "Just remember, I'll do anything to protect him and his reputation. Anything . . . Kevin's welfare comes first."

Martin looked bored by the conversation. "Hasn't it always been that way, Lydia? Hasn't it always been Kevin?"

Kate kept pace with Michael, as they followed a dirt road toward Charleston. "I don't understand how you intend to stop him? Don't you think your own uncle would recognize you?"

Pushing her behind a large tree, he looked beyond it and whispered, "Will you stop chattering?"

Startled by his actions, she searched Michael's face for some clue to explain his behavior. Following his line of vision, Kate slowly turned her head to see beyond the treeline. It was a farm of some kind.

"Last time I came through here, the place was deserted. C'mon," Michael said in an undertone, while taking her arm and bringing her back to the road. "Let's see who our neighbors are."

She couldn't help a shiver of aversion as they made their way closer to the farm. A run-down shack served as a house and the barn was patched in so many places, it was hard to tell exactly where the few chickens were coming from. "People live here?" she asked, while carefully watching where she placed her feet.

Michael didn't answer her as he stopped in front of the house. Just as he was about to place his foot on the first step, the wooden door slowly creaked open. First a rifle appeared, and Michael quickly pushed Kate behind him. She held on to the back of his shirt, yet her curiosity was too strong to remain hidden. Peeking around Michael's shoulder, she saw a heavyset black man eyeing both her and Michael with suspicion.

"You got business here, mister?" he asked Michael.

She felt Michael take a deep breath. "That could be," he answered noncommittally. "Keep any horses on the place?"

The farmer straightened his shoulders and lowered the barrel of his rifle to be in direct line with Michael's chest. "Only horses 'round here's for the fields. You best keep on going, mister."

Kate tugged at the back of Michael's shirt. Couldn't

he take a hint?

Ignoring her silent communication, Michael leaned his elbow on the splintered wooden railing. Although he looked casual, Kate could feel the tension in his body. "Be careful with that rifle," he said in a calm voice. "We don't mean you or your family any harm. I was just curious to see who had taken on the place after so many years."

"You from around here?" the man asked, the tip of the rifle lowering a fraction.

Michael nodded. "My family has a cabin up the road . . ."

"Haphazard?"

Surprised, Michael again nodded.

"You a Sheridan?" The man's eyes looked intensely into Michael's. "The young one?"

Instantly he was alert. "Do I know you?" Michael asked.

The black man lowered the rifle and smiled. "You owe me two bits, Mickey Sheridan. I've waited some long years to tell you that."

Feeling safe, Kate left Michael's back and looked at him. He was staring at the black man, a look of confusion on his face.

"You dared me to let old man Clemen's pigs out the week after you done it. You'd already gone back to Charles'ton and never knowed I got caught. Couldn't sit down for three days after that whuppin' my . . ."

"*B.D.?*" Michael looked at the robust man and laughed. "I can't believe it! My God, that must be fifteen, twenty years ago!" He came up onto the porch and shook his head as he smiled at his childhood friend. "How long have you been out here? Wiley never said

236

a word."

B.D. Reynolds's grin was so infectious, that Kate found herself smiling. "Been sharecroppin' near a year. Me 'n' my family plans on makin' a new beginnin' out here." His eyes suddenly became serious. "Sure did give a scare, Mickey. Thought them Night Riders was back visitin' in the daylight."

"Night Riders?" Kate found herself asking.

Both men looked down at her as if just remembering that she was standing there. Holding out his hand, Michael brought her up the three steps, once more noticing the way Tommy's pants clung to her long legs. "Kate, I'd like you to meet the best fisherman I know— B.D. Reynolds."

Instinctively, Kate extended her hand. She saw the worried expression on the black man's face as he looked first at her, then at Michael. Confused and embarrassed, she slowly lowered her hand to her side. "I'm happy to meet you, B.D." She said his name with a hint of a question.

Wanting to make up for the awkward moment, Michael said quickly, "Bartholomew . . . ?" He looked at B.D.

"Dominick." The large man promptly supplied the name. "Was Mickey here and his brother Kevin who stuck me with B.D. Said it was easier than the other way." He looked at Michael and grinned. "It sorta never came unstuck."

Michael laughed and looked across the yard to the dense woods. "We sure had some good times out here, didn't we? I wonder why Wiley never told me you were back?"

Not hearing a reply, he turned to his friend and saw

237

B.D. was no longer smiling.

"Mickey, when's the last time you seen Wiley?"

Thinking of his father's old servant, Michael answered honestly, "I don't think I've seen your uncle in eight or nine months. I haven't been . . ." He didn't want to explain his banishment from his own home. "Why? Is something wrong?"

B.D. shrugged his shoulders. "Wiley says there's trouble in the big house, since your daddy died." Shaking his head, he said sincerely, "Sorry to hear 'bout that, Mickey. Your daddy was a fine man."

Nodding, Michael came closer. "Tell me what Wiley said. It looks like I'm going to need your help, B.D., but I promise you won't be putting you or your family in trouble."

Pushing open the old wooden door, the larger man jerked his head toward the inside. "First, Mickey Sheridan, you'll have to pay up them two bits. You was a hell raiser as a young'un, and I got a feelin' in my belly you ain't no different now."

Taking Kate's hand, Michael led her to the front door. Just before he entered the house, he looked into B.D.'s eyes and whispered, "You and I, my friend, might be able to do business totaling far more than two bits."

Bartholomew Dominick Reynolds shook his head and laughed. "I knew it! Somehow's I knew you'd never lose that streak of trouble. What'cha got yourself into now?"

"I don't believe we're doing this!"

238

"Keep quiet!" Michael gritted out through clenched teeth as he brushed a tree branch away from his eyes. "You insisted that you come, remember?"

She couldn't clearly see his face, for even the moonlight didn't penetrate through the thick woods where they were hidden. Tying the reins from one of the old horses they had borrowed from B.D. to a branch, Kate brought out the cloth from the saddlebag. "But this?" she insisted. "I never agreed to this!"

"Just be quiet and put it on."

Seeing Michael don his own costume, Kate shivered in revulsion. "I don't think I can, Michael," she whispered. "Do you have any idea what this thing stands for? How disgusting it is?"

She could hear the anger in his voice. "Of course I know! Who better to blame for the robbery than the Night Riders? Damn it, Kate. We discussed this back at B.D.'s when you and Leah were sewing the damn things!" She saw him pull the white piece over his head. "Either put it on now, or stay hidden. I don't have time to argue."

Kate backed into her horse. "God, Michael, even in the dark, you look frightening. And you sound so . . . so threatening!"

"That's the purpose," he whispered in a frustrated voice.

Stepping away from the horse, she brushed back her hair from her face and asked, "Can you imagine how people felt seeing this? How horrified they must have been?"

"Kate," her name was said with a strained patience, "we can discuss the human condition another time.

Martin's going to be coming down this road any minute. If you're not going to put it on, at least be quiet!"

Kate knew it was the perfect disguise. Unless they were shot, no one would ever know who they were. She knew it, yet her fingers were shaking as she brought the sheet over her head and tied it with the thin rope at her waist. Something deep inside her felt outraged, even betrayed, that she would wear the guise. Looking at the white figure at her side, she held the headpiece to her face. He doesn't know, she told herself, how hated this is, how revolted decent human beings are by what this represents. Slipping the white material over her face, she adjusted the holes for her eyes and breathed deeply. Michael's right, she told herself again. Don't think about anything, except that the Night Riders are the perfect group to blame for the robbery. Their actions tonight will throw everyone into chaos. Whoever these Night Riders are, they'll be confused and angry. And those others who hear of it will be furious that the Klan is now making trouble for a wealthy white man.

"Are you okay?" Michael's whisper was gentle, and Kate nodded.

He handed her a rifle. "Remember, don't try and shoot it. Just aim it at Martin. I'll take care of the rest."

"Why do I get the gun that doesn't work?" she asked in a worried voice.

"I told you. B.D. only had the one. Yours is for show. Just intimidate him with it . . . and keep your mouth shut. I don't want him to hear your voice."

The white sheeting disguised Kate's astonished expression. "What about your voice? He's your uncle. He's never even heard of me, let alone . . ."

"Shh!" Michael tightly grabbed her shoulder to silence any further discussion. "I think this is it. Mount up!"

Sitting atop the old horse, Kate thought she might scream as she listened to the sound of horse and carriage. They were coming closer . . . so close! Just as she imagined them driving right up to her, Michael spurred his horse and shot out of the woods, yelling in a deep voice, "Hold it right there!"

Her brain had ceased to function; her limbs were suddenly paralyzed as she clutched the old worn pommel . . . she was frozen with fear!

Chapter 16

Masterson's heart beat furiously inside his chest as he eyed the robed figure. Attempting to loosen the man's hold on his horse, he jerked on the reins.

"Now see here!" he exclaimed in an angry voice when it was obvious the bandit was stronger. "Let loose that horse immediately!"

A slow chill ran up his back and settled at his neck as he heard the hooded figure speak.

"Hand over your money, old man."

"I will not!" he stated boldly, despite his growing fear.

Still holding the reins, Michael brought his gun in line with Martin's chest. "You'll hand over your money . . . or you'll die," he said in a slow, husky voice. Damn! Where was Kate?

Thinking of what was inside his jacket pocket, Masterson nearly shouted, "This is outrageous! Decent citizens robbed at gunpoint!"

His own anger matching his uncle's, Michael almost growled, "Shut up and do as I said. Your money or your life . . . make your decision."

Behind the white sheet, Michael's jaw clenched in anger. It was hard enough to be so close to Martin without listening to him talk of decency—a virtue he knew nothing about. Something inside of him wanted his uncle to refuse, to give him a reason to end the nightmare now.

Realizing he couldn't talk his way out of it, Masterson slowly reached into his jacket. He mentally cursed himself for bringing such a large amount of money. It was because of the jewels—knowing they were worth a fortune, he'd felt safe in taking more than the normal amount of cash. Although he might have been rash in that decision, he wasn't a fool. Instead of his money clip, Masterson's hand revealed a small revolver.

With an evil grin, he pointed it at the Night Rider and whispered, "Now what? Get the hell out of here before I put a third hole in that goddamned sheet!"

Gloating over his good fortune to have brought the pistol, he was unprepared for the pressure of cold metal behind his right ear. His heart actually stopped beating for a few seconds as he listened to the accomplice's voice coming from behind his head.

"Go ahead, mister. Make my day . . ."

Martin stared at the terrifying figure in front of him, not daring to turn around.

"Throw it to the ground," the first man ordered.

His mind working furiously, Masterson didn't make a move to follow that command, and from behind him he heard the deadly click of a hammer being pulled back. Quickly, he threw the gun out toward the woods.

"Now," the first figure stated calmly, "I will repeat

this for the last time. Hand over your money."

Without the slightest hesitation, Martin reached into his jacket and withdrew his money clip from the inside pocket. Holding it out to the man in front of him, he stuttered, "That's it . . . that's . . . that's all I have."

Taking the money, Michael looked at his uncle and said, "Get down."

"You have my money! What more do you want?"

"I want you to get out of that carriage. *Now!*"

Masterson felt a nudge at his ear. He scrambled out of the carriage and watched in horror as the first man came closer to him. Using his horse, the thief slowly pushed him back toward the thick woods. "You said if I gave you the money, you wouldn't kill me!"

So great was his fear that he barely noticed the other figure dismount, pick up his small pistol from the ground, and throw it deeper into the woods. Frightened, Masterson kept backing up—away from the horse and closer to the woods. The second figure, a smaller man, came up to the first and Martin watched as his money was exchanged. It was all he saw before the horse was again breathing in his face. He could smell the nervousness of the animal . . . and he could smell his own fear as his back hit the hard trunk of a pine tree.

"You don't die today, old man. Not on the road to Dorchester . . ."

Before Martin could react, the second man rode up to the carriage and hit the horse's rump, while yelling for it to take off. In dismay, Masterson watched as his horse and carriage did exactly that.

Stranded, Martin Masterson glared as the two hooded white figures quickly disappeared into the night. Shaking his fist in their direction, he attempted to overcome his fear. Enraged, he shouted, "I'll see both of you bastards hang! Do you hear me, you cowardly sons of bitches! Do you hear me? *Hang!*"

"Lordy Bejesus!"

Even though B.D. had prepared himself for it, the sight of the two white-robed riders galloping in his direction was enough to take him into the afterlife. Holding on to a pine tree branch, he stayed hidden at the entrance to Haphazard, and it was only when he recognized his own horse that he slowly left his hiding place.

Grabbing the reins as the taller rider pulled up the horse and slid off its back, he nodded as Michael ripped the hood off his head. "I take it by that smile, Mista Masterson came through for ya," he said in a nervous voice.

His grin widening, Michael helped Kate dismount and whispered, "We didn't leave Mister Masterson any choice in the matter. Did we, Katie?"

Both men watched as Kate pulled the hood away from her face. Even in the moonlight, her smile was brilliant. "Judging from the weight of what's inside my blouse, I would say Mr. Masterson is considerably poorer."

Instinctively, Michael placed an arm around Kate's shoulder and ran a hand over the lathered rump of the old horse. "They served us well, B.D. Take good care of them and we'll settle up tomorrow." He winked at his nervous friend. "We have to replace your sheets, remember?"

Shaking his head, B.D. found no humor in Michael's remark. He was still doubting the wisdom of helping to rob a white man, even an evil one. Leading his worn horses, B.D. started walking down the road. He looked back at the couple only once. "I knew you was goin' to be trouble," he whispered in a worried voice. "I jus' hope it don't find the rest of us any too soon."

Squeezing Kate's shoulder, Michael led her up the crushed oyster shell drive. As if by silent agreement, neither spoke as they rushed through the darkened woods—each filled with a sense of urgency. They were almost running by the time they reached the house.

Flinging the door open, Michael let Kate enter first, then followed her. He closed it, bolting the lock for the first time since they'd come to Haphazard. The cottage remained dark until Michael lit an oil lamp and brought it closer to Kate. Seeing her standing before the fireplace, her dark hair contrasting with the whiteness of her costume and her flushed cheeks, Michael had to fight the urge to take her into his arms.

"We did it, Kate," he pronounced, excitement showing in his eyes. "Now, let's see what we've got."

"First build a fire," she whispered in a tiny voice.

"A fire?" Michael started to protest until he suddenly realized the cottage was cool. In a magnanimous mood, he hurried to do her bidding.

As Kate watched the small flames grow larger, she seemed hypnotized by them. When they had grown to such an extent that she could feel the heat, she gathered the material at her hips and pulled the offensive garment off her body. Rolling the white muslin into a ball, she tossed it on top of the flames. She watched the

246

edge of the material darken to a spreading brown, until the flames licked at the sheet and began to consume it.

Satisfied, she was about to turn to Michael when another sheet joined hers. Smiling, she looked to her side. Whatever she was about to say caught in her throat as she gazed into his eyes. He looked so incredibly handsome in the firelight. His golden hair was brushed back off his face, his eyes revealing understanding, then excitement, and something else that made Kate grow warm. She knew it had nothing to do with the heat coming from the fire.

Confused, she returned his smile and said, "C'mon, let's see how much of a gambler Martin really is."

Nodding in agreement, Michael picked up the lamp and followed her to the bed.

He watched as she unbuttoned her shirt and pulled it out from her pants. His eyes lingered only momentarily on her chemise before lowering to the stack of bills that tumbled onto the mattress.

Picking up a handful, Kate held them up for him to see. "Michael, look!" she directed in an awe filled voice. "We're stinking rich!"

His lower jaw dropped in astonishment. Never did he think Martin would be carrying this much! Sitting down on the bed, he slowly picked up a fistful of money. "He must be crazy. He could have been . . ."

When he didn't finish his sentence, Kate giggled and supplied the last word. "What? Robbed?"

Their eyes met and, suddenly, all the tension, all the excitement, all the danger was abruptly released. Simultaneously, they both burst into laughter.

"I should count it," Michael managed to get out breathlessly.

Kate nodded while collapsing back onto the bed. "You do that, Michael," she giggled. "God! I wish I could have seen his face!"

Gathering the bills together, he shook his head. Still laughing, he said, "Kate, it almost made up for everything to have witnessed Martin's expression when you put that rifle to his head."

In a deep voice he mimicked her, *"Go ahead ... make my day.* It scared the hell out of me ... and I knew the rifle was broken!"

She covered her face with her hands and burst into fresh laughter. "It was the only thing I could think to say! I almost died when he pulled out that gun."

Suddenly, she sobered and raised herself up on her elbow. Seeing the happy look on his face, Kate whispered contritely, "I'm so sorry I froze on you. But you just burst out of those woods. You didn't even say you were going."

His hands became still, forgetting the growing stack of money. "Kate," he whispered her name like a soft caress, "you were wonderful. You might have just saved my life ... again."

Embarrassed, she handed him the strangely larger-shaped bills and asked, "So tell me, Mr. Sheridan, how much money is there?"

She waited patiently while Michael returned his attention to the money. Within less than a minute, he slowly raised his head and stared at her. "I don't believe it," he said finally. "There's twenty-seven hundred dollars here!"

Kate's mouth dropped open in amazement. "Twenty-seven hundred?" she repeated.

As Michael nodded, her grin spread even wider. "No

wonder he put up such a fight! Old Martin took a gamble and lost before he ever got to Dunnemores."

"I can't believe he was carrying this much," Michael said, while staring at the money. "It isn't like him, at all. He's usually too stingy to risk losing more than a couple hundred."

She sat up straighter. "I think it's a strong indication that he has the treasure. If this is unlike him, then something must have happened to have changed his behavior. Wouldn't discovering a fortune in jewels make you feel confident? Don't you see? It didn't matter to him if he lost it gambling. He has the treasure, Michael. I'm sure of it."

Slowly he acknowledged her reasoning. "I think you're right. For Martin, twenty-seven hundred dollars is a lot of money to risk."

Kate kicked off her shoes and crossed her legs, Indian-style, in front of her. Widening her eyes, she giggled. "And now it's all ours!"

Looking at her, Michael forgot his uncle and chuckled. "That's right, it is, isn't it? You seem very pleased with yourself, Kathleen Anne."

She lifted her chin and grinned. "I can't help it. I guess I'm just a happy thief."

Handing her the money, Michael rose from the bed. As he walked into the kitchen, he said, "We're not thieves, Kate. That money was never Martin's to begin with. It belongs to my family."

Liking the way Michael absolved them of any guilt, Kate propped a pillow behind her head and stretched out her legs. Fanning the thick stack of bills in her hand, she waved them in front of her. "Do you know what's the first thing I'm going to buy with this money?" she said into the darkened kitchen. Not waiting for a reply, she continued, "A change of clothes! When can we go into Charleston?"

Michael came out of the kitchen area carrying a tray. As he came closer, Kate could see it held a bottle of liquor and two glasses. She stopped fanning herself as she watched him place it on a small table by the bed.

Pouring the amber liquor into a glass, he smiled as he handed it to her. "Kentucky bourbon. I found it yesterday. I was hoping we'd have something to celebrate tonight."

Accepting the small glass, she continued to stare at him as he poured his own. She watched the play of his arm muscles as he returned the bottle to the tray and noticed he had unbuttoned his shirt while in the kitchen. There was a subtle difference even in the air that surrounded them. The exhilaration of the robbery was exchanged for an excitement that was quietly taking place between them. Kate could feel it, as if it were a tangible thing.

He sat on the edge of the bed, close to her hip, and raised his glass. "To us, Kate," he whispered, a seductive smile appearing on his lips. "We're quite a team."

She found her hand was shaking as she raised her glass in the toast. Sipping the strong bourbon, her eyes held his. What was he doing, she wondered. It wasn't like Michael to be seductive . . . she had always been the one to entice him. He was obviously making it clear they just changed roles.

Overwhelmed by the naked desire she could read in his eyes, she clumsily handed him the money. "You . . .

250

you'd better put this away somewhere," she stammered, and held out the bills to him. His hand wrapped around hers and brought it to his chest. Feeling the heat from his body warm her fingers, Kate couldn't control a gasp, for the heat turned into a delicious fire that quickly ran up her arm and curled around her heart.

She felt dizzy as she sensed, rather than saw, him take away the money and remove her glass. Kate felt helpless to stop him, and frantically questioned whether she should.

Michael's heart was expanding with a strange emotion. Kate, his Katie, so bold and shocking one minute, so shy and frightened in the next was now afraid of him, or something he represented to her. Unhurried, he brought his fingers up to her face and ever so gently ran them across the bridge of her nose, lightly caressing each tiny freckle. His fingers wrapped themselves around her neck and, slowly, he brought her face closer to his. Leaning his head toward hers, Michael stopped inches from her lips. Still holding her vision, he whispered into her mouth, "Whatever it is that frightens you, Kate, let it go . . . You know I won't hurt you."

Feeling his lips brush hers in a tender kiss, Kate moaned with a mixture of pleasure and fear. As the pressure on her mouth deepened, she fought the battle within herself. Part of her wanted to give in to him, to partake of the beauty she knew would come, yet a stronger, more primitive section of her brain was telling her to disregard her feelings and protect her heart.

251

He instinctively knew she was fighting him, for he had already experienced the thrill of Kate's kisses, and she was responding like a virgin. Frustrated by his need to reach her, he muttered hoarsely, "Trust me, Kate. You can trust me . . . I won't hurt you."

If he had said anything else, she might have relented and melted into his arms. It was his entreaty to trust him that made Kate pull back. Her eyes filling with tears of pain, she cried, *I can't!* Don't you understand that? I can't trust you!"

She scrambled off the bed and started for the kitchen—anywhere to get away from the hurt look in Michael's eyes.

Letting her go, he stared at the pillow for a moment before asking over his shoulder, "Who was it, Kate? What did someone do to you to make you so afraid?"

She stopped walking when he spoke. Hugging herself, she slowly turned around and fought the burning in her throat, the threat of tears that seemed impossible to hold back. She watched Michael's slumped shoulders rise and fall with each deep breath as he waited for her answer. What could she tell him? That it was all right, as long as she was in control of their relationship? That she was terrified for another to gain control over her heart? That she didn't think she would survive loving another man? She owed him something, for Michael had come a long way himself since she'd met him. He was changed—open and caring—probably for the first time in his life. Finally, she decided she owed him the truth . . . at least a part of it.

"I was . . . I was married," she said in a tiny, halting

voice. "A long time ago."

Michael spun around and faced her. The tears she'd been holding back fell freely as she took in his shocked expression. *"Married?"*

She nodded, and he quickly stood up. "You're a widow?" he asked slowly, feeling as if someone had kicked him in the gut. She loved her dead husband.

Tightening her arms, Kate wiped her eyes on her shoulder. "No. No, I'm not a widow. I'm . . . I'm divorced."

"You're . . . divorced?" He said the words with even more shock than before. "Don't you think you could have managed to tell me this earlier than now?"

For some strange reason, she felt as if her former marriage was a betrayal of Michael—which was ridiculous. Hoping to make him understand, she took a step toward him and said, "It was too painful to remember, and I was trying to forget. It was a long time ago, Michael . . ."

"Who was he? How long ago?"

She closed her eyes as his questions shot across the room. She'd tell him. He was right—she had led him on, without telling all of her past. She could let go of part of it, but not all. Never all . . .

Opening her eyes, she straightened her shoulders and gathered her strength. "His name is Jonathon Ashford, and I left him over five years ago."

Michael's jaw hardened at the sound of the man's name. An unreasonable jealousy took hold of him. "And why did you leave him?" he demanded, irrationally wanting the man to have been a monster, so he could wipe away any memory of him.

253

Kate swallowed several times. She should have expected the question, yet it was the most painful of all. She wouldn't lie, but she refused to voice out loud what had been buried for so long. Her mouth quivered as she drew in a deep breath. "I left him because he was . . . he was . . . unfaithful."

An immense relief washed over him as he stared at her, silently taking in what she had told him. It explained everything. What amazed him was that Kate, proud Kate, had overcome that humiliation. Never had he met a woman with more of a joy for life . . . until now. He felt very protective, very possessive, and wanted to return the joy to her.

"Come here," he softly commanded. When she didn't move, he held out his hand. "Kate?"

He whispered her name as a soft plea, and she was unable to refuse. Slowly her hand reached for his. When their fingers touched, Michael quickly tightened his hold and drew her into his arms. Clasping her firmly to his chest, he buried his face in her hair and soothed her. "I won't hurt you, Kate. Don't be afraid. I promise to give you time. I promise."

Feeling her slowly wrap her arms around his waist, Michael tightly shut his eyes. It was all new to him, and frightening. It was also crazy, and he knew it. Their whole relationship was backwards. They'd made love, without really knowing each other. He wanted more. For the first time in his adult life, he wanted more.

Waiting until her sobs became occasional whimpers, Michael squeezed her before leaning back so he could see her face. Wiping away the moisture at her cheeks, he looked into her incredible blue eyes and smiled.

"Have you ever been courted proper, Miss Kathleen?" he asked while taking her hand.

Starting to hiccup, Kate couldn't help the giggle that escaped her lips. She shook her head. "I don't know," she admitted, "what you'd consider a proper courtship."

He stood away from her and assumed his full height. With his shoulders straight, he brushed back his hair and slowly bent over her hand. She gasped at the astonishing tenderness of his lips as they brushed her fingers. Lifting just his head, he smiled into her face and winked.

"You're about to find out, Miss Kathleen . . . and there hasn't been a woman born yet who can resist a Southern courtship."

Miles away, Lydia Sheridan stood in the drawing room of her palatial home and calmly listened to her brother's ravings.

"I tell you, it was those damn Night Riders! If I get my hands on them, I'll wring their bloody necks. To hell with a hangin'!" As Martin Masterson paced the thick carpeting, Lydia poured him a brandy.

Handing over the thin crystal glass, she was startled when Martin shouted, "Wiley! How the hell long does it take for one lazy buck to get the sheriff here?"

Lydia looked at the old servant hovering by the doorway. Nodding in his direction, she said in a quiet voice, "Never you mind, Wiley. Just wait on the porch for Primus and the sheriff."

Standing next to Kevin, she patted her son's hand as

255

he brought his arm around her shoulder. She could always depend on Kevin to remain calm.

"Uncle Martin, you never said how much they took."

Masterson looked away from his nephew and sister. Polishing off the brandy, he mumbled, "Twenty-seven hundred."

Kevin felt his mother stiffen. "I beg your pardon, Martin?" she said in a low, angry voice. "I don't believe I could have heard correctly."

"You heard right, Lydia," he said defensively. "Twenty-seven hundred dollars. Taken! By some white trash rabble!"

Lydia Sheridan breathed deeply, attempting to control the rage that was threatening to explode. She glared at her brother's dirt-covered face, his mud-splattered clothing.

"Why ever would you have been carrying that kind of money on you? Surely you couldn't have been planning on gambling it all."

She remained calm, even though her fingers itched to slap her brother's cheek when he slyly looked away. He couldn't meet her gaze.

"I . . . I felt lucky tonight," Martin offered weakly as he reached for the decanter of brandy.

Watching him, Lydia quickly made up her mind that something would soon have to be done about dear Martin. For the last two weeks, since Michael's death, he'd been acting strangely. Now, it appeared, he was also a liar. In that same amount of time, Kevin had grown stronger. Perhaps, fortune was finally going to shine on her. Again, patting her son's hand, she stepped away from his embrace.

"You felt lucky tonight, Martin?" she asked quietly.

4 FREE BOOKS

GET
FOUR
FREE
BOOKS
(AN $18.00 VALUE)

ZEBRA HOME SUBSCRIPTION
SERVICE, INC.
P.O. Box 5214
120 BRIGHTON ROAD
CLIFTON, NEW JERSEY 07015-5214

When he didn't answer, she smiled in a sympathetic manner. "You best be more careful. It looks like Lady Luck has abandoned you . . . not embraced you."

Kevin couldn't understand why his uncle looked so frightened. Yet before Martin could respond to his sister's strange statement, all heads turned as Wiley led the sheriff into the room.

Chapter 17

"The blush of your lovely lips reminds me of the center of a magnolia, so pink, so fragile . . ."

Rolling her eyes to the branches overhead, Kate laughed out loud. *"Please!* The center of a magnolia?"

Michael couldn't help joining in her laughter as he walked next to her. Carrying their picnic lunch, he looked down at Kate and remarked, "Well, you asked how a man would compliment a woman. He would compare her to something beautiful, preferably something in nature, so she would believe her beauty had come to her naturally."

"It sounds contrived, Michael," she pointed out as they followed a path lined with wildflowers. "What about a woman's other attributes? What about her strengths, her resourcefulness? Doesn't that count?"

"Kate." He said her name with a strained patience. "It hardly sounds romantic to tell a woman that you admire the way she can start a fire from nothing, or that the way she handles her underwater breathing apparatus boggles the mind."

Again, she giggled. "It's nice to know I boggle your mind, Michael. You don't want to try for another discussion about me coming from the future, do you? Now that would really boggle your mind."

He groaned aloud. "That is the very *last* thing I wish to discuss today." Reaching the small stream, he placed the basket on the ground and shook out a blanket to cover the grass and pebbles that lined the water. "I promised you a courtship," he pronounced with a smile. "Why don't you stop analyzing it, Kate, and just enjoy it."

It was on the tip of her tongue to say that she'd never been courted before, at least not like this. How could she explain that in her time most men had lost this art, this patience with courtship. Would he believe her explanation that silly phrases and gallantry were shunned by the modern male, and that three dates seemed sufficient time before something more intimate was required? Dropping to her knees, she settled herself on the blanket and decided to take his advice. Why not just enjoy this lapse into the past, when the only requirement was that she let a man please her.

Concluding that she was in an enviable position, she smiled up at Michael and asked, "Is this where you and Kevin went fishing? It's really beautiful."

Nodding, Michael sat down and placed the basket between them. He looked out to the moving water and smiled, as if recalling memories. "We also went swimming here. It isn't deep until you go farther upstream."

Inhaling the smell of the woods, Kate slowly let out her breath and leaned back on her elbows. "You were right, the other night, when you said this was an ideal place to grow up. I envy you."

He was mesmerized by the picture she presented. Reclining on the blanket, her long, dark hair was thrown back over her shoulders, revealing the column of her throat. His mouth ached to kiss her soft skin. The white blouse was stretched across her breasts, outlining their fullness, and his hands itched with a longing to touch them. Turning his concentration to the picnic basket, Michael brought out their food. He realized, as he placed a filled plate by her side, that Kate had turned everything around without even trying. It was as if she were unconsciously courting him, for the responses taking place inside his body were exactly those he had wished to instill in her.

Recognizing that he would have to work harder, he cleared his throat and said, "Have you ever been told, Miss Kathleen, that you have a keen mind, a disposition that soothes a man's soul, and a smile that would drive a strong man to weakness?"

Bringing the thick ham sandwich to her mouth, Kate stopped in midair and stared at him. Suddenly, laughter bubbled at her lips and she chuckled while gazing at him with fondness. "Now *that,* Mr. Sheridan, has to be the height of courtship exaggeration . . . a disposition that soothes a man's soul?"

He liked her laughter. "I can see you're going to make this difficult, if you continue to question each of my compliments. The proper response is, 'Thank you, Michael.'"

Breaking off a piece of bread, she popped it into her mouth and grinned back at him. "Thank you, Michael," she responded. "And may I say that I, too, am impressed with the keenness of your mind, the evenness of your disposition, and allurement of your smile . . ."

He shook his head and chuckled. "You really understand nothing of this, do you? *I'm* the one who gives the compliments. You're supposed to accept them and look properly embarrassed—not laugh at them and throw them back at me."

"But you're laughing!" she protested. "And you have to admit you've already accused me of not being of sound mind, told me I was argumentative, and stated that I can't take anything seriously . . ."

"That was *before* I was courting you," he interrupted with exasperation. "Now it's different."

"Oh." Even though she enjoyed teasing him, she sensed he was becoming impatient. Trying to look "properly embarrassed," she shyly murmured, "I'm new at this. Thank you for your compliment, Michael."

He stared into her eyes and found only sincerity. Nodding, he opened a jar and poured her a glass of cooled, sweetened tea. "Perhaps later you might like to explore the stream," he offered. "As long as we don't wander too far from this spot, we should be able to wade quite comfortably."

Swallowing, Kate nodded. "That sounds wonderful," she admitted. "We'll make it an adventure . . . like when you and Kevin were children."

An hour later, Kate had reason to regret her words. Michael had insisted that he unhook her shoes, drawing them off her feet with an agonizing slowness. And it was anything but childish thoughts that raced through her mind as she hiked up her skirts and waded out to meet him in the stream. As the cool water brushed her ankles, her breath caught at the back of her

261

throat when she looked at Michael. His shirt-sleeves were rolled up, along with the cuffs of his pants. For the first time since they had come to Haphazard, he looked truly relaxed.

"Watch your footing," he gently advised. "Some of these rocks can be slippery."

No sooner had his warning been issued when Kate's heel slid off an algae-covered rock and Michael grabbed for her arm. He caught her up against his chest, holding her there while she lifted her face to his.

Kate was only aware of the buzzing sound of the insects, the rushing of water at her feet, the fact that Michael's lips were so very close to her own . . . and that her hands longed to inch their way up his chest and encircle his neck. She could feel his heart beating behind her palms, sending a tremor through her own body.

Staring back at her, Michael took a deep breath. It was a supreme act of willpower not to lower his head and kiss her waiting lips. But that was not part of his plan—not yet. He wanted to build a trust between them, for both of them had been hurt, both of them abused. They each needed confidence, dependence, and faith that the other would not mistreat what was growing between them. No. It was better to take it slowly and build a firmer foundation.

He gently set her from him. "You must be careful, Kate," he warned in a low voice.

Feeling somehow deprived, she could only nod, for her mind was also issuing a warning to be careful. The thought was unexpected, truly unbelievable. She was standing in the middle of a stream and suddenly afraid that she might be falling in love.

262

She watched him through dinner, waiting for him to make a comment about her leftover beef casserole that she had burned in the damn oven. He said it was delicious. She watched his face when she suggested that she needed money to buy clothing when Kevin returned. He smiled and announced that she was entitled to a fair distribution of the money they had taken the night before. At every turn she tested him, almost hoping that his politeness would give way to annoyance . . . anything that she could wrap around her heart and protect it from him. But he was persistent in breaking away her barriers. By the time he tucked her into bed and whispered a soft good night before placing a chaste kiss on her forehead, she thought she would go out of her mind. What was he doing to her? What the hell was he doing? It was a question she asked herself at least a dozen times as she fought for sleep. Tossing and turning, Kate stared at his shadowed form asleep on the couch. She knew, without a doubt, it was going to be a very long night.

The banging was loud and insistent. Kate bolted upright in bed just in time to see Michael buttoning his pants and hurrying to the door. Positive there was a lynching party outside, Kate's heart quickened as she unconsciously brought the blanket up to cover her neck.

"Who is it?" Michael demanded through the door, his voice low and menacing.

"Kevin! Now, will you open up?"

Michael glanced at Kate and relief washed over both of them.

Unlocking the door, Michael quickly threw it open to admit his brother. "Kevin, what the hell are you doing here? You said the end of the week!"

Rushing into the room, Kevin noticed Kate still abed and lowered his eyes. "I apologize, Kathleen, but I have news that couldn't wait."

Michael's eyes narrowed as he brushed the hair back off his forehead. "What is it? What couldn't wait?"

"Martin was robbed the night before last. On his way to Dunnemores."

Kate had to bite the inside of her cheek. "Really?"

"I would have come yesterday, but I was afraid of attracting attention." Walking farther into the room, he removed his riding gloves and nodded. "He came home in such a state . . . let me tell you. Said they were Night Riders. Can you imagine? And what's worse, for some reason he had twenty-seven hundred dollars on him!"

Noticing the sly looks that were exchanged between his brother and Kathleen, Kevin felt a shiver run up his spine—a sensation that had nothing to do with the morning's chill.

His eyes darted from one to the other. "You didn't . . . !" He shook his head, as if dismissing the ridiculous thought, then saw the confirmation in Michael's eyes. "You two . . . No, tell me I'm wrong . . ." he sputtered.

Grabbing his shirt from last night, Michael slid his arms into it. Leaving it unbuttoned, he placed a firm arm around Kevin's shoulders. "Come," he said to his startled brother. "Let's give Kate some privacy to dress. You and I can put on a pot of coffee and discuss this. It really isn't as terrible as it sounds—once you think

264

about it."

Kate frowned as she watched the two men enter the kitchen. What if Kevin didn't agree with their plan to harass Martin, she thought as she scrambled out of bed. What if he turned them in? Gathering her clothes, she shook her head. No, he wouldn't do that. He would never turn in his brother. But what about her? She wasn't family. Rushing to the couch, she hid any sign that would indicate where Michael had spent the night. Let Kevin continue to assume that they were married, she decided. He might be more sympathetic. As Kate stood in front of the fireplace, she looked into the cold ashes of last night and felt a twinge of guilt. Not for the robbery—Martin had deserved that—but for using Michael to ensure her own safety.

Taking off Michael's oversized shirt that she had again slept in, Kate remembered his kindness of yesterday. He had been solicitous, courteous, making every effort to put her at ease. He had been acting like a . . . a gentleman, she realized and smiled with affection. As she grabbed her worn underwear, Kate couldn't help shrugging her shoulders— And she had spent the better half of last night fighting the urge to join Michael on the couch. Compared to his gentlemanly attitude, her fantasies were positively wanton! Hearing the masculine voices coming from the kitchen, she scolded herself for her foolishness and quickly started to dress—eager to find out Kevin's plans.

Ten minutes later, both men stood as Kate entered the kitchen. Shyly acknowledging Kevin, she sat down in the chair Michael was holding out for her. An awkward moment of silence ensued as Michael left them to pour Kate a cup of coffee, and she found herself clutching her hands in front of her until he returned.

Seated next to her, Michael casually slid an arm around the top of her chair and smiled. "Kevin thinks we've acted irresponsibly," he said while pushing the sugar bowl across the table to her. "I told him you wanted to wait for him to return and discuss it, but I had insisted."

Touched by his statement, which was meant to protect her from any further incrimination, Kate returned his smile before looking at Kevin. "Michael and I are partners in this. I accept equal blame for what happened the night before last—and I'd do it again if I had to."

"*Why?*" Kevin was shocked. Despite her appearance and the circumstances surrounding her relationship to Michael, Kathleen had seemed a lady. "I know Michael hates our uncle, but to involve you in a robbery is unforgivable! Do you realize the sheriff has been called into this? Martin wants to go to the Major General's Office and report it. You know how they're looking into this Night Rider thing that's spreading from Tennessee. He wants to call in the Federal Government!"

"He would," Michael interrupted, his mouth showing his distaste.

Kate was suddenly confused. "What are you talking about?"

Michael's annoyance was obvious. "The commander of our military district," he explained. "Unlike the North, Kate, we continue to be punished and our State Governments have been abolished. The Confederacy has been divided into five military districts until we

266

meet all the requirements to be readmitted into the Union."

Watching Kate digest the information, Michael couldn't help wondering why such an intelligent woman wouldn't be knowledgeable about current events. Where had she been, not to have known what was happening to her country?

Michael's brother impatiently ran his fingers through his dark brown hair. "I still cannot believe the two of you held up Martin! One of you should have had the sense to stop the other." Kevin's handsome face was red with anger, his blue eyes shouting accusations at both Kate and Michael.

Kate held the cup of coffee in her hands, enjoying the warmth as it spread through her fingers. "Kevin, how much did Michael tell you about the treasure?"

"Just that it was supposed to be in the trunk Martin removed from the *Rebel.*"

Kate looked at Michael for confirmation, and he nodded. "He didn't describe it?"

She saw Kevin shake his head. "Not really—just that there was supposed to be some jewels he had discovered . . ."

"*We* had discovered," Michael quickly interjected.

Kate couldn't suppress the smile. He was learning . . . Forcing her attention back to Michael's brother, she leaned closer to him. "Not just 'some' jewels, Kevin. A fortune in jewels. Emeralds, amethysts, diamonds, a large gold cross studded with emeralds—a hunk of gold the size of a small bowl. Uncut jewels the size of a child's fist. It's worth a fortune . . . and Martin's got it."

Kevin leaned back in his chair, his lower jaw slack as

he stared at both Kate and Michael. At his silent plea for affirmation, Kevin abruptly closed his mouth and pushed back his hair as Michael nodded.

"It's . . . it's true?" he managed to verbalize. "There really is such a treasure? And Martin has it?"

This time both Kate and Michael nodded in unison. "As Kate pointed out," Michael said, "the fact that Martin was carrying such a large sum of money shows that he wasn't all that concerned about losing it. You know that description doesn't fit Martin. Obviously, he has the treasure to fall back on."

Kevin was silent as he tried to take in everything. Slowly, he raised his head and asked, "Where do you think he has it?"

Feeling they had just gained an ally, Kate and Michael quickly smiled at each other. Turning back to his brother, Michael said, "It's in the house. I'm sure of it."

"Where? I'll check the wall safe tonight, but I can't imagine . . ."

"Forget it," Michael interrupted. "Because you could check the safe is exactly why Martin would have chosen a different spot. My bet is it's in his room. Is he still using Father's bedroom?"

Kevin nodded, then shook his head. "I don't know how I'll be able to get in there. It's always locked when he's away, and the only other person with a key is Mother. How could I explain why I wanted to get into the room?"

Michael smiled. "You don't have to . . . I'll get in there."

Kevin was clearly shocked at the suggestion, yet

before he could respond, Kate's equal surprise turned into delight as she giggled and added, "And so will I!"

Without giving Kevin a chance to recover, Michael hurried to explain. "Kevin, I want you and Denny to start spreading a rumor along the wharf that I had discovered Old Tom's treasure. Make sure everyone, especially Martin, hears about its legend."

"What legend?" Kevin demanded, clearly trying to regain some sort of order to the conversation. How had he ever let himself get dragged into this? He barely had time to wonder as Michael again started to speak.

"Doña Marina was Cortez's translator and mistress. She gave him a son, yet Cortez left them and returned to Spain. The legend says that when Doña Marina was old and her heart longed for the explorer, she sent him a tribute. The ship carrying it was lost in a hurricane and it's said the treasure will bring the finders their heart's desire." He stopped and grinned at Kate. "Tell Martin that whoever takes the treasure from its rightful owners will be plagued by back luck. That should explain what's going to happen to him. Right, Kate?"

She was staring at him. This man, this changed man was Michael. When he had smiled at her after saying the treasure would bring your heart's desire, she had the strangest feeling Michael was thinking of her, not revenge as he had said earlier. Realizing he was waiting for an answer, she nodded and murmured, "Right, Michael. That should explain it."

Although confused by what his brother and Kate were saying, Kevin hadn't missed the silent exchange between them. Whatever their problems were on the island, it seemed that they had resolved them. Seeing the tenderness that passed from one to the other, he felt suddenly alone—as if the two of them, for an instant, had shut him out. He felt a twinge of envy for his younger brother. Incredible as it might be, Michael, it appeared, was in love.

The envy passed quickly and was replaced by happiness. There wasn't a man alive who deserved love more than Michael, Kevin readily admitted. He wasn't blind to his mother's favoritism and, even though he had tried to make her realize it, Lydia Sheridan had continued to treat her younger son as if he was never quite worthy to receive her love. Kevin had shared Michael's pain, had understood his wild escapades were only cries for attention—even negative attention—and had tried to make him understand. Their father had grasped the problem and had gone out of his way to make up for Michael's lack of motherly love. But it never quite compensated for the long-standing hurt that Michael had carried around with him since childhood.

Seeing the warmth in Kate's eyes as she shyly looked away from his brother, Kevin grinned. Maybe now, Michael could let it go. He had a feeling Kate's love was going to make up for all those lonely years. He prayed she was strong enough to break through Michael's barriers and give to his brother what had always been denied him.

Very pleased by the change in Michael, Kevin smiled at the couple and said, "Would anyone care to inform *me* what's going to happen to Martin?"

Kate giggled and pushed her hair back over her shoulders. Leaning into the table, she widened her eyes and whispered, "We're going to haunt him!"

Kevin only blinked, too stunned to respond.

Parts of Charleston reminded Kate of footage she had seen of Europe during World War Two. Although Michael had said the city was quickly rebuilding, she could only imagine what it was like during the Civil War. Keeping the brim of his hat low over his eyes, he steered her toward the shops and told her how the Federal Government had rained artillery on the city for a year and a half, and had blockaded its ports until Charleston's economy was in ruins. Listening to his impassioned voice, she had the distinct feeling Michael wanted her to understand what had happened during the war.

Before reaching the shops, they passed homes that made Kate stop and stare. They were mansions, most three stories high, with columned Greek Revival facades. Balconies were everywhere—many of them fine wrought iron. She noticed in each home that there was a great attention for detail. It could be seen in the many cornices and gable ends, chimneys, roof tiles, and gateposts. Never had she seen such magnificent homes and several times Michael had to pull her away from a particularly exquisite one.

Walking on the cobblestone street, he led her around black hucksters, who were musically crying out the quality of their wares. Smiling, Kate breathed deeply of the endless breath of fragrance coming from the many gardens. It was an intoxication that seemed to mingle with the smell of the river, marshes, and the sea mist.

Charleston was a place with sights, sounds, tastes, and aromas all its own. As they made their way toward the business section, Michael pointed out each tree and flowered bush that they passed: crepe myrtle, mimosa, chinaberry, and the fragrant tea olive. She was fascinated by the gentility, the seductiveness of the city.

"Get whatever you want, Kate," he said when they'd stopped in front of a shop advertising women's fashions. "I'm going to see about buying another horse and renting a carriage. That old mare of B.D.'s isn't going to make too many more trips into the city."

"You're going to leave me?" she asked, panic starting to rise as she viewed the window display.

Michael pulled at the rim of his hat as he glanced up and down the street. "You'll be all right," he assured her. "Besides, I'm going to meet Denny and Kevin and make sure everything is in motion for tonight. Go on, Kate," he said, while squeezing her hand. "It's time you had your own clothes." He smiled. "Buy something pretty. You deserve it."

Letting go of his hand, she self-consciously smoothed the front of her worn blouse and looked to Michael for reassurance. Seeing him nod, she took a deep breath and placed her hand on the door handle.

"Kate?"

She looked back at him.

"Don't forget the feathers," he reminded her.

Briefly closing her eyes, she whispered, "Right . . . the feathers," just before entering the old-fashioned shop.

Kate felt transported. It wasn't like meeting Helene, and taking her word that it was 1868, nor like listening to Michael as he talked about the war. She'd been

272

isolated until now. This shop was another time, another place, and she had brief flashes of modern department stores, small funky boutiques where rock music blared as you browsed through racks of clothing. There were no racks here—just bolts of fabric, rows of pattern books, and a few headless mannequins. She was lost, unsure of how to proceed.

"May I help you, madam?"

Kate turned away from a mannequin and looked into the pleasant face of a middle-aged woman. Trying to appear friendly, Kate smiled and said, "I certainly hope so. I need clothes."

The saleswoman looked at Kate's skirt and blouse and nodded in agreement. "Don't we all, dear? Forgive me, but there are less expensive shops. If you like, I can . . ."

Now that she was inside the place, Kate cringed at the thought of going elsewhere. "I have money," she quickly interrupted, and pulled out a stack of bills from her skirt pocket.

Mamie Legare's eyes widened as she mentally estimated the small fortune. It had been too many years since she'd seen that kind of money. Before the war, she hadn't been able to keep up with the orders from Charleston's aristocracy. Now, after years of watching her customers disappear, she was finally starting to build up her business once more. Wanting to settle something in her mind, she narrowed her eyes and looked at the young, nervous woman.

"You're from the North?" she asked, a trace of disdain in her voice.

Remembering Kevin's lecture on the ride into Charleston about the resentment she would meet if her

273

northern accent was questioned, Kate squared her shoulders and said truthfully, "Originally yes. But it's been ages since I've been to New Jersey."

Ignoring the fact that the young woman's attire said otherwise, Mamie Legare was satisfied that she wasn't really dealing with one of those obnoxious "carpet-bagger" people. She seemed to be a nice young lady. Her active imagination, so needed in her line of business, went to work inventing a background for the pretty girl. Probably lost her clothes on the rail-road . . . Could have happened to anybody. Once more eyeing the money in the young woman's hand, she was convinced that the poor thing had been through some disaster. Hadn't they all been through the fires of hell in the past eight years?

Reaching for her measuring tape, Mamie said, "Now you just put that money away, dear. We're going to outfit you from head to toe."

Before Kate could protest, the stocky woman encircled her tape around Kate's chest. Standing face to face with the saleswoman, Kate smiled weakly. "I don't think you understand. I . . . I just need something to wear for right now. Maybe later . . ."

Marking down the bust measurement, Mamie quickly brought her tape to Kate's waist. "I might have something in the back you could take with you today, but don't upset yourself, anything else will be ready by the end of the week."

"But . . ."

"It's been ages, dear, since I've had carte blanche," Mamie said with a dreamy look in her eyes. "I can hardly wait to show you the newest patterns."

Kate looked at the woman's hopeful expression and

didn't have the heart to disappoint her. Attempting to smile, Kate nodded in defeat as her arm was measured from shoulder to wrist.

Glancing at the elegant lines of the young lady's face, Mamie introduced herself. "I'm Mamie Legare, and I can't tell you how pleased I am that you chose my shop."

Knowing it was her turn, Kate swallowed before saying, "How do you do? My name is Kathleen . . ." She hesitated and glanced at the pattern books displayed on a nearby table, searching for a last name among the gilt lettering. "Bonaparte," she said quickly, and inwardly cringed when she realized how stupid that must sound.

Mamie held her tape in front of her as she studied Kate. It was the eyes, she thought, as her excitement grew. Feeling she was in the presence of a celebrity, Mamie almost gushed, "Why, that's right, isn't it? Napoleon's brother, Joseph, wasn't it? Why, he did live up there in New Jersey. I remember hearin' how he'd this palace on the Delaware River and filled it with his brother's treasures . . ."

Kate's eyes widened. "Really?" Recovering quickly, she added, "I'm . . . I'm just surprised you heard about all that." And wondered why she'd never heard it.

Gathering her tape and draping it around her neck, Mamie leaned closer and said under her breath, "Before the war, Charleston regularly entertained royalty. We'll do it again, I'm sure. While there's breath, there's hope." Brightening, she placed a hand on Kate's elbow and steered her toward the bolts of expensive fabrics. "Why, look, it's startin' already. And right here in my own shop! You're goin' to need several

275

ball gowns, once everyone hears you've come visitin'."

Pulling out a long length of midnight-blue satin, Mamie held it up in front of Kate. "He was the king of Spain, wasn't he?" she asked, greedy for any gossip.

Startled, Kate said, "I beg your pardon?"

"Joseph. He was too old to be your daddy. I recollect him dyin' around '44. Isn't that right?"

Realizing how disastrous her lie was becoming, Kate tried to smile. "That's right," she murmured, not knowing if it actually was. Seeing no way out, she muttered, "He was my uncle . . . on my father's side."

"Why, you must be Jerome's daughter! Funny, I only heard of a son. But then, what do I know of royalty?"

Kate thought Mamie knew a great deal, certainly far more than herself. Hoping to be extricated from this insane mess, she replied, "We've always tried to keep a low profile . . . our side of the family."

Mamie Legare looked as if she had just received the Ten Commandments from God. "I knew it!" she stated with authority. "Napoleon's niece! It's in the eyes, and color of your hair. All them Corsicans have it."

Startled, Kate clutched at her dark hair while wondering how the woman would know such a thing. *Napoleon's niece!* Dear God, why had she ever said that last name? Walker was a good name, an American name . . . It was Michael's and Kevin's fault. On the ride into Charleston, they'd filled her with all that talk about hostility toward northerners and how she shouldn't let anyone know her last name, considering they were planning something illegal.

"This is your color, my dear," Mamie said in an excited voice, almost bursting with her wonderful piece of gossip. Her business would soar when she let it out that Napoleon's own niece was her customer. "It draws attention to your unusual eyes."

Feeling like Alice after she had fallen down into Wonderland, Kate looked at the smiling woman, the luxurious fabric, and quietly, almost meekly, asked, "Do you have feathers? I need feathers."

Considering the craziness of the conversation, it hardly seemed an unreasonable request.

Chapter 18

He was waiting for her. Standing beside a handsome carriage, Michael grinned as she left Mamie Legare's shop. Immediately, he rushed up to meet Kate and removed the packages from her arms.

"I see you were successful," he commented while taking in her dove-gray outfit.

Jerking on the short jacket that ended at her waist, Kate whispered, "Let's get out of here! You won't believe what happened."

He watched her nervously pull at the heavy, intricate lace that made up her collar and quickly put the wrapped packages in the back of the carriage. "C'mon," he said, supporting her as she stepped up to the seat, "I can hardly wait to hear what you've gotten yourself into this time."

Kate clamped her mouth closed as she watched Michael walk around the horse and climb up next to her. Surreptitiously, she glanced back at the shop while trying to control the volumes of slips and material that seemed unmanageable. A tiny whimper escaped her

278

throat as she saw Mamie standing at the window with a huge grin plastered across her mouth.

Sitting up straighter, Kate tried to smile and brought her hand up in a farewell wave. She could almost hear Mamie's mind grinding with fresh news for the gossip mill. As Michael pulled away from the shop, she leaned closer to him and said, "It wasn't my fault!"

Slowing for another vehicle, he pulled his hat brim down even lower and said, "What wasn't your fault? Kate, what happened now?"

"Mamie, the owner of the shop. She thinks I'm Napoleon Bonaparte's niece."

"What?"

She had to grab the edge of the seat as Michael abruptly drew back on the reins. "I told you . . . it wasn't my fault. You said, 'Don't use your own last name.' . . . I didn't."

From the corner of her eye she could see Michael shaking his head as he urged the horse on. "I said don't use your last name. I *never* said to use the emperor of France's last name! The whole purpose was not to draw attention to yourself."

"Well, I didn't do it on purpose, Michael. She wanted to know my name, and there it was . . . on the binding of a pattern book! It was out of my mouth before I knew it."

Miserably watching the crowded street, Kate suddenly felt the movement of Michael's shoulders. Glancing to her side, she was shocked to discover him silently laughing. Realizing he was found out, he chuckled openly and, nervously, Kate joined in.

"Napoleon's niece!" he exclaimed between bursts of laughter. "Tell me, who's your father?"

"Jerome," Kate giggled. "That's what Mamie said—"

"Jerome!"

Kate nodded, very pleased that Michael was taking it so well. Obviously, he thought it was funny, and she really was swept along by Mamie. "The woman said Joseph was too old to be my daddy, so it must be Jerome. I swear I've never met a person with such knowledge of royalty. How does she do it?"

Steering the carriage toward the waterfront, Michael chuckled while shaking his head. "Lineage is very important here. We love to look down on the British for their obsession with royalty and titles. Yet for all our independence, we're more impressed with them than the English themselves."

As he was talking, Kate looked out to the street and noticed several men lifting their hats in an old-fashioned gesture as their carriage passed. It took several more seconds to realize they were acknowledging her and showing their interest. She smiled, thinking that in her time men had forgotten this courtly gesture—they tended to avoid eye contact on the street and anything else that might invade their space.

She wasn't alone in noticing the men. As Michael pulled on his already lowered hat, his stomach tightened as he viewed the attention paid to Kate. Being with her almost constantly, perhaps he'd taken her beauty for granted. And yet now a surge of jealousy invaded his system, making him want to throw off his hat and glare at those who dared to stare. Frustrated, he could only lower his voice and say, "You look lovely, Kate. I forgot to tell you that."

She turned away from the street and smiled at Michael. "Thank you," she said shyly as she smoothed the pale-gray silk. "Some poor woman is going to be furious at Mamie for selling me this suit. I guess she thought Jerome's daughter needed it more."

Michael chuckled. "My bet is Mamie Legare couldn't wait until you left so she could spread the word that she now caters to royalty."

Kate gasped in surprise. "You're right! What are we going to do?" Without waiting for his answer, she said, "We'd better get back to Haphazard and stay hidden."

Shaking his head, Michael turned onto a street that bordered the ocean. "We're going to Denny's. No sense in traveling all the way to Haphazard when we'll just be coming back tonight."

Breathing in the tangy sea air, Kate showed her surprise. "Denny's? Why didn't you tell me before?"

He gave her a patient look. "I really didn't have the chance, did I?"

She tilted her head and inhaled deeply as she watched the waves roll in toward the wharf. "Where's the *Rebel?*" she asked, while viewing the anchored ships in the distance.

"Keeping an eye on your investment?"

Kate grinned. "You might say that," she replied in a soft voice.

He nodded toward the ships. "Denny said they're doing some minor repairs."

"Why don't we drive by and see?" Kate offered, knowing how much he must miss the ship.

Michael shook his head as he steered the carriage onto a side street. "I think that would be drawing a bit too much attention, don't you? Remember, I'm supposed to be dead."

Kate's shoulders slumped. "That's right. God, this is really getting confusing. No wonder Kevin's ready to tear his hair out. First you pose as Kevin, then you're Michael—and now you're dead."

"You say it like I really am," Michael noted sourly.

"And what about me? I tried to pass myself off as Helene Barnett, then I confess and I'm Kate. I'm supposed to have died with you and yet now I'm Kathleen Bonaparte—who's soon to transform into the resurrected Doña Marina. Poor Kevin! It sounds incredible to me . . . and I thought up half of it!"

Michael laughed as he stopped the carriage in front of a single home that bordered the street. He looked into her eyes and said softly, "You are incredible, Kate. I've never met anyone like you before."

She felt as if he'd kissed her. His voice was a seductive caress that sent velvety tendrils of excitement sweeping through her body. He was pulling her to him with his eyes and Kate was helpless to break the magnetic hold. She unconsciously bit her bottom lip then whispered, "And you never will again."

She saw his broad grin as he studied her mouth and knew she had just made an admission. It was useless to fight the attraction that existed between them. And in all honesty, she didn't want to any longer. She wanted to stay with him for as long as possible . . . Of course, she silently admitted, she intended to make sure that was also what Michael wished.

Pleased to have resolved the problem between them, Kate was the first to break the silence. "If this is Denny's home, I think we'd better go in, or any minute now we'll be drawing quite a bit of attention."

Looking around the street, Michael reluctantly nodded and climbed down from the carriage. He helped her out, letting his hand linger on her back. Kate's every nerve ending was sensitive to him, and she briefly closed her eyes to savor his touch. Tonight, she thought as Michael led her to the front door, was going to be very interesting . . . in more ways than one.

Flirtatiously smiling at her, he knocked on the wooden door. "According to legend, many of these houses were used by pirates when they were welcomed in the city. They're built of coral limestone blocks cut in Bermuda."

Kate looked over the two-storied white stone house with its deep-blue shutters. "I thought you didn't believe in legends," she remarked, the air charged with the electricity taking place between them.

Devouring her mouth with his eyes, he said softly, "Only some, Kate. Only some . . ."

He was talking about the legend of the treasure. She knew it! Was he telling her that the legend was fulfilled? That she was his heart's desire? Before she had a chance to question, the front door opened and she was startled to hear a woman's small scream.

"Michael!"

Kate was further amazed to see Michael enveloped into the arms of a short woman who closely resembled every picture she had seen of Santa Claus's wife. After much hugging and exclamations, the woman pulled back to see Michael's face and noticed Kate for the first time.

Kate's mouth hung open when the woman slapped Michael's rear and demanded, "Where are your manners? Come in this house and get that young lady out of the sun!"

Throwing Kate a sheepish look, he shrugged his shoulders and placed a gentle hand on her elbow. As he led her into the woman's cool home, Michael said, "Rose Pringle, I'd like to present Miss Kathleen Walker."

Kate smiled into the warmth of the older woman's eyes. She immediately liked her. Anyone who could get away with that kind of behavior with Michael had her admiration. "How do you do, Mrs. Pringle? Thank you for letting us spend some time with you."

"It's a real pleasure to meet you, child," she said warmly, a twinkle showing in her blue eyes. "My Denny's already told me about you. I don't mind sayin' I've been real anxious to see you in person."

Wondering what Denny might have said, Kate couldn't help grinning as the woman good-naturedly pushed Michael aside.

"Come on back," she said, taking Kate's wrist. "I'll fix some nice cool jasmine tea and we can talk." Over her shoulder she remarked, "I thought I saw packages in that carriage. You get out there and get 'em, Michael. You hear?"

Swept away with Rose, Kate barely managed to control her laughter. She certainly liked this woman's style.

Rose Pringle poured the tea while studying the young woman at her table. Kathleen Walker was as pretty as her brother had described: dark hair almost as black as the night, except when the sun brought out a hint of brown; a healthy complexion enhanced by an attractive sprinkling of tiny freckles, a mouth that showed easy laughter, and astonishing light blue eyes that reminded Rose of springtime. It was the girl's mouth, though, that she appreciated most, for it told a great deal. Here was a young woman who could be strong, yet knew the value of laughter.

"So what do you think of our city?" Rose asked while placing her mother's silver sugar bowl on the table.

Aware of Rose's scrutiny, Kate took a deep breath and smiled at the older woman. "It's very . . . charming. The gardens are beautiful," she quickly added, hoping she'd passed inspection.

Rose settled her weight onto a sturdy wooden chair and sighed. "Oh, you should have seen them before the war. Child, there's Magnolia Gardens—named for a magnificent row of magnolia trees stretching to the river. You get Michael to take you there. And, of course, there's Middleton Place. It used to be the oldest garden in the entire country."

"Used to be?" Kate asked as she watched Rose place three teaspoons of sugar into her tea.

Sliding the bowl in front of Kate, Rose frowned. "When them Federals swept through the area, they burned the plantation house. The Middletons can't keep up the place. From what I hear, it's startin' to show its neglect." Shaking off the memories from the war, Rose forced a smile. "But you should still see it— huge lakes shaped like butterflies, drifts of azaleas and camellias . . ."

"Why, Rose, I didn't know you'd been to the Middletons." Michael deposited Kate's packages onto the dining room table and walked into the kitchen.

Quickly standing up, Rose Pringle pouted like a

young disappointed girl and brought another glass to the table. "Watch your manners, Michael Sheridan. I was just describing what I'd heard, is all."

Sitting to Kate's right, Michael teased, "You mean that wasn't you I took out on that midnight stroll down to the butterfly lakes? You weren't the one who stared at the stars and swore your undyin' love—"

"You hush! Hear?" Rose swatted his shoulder while trying to control her laughter. Pouring his tea, she finally giggled. "You know Willis Pringle was the only man I counted any stars with, or declared my undyin' love. Now drink this and cool down." In a show of fondness, she playfully ruffled Michael's hair before walking back to her seat.

Kate watched in amazement as Michael left his hair falling onto his forehead. What truly startled her was the look on Michael's face as his eyes followed every movement of the older woman. His expression clearly showed love while his eyes seemed to hungrily devour Rose. With a flash of insight, Kate realized that here, in Rose Pringle's home, Michael had found the maternal affection that had been denied him in his own.

"It's on the Ashley River," Rose continued, as though there had never been an interruption.

Kate blinked a few times before she realized what Rose was talking about. "The Middleton Place?"

Nodding, she looked at Michael and ordered, "You take Kathleen. You hear? It's famous and everybody should see it once."

"What about you, Rose?" Michael asked. "When are you going to see it? Why not come with us?" He smiled at Kate, as if silently asking her approval.

Rose watched the interplay between the two young

people and her heart soared for Michael. How she loved him, for he was the son God had denied her and Willis. Deep in her heart she hated Lydia Sheridan for the way she had treated Michael, yet honesty made Rose admit that it if wasn't for Lydia's coldness, Michael might never have entered her life. And what an empty life it would have been without him. She'd treated his wounded pride, tended his scratches after he'd been in a fight. She'd listened to his complaints, endured his teasing, and had tried to curb his rebellious nature. In return, he'd lavished her with love. Not that he had ever said the words. But he'd shown her, in countless ways. Why, just last year, when Denny was in Savannah and she'd come down with the grippe, Michael hadn't left her side. That was the first time she'd ever thought about what would happen to Michael when she was gone. She'd given him all the love in her heart, but she also knew that wasn't enough. He was a grown man now and it was time for him to take a wife.

While sipping her tea, she glanced at Kathleen. Michael probably didn't even know that he'd found his mate. Never had she known him to ask for any woman's acceptance on anything. The dark-haired Kathleen had already tamed him, and Rose would give anything to learn how she'd done it. Seeing the knowing smiles that passed between them, Rose made up her mind to help them along the way to true matrimony. That ceremony Denny had said took place in Bermuda didn't amount to a hill of beans in her eyes. They needed a *real* wedding, like hers and Willis's. And if she was correct in suspecting what those smiles meant, she knew just how to do it.

Filled with a sense of purpose, Rose Pringle faced the young couple and asked, "Now, what is this craziness my Denny was tellin' me? You two plannin' on being' *ghosts* tonight?" She shook her head sadly. "I was prayin', Michael, that strain of lunacy on the Masterson side would pass you by."

A summer rain shower briefly washed the city, leaving the night crisp and clean and ladened with the intoxicating scent of blooming flowers. The streets were nearly empty as midnight approached, making the sound of the carriage all the more pronounced, as it slowly wound its way toward the more fashionable section of town. Although nervous himself, Denny couldn't help grinning as he listened to the low tones coming from inside the cab.

> "'There's something strange—
> In the neighborhood—
> Who you gonna call?
> Ghostbus—'"

"Kate! Will you stop singing that ridiculous song?"

Clutching Rose's heavy black cape around her shoulders, Kate huddled into a corner of the closed carriage. "It's not a ridiculous song," she insisted. "It's a great song . . . I happen to think it's quite appropriate for tonight."

Michael's face showed the tension he'd been under since Denny had driven up to Rose's home in the carriage. "It's getting on my nerves," he remarked without looking at her.

288

Kate blew the edge of a feather away from her cheek. "Why do you think I keep singing it?" she demanded in a whisper. "Don't you think I'm nervous, too?" She touched the many feathers that Rose had pinned in her hair to resemble a headdress. "And why do I have to wear all these things? In a good wind I might just take flight."

Michael glanced impatiently at her costume. "I told you—Doña Marina was a Mayan Indian. She would have worn feathers."

"Just because she was an Indian, you assume she wore enough feathers to choke a rooster? Talk about an ethnic slur!"

"Kate! *Will* you stop chattering? If you don't want to go through with it, just say so. Only please stop the singing and all this nonsense."

"Nonsense?" She rose higher in the seat. "What nonsense? Don't I have the right to be nervous? If singing calms me down, then I don't think you should call it nonsense." She arched one eyebrow. "You might want to try it. You look pretty tense yourself."

The look he gave her spoke volumes and he settled back in his seat without answering. Kate tried to do the same, but soon her mind returned to the one thought that had planted itself in her brain. What would they do if they got caught? She hadn't really entertained the possibility until Denny closed the wooden door behind her and Michael and steered the carriage away from the back of Rose's home. What the hell would they do?

Envisioning herself thrown into an antiquated jail and at the mercy of Martin Masterson, she unconsciously started humming, "Who you gonna call . . . ?"

"Kate!" The annoyance in Michael's voice was clear.

289

Jerking upright, she glared at him. "I can't help it! It's the only song I can think of right now. What are you doing?" she asked as he reached across her and turned down the oil lamp that hung on one wall of the carriage.

When the small cubicle was dark, he slowly lifted the curtain by her shoulder and peered out into the night. "Only a few more blocks," he quietly observed. Replacing the dark curtain he turned his head and stared at Kate. He could barely make out her face, yet every detail was already etched in his brain. Moving his lips closer to hers, he whispered into her mouth, "We're both nervous. Forget your song, and concentrate on this . . ."

His lips moved over hers in a gentle caress, taking away her tension and replacing it with a yearning for more. As if reading her mind, he deepened his kiss, gently pushing her head back against the cushioned seat. He wanted her to know just how much he needed her. He wanted his mouth to convey the desire that had intensified over the last few weeks. Feeling her respond as she arched her breasts into his chest and wound her arms around his neck, Michael knew her surrender was near. By not pushing, he was dissolving the barrier she had erected against him, for he felt more than a sexual urgency in her. He felt the beginnings of trust.

It was Michael who heard Denny's soft knock on the top of the carriage. Inhaling deeply, he nibbled at Kate's lower lip before pulling back from her. "We're there," he whispered, while pushing a feather away from her cheek.

Kate felt dizzy with the intensity of emotions that shot through her body. A white-hot coil of desire in her

290

belly snaked its way to her extremities, making them feel heavy. How she wanted him! In a few short weeks, Michael Sheridan had become an important part of her life. It went beyond affection, beyond sexuality, yet she was still afraid to place a label on it. She only wanted to concentrate on the moment, on this night—forevers never lasted.

"Are you all right, Kate?"

She sat up straighter and tried to replace a few feathers that Michael's kiss had loosened. Nodding, she said, "We're here? This is your home?" she asked, unsure of how to handle what had just happened.

He pushed the small curtain to one side and looked out. "Actually, we're beyond my home. Denny didn't want to stop in front of it."

Suddenly her heart started hammering against the wall of her chest, her palms felt moist, and her limbs trembled. What had sounded like fun when they discussed it at the cabin, now seemed like childish naïveté. What if Martin had a gun in his room? What if Michael's mother discovered them? What if Kevin wasn't waiting for them as he promised? What if . . . ?

"Kate, c'mon." He reached for her hand and felt her instinctively pull back. "What's wrong with you? We've got to get out and let Denny take the carriage away before it's spotted."

"Michael, listen to me," she urgently whispered. "This is crazy! You know it's crazy! We're going to get caught . . . I can feel it. Why don't we just go back to Rose's?"

She sensed his irritation. "Look, I'm going through with it. I don't care about this ghost thing. I didn't want you to do it in the first place, but I'm going into that

291

bedroom and look for the treasure . . . with you, or without."

He slipped out the door and she felt the shifting of the carriage as his weight was removed. It was all she needed to follow. "Wait!" she whispered, as she gathered up the cloak and started toward the door. "This was my idea in the first place!"

She stopped speaking as she saw a strong hand reach back inside the carriage. Grinning at the certainty of his action, she placed her fingers inside his open palm. He knew her too well.

"This is your home?" she demanded in a shocked whisper.

Michael nodded as he stopped at a black wrought-iron gate and ran his fingers over the nearby bricks, appearing to search for something.

Kate squinted in the darkness as she viewed his family's residence. It was magnificent. As large as any plantation house she had seen, it had been built sideways. The part facing the street was all wood and windows, with a high brick wall to ensure privacy.

"Ahh . . . here it is," Michael announced as he jiggled a brick loose and slid it out from the rest. Holding the formed mortar in one hand, he reached into the empty spot and brought out a key. "Thank God for the Sheridan men," he said prayer-like.

Before Kate had a chance to question his remark, he unlocked the iron gate and quietly opened it. Without waiting to be told, Kate followed right behind him, unconsciously holding on to the back of his shirt for protection. She glanced up at the huge white home and had to gulp back her admiration. Now that they were inside the gate, she was able to see that the front of the

292

house faced a lovely small garden. Even in the faint moonlight, she was able to make out the intricate, precise plantings. It was beautiful, yet strange. Coming from the North, it appeared foreign and exotic— This side area was maintained as perfectly as a wealthy northerner's manicured front lawn. Imagining its beauty in the daylight, she clung to the material at Michael's back as they left the secluded piazza and came closer to the house.

"Michael!"

Both she and Michael jumped at the sound of his whispered name. The first to recover, Michael took her wrist and led her in the direction of the voice. "Kevin!" He clasped his hand on his brother's shoulder and whispered, "Is everyone asleep?"

Nodding to Kate, Kevin looked at Michael. "Are you sure I can't talk you out of this? No one's used that passageway in thirty years."

Michael grinned. "We used to play in it, Kevin. How many times did I hide from Mother in it? She swore I'd left home."

Shaking his head, Kevin looked up at the house and said, "Nothing good's going to come from this, Michael. I just know it!"

Kate's heart skipped a beat as Kevin echoed her own misgivings. Yet she was in this now. She was Michael's partner and felt obliged to support him. Straightening her shoulders, Kate reached for Michael's hand and clasped it tightly within her own. "We're determined, Kevin," she said with more bravery than she felt.

Michael's brother let his breath out in a long, frustrated rush. "All right, then. Let's go."

Kate didn't even notice what the inside of the house

293

looked like as she was hustled into a room by both men. Once inside, Michael led them to a paneled wall. Stopping in front of the middle panel, he looked up at a portrait of a man. In the dark silence, both she and Kevin watched as Michael ran his hand along the edge of the carved wood. Within seconds, she heard a soft click coming from the wall. As if on a spring, the panel moved slightly. Turning his head to Kate, he lifted his eyebrows and grinned. "Paine and Eugenia Sheridan were not known for their marital bliss. We have my great-great grandfather to thank for this."

He pushed on the panel and it widened. Kevin entered first and struck a match against the wall. Using its flame to light a small lamp, he held it high as he waited for Kate and Michael to follow. The passage-way was narrow and dirty. It was nothing more than stairs, and Kate had no idea where they would lead. Holding the hem of her clothing off the stone steps, she followed Kevin. Michael was right behind her.

Fighting off a feeling of claustrophobia, Kate whispered, "Your great-great grandfather built this? Why?"

From behind her, Michael chuckled softly. "This is the Sheridan men's secret—passed down from father to son. When you become of a certain . . . ah, age, you're introduced to this passage into manhood."

"Shh!" Kevin made his disapproval known.

Ignoring his brother, Michael continued in an even lower voice. "Many a Sheridan male has used these steps to keep his comings and goings secret. I believe you're the first female to use them."

Kate stopped dead in her tracks and turned around to Michael. "Do you mean to tell me all the Sheridan

294

men cheat on their wives?"

"Will the two of you be quiet?"

Kate and Michael both glanced up at Kevin. Holding the lamp above his head, he appeared nervous and annoyed. Kate understood completely. She felt that way herself. Imagine generations of men sneaking out on their wives and mothers . . . and feeling justified. This had to be the height of chauvinism!

Giving Michael a look that said she'd continue the conversation later, she again turned to Kevin and nodded. Satisfied that the couple would remain silent, he continued up the stairs.

They exited in a small dressing room that smelled of cigars and bay rum. As Kevin held the lamp, Michael slowly pushed aside a row of suits and jackets. When all three were clear of the clothing, Michael motioned to Kevin and Kate that he would proceed alone into the master bedroom.

Kate held her breath as he inched the door open. Satisfied with what he saw beyond it, he smoothly entered the room.

With the agility of living for many years on board ship, Michael walked into his father's bedroom. Nothing had changed since his death, except now another man slept in his bed. Listening to Martin's even breathing, Michael drew closer. Immediately, a red haze of anger settled before his eyes. Martin Masterson wasn't good enough to shine his father's boots, let alone take possession of his home and business. And now he slept peacefully in Joseph Sheridan's bed. His indignation was increased as he remembered how Martin had nearly ruined him and almost destroyed Kevin by his manipulations.

Breathing deeply, Michael realized he'd forgotten about the shares. He'd been so close to obtaining them, but he'd been sidetracked by Kate . . . and by the treasure. Now the revenge he had desired so intensely came back as a flash of lightning briefly lit the room. He would not again be sidetracked from his original plan of revenge. Martin had caused enough heartache and misery for his family. It would be so easy to place a pillow over Masterson's face . . . to end right now . . .

As the distant rumbling of thunder followed the lightning, Martin stirred in his sleep, and Michael stepped back to his father's chair. Maybe not now, he thought, but soon— Soon he'd have his revenge.

He began searching the room, remembering every inch of carpeting, every placement of furniture. And, yet, nothing . . .

As another flash of silver-white light entered the room, Martin shifted in his bed to the accompanying thunder. Just as Michael was about to check his father's desk, he heard a familiar, hated voice.

"Who is it? Who's there?" Martin demanded in a thick, hoarse voice, as he leaned up on an elbow.

Michael froze. He knew that in the next flash of lightning, Martin would see him. Just as he was about to attack his uncle, the dressing-room door fully opened and an apparition in white floated into the room. She was beautiful, clothed in a flowing white dressing gown, her dark hair streaming over her shoulders, her face hidden by the light that Kevin must be holding behind her. He was as startled as Martin by the shadowy silhouette that showed a lovely woman with feathers arranged in her hair and holding a larger one in her hand.

296

She came a fraction closer to the bed.

"I want my treasure back," she whispered in a soft voice. "Give it back. It doesn't belong to you. Give it to me . . . before it is too late to save you . . ."

For a man of such advanced years, Martin Masterson showed the energy of a much younger man as he bolted off the bed and scrambled to the door. Dressed in a long nightshirt, he fought with the lock while whimpering in a frightened voice, "Go away . . . Do you hear? *Go away!*"

Finally working the lock free, he flung open the door and ran into the hall screaming, "Lydia! Kevin! Help me! It's that Aztec witch! She's comin' for me!"

Michael quickly closed the bedroom door and hustled into the dressing room where Kate and Kevin waited for him. Arranging the clothing back into place, he watched them enter the passageway and closed the panel behind them. Following the light in Kevin's hand as he led them back down the stairs, he excitedly whispered, "You both were wonderful! Absolutely wonderful!"

His two favorite people in the world joined voices as they scurried toward their escape. *"Shh!"*

Chapter 19

Lydia Sheridan clutched her robe tighter to her chest and glared at the frightened man standing in the doorway. Moving about her husband's bedroom, she tried to control her voice. "There's nothing here, Martin. It must have been a nightmare."

"It was no nightmare, I tell you! Something was in here. I *saw* her!"

Lydia glanced beyond her brother and noticed the house servants huddled in the hallway. There was fear in their large, probing eyes. "What you saw, Martin," she said calmly, "was probably the lightning. It caused the furniture to appear threatening."

She nodded to Wiley. "Everyone go on back to bed. We've lost enough sleep this night." She waited until they had followed her order before pulling Martin into the bedroom and closing the door. "Have you lost your mind?" she demanded. "You saw *nothing!* Do you understand? There was nothing in this room!"

Martin's eyes darted nervously to each piece of furniture. "I don't care if you believe me. I know what I saw. It was that Indian woman . . . Doña Marina. And she . . . she threatened me!"

His sister's eyes narrowed. "You're senile, Martin," she pronounced in a derisive voice. "Have you any idea how ridiculous you sound screaming about an Aztec witch coming to get you? Why would an Aztec, of all people, threaten you? They don't even exist anymore."

"How would I know?" Martin asked evasively as he sat in the overstuffed chair by the window. "It *was* her ghost, though. She had all these feathers on her, like . . . ." He stopped speakinge as the door opened.

"Mother? Uncle Martin? What's all the confusion about?" His hair out of place, and dressed in a green satin smoking jacket, Kevin entered the bedroom and shut the door behind him. "I wasn't sure if there was a fire, or what, with everyone yelling." He tightened the sash at his waist. "What's going on?"

Lydia glanced at her brother. "Not everyone, dear. Just your uncle. He claims to have seen a ghost."

Kevin managed to look both astonished and amused. "A ghost? Here, in this house?"

"There's no need to smirk, boy! I know what I saw." Martin might have to take Lydia's ridicule, but not her son's.

Kevin's mother bristled at Martin's tone of voice. "If you're so frightened of this room, perhaps you'd prefer to spend the night in another? You can always use Michael's."

Martin sat up straighter. "Never! He's tied into this. I know it!" He looked at Kevin. "You remember that story Denny Moran was telling us? About that Aztec princess and how she'd bring bad luck to anyone who had her treasure?"

299

"What treasure?" Lydia demanded. "What are you talking about?"

"It was Michael, that worthless bastard, who disturbed it, or . . . or something," Martin mumbled, furious that he had even brought up the story. "And now *I'm* involved because his ship is part of the Sheridan Line." It was the best he could come up with, considering Lydia's eyes were boring into his.

"The *Rebel* belonged to Michael alone," Kevin stated defensively. "It was never part of the line. You probably fell asleep thinking about Denny's story and had a nightmare."

Lydia pushed a stray lock of hair behind her ear. "That's exactly what I told him."

"She was here! I'm not losing my mind!"

"Where?" Kevin asked. "Where exactly did you see her?"

Martin reached out a bony, arthritic hand and pointed to the dressing-room door. "Right there. She was standing right there."

Meeting his mother's eyes, Kevin smiled slightly. His expression clearly told her that they would pacify Martin. As he walked to the closet, Kevin picked up the candelabra from the dresser and opened the door. Holding the light high, he looked inside. "There! Come see. There's nothing in here."

Kevin could hear his mother and Martin coming closer to him. He looked over his shoulder and saw his uncle peering around his mother.

"She was there, I tell you," he insisted in a doubting voice. "I saw her . . . I saw something . . ."

His mother walked around Kevin and entered the

closet. When he turned back to the small room, his heart skipped a beat as he saw her bending down to the floor. He tried to keep his hand steady while holding the light as she slowly stood up and held out a small blue and white feather . . . just like the ones Kate had been wearing!

Witnessing her strange expression, Kevin felt as though she had just reached inside him and had seen him for the liar he was. For his brother's sake, he didn't look away.

Lydia's watchful gaze went from Kevin to Martin and then back again. Her smile was mysterious, her expression calm, as she said, "I'm going to have to talk to those girls about checking their feather dusters. I believe some are in need of replacement."

"You were magnificent, Kate! I knew it was you, yet for a moment there I think I actually believed Doña Marina had come back to reclaim her treasure." Michael shook his head in admiration.

Smiling at Rose Pringle as she took her heavy cloak, Kate let the material slip down her arms and muttered, "Sorry, Michael, just plain old Kate Walker here."

Ignoring the sarcasm in her voice, Michael turned to the older woman. "You should have seen her, Rose. She was wonderful!" His voice became low and whispery. "Give back the treasure before it's too late to save you."

Kate grimaced at his poor imitation of her. "It just so happens I was scared to death—"

"Making up that last part was a masterpiece," he

interrupted and again turned to Rose. "You should have seen old Martin fly out of bed! God, it was so satisfying . . ."

"Rose? Would you excuse us for a moment?" Kate asked politely. "I'd like to have a word with Michael." She glared at the tall, handsome man who was beaming at her with admiration. "Before he gets too excited."

Without a word, Rose walked to the double French doors that separated her parlor from the rest of the house. Just before closing them, she looked at the young couple and said, "Thank God you're both safe. My prayers were answered."

Waiting until they were alone, Kate spun around and slapped Michael's shoulder. "What's wrong with you?" she demanded. "All three of us could have been caught! And you're strutting around like the damn Pink Panther!"

"The who—?" Shocked by her actions, he looked like a little boy whose ice-cream cone had just fallen into the dirt.

"Never mind," she said impatiently, realizing he wouldn't have any idea who she was talking about. "What the hell did we gain tonight by all this, Michael? So we scared an old man. Wonderful! Did we get the jewels? Did we even find out if they're in that room?"

She ignored the clenching of his jaw and continued, too worked up to stop. "Have you any idea how frightened I was when Martin woke up? I could barely breathe when he looked right at you and began speaking. Kevin had to *push* me out of the dressing room!"

Angry that she had taken all the joy out of the evening, Michael's eyes narrowed dangerously. "If I remember correctly, this entire charade was your idea. It was your suggestion."

"I know it was. And it was stupid!"

"I disagree. I think it was brilliant . . . and I intend to go back."

Kate's eyes widened; her lower jaw dropped. Swallowing several times, she whispered in a shocked voice, "You can't be serious!"

Michael walked away from her and stopped at Rose's large fireplace. Examining a vase Denny had brought his sister from the Orient, he leaned a hand on the mantel and looked back at Kate. "I'm very serious. We did it once. I can do it again." His voice hardened. "And perhaps this time I might discover your precious jewels."

She felt as if his fist had connected with her stomach. "You think that's the reason I'm upset? Because we didn't recover the treasure?"

"Is there another? Everything else went as planned."

How could she tell him that she'd feared for his life? That in those agonizing moments when Martin demanded to know who was in his room, she would have done anything to have protected him? That the horror of losing him had momentarily paralyzed her? Why did he think it was only the treasure that mattered to her? Didn't the last few weeks prove anything to him? Couldn't he see that she had changed? That *he* had changed? It was as if their roles had been reversed. She was now the cautious one, while Michael threw caution to the wind.

Disappointed in him, she said with a heavy heart, "You're an even bigger jackass than when I first met you."

Insulted, he drew himself up to his full height. "I beg your pardon, madam?"

Kate looked at him sadly. "As well you should, Michael." She walked toward the doors. "I think I'd like to go back to the cabin now. I've had enough of Charleston."

From behind her, she heard his voice. It was filled with authority. "We're staying here for a few days. I made the decision to remain in the city."

Slowly, Kate turned back to him. He was still in front of the fireplace, and her heart ached as the light from the flames reflected off his pale hair. She wanted to tell him he was wrong about her, but her pride kept the words lodged in her throat. She shouldn't have to tell him. After everything they had gone through together, he should know. Instead, he still believed her to be a greedy, conniving woman.

Attempting to overcome her hurt, she summoned up her anger. Anger was easier to deal with than what was happening to her heart. "*You* made the decision to remain in the city? You didn't even think to consult me?"

He lifted his chin. "It's too dangerous to keep going back and forth from the cabin. I've been lucky so far no one has recognized me. This way I can stay hidden and be close enough to find out what's really going on . . . instead of waiting for Kevin's visits."

Michael recognized the anger in her eyes, the tightness around her mouth. He didn't dare tell her that his decision to stay in Charleston was made only moments ago. He had been too eager to get her back to the seclusion of the woods, for he'd felt tonight she would finally be open to him. Whatever her dark

304

secrets were, he had hoped the two of them were beginning to trust. When she'd made her hurtful remarks about not finding the jewels, it was then all of his own doubts had come rushing back. Kate only wanted the treasure, not him. He was only a means to reclaiming it. No wonder she had been so good at playing Doña Marina—she was a brilliant actress. And, besides, Kate had diverted his attention for too long away from his main goal . . . regaining the shares and destroying Martin.

To Michael, it appeared as if all the fight had suddenly gone out of Kate. Her shoulders slumped downward in weary defeat. Without looking at him, she slowly removed the feathers from her hair and walked toward the doors. "I'll . . . I'll find out from Rose where I'm to sleep. Suddenly, I'm very tired."

His mouth opened in an attempt to call her name, but no words came out. Instead, he watched her retreating back as she left the room and immediately felt her loss.

When she awoke the next morning, Kate was disoriented. It took her a moment to realize she was in Rose Pringle's home. And for the first time since the day she had been brought back to the 1800's she was alone. If Michael had spent the night in this house, he had not spent it on the second floor. She'd stayed awake for hours last night, just listening for his step outside her door. It hadn't come.

As she descended the stairs less than a half hour later, Kate acknowledged that a deep depression had taken hold of her. She didn't bother to shake it, for it was long overdue. She had come to this time filled with acceptance, hoping to make the best of the situation. What she had found was a bitter man who had lost the joy of living. Forgetting her own troubles, she had tried to teach him that life was precious and he was wasting it on revenge. Judging from last night, it was obvious her skills did not lay in teaching, for Michael's suspicious nature was a harsh disappointment. It had been so easy for him to believe the worst of her.

"Kathleen! I hope you slept well."

Startled out of her daydreaming, Kate smiled into Rose's warm, friendly eyes as she met her at the bottom of the stairs. "Yes, I did," she lied. "Thank you again for taking us in."

"Nonsense, child. My home has always been open to Michael. That now extends to you." Nodding toward the kitchen, she added, "You must be near starving. Michael ate over two hours ago."

Instinctively, Kate's eyes turned toward the parlor in search of him.

"He's gone, dear," Rose said quietly. "He and my Denny went to meet Kevin. They thought it best not to have too many strangers coming here." Seeing the wounded expression on the younger woman's face, she was sympathetic. "Why don't you have some breakfast? Maybe we can straighten this out over coffee."

Kate couldn't help the smile from forming at her lips. Rose reminded her of her grandmother. She, too, thought food would make everything better. Needing the same comfort she had once found as a child, Kate willingly followed Rose into the kitchen. As she inhaled the fragrant aroma of freshly brewed coffee, she wondered if there wasn't something to be said for these older, wiser women. Already she felt stronger.

Having nourished Kate internally, Rose decided to work on the younger woman's exterior. "Didn't you say yesterday that Mamie Legare wanted you to come back for a fittin'?" At Kate's nod, she continued. "Well, I say we pick ourselves up, get out in the sunshine, and breathe in some fresh air. You don't mind walkin', do you?"

"No," Kate automatically answered. However, the very last person she wanted to see today was the nosy dressmaker. "I don't think I'm up to Mamie Legare," she admitted. "If you want to go for a walk, though, I'd love to accompany you."

Rose's blue eyes twinkled. "She said she wanted you back in. That's what you told me at supper last night. I've never been there, Kathleen. You gonna deny me the pleasure of walkin' in with you?"

Looking at the woman, Kate knew it would be hard to deny her anything. No wonder Michael loved her. "If you remember, Rose, I also told you that she thinks I'm Napoleon Bonaparte's great-niece. After last night, I don't think I'm up to playing another part just yet."

Rose stood up and took away Kate's half-filled cup of coffee. "Why, you wouldn't have to do a thing, 'cept stand there and let the woman do her job. I'd do all the talking. None of them fine ladies knows me." Holding a saucer in her plump hand, she used it for emphasis as she lifted it in the air. "I could say I was your companion. Why, that's it, of course! A companion, who not only looks after your welfare, but serves as your personal maid."

Kate was shocked. "I wouldn't want anyone to think you were my *maid*—"

307

"Why not?" Rose cut in. "I would think it'd be perfectly natural for a Bonaparte to employ one. Besides, if you knew how dull my life has been, you wouldn't be able to refuse me this. Why, I depend on Michael to bring me excitement . . . and now I have you."

Kate grinned at the gray-haired woman's expression. There was a peculiar mixture of pleading and stubbornness. Knowing she was going to give in, Kate cleared the rest of the dishes from the table and stated, "I have the strangest feeling that with both Michael and myself in your home, you're going to yearn for those days of boredom."

Rose's voice told of her excitement. "Does that mean we can go to Mamie Legare's?"

Kate nodded and laughed. "If it will make you happy, Rose, we'll go."

Rose Pringle quickly turned to her breakfast dishes, not allowing Kate to see the triumph in her eyes. It was all goin' as planned, she thought happily. Sometimes, meddlin' was downright fun.

Build a fence around the South and you'd have one big madhouse. Somewhere in her past, Kate had heard that saying. Within thirty seconds of entering Mamie Legare's establishment, she had reason to believe the validity of that statement. As soon as Mamie had sighted her, she'd announced in a loud voice, "Miss Bonaparte! How very nice to see you this morning!" Whereupon, from behind bolts of materials and curtained dressing rooms there came a crush of southern womanhood accompanied by a calliope of high-pitched squeals.

Kate could only blink as women of all ages, sizes, and state of dress surrounded her and began speaking at once.

"Miss Bonaparte, what a pleasure! I'm Divinia Allston—that's the two l's, not the one. I would be honored if you'd—"

"Why, we are *all* just honored, Miss Kathleen, to have you visit our fair city. My daddy, Marston De Bose, met your uncle when he was in—"

"Lisbeth De Bose! Your daddy never did no such thing! Why my great-great grandfather wrote down how we Meades are directly descended from Scota, a pharaoh's daughter, who drifted out of the bullrushes and straight up to what is now Scotland—and found it. If anyone should address Miss Bonaparte, it should be—"

"Amanda Vanderhorse, Miss Bonaparte. Could I extend an invitation to visit Mr. Bullwinkle's bakery after your fitting? Or perhaps I could leave my calling card tomorrow? Might I inquire where you're staying? The Vanderhorses and the Warings settled Charleston with—"

"The Olephants were with William the Conqueror . . . The *real* beginning of civilization, Amanda. I would think that gives me the right to—"

"*Ladies!*" Rose's voice sounded like a haven of sanity, and Kate turned to the small woman at her side . . . along with the rest of the women. "Ladies," Rose continued in a much lower voice, "Miss Kathleen is here for a fittin'. She will be stayin' at the Charleston Hotel and any of you that wishes to leave your cards are welcome to do so. However, I must tell you my mistress is here for relaxation—a . . . a holiday, you might say."

The women backed off and nodded their understanding. Centering their elaborate hats back on their heads, or holding lengths of material to their half-dressed bodies, both young and old made a path for Kate to continue into the shop. Accompanied by Rose, Kate took a few hesitant steps forward until her eyes met those of Mamie Legare. The shop owner was beaming with pride.

"I'm here as you requested, Miss Legare," she said in a controlled, soft voice, positive Mamie had planned the entire episode to reestablish her trade. "If you aren't too busy I'd like to conclude our business." It was strange that she was picking up the more formal speech of the era. Maybe it wasn't, she thought as Mamie rushed to her side and steered her into a dressing room. Thanks to Mamie Legare and Rose Pringle, she was about to play another role. Kathleen Bonaparte— How ridiculous that these people believed it all! And what about Rose? Where did she come up with that story about the Charleston Hotel? What were they going to do if those women actually did leave their calling cards there? Who could afford to stay in a hotel?

Turning to her older friend as she reached out to hold the gray outfit Mamie had sold her yesterday, Kate gave her a look that said, *Wait until I get you outside!*

Rose Pringle correctly interpreted Kate's expression, yet chose to ignore it. She was having too much fun.

As Kate and her "companion" left the dress shop, she smiled or nodded to the staring women. This time they respected her privacy and felt honored if they happened to be the one graced with her acknowledgment. The objects of the intense curiosity weren't even out the door before they heard the buzz of animated whispers. Kate didn't know it, but she had just infused the old city of Charleston with an excitement that it hadn't seen since before the war. The old guard wanted to believe her story. In truth, they needed it to wipe away their humiliation and defeat of three years earlier. It mattered little that Kate was a Yankee. She was a genuine celebrity, come to visit their city—just like before the bad times. The psychological weapon they had flung into a northerner's face of commonness and mongrelism did not apply. Here was a young woman with an enviable lineage—granddaughter of Joseph Bonaparte who was brother to the former emperor of France. And she had chosen Charleston for her holiday. It was proof positive that the South would again rise to her former glory. And the women of the most respected families in the city were about to engage in a heated argument over who would be the first to begin their own social reconstruction.

Kate waited until they had passed three stores before she spun on Rose. "I don't believe it!" she whispered. "How could you say I'm staying at a hotel? *Now* what are we going to do?"

Right there on the street, Rose threw back her head and laughed. "Did you see 'em?" she asked gleefully. "They were bumpin' into each other tryin' to get to you, so they could recite their damn kennel papers!" She shook her head. "Believe me, Kathleen, it was worth it."

Kate was taken aback. "You enjoyed that, didn't

you? You liked riding roughshod over those women."

Rose brought her rounded chin up higher in defense. "That I did," she admitted. "My Willis was as fine as any of their men, probably finer than most, yet he was snubbed by their ilk. I always felt bad about that. My husband was a hard-working, honest man—good enough to do business with, but not equal enough to share a cigar. He never said as much, but I know it bothered him. Especially durin' the war."

Rose gathered her shawl around her ample shoulders. "To listen to them, there were no enlisted men in the Confederacy. No infantry. No artillery. Only the cavalry, with fancy plumes in their hats, leading charges. Well I ask just who the blue blazes followed those commands to charge? My Willis, that's who!"

Seeing a Union officer coming out of a nearby shop, Rose stopped speaking until he had passed on. "They got us into it, them highfalutin landowners. And look what's happened? We're under military rule until Washington says we're good enough to be brought back into the Union. Me and Willis never owned a single slave. Not a one! Them bluebloods, with their crazy lineages, had us start a war without ownin' a single cannon factory. What's crazier than that?"

Kate could almost feel the anger and pain coming from the tiny woman who had lived through hell, yet come out alone. "Did your husband die in the war?" she asked softly.

Rose shook her head. "Every night I say a prayer of thanksgiving that my Willis didn't go to his Maker on some battlefield. He came home to me and we had three months together before he went peacefully in his sleep." She tightened her face and looked directly into

312

Kate's eyes. "I'm not a traitor, like some of them up North are callin' us. I supported my man in battle and he fought for his State. But I will tell you that Willis and Denny and Michael sat up many a night discussin' the madness of goin' to war. And I agreed with them. Those women in there—Kathleen, they *still* think they were right. They still believe it was honorable. Too bad they can't ask some dead boy if he thinks it was honorable to have died fightin' their war! And for what? So the landowners could keep the old ways?"

Seeing Rose was working herself up, Kate tried to diffuse her anger before they attracted more than stares. "Did you hear that old woman say she was descended from a pharaoh's daughter? She wasn't serious, was she?"

Rose put behind her the painful memories and smiled. "That was Marbelle Meade. I heard she's the craziest of the bunch. I'm tellin' you, Kathleen, all of 'em are beset by who's got the best kennel papers in town." She started walking in the direction that they had come. "It looks like they think you do right now."

Keeping pace with the smaller woman, Kate again asked, "And what do we do about the Charleston Hotel? What happens when I'm not there?"

Without looking at Kate, Rose stated, "But you will be. And so will I. We're movin' in this afternoon."

"What?" Kate stopped walking and stared at the older woman. She sounded as absurd as the shrieking women in Mamie Legare's shop.

Rose took Kate's wrist and brought her along with her. "My Willis didn't leave me penniless, you know. I always wanted to know what a suite in that fancy place looked like."

"I won't allow you to spend your money like this! What about Michael? What's he going to think? It isn't what we had planned. This whole thing is getting out of hand. It's . . . it's insane!"

Rose continued to lead her back toward her home. Without stopping for rest, she said, "I'll spend my money any way I choose. And what about Michael? Where is he, anyway? If we do this, you'll be invited into the best homes in Charleston . . . maybe even the high and mighty Lydia Sheridan's. It's a lot safer way of findin' out what's goin' on than dressin' up as ghosts!"

Suddenly, it all made sense to Kate. Rose wasn't after the women she had met today, as much as Michael's mother. The deep resentment Rose carried was for Lydia Sheridan. Smiling slightly, Kate linked arms with the smaller woman and said, "Rose Pringle, I do believe you're as devious as I am."

Lifting her face to the lovely girl at her side, Rose giggled. "You're not devious, child. What we share is the ability to combine business with fun. If men wouldn't take everything so seriously, a great deal of heartache could be avoided. I fully expect to enjoy myself in this adventure, and so will you. I saw it in you right away, Kathleen. You have the gift."

"What gift?" Kate asked, intensely curious.

"You've realized the really important things in life aren't money or lineage, or any of those things others crave. It's people. You've learned how to live, Kate. For someone so young, that's a gift."

A chill ran up her back as Kate listened to Rose repeat her mother's words: *It's your time . . . Live, Katie . . . enjoy life.* Holding back the tears, she felt the moisture building in her eyes. Her mother was right, and so was Rose. It was people. That was what was important. And the most important person in her life was Michael. It wasn't the treasure. She could only prove it to him one way. She'd get the treasure herself, and give it to him. Maybe then he could let go and realize what was important in his life.

Determined, she quickened her steps. "We'd better hurry, Rose, if we want to start this adventure before Michael gets back."

Nodding her approval, Rose Pringle kept up with the younger pair of legs. She had packing to do and notes to write. She felt no guilt at leaving the men to fend for themselves. Nor did she feel any guilt in manipulating Kate and Michael's lives. She'd heard their argument last night. What they needed was a little distance. Everyone knew absence made the heart grow fonder. Why, didn't she have to go all the way to her aunt Fern's in Harleyville before Willis proposed? And he wasn't half as stubborn as Michael Sheridan!

Chapter 20

"She's *where?*"

Seeing the muscles in Michael's face expand with anger, Denny Moran quickly picked up the piece of paper. "Kate's stayin' at the Charleston Hotel. Here," he hastily offered, "read it yourself."

Grabbing the paper from his first mate, Michael's eyes scanned the note written in Rose's handwriting. To properly fulfill social obligations?

"What social obligations?" he demanded aloud.

Denny shifted and pulled on his worn leather belt. "Ah . . . if you read on, you'll see. Somethin' about the ladies from the best families comin' to call on Napoleon's great-niece—"

"Damn it! No, damn *her!*" Michael crumbled the note and threw it into a corner. "I can't leave that woman alone for a minute. She's always getting into trouble!" He started pacing the small kitchen, and Denny was intelligent enough not to speak.

Unclenching his fists, Michael spun around to the older man waiting patiently by the table. "I'm going

316

over there and drag her back here!" he announced.

"You can't do that," Denny said quietly, obviously not fazed by his captain's anger. He'd seen it too many times in the past. "You're supposed to be dead. Remember?"

Michael ground his back teeth together in frustration. "Then you go."

"Not me," Denny pronounced. "I'd get thrown outa that fancy place faster than spoiled meat."

Michael gripped the back of a chair. "Then I'll get Kevin to go. I'm not going to let her get away with this, Denny." He glared at the older man. "She's free to create all sorts of trouble, and I'm helpless to stop her."

Denny walked around the table and sat down. "Don't you think you might be exaggeratin' a bit there? Miss Kate's no fool. Maybe it's just like Rose said—all them ladies want to meet Kate and the hotel seemed the best place."

"Why did she have to go back to the dress shop today?" Michael asked, while ignoring Denny's explanation. "If they think she's Napoleon's niece, every dowager in the city is going to be standing in line to see her. Whatever happened to keeping a low profile?"

"Well, at least she's not alone. Rose will look after her."

Michael rolled his eyes toward the ceiling. "And who's going to look after Rose? She can be as bad as Kate for starting trouble."

Bringing his elbows onto the table, Denny rested his chin on his raised hands. "You might have somethin' there," he said thoughtfully. "Once Rose gets an idea into her head, she can be right stubborn about it."

Michael sat down heavily onto the chair opposite

317

Denny. Looking at his mate, he said in a tired voice, "Between Rose and Kate, there's sure to be trouble . . . I just know it. We'd better find Kevin again—and quickly."

Kate watched as Rose Pringle slowly walked around the elegant suite of rooms. Her plump hand caressed the needlepoint sofa, the ivory moiré chairs, a magnificent satinwood commode. "It's money well spent," she breathed blissfully as she examined the intricate shrimp-colored draperies. "Don't your feet just sink into this carpet?"

Kate glanced down at the flowered rug. "Rose, this is too much. I can't allow you to spend your money like this—"

Primly sitting on the edge of a chair, Rose inhaled deeply. "Fresh flowers, too. Can you smell the oleander?"

Impatient, Kate moved farther into the expensive suite. "You're not listening, Rose. I said—"

"I heard every word, Kathleen," Rose promptly interrupted. "Did you see the balcony off your bedroom? Imagine waking up every morning to that garden outside?"

"Rose, we don't need anything this elaborate. You should save the money your husband gave you."

"Hush, girl! A body deserves some pamperin' after years of hard work. I just wish my Willis could've seen this. He'd have been mighty impressed."

Just as Kate was about to sit down and try to talk some sense into the generous woman, someone knocked on the door. Kate froze and both women stared at each other.

"You sit here," Rose whispered, "and I'll answer it!"

As Kate nervously did as she was instructed, Rose smoothed the material of her black hooped skirt and reached for the door handle. Holding her breath, Kate tried to appear casual as she waited to see who was beyond the door.

A young hotel porter stood with his arms full of boxes. "Delivery for Miss Bonaparte," he announced from behind the stack.

Rose quickly reached for the top hat box and said, "Come right on in, my boy. Why don't you take them into Miss Bonaparte's boudoir?"

Kate's astonishment over the delivery caused her to stand up. It was on the tip of her tongue to tell the young man he had made a mistake. Her clothes from Mamie Legare weren't supposed to be ready until the end of the week. She smiled faintly as the porter left her bedroom and pulled a small stack of envelopes from the pocket of his red jacket.

"These were left at the desk," he said to Rose. "And these," he turned to Kate, "I was told specifically to place in your hands."

Kate accepted the two larger envelopes and thanked the boy as Rose ushered him to the door. Curiosity made her rip open the first. It was a formal note from Mamie Legare telling her that she had taken it upon herself to send along a few items for Kate's wardrobe. She also mentioned that she was so grateful Kate had chosen her shop that the woman would be honored if Kate would accept them as a small token of her appreciation.

Shaking her head, she showed the note to Rose. "Do

you believe this? If you're poor, I don't believe Mamie would want you giving her shop a bad name by standing too close to the door. But if she thinks you're wealthy, and you don't really need it, she's willing to give you the shirt off her back. It makes no sense," she said, sitting back down.

"Sure it does," Rose remarked while opening one of the smaller envelopes. "She's payin' you back, is all. You brought all them women into her shop again. My bet is every one of 'em ordered a new gown for when they entertain you. Well . . . !" Rose dropped to a chair and smiled as she read the note she'd just opened.

"It says here that Mrs. Alexander Dunbar requests the honor of your presence at a tea on Thursday . . ."

"But that's the day after tomorrow!" Kate protested. "I can't go! What will I say to those women?"

Rose didn't answer as she tore open the remaining four envelopes. Holding the engraved cards in her hand, she announced, "Looks like you're goin' to be busy until next week. They sure didn't lose any time in makin' plans, did they?"

Feeling miserable, Kate closed her eyes and sunk deeper into the chair. "What have we started, Rose? I can't pull this off."

Choosing to ignore the younger woman's lack of enthusiasm, Rose said, "Still, nothin' here from Lydia Sheridan. It's early yet. If she isn't at that tea party, we've got to make sure we find a way for you to meet her. What's that one in your hand say?"

Gazing down to the last envelope, Kate absently tore it open—expecting to see another invitation from one of Charleston's elite matrons. Reading the signature at the bottom of the heavy paper, she sat up straighter.

320

"It's from Kevin," she said in a surprised voice. "He's inviting me to have dinner with him downstairs."

She looked up at Rose in time to see the older woman smiling. "Wait until Mrs. Lydia Sheridan gets wind of that," she whispered in a mischievous voice. "I expect we'll be hearin' from her soon enough."

"Rose, you look like the cat that swallowed the canary. Sometimes I worry about what you're plan—"

"Let's find out what Mamie sent over," Rose interrupted while standing up. "And we're going to have to do somethin' about that hair of yours before tonight."

Coming to her feet, Kate asked, "Why do you always interrupt me? And what's wrong with my hair?" she demanded, while grabbing a handful at her shoulder so she could examine it.

Already making her way into the bedroom, Rose gently remarked, "Why, it's lovely, dear. Just too straight and plain. I'll fancy it up a bit with the iron. Remember, Kathleen, you're royalty now."

Letting her straight, dark hair fall back to her shoulders, Kate closed her eyes and groaned.

"Why, Kathleen, you look enchanting," Kevin remarked while leading her into the hotel's dining room.

Kate smiled her thanks while nervously trying to avoid the stares of strangers as they passed. Just like in Mamie's shop, she could hear whispers following her. "I'm afraid, Kevin," she said in a low voice, "it will be all over the city tomorrow that you dined with Napoleon's niece."

Following the maitre d' to their table, Kevin leaned closer and whispered, "My reputation can withstand it. You should get used to the attention, though. Already the city is buzzing with news of you."

Kate smiled and shook her head slightly in amazement. As they were seated she could actually feel the stares of the other diners. What did they expect her to do? Break into the first verse of the "Marseillaise?" She looked directly into the eyes of an elderly woman and smiled.

The matron appeared startled, then quickly recovered and smiled back while nodding. From the corner of her eye, Kate watched as the woman excitedly addressed her husband.

"I think you've made Mrs. Dunbar's evening," Kevin remarked while placing his napkin across his knee.

"Mrs. *Alexander* Dunbar?" Kate asked.

Kevin nodded.

"She's invited me to a tea on Thursday," Kate said while favoring the woman with another smile.

"It doesn't surprise me. You're already famous."

Turning back to Kevin, Kate leaned closer to the table. "You don't approve, do you?"

Kevin shrugged. "I'm not like you and Michael. Excitement seems to follow both of you. I prefer a quieter life."

She decided not to explain that this particular adventure was Rose Pringle's idea, not hers. Wanting to change the subject, she asked with a false calm, "How is Michael?"

A waiter politely interrupted them to ask Kevin if he wished a drink before dinner. Kevin looked to Kate.

Feeling she was going to need fortification before

this evening was over, she said to the waiter, "I'll have a bourbon and ginger, with a twist of lemon."

Both the waiter and Kevin stared at her. Embarrassed, Kate cleared her throat. "A glass of wine would be fine." It was probably the ginger ale, she thought. Maybe they'd never heard of it.

"You were asking me about Michael," Kevin said after the waiter had left. "Actually it was his idea that I come tonight and speak with you. He was very upset, Kate, when he discovered you'd left."

She nodded. "I thought he might be."

"Then may I ask why you did it?"

Kate looked down to the skirt of her orchid silk gown. "It's this ridiculous Bonaparte thing! Kevin, everyone thinks I am this woman . . . Napoleon's great-niece!"

He nodded. "Michael explained that part. What he wants to know is why you're here. He seems to think it had something to do with an argument the two of you had last night."

Kate gave Michael's brother an exasperated look and shook her head. "That had nothing to do with it. I was angry last night because Michael seems obsessed with destroying your uncle. Nothing else matters to him. Did he also tell you that he intends to go back into Martin's bedroom?"

Kevin's mouth opened in shock.

"I can see he forgot to mention it," Kate remarked as the waiter returned with their wine.

Waiting until he had approved the selection and their glasses were filled, Kevin leaned closer to Kate and whispered, "If he goes back, it would be disastrous. My mother found one of your feathers last night."

Kate inhaled with fear. "What did she say?"

"She said the cleaning girls needed to replace their feather dusters. But it was the look she gave me. I'm not so certain she doesn't know about the passageway."

"We have to stop him, Kevin, before he destroys himself along with Martin."

Kevin relaxed back in his chair and casually sipped his wine. "You do care for him, don't you?" Observing a flattering blush appear on Kate's cheeks, he added, "I apologize for my rudeness, but there just isn't time for propriety now."

Kate nodded. She could see Michael in the man across from her. The resemblance was in the eyes and the mouth. Kevin was less guarded than Michael, though, as if he'd come to some understanding with himself and was comfortable with the man he'd found. He might even have been the perfect husband for Helene Barnett if she and Michael hadn't interfered. "I feel something for your brother," she quietly admitted. "I don't know what it is— A good deal of the time he gets on my nerves."

Kevin chuckled. "I seem to recall Michael saying the same thing about you. But I do know my brother, and I believe he also cares for you. He wouldn't be this upset over you leaving if he didn't."

Kate's heart expanded with Kevin's words. If only she could believe him. But she, too, knew Michael, perhaps even better than Kevin. Whatever Michael had begun to feel for her had died last night when he'd accused her of only caring about the treasure. Just like herself, Michael, too, had a problem with trusting. Perhaps Kevin might be able to help them both.

She picked up her wine and eyed the handsome man

across the table. "Did you really mean it when you said your reputation could withstand being seen with me?" she asked softly.

"Of course. In fact, right now I'm probably envied by every man in the room."

Kate smiled. "Would you like to be my escort while I play the part of visiting royalty?"

Kevin viewed her with speculation. He'd seen that same scheming look on Michael's face too many times in the past. "What exactly do you have in mind? And where will I be escorting you?"

Kate's eyes shined with mischief. "Dunnemores," she announced. "It's a much safer way to meet Martin and find out if he has the jewels."

Kevin swallowed several times. "Dunnemores? Kathleen, you can't go into a gaming establishment. It isn't done!"

The lovely woman at his table shook a fall of riotous curls that hung down her back and gave him a secretive smile. "Maybe not for the common womanfolk, Kevin. But I don't think they'll turn royalty away, do you?"

Over the next few days, Kevin accompanied her everywhere. They were constantly seen together at teas, small dinner parties, and the theater. Always a good student, Kate had sent both Kevin and Rose to dig up any books on her new "family." She devoured anything she could get her hands on, including the current emperor of France, Napoleon III's *Napoleonic Ideas*— a book idealizing the career of his famous uncle. She brushed up on French literature, painting, and music. Within days she could speak with authority on realism versus romanticism using Gustave Flaubert's *Madame Bovary* as a poetic example. She could discuss Jean Auguste Dominique Ingres's new approach to neoclassical painting and the excitement found in the work of Eugene Delacroix, the most famous French romantic painter. She stunned her listeners by saying she preferred the lesser known work of the young, new Impressionists—Monet, Renoir, and Degas—who rejected the idea that a painting should tell a story. Not wishing the label of Francophile, when pressed, she would admit a fondness for Beethoven and Frederic Chopin's compositions for solo piano. At her next gathering, Chopin's "Fantasia" was playing when she walked in.

Only Kevin knew she was bluffing her way through every encounter, and for three straight days Kate gave flawless performances. Not even Kevin knew she was near ill with stage fright, that she was terrified someone would challenge her newly acquired knowledge. No one did. The city of Charleston was enchanted by its charming outspoken visitor. In their eyes, Kathleen Bonaparte could do no wrong.

"I'm beginning to understand why Michael is so exasperated with you," Kevin whispered, raising the oil lamp to light the stairway. "What I fail to comprehend is how you managed to talk me into this."

"Shh! We don't want to announce our second visit, do we?" Lifting the hem of her costume, Kate carefully followed Kevin up the narrow stairs. "We're doing it to protect Michael," she muttered under her breath, and prayed for the courage to go through with this hasty plan.

Someone had to protect Michael from himself. It would be sheer madness for him to reenter Martin's room. Michael was determined to search for the treasure and, in doing so, he was sure to be caught. She, on the other hand, only wanted to harass Martin and her brief encounter with him tonight was just the beginning of her plans. What did surprise her was Kevin's assistance. Although reluctant, he had promised to help her, once he'd heard her reasoning. Agreeing that Michael's emotions ruled him where their uncle was concerned, Kevin had also conceded that Kate's systematic harassment would produce the desired effect of driving the older man to rid himself of the jewels. All they had to do was be patient . . . and never to let Michael know what they were doing.

The familiar scents of cedar and bay rum mingled together in the closet as Kate gathered the bright feathers in her hand. This time she was determined that no loose reminders would be found. Clutching them, she turned to look at Kevin as he held the lamp between them. They had already discussed how he would keep the light behind her head to form a halo of sorts, thus ensuring her face would be cast in shadow.

Swallowing several times, she tried to smile at Michael's brother and hoped her eyes would convey her thanks, for she feared speaking now that they were outside the bedroom.

Nodding to her, Kevin let her know he understood and motioned to the closet door. Kate took a deep breath, reached out her hand, and slowly opened it.

Fear made her senses more acute. She could feel the old man's presence across the room. His erratic breathing indicated a fitful sleep, and she gathered her courage as perspiration collected in the creases of her palms.

"You have no right to my treasure, Martin Masterson," she said in a low, husky voice. "I want it back."

He was dreaming again. This time he could hear the Mayan witch as she said his name. Taking in a long, shuddering breath, he settled himself more comfortably and raised the cover to his shoulder. Drifting in and out of sleep, he cursed the Fates that had robbed him of his strength and now sought to play with his mind. He would not listen to the low voice inside his head, for it was only a dream talking, and the price one pays for living past three score.

"I have come to give you another chance. Return what you have taken from me."

A slow chill ran up his spine and down the back of his arms. Opening his eyes, he forced himself to look toward the closet. His mouth hung open in fear, and his heartbeat increased as he reacted to the vision standing across from his bed. She was back!

"You have robbed me of my treasure. Return it before it's too late."

"Go away!" Masterson whispered in a frightened, raspy voice. "Get away from me!"

She held her feathers out to him. "I have come to warn you. You have five days to give me what is mine . . . no more. Then, I will come for you."

"Lydia!" Strangled by fear, Martin crawled off the bed and ran to the door.

Fumbling with the lock, he heard Doña Marina say, "Five days . . ." and then the halo around her head disappeared. Thrust into darkness, Masterson's fear only increased. Flinging open the door, he ran down the hallway.

"My God! Somebody help me . . . She's back!"

They thought he was losing his mind. He could see it in the faces of the servants, read it in his sister's eyes. Even Kevin treated him like a senile old fool, and Kevin had been with him yesterday when he'd discovered the feather lying innocently on the seat of his carriage. Gazing down at the open drawer of his office desk, a tremor began in his fingers as he attempted to pick up the blue and white feather that matched the others. It was another warning. She was counting off the days.

He would not believe in this witchcraft. Perhaps it was the believing that made it so real. Although his nerves were frayed to a breaking point, he was determined to hold on to his sanity. She would not defeat him.

Slamming the drawer shut, he walked over to the liquor cabinet and poured himself a healthy drink. Letting the fiery liquid enter his system, he realized that he must somehow show the others that he had not lost his grip on reality. He must go through with his normal routine—and get rid of the treasure as quickly as possible.

Now that he had a plan, he felt safe. Doña Marina, or whatever her name was, could leave all the feathers she wanted. She no longer had power over him. Martin Masterson was flesh and blood . . . and he'd never yet been beaten.

*   *   *

On Friday evening Rose Pringle held the cape that matched Kate's midnight-blue evening gown. She had to admit Mamie Legare had outdone herself this time. Kathleen looked magnificent as she waited for Kevin to pick her up.

"Everything's goin' so well," Rose again lectured. "Why do you have to mess it up by goin' to that place?"

Kate checked her face in the mirror and smiled. "I've spent three days leading up to tonight. Trust me, Rose, no one's going to be as shocked as you think. They already believe I'm a bit eccentric. Showing up at Dunnemores will confirm it."

"But, Kathleen, Dunnemores is a . . ."

"Respectable place," Kate interrupted. "Michael says so."

Rose's eyebrows came together. "Hmmph! Respectable, huh? I've never known Michael to spend so much time in a respectable place before. Why, I've heard . . ."

Kate kissed the older woman's cheek. "Don't worry, Rose. I know what I'm doing. For the first time since we started this Bonaparte thing, I know what I'm doing. At least tonight I won't have to fake it."

"What do you mean, fake it?" Rose demanded as a knock sounded at the door.

As Kate moved to answer it, she turned back to Rose and winked. "Wait up for me and I'll tell you if all those shameful stories you heard about Dunnemores are true."

Rose was too flustered to reply. After tonight's shocking performance, Lydia Sheridan was sure to come callin'!

Chapter 21

Kate knew she would never get used to her celebrity status. It would have surprised Kevin to realize she was more like him than he had thought. She didn't enjoy the stares from those who scrutinized her every movement, nor being stopped three times before she and Kevin could make their way out of the hotel.

Kevin, dressed in impeccable evening clothes, took her elbow as they stepped out to the street. "Kate, I have to tell you something," he whispered in a nervous voice.

Kate recognized Denny's carriage as it pulled up to the front of the Charleston Hotel. Smiling, she glanced up to greet Rose's brother when her eyes widened in shock. She felt frozen in place, incapable of movement, as she identified the driver. *Michael!*

"That's what I wanted to tell you," Kevin muttered, as Kate continued to stare at his brother.

Michael was disguised behind a seaman's jacket that was at least two sizes too big for him. The old ratty hat that he'd been using to hide his upper features was back in place, slouching over his eyes. As he carelessly hopped down to the street to open the carriage door, Kate could see a three-day growth of whiskers covering his face. If she hadn't identified the hat, and recalled how he had looked on the island without the benefit of a razor, she never would have recognized him.

Kevin had to apply a slight pressure to her back in order to make her move toward the open carriage door. Her throat could form no words in reply to Michael's polite, "Evenin' ma'am."

Although it was evening, there was still traffic outside the Charleston and somewhere, in the chaos of wild emotions careening through her brain, came the sane thought that here, on the street, was not the place for a confrontation. Furious that he would take such a dangerous risk of being discovered, she briskly nodded to Michael and accepted Kevin's assistance into the carriage.

"I wanted to prepare you," Kevin said as they made their way out of the city. "There was no talking him out of coming tonight."

Kate tried to slow the pounding of her heart by taking deep breaths. "Why is he doing this?" she demanded while shaking her head. "How long can he hope to go unrecognized?"

Kevin turned to the woman at his side. As he regarded her in the faint glow coming from the carriage lamp, he thought how much he'd enjoyed accompanying her throughout the city. In the past few days he had become quite fond of Kathleen Walker, and decided to speak honestly.

"Frankly, Kate, I think Michael's patience with being dead is near an end. He's been intolerable to be

332

around since you've left." He looked directly into her beautiful eyes. "It doesn't sit well with him that we're constantly together. I believe he's jealous."

He watched her eyes widen with amazement. "Michael? Jealous?"

Kevin nodded. "That surprises you? Do you realize I've had to report to him every night after I've left you at the hotel? If I didn't, he threatened to come back to the house . . . and haunt me!"

Kate couldn't suppress a grin. It sounded like something Michael would say.

"And tonight," Kevin continued, "when he found out where we're going, both Denny and I had a devil of a time talking him out of confronting Martin along with you. I tell you, Kate, he isn't going to stay in the shadows much longer."

The smile left Kate's mouth. "What would happen if your uncle knew Michael were alive? What could Martin really do to him?"

Kevin took a deep breath and briefly closed his eyes. "He would immediately have Michael arrested for kidnapping and possible manslaughter."

"What?" Kate jerked upright in the seat. "What are you talking about? Whose murder?"

"Helene Barnett's. He did kidnap . . ."

"He kidnapped *me,* not Helene! And she isn't dead . . . she's at her aunt's, or some convent . . . I don't know exactly where she is right now, but she isn't dead! Dear God, does Michael know this?"

Kevin glanced out the window of the carriage. "My brother has some sense of self-preservation. It was the one reason he agreed to be your driver tonight, and not your escort," he said as the carriage slowed to a stop.

333

Kate leaned forward to look out her own window. "Are we there?" she asked, seeing nothing but the dark woods where she and Michael had committed their first crime.

Feeling Kevin's weight shift as he opened the carriage door, Kate turned back to him in time to see his look of sympathy. "I also had to promise that I would give him the chance to speak with you in private. Don't worry, Kate, I'll be right outside."

She felt like a helpless victim. A huge wave of apprehension rolled over her and took hold, as Kevin disappeared and Michael stood at the carriage door. Without saying a word, he entered the cab and shut the wooden door behind him.

"You . . . you look different," Kate stupidly mumbled.

Sweeping the hat off his head, he ran his fingers through his hair and appraised her costly gown. She detected almost a sneer as he remarked, "So do you, Kate. It looks like you finally got the clothes you craved so dearly."

She inhaled with self-righteous anger. "What is that supposed to mean?"

He shrugged. "Ever since we met, your main goal has been to change your status in life. I just never thought you'd go this far . . . Miss Bonaparte."

Her eyes deepened with indignation. "You know this wasn't my fault. I explained to you about the pattern book . . ."

"What I would like to know," he interrupted in an equally angry voice, "is what the hell you think you're doing flaunting yourself all over Charleston?"

"Flaunting myself?"

"You heard me! As if it isn't bad enough that everyone in the city is already talking about you, now you intend to make a spectacle of yourself by going to Dunnemores. I won't allow it!"

Michael immediately knew he'd made a terrible mistake as he watched Kate's expression change. After blinking in disbelief, a sudden calm relaxed her features.

"You won't allow it?" she asked with a smile. "What do you intend to do, Michael? You've already kidnapped me once before. I wouldn't think you'd make that mistake twice."

"Stay out of what isn't your business, Kate," he tried again. "Leave Martin to me."

"Martin is my business," she said in a hard voice, not wanting to react to Michael's nearness. The short stubble of beard reminded her of the man who'd made love to her on a deserted beach. It seemed like a dream now. Where had that endearingly tender man gone? "Martin is my business," she repeated. "And so are you. We're supposed to be partners. Remember? Why is it in this partnership you make all the decisions? I'm going through with this tonight, whether you like it or not."

As Kevin knocked on the door, Michael glanced with annoyance at his brother's appearance. "Whatever you two decide, you'd better do it quickly. I can hear another carriage coming up the road."

Michael looked at Kate and experienced an attack of pure frustration. He knew he was helpless to stop her. Not having time to reason with her, he said quickly, "Don't do it, Kate. Martin's a dangerous man. He isn't the fool you imagine him to be . . ."

"I have a plan," she said confidently.

"What plan?" he demanded after he'd stepped out of the carriage.

Kate smiled knowingly. "Don't worry," she said softly while giving him a confident smile.

In a foul mood, Michael jammed his hat back on his head and whispered, "Not only will I worry, but I'll be watching you. I've already arranged it with Terry Dunnemore."

Kate managed to appear calm. "Be my guest," she invited. "You might learn something."

His body was so rigid, Kevin had to push Michael toward the horse. "*Will* you get going? I have no desire to explain why we're stopped out here."

Shrugging off his brother, Michael glared at Kate. Had she no fear at all? Abruptly turning away, he climbed back into the driver's seat while vowing to teach her a badly needed lesson. She was stubborn, headstrong, conniving, greedy, a liar . . .

"Aughh!" His voice rang out in the night as he flicked the reins over the horse's rump. Kate dearly needed a taming . . .

Admission into Dunnemores proved easy—almost too easy—and Kate had a nagging suspicion that she was expected. Probably Michael's friend, the owner, was already warned of her arrival. Her immediate impression was that the establishment resembled every bad interpretation of a brothel she had seen in period movies. There was a great deal of red mixed with the deep mahogany wood—from the red and black flocked wallpaper to the scarlet tassels that created an arch over each doorway.

Standing under a huge chandelier in the wide foyer, she sensed Kevin's deep embarrassment and leaned closer to his shoulder. "I would like to go straight into the gaming room," she whispered, "and avoid the . . . well, any other rooms."

It was a small lie, for she was dying with curiosity to actually see what other "entertainments" Michael had told her about, but noticing Kevin's immense relief, she felt it was a small price to pay. Maybe another time, she told herself as Kevin removed her cape and handed it to a formally dressed Negro servant.

Placing her hand on Kevin's arm, Kate let him lead her toward a side room. As they stood at the entrance, they could hear the slow dwindling of conversation as their presence was noticed.

Terry Dunnemore stopped shuffling the chips in his hand and, along with every other man in the place, looked at the delicious vision about to enter the room. On the arm of Kevin Sheridan, she slowly looked over the roulette and blackjack tables, past the faro players and the bar. Immediately, Terry felt an admiration for the beauty as she glided into the room and graced each man she passed with a charming smile. Most were too stunned to do more than stare.

Michael was right, Terry thought, as he placed the poker chips back on the table and stood up. Kate Walker was no ordinary woman. After scaring him half to death this afternoon by his appearance, Michael had prepared him for this evening's visitor. His first impulse was to bar her entrance until Michael had clarified the purpose of her call. His friend had explained how Miss Walker was posing as a Bonaparte, and how the elite of the city had taken her to their bosoms. Although he relished a good joke, it wasn't enough to open his establishment to a curious woman only interested in spreading her reputation. What Michael had to say next, however, had given him reason to change his mind.

For two years, Martin Masterson was a steady customer, losing enough to compensate for his foul temper. In the last week, though, he'd heard rumors of Masterson loudly complaining that perhaps Dunnemores couldn't wait until you got there before it took your money. No one believed his grumblings, yet Terry resented the blemish on his reputation. He'd worked hard to reestablish his business—a business built on honesty. He'd learned that in gambling, the percentages were always in favor of the house and there was no need to risk anything underhanded. For days he'd been pondering the best way to respond to Masterson's implications and this afternoon Michael had supplied the answer. He'd let the royal impostor do it. If she was as good as Michael said she was, then Masterson would get his comeuppance . . . and by a woman, no less. It was perfect.

A willing participant in the farce, Terry Dunnemore smiled as he made his way to the couple. She was stunning, he thought, as he came closer. The wide gown of night-blue was an enticing contrast to the creaminess of her skin. Her dark hair was pulled back from her face and held by two small combs with sprigs of oleander attached. She was a combination of simple elegance and feminine confidence.

Stopping in front of her, he watched as she extended her hand in a graceful offering. For some reason, even though he knew she was no Bonaparte, he found himself automatically bowing over her white-gloved fingers in a formal salute. As he raised his head, he noticed her unusual eyes, the pale freckles on her cheekbones, and the natural sensuality of her mouth. Ah, Michael, he thought with an immediate envy, you don't stand a chance against her.

Reminding himself that Michael was a long-standing friend, he cleared his mind of carnal thoughts and introduced himself. "Welcome to Dunnemores, Miss Bonaparte. I'm Terrence Dunnemore."

Under the fingers of her left hand, she could feel the tension leave Kevin's arm and she favored the attractive man who stood before her with another smile. "Thank you, Mr. Dunnemore, for permitting me to visit your establishment." She looked about the large room. "I'm very impressed."

Terrence Dunnemore acknowledged her compliment with a nod, as she continued. "I'm from New Jersey and there is talk of building several casinos along the shoreline. I was interested to know what one might look like."

"I hadn't heard that," Dunnemore said while shaking Kevin's hand. "Maybe I should travel north to see if I might extend my business."

Looking at Kevin, he added, "Your uncle is here tonight. Perhaps you'd care to join him at the blackjack table?"

Kevin glanced at Kate and she nodded, positive now that Michael had already talked to Terrence Dunnemore about her. As they walked through the room, she continued to smile at the startled men. She found it odd that many were dressed in Northern uniforms and they were sitting next to civilians. It appeared as though the green grass of the battlefield had been replaced by the green felt of a gaming table. She couldn't help but wonder how many of them were still fighting the war, and what the nightly outcome was.

Even though he was dressed in a black suit, instead of a nightshirt, Kate had no trouble recognizing Martin Masterson. As they neared, she watched as he rose from his seat. He was older than she had thought on the nights they had haunted him. Bent at the shoulders, he stared at her from small, calculating eyes. Under other circumstances she might have been upset by his perusal, but tonight she was confident. Here, in this amusingly decorated casino, she was in her element. Here she was superior to almost every man in the room . . . and that included Martin Masterson.

She smiled into his cold eyes as Kevin introduced them. "Uncle Martin, may I present Miss Kathleen Bonaparte?"

As if it were her due, Kate extended her hand for his attention. She had to bite the inside of her lip to stop a grin as Masterson lowered his head and bowed over her held fingers. *Ahh . . . royalty,* she thought. This could get habit-forming. Right now, though, it was very useful.

"How do you do, Mr. Masterson? I hope we haven't interrupted your entertainment this evening."

Martin cleared his throat. "No . . . no, you haven't."

"Might we sit with you?" Kevin asked, already holding out a chair for Kate.

Seeing no way out of it, Masterson gave his consent as his nephew seated the young woman between them. Just as he was about to crush his cigar out, he saw a small, gloved hand touch the sleeve of his suit.

"Please don't on my account. I do so love the aroma of a good cigar." It was a blatant lie, yet worth it when she saw Masterson's look of approval. Turning to Kevin, she said, "Might we have something to drink? At dinner tonight the fish was so salty I swear I can still taste it."

Overhearing her remark, Terry signaled a waiter and within less than a half a minute a tray containing filled champagne glasses was presented to the trio. Accepting a fragile crystal glass she beckoned Terrence Dunnemore to bend his head. In a low voice she spoke to the casino's owner while feeling every eye in the room on her.

Nodding, Dunnemore straightened, picked up a glass of champagne and addressed his customers. "Gentlemen! If I might have your attention, please?" Seeing he'd already had it before he'd even made the request, Terry continued. "Miss Bonaparte asks that you forgive her intrusion and begs you to continue, as if she weren't here." He smiled. "In return, she promises never to reveal that you were."

Kate heard the laughter and a few shouts of "Bravo!" or "Vive la France!" Raising her glass in a toast, she smiled at the roomful of pleased men. She hadn't ruined a perfectly good evening for them . . . and she was about to make it much more interesting. As the men settled back to their games, Kate couldn't help but wonder where Michael was hiding—and what he was thinking.

Standing behind a smoky glass window in Terry Dunnemore's office, Michael intently watched his brother and Kate. He had felt an immense surge of possessiveness when she'd entered the room, for the masculine interest was almost a tangible wave that quickly spread through Dunnemores. It hadn't been just curiosity either. Kathleen was an exotically beautiful woman. He resented that he must stay hidden and allow others to stare. In all truth, he couldn't blame them, and again admitted a grudging admiration for Kate. In her typical fashion, within a matter of minutes, the lovely Kathleen Walker/Sheridan/Bonaparte controlled the room. Leaning his arm against the window frame, he continued to watch her as she conversed with his uncle. Be careful, Kate, he silently warned. Martin is no fool.

"Are you here to observe, Miss Bonaparte? Or do you wish to play?"

Taking her eyes away from Masterson's arthritic fingers, Kate smiled up at the casino's owner. "I was thinking, Mr. Dunnemore, that I might try my luck at your table."

Seeing the man's grin, she reached into her purse and brought out a stack of money. "I would like to buy a hundred dollars worth of chips, please."

Kevin cleared his throat, yet she ignored him. It was part of her share of the robbery. It also seemed to her the height of irony that she would use Martin Masterson's money to defeat him. She knew Michael, wherever he was hiding, would appreciate it.

She played conservatively at first, losing occasionally to the house. She also passed up cards that helped Masterson win. Sensing Kevin would be upset by her plan, she took her time about setting it into action. When she had lost seventy dollars, she finally heard Masterson's gloating remark.

"I beg your pardon?" Kate asked politely.

The old man shook his gray head while chortling back his reply. "It was nothing."

"Please," Kate insisted in a slightly louder voice.

Feeling very secure in his position, and luckier than usual with the cards, Martin looked at the woman next to him and said, "I was only remarking to myself that your less than inspired showing tonight proves a woman's place is still in the drawing room, rather than a gaming room."

Kate was so pleased with Masterson's chauvinistic remark, she could have kissed his wrinkled cheek. Having heard about his reputation from Michael and Kevin, she had depended on Martin to set himself up. As if thoroughly enjoying his observation, Kate smiled at the old man while noticing the attention being paid to both of them from those close enough to overhear it.

"But I've only just started, Mr. Masterson. I don't believe Lady Luck takes into account whether one is male or female before deciding to bestow her favors. I would ask that you give me the time to prove my worth."

"Yes, Martin," a distinguished elderly man insisted. "Miss Bonaparte has only started. Her chances of winning are as good as yours. Why she might just come out ahead of you tonight."

Several others laughed their approval and patted the back of the speaker. Kate could see a controversy brewing and she delighted in starting it, for it was going exactly as she had planned.

Not at all happy with being the object of ridicule, Masterson turned to fully face the young woman at his side. "Would you care to wager, madam, which of us leaves this table a winner?"

She picked up her glass of champagne and delicately sipped. "It wouldn't be a fair wager, sir. You have already accumulated a good amount of winnings." She looked to the large stack of chips in front of him.

Sensing her indecision and cautiousness, he hurried to add, "We shall begin even, then. How much will you start with?"

Replacing her glass onto the table, Kate opened her purse and brought out another hundred dollars. She placed it next to her small pile of chips. Allowing the tiny red disks to filter through her fingers, she said, "I have one hundred and thirty dollars, Mr. Masterson. Not a great deal of money, I'm afraid."

The cold, calculating look in his watery eyes turned to pure greed. "It's quite enough to prove my point, madam."

Refusing to be goaded into an argument, Kate retained her poise and gave the answer all were waiting to hear. "On behalf of my gender, I accept your challenge, sir."

She heard a murmuring of approval as Kevin leaned closer to her ear. "Are you sure of this, Kate?" he whispered.

Smiling, she patted his arm as Martin stood up to stretch his legs and receive some good-natured teasing from his peers. "Stop worrying," she whispered back to Kevin. "I know what I'm doing. If you're nervous, why don't you go to the bar and have a drink?" Casting her eyes about the garishly appointed room, she added, "And why don't you get one for your brother . . . wherever he's hiding. I'm sure by now he can use one."

She played ruthlessly, making sure either she or the

344

dealer won—and it was made so much easier since only one deck of cards was used, instead of the several decks she'd had to memorize in the past. She allowed Masterson no mercy, despite his constant grumblings and accusations. They had already changed dealers three times because Masterson had questioned the men's honesty. Martin Masterson's loud, boastful attitude had turned nasty and Kate's dislike of the man grew stronger with each hand played. She decided, after the man again demanded another dealer, that she was tired of the game . . . and of him. It was time to play her real hand.

Leaning back in her cushioned seat, she visibly relaxed as she gazed at the angry, frustrated man next to her. Together, the two of them had attracted almost every player in the room. She'd heard them place private bets between themselves and Terrence Dunnemore, who now seemed more of a bookmaker than a casino owner. Nor had her concentration on the game been so intense that she hadn't heard the odds constantly changing. It must infuriate Martin to know she was now favored to win.

"I insist on a new dealer!" Martin demanded before throwing back another whiskey and water. "You, Dunnemore! You deal—"

Kate straightened and picked up a deck of cards. Holding them out to the old man, she said in a calm voice, "If you question the integrity of every dealer, perhaps you would be more comfortable dealing them yourself? I will play against just you, Mr. Masterson. Surely you trust yourself."

Amid the excitement her offer had caused, Terrence Dunnemore's voice rose above the rest. "Now wait a minute! I'm not letting Masterson loose with my money. What if . . ."

"Mr. Dunnemore, Mr. Masterson and I will use our own money," Kate politely interrupted. "With your permission we would only be using your cards, and he will be seated across from me—instead of at my side." She had acquired over four hundred dollars and estimated Masterson's chips had been reduced close to that amount. They were evenly matched . . . Well, almost, she thought happily as Terrence Dunnemore could find no objection to her proposition.

Michael knew he would not be able to remain in Terry's office for much longer without yelling out his frustration. He'd practically worn the smoked stain off the glass as he'd pressed his face against it to see better. Already he had opened the office door in an attempt to at least hear what was going on outside the small room. Just from the noise and the excitement in the air, he knew Kate was doing what she did best—creating trouble. Only now, he admitted with a supreme relish, it was happening to his uncle. God! He wished that he could be out there next to her. Not that he wanted to take away from her accomplishment. On the contrary, he only desired to witness her moment of victory. Smiling, in spite of the tense knot in his stomach, Michael was assured of Kate's triumph. She was a far superior player than his uncle . . . Hell, he grudgingly acknowledged, she was better than any man he'd ever known . . . including himself. Grinning, he pressed closer to the window.

In less than half an hour, Kate had consistently reduced Martin Masterson's chips to a lonely few. She watched no one but her opponent, taking note of the slight tremor in his hands, the quick beading of perspiration on his brow. She had merely blinked at his muffled oaths and curses, and demands to know how she did it.

Ready to play her final hand, Kate carefully placed her ante onto the green felt. It was five hundred dollars—four hundred and twenty dollars more than Masterson had in front of him.

"Madam, I cannot cover your bet," he said with a strangled anger.

Kate leaned back in her chair and steepled her fingers under her chin. "There must be something you have, besides money, that would entice me to continue playing." Her eyes never left his.

"Dunnemore will credit me with the additional money," Martin stated while looking at the casino owner for confirmation.

Kate quickly waved her hand in dismissal. "I'm afraid that won't do, Mr. Masterson. Have you nothing on you? Some jewelry? A watch, perhaps? I did promise my maid a new piece for her brother."

Automatically, Masterson's hand went to the fob at his waist pocket. Bringing it out, he glanced downward. The piece had been his father's, and his father before him. He hesitated placing it on the table, for the woman's luck had been exceptional—and he would loath parting with the heirloom. Besides, Lydia's rage would be fierce. She intended it for Kevin.

To lose would be a public humiliation, and there were too many here tonight eager for it. Knowing he had to play it out until the end, he cursed the confident woman opposite him and reached into his jacket. Slowly, he withdrew from the inside of his coat a small object wrapped in cloth, and he didn't know whether he was damned or blessed for bringing it with him. His intention was to find a suitable buyer from the wealthy Northerners who frequented the gaming hall. Perhaps it was fortunate he'd not inquired earlier, for now it seemed his salvation.

Kate's breath caught at the back of her throat, her heart pounded against the wall of her chest, and the hair on her arms rose in anticipation. Her eyes were glued to the aged fingers as they removed, with agonizing slowness, the white cotton covering.

Oh my God! The light from the overhead chandelier picked up rays of green hues as the uncut emerald was revealed for inspection. She swallowed several times, attempting to bring moisture back into her mouth as the crowd pressed closer to see for themselves. Never had she dreamed he would have it with him! She'd only hoped to goad him into a rematch with higher stakes.

"I believe this will cover your bet, madam."

She drew her eyes away from the emerald and concentrated on Michael's uncle. She refused to look at Kevin for fear his expression would give them away. "Yes," she said in an unnaturally calm voice. "I agree."

Michael watched as Ryan Barrington left the crowd and slowly made his way to the office. It had been sheer luck that he'd recognized his friend and fellow blockade runner standing at the bar. Desperate to find out what was going on with Kate, and just as anxious to speak with Ryan, Michael had chanced discovery in order to pull one of Terry's waiters into the office and send him back out with a note for Louisiana's state representative. After a near comical reunion, the two men had hastily discussed Michael's death and resurrection. With a promise to quickly return with a report, Ryan had left the office and joined the crowd surrounding the two players.

Nearly pulling Ryan back in, Michael demanded, "Well? Tell me! What's she doing?"

Ryan straightened his jacket and leaned against the closed door. "I would say, my friend, she's doing quite well."

Michael grinned widely as he glanced back through the window. "She's winning, isn't she? God, Ryan, I've never met anyone like her in my life."

Watching his young friend, Ryan recognized the look in Michael's eyes. It went deeper than admiration. "She reminds me," he said quietly, "of my wife. Brianne also has a fondness for emeralds."

"Emeralds?"

"Why, yes. That's what your uncle came up with to cover his ante." He watched as Michael tightly grasped the frame of the window.

"Damn that old bastard!"

Seeing the pain in his friend's face, Ryan placed his hand on Michael's shoulder. "Listen," he whispered in a comforting voice, "there's a better way to solve your problems. Come with me to Washington. I have a friend there who's starting to investigate some of the injustices in the South. From what you've told me, I think he'd be very interested in your story."

Michael turned his head and noticed, for the first time, the threads of gray at Ryan's temples. "Who is he? Who in Washington would care about my father's reputation?"

"His name is Frank Adams. He served under Grant and formed a very effective information-gathering organiza—"

"A Yankee spy? You think I'd trust someone like that to extract justice?"

Ryan shook his head sadly. "The war's over, Michael. Frank Adams is probably the one person who can help you. I know for a fact that he'd be interested in finding out how Martin Masterson accumulated all that wealth for your family." He looked out the stained-glass window. "You can't do it alone, you know. Especially if everyone thinks you're dead. Christ! I'd only heard tonight of your demise . . . and here you are. Your hands are tied in Charleston, Michael. Come to Washington. At least give me a chance. I might be able to help you."

Following Ryan's line of vision, Michael turned his head and looked back at the players, his eyes appearing cold and hard . . . and old, too old for such a young man. Could he leave Kate?

Of their own accord, the crowd hushed as Masterson picked up the deck. Kate was oblivious to the many bodies that encircled them. Although her ears didn't pick up the clinking of glasses, she was unaware that even the waiters had left their posts to see the outcome. She had even pushed the emerald out of her mind. Nothing mattered to her except the cards. Now, if only her hands would stop shaking . . .

Masterson dealt her two eights. His fingers quickly moved to place a card facedown on the felt in front of himself and cover it with a seven of diamonds. As she stared at the small figures, her mind whirred like the drive of a computer scanning her mental screen for those cards already played. There were three face cards and two aces still in the deck. It was that unknown, hidden card that nagged at her brain. If he had one of the face cards in the hole, he would have seventeen. Everything depended on that card facing the table. With a boldness born of practice, she took a deep breath and said, "I'm going to split the eights."

She heard a unanimous gasp rise around her. Unfazed by the crowd's reaction, she stared at her opponent. She could tell he thought she'd just revealed her inexperience, for he was positively gloating over his seven of diamonds.

Kate knew her limitations. She was a card counter. She couldn't control the sequence in which the cards were drawn. Yet, instinctively she'd felt it was the right decision. Masterson dealt her two cards, one on top of each, now separate, hand.

The old man and the young woman eyed each other for at least ten seconds before Kate slowly lowered her eyes to the felt table. She had been dealt the queen of spades, giving her eighteen. With only a moment's hesitation, Kate took a deep breath and identified the card resting on her second hand. The ace of hearts . . . nineteen. She exhaled slowly and raised her eyes to Martin's hand. Drawing out the suspense, he slowly turned over his hidden card. A four of clubs.

Kate drew on every bit of training from her past to keep her face impassive. He had eleven; all he needed to draw was a face card . . . and there were two more in the deck.

Confident, already gloating over his victory, he casually held the deck of cards in front of him and flipped over his last card.

351

The ace of diamonds . . .

Shutting out Masterson's ashen complexion, Kate closed her eyes and sagged back against the chair in relief. He'd gone over. She'd won the emerald!

"I don't know how you did it, but I congratulate you on your skill."

"That was the most remarkable hand I've ever seen."

"Brilliant! Splitting your eights . . ."

She smiled, accepted Kevin's quick kiss, yet didn't pay attention to any of them. Her eyes were locked with Masterson's. His movements were unsteady as he pushed himself away from the table; he appeared to need its support to remain upright. The color in his face had returned with an intensity, and his eyes glared a hatred that couldn't be veiled.

"Had you lost, madam, I would have demanded payment upstairs," he spat out in a hoarse voice. "I imagine a woman like you is skilled in many areas."

The surrounding laughter and excited conversation ceased, and Kate was aware of disapproving murmurs directed at Michael's uncle.

Straightening her shoulders, she remembered his earlier statement about a woman's place and lifted her chin. "Had I lost sir, I would hope I could be as gracious here as I'd try to be in any drawing room." She inclined her head in a regal manner. "Thank you for tonight's entertainment."

She was too excited to sleep and quietly slipped out of bed to turn up the lamp. After all the celebration and champagne, Kate knew she should rest, yet she wanted to look at the emerald just once more. Searching under

352

her mattress, she brought out the stone and unwrapped it. Inhaling with satisfaction, she shook her head. It was real . . . and in her hands. Just as she was about to turn it over, a weird, frightening sensation took hold of her and she felt the eerie presence of another. Chills immediately broke out at the back of her neck and ran up her scalp. Afraid, yet compelled, Kate slowly turned her head and looked over her shoulder.

He leaned almost casually against the French doors that led to the balcony. With his arms crossed over his chest, he continued to study her through hooded eyes. He didn't move—just stood there watching her. It was like the haunting . . .

Her mouth opened, yet no sound immediately emerged. It took a few seconds for her heart to slow down and her stomach to settle. She tried again, this time uttering his name with a mixture of fear and anticipation.

"Michael!"

Chapter 22

"I came to congratulate you."

Kate slid off the bed and clutched the emerald to her chest. "Well, you just about scared the hell out of me! Do you have something against using a door?"

Grinning, Michael pushed himself away from the balcony. "I did use one. It just wasn't the one you were expecting."

She wished she had on a robe, instead of the sheer white lawn nightgown that Mamie had sent over. Crossing her arms over her chest in an effort to hide herself, she tried to appear casual as she walked across the carpet. "Where were you hiding tonight?" she asked, picking up a matching wrapper from a chair and quickly pulling it around her.

Michael came closer. "I was in Terry Dunnemore's office. To be truthful, I could hear more than I could see."

Kate turned around and faced him. He looked just like a pirate from an old Errol Flynn movie: his beard was overgrown just enough to make him dashing

354

instead of unkempt. His white shirt was unbuttoned to the middle of his chest and his black pants were tucked into high riding boots. A sun-bleached lock of blond hair fell over his forehead and his eyes held a look of excitement. All he needed was an earring and he would be ready to plunder.

Grinning at her mental image, she circled around him. "Michael, you change roles as easily as I do. What happened to my surly carriage driver?"

His eyes narrowed and he looked down at his clothes. Shrugging, he said, "I stopped by Rose's home before I came here."

Kate nodded. "Which brings us back to your reason for sneaking into my bedroom. I believe you said something about congratulating me?"

He watched her nervous movements as she stayed far away from him. He also saw that her fingers were tightly clasped around the emerald. "I've already said it once, but it bears repeating. Congratulations, Kate. From everything I've heard, it was a magnificent performance." He inclined his head in acknowledgment.

She tried to detect some sarcasm but could find none. "Thank you," she said quietly. "Does this mean you're no longer angry with me?"

He threw back his head and laughed. "How could I be angry with you? You did exactly what you set out to do. Not only did you discover that Martin has the treasure . . . you regained part of it." His eyes turned serious. "I'm not angry with you, Kate. I admire you."

She blinked a few times in disbelief. Surely she couldn't have heard correctly. "You *admire* me?"

He nodded and took a step in her direction. "You are

355

the single most remarkable woman I have ever met. I was so proud of you tonight . . ."

Kate stepped backward. Flustered by his unexpected praise, she muttered, "I . . . ah, I never expected him to have the emerald. I was only trying to goad him into a rematch. He was—"

"He was beaten," Michael finished, coming closer. "And you were magnificent," he stated, grinning as he watched her backpedaling away from him.

She shook her head and pulled her robe tighter, as if for protection. What the hell was he doing? She felt like he was stalking her around the bedroom. "I was . . . I was scared to death he had a . . . a face card in the hole. I . . . ah, I didn't know. It was . . . luck. That's it," she stammered. "It was luck."

Michael's grin widened as he continued to follow her retreating steps. "Ah, no, Kate. It wasn't luck. It was skill; you set him up perfectly. Be proud of your accomplishment. I am."

She swallowed several times. Why did he have to look so damn handsome? And where was Rose when she needed her? Instinct was telling her to erect a barrier between herself and Michael, for the image of a pirate about to plunder was suddenly more vivid than before. "Listen," she said, hearing the near desperation in her voice. "You should have seen Kevin. I thought he would faint when I pulled out the money from the robbery. Then he almost fell off his chair when Martin took out the emerald. I was afraid to look at him, for fear that he would give it . . ."

In three quick strides he closed the distance between them and slammed her against his chest. "Shut up, Kate. You always did talk too much," he breathed into

356

her mouth.

As she inhaled with shock and indignation, he quickly slanted his lips over hers to stop any reply she might make.

His kiss jolted her with its overwhelming urgency. His tongue teased her with its sensual exploration as his arms pulled her even closer into the firm muscles of his body. She felt his hands roam over her back until they cupped her buttocks and lifted her against his hard arousal.

Gasping for breath, she pushed back from him. "Michael . . ." Gazing into his desire-filled eyes, she was unable to form any other words as his hands slid up to her shoulders.

Holding her firmly against him, he pushed the thin material of her nightgown down her arm and lowered his head. He feathered her exposed skin with warm kisses. "Not now, Kate," he whispered in a raspy voice. "God Almighty, don't talk now." Taking a deep breath, he searched her eyes and said, "I want you, Katie. Don't deny me . . . don't deny us."

She continued to stare and was unable to move. Her mind was warning her of the danger to her heart, yet her heart commanded her to recognize her own need and see it reflected in Michael's eyes. In a fraction of a second, her body made the decision as her fingers dropped the emerald into her pocket and slowly lifted to the buttons of his shirt. Pulling it away from him, Kate gasped as she viewed his chest. Her breath slowly left her lungs as she lay her cheek against him and felt the rapid beating of his heart.

"Michael . . ."

She breathed his name against the fine hairs on his

357

chest, setting off an intense flame of desire throughout his body. Sensing her surrender, Michael lifted Kate into his arms and brought her to the bed.

It was frantic and feverish, their bodies ruling their minds, demanding the release of a passion kept too long, too tightly under control. Each brush of skin, each stroke of the hand brought them closer to a frenzied breaking point. When she could no longer endure the exquisite pleasure of his kiss, the fine grazing of his beard against her skin as he ravaged her with his mouth, Kate opened herself to him. An astonished moan escaped her lips as she took him inside her. His searing heat warmed her, both physically and mentally, and she opened her eyes, memorizing the breathtaking image of Michael.

Holding her arms above her head, his fingers tightly intertwined with hers. She received and held him with a silkiness that aroused a fierce possessiveness within him. Never would he let another take his place. She was his . . . and he thrust deep within her to lay his claim. He felt all-powerful as he watched Kate gasp and sink her head back into the pillow with each pleasure-filled stroke. Committing to memory the way she bit her bottom lip to keep her voice under control, the way her blue eyes darkened with desire, Michael was engulfed with a rush of emotions. He wanted to take her with him, to release her tight hold on control, and he quickened his pace. He would prove to her tonight, and forever, that she was his alone.

The tight cluster of passion seemed to explode inside of Kate, sweeping her outside her body. She could hear Michael calling to her and she clung to his shoulders, unwilling to journey alone. Using her body, she strove to bring him with her, to free him from his earthly hold. She longed for him to soar with her—to where the pleasure was overpowering, the pain of loneliness a forgotten memory.

They were not two, but one, as together Kate and Michael left the reality of that room and briefly entered a spiritual place . . . a place where their bodies melded and their minds fused. Its intensity was a shattering, white-hot fulfillment that created exquisite aftershocks until slowly releasing them to a soothing gentleness. It was their time, claimed from eternity, a precise moment that would bind them forever.

Kate was afraid to break the silence, for fear that spoken words would reduce the magnitude of what they had just experienced. She lay quietly, with her head resting on Michael's damp shoulder, and listened to the sound of his breathing. Slowly caressing the growth of whiskers on his chin, she felt an aura of peace, a completion to her life that she'd never known before.

Michael inhaled deeply and closed his arm more tightly around her. "I would say this bed is far superior to any beach."

Kate grinned and nodded. She could hear a chuckle rising from his throat.

"I can't believe I almost miss that damn duck! For some reason, he made me feel lacking . . ."

Snuggling closer, she whispered into his chest, "If he were here now, Michael, I'm sure Casanova would have applauded."

He tilted her face up to his. "He would have, wouldn't he?" he asked seriously as he searched her eyes.

359

Nodding, Kate pushed the hair back off his forehead and lightly kissed his lips. "You were remarkable," she quietly noted.

"*We* were remarkable," he corrected. His gaze was intense as he held her closer. "I've never experienced anything like that before . . . not ever, Kate. And I certainly never expected to find it with a wife."

She tensed, and tried to push away from him but his hold on her tightened. "Don't," he pleaded in a soft voice. "Does it bother you so much to think of us as married?"

She couldn't answer him. Why did he have to talk? Why did he have to ruin everything?

"You're pulling away from me, Kate. I can feel it."

She shook her head in denial, yet her body refused to relax. Capturing her face within his palms, he stared into her eyes and softly asked, "Can't you tell me? Maybe saying it out loud will finally exorcise it."

She pushed harder and this time he released her. Scrambling out of the bed, she picked up her robe and quickly put it around her. "I don't want to talk about it," she said with a finality. "It's over."

"It isn't over," he countered, sitting up and pulling the sheet to his waist. "If it were over, it wouldn't be coming between us. You know what you're doing, don't you? You're making me pay for that man's sins."

Crossing her arms over her chest, she looked back at him. He was right. He wasn't Jon, yet he was still a threat . . . simply because he was male. And he wanted something from her that she vowed never to again give. Her trust.

"At least sit here on the bed, so we can talk," he offered. "Don't put any more distance between us than there already is."

She conceded to that. She would talk to him, try to make him understand, but she couldn't reveal the dark secret she'd carried inside for so many years. She couldn't relive that shame—even for Michael.

His heart went out to her as she hesitantly sat on the edge of the bed. She was too important to him to let some faceless stranger control her life. He wanted to free her of the man, to break the strong hold her first husband still seemed to have over her.

Taking her hand, his thumb gently caressed her fingertips. "Tell me his name again. What was he like?"

Her shoulders slumped in defeat, as if just remembering the man's name was painful. "Jonathon . . . Jonathon Ashford," she murmured.

"And what was he like?" Michael again asked, realizing that her answers were also going to be painful to hear.

She stared at the flowered patterns on the rug. "He was an actor."

"Was he good? Was he handsome?"

She nodded.

"How did he treat you? Was he kind?" Each question was torn out of him; each answer dragged from her.

"At first, until we moved to California."

"What happened there? What changed him?" He watched as she took her hand from his and pushed dark strands of hair away from her face.

"A lot of things: success, a different life-style." She shook her head and shrugged. "I don't know, Michael. I don't want to go on with . . ."

"You said he was unfaithful to you," he persisted. "You said it was the reason you divorced him. Is that why you're so afraid? Is that why you can't trust . . ."

Holding her hand up, she interrupted his interrogation. "Just stop it, all right? You don't have the right to ask these questions. What gives you the right?"

He grabbed her hand and pulled her closer to him. "I have the right, Kate. I want to know everything because . . . because I love you!" His face was contorted with the emotion and pain his admission had cost.

She tried to free herself as tears sprang to her eyes. "Don't love me, Michael! Please . . . I'll stay with you. I'll do anything you want, but don't put that pressure on me. I couldn't take it again . . . I couldn't go through it again . . ."

"Why?" he demanded, his own eyes filling. "What did he do to you?"

"He betrayed me!" she nearly screamed, no longer able to fight the tears.

Holding her by the shoulders, he said gently, "You found him with another woman. Kate, you're not the first . . ."

She almost laughed with derision.

"What? Damn it, Kate, what happened?"

He felt her withdraw from him and knew if he didn't break through now, there would be a part of her forever closed to him. He refused to accept that. "Kate, I never learned how to love, but it seems you've forgotten. You're building a wall around you." He ran a hand through his hair in frustration. "If you continue, soon it'll be too strong for me to break through. Why can't you trust, Kate? *Why?"*

Silence.

Gently shaking her shoulders, he again demanded,

"What happened? What was in that room when you saw your husband and another woman? Tell me," he pleaded. "Can't you see that you need to get it out of you? Say it aloud! Say it and be done with it forever!"

She covered her face with her hands as the vivid picture that she had pushed to the back of her mind quickly rose to the surface. Again, she experienced the shock, the betrayal, and the destructive humiliation that had nearly destroyed her. "It wasn't a woman," she sobbed. "He wasn't with a *woman . . .*"

Michael's eyes widened in confusion until realization finally came. "Oh, God," he breathed aloud, and quickly pulled her to his chest. Soothing her, he stroked her hair and let her cry. He listened as she haltingly told him the rest: how she had needed to prove her femininity, how she had nearly lost herself in her search for revenge, and, finally, how she had fled from California and started to rebuild her life in the safety of her mother's home. He experienced anger, sympathy, and hope.

Pushing her hair behind her ear, he whispered, "It's finally over, Kate. That man, that memory—they don't have the power to hurt you any longer. You're free. You're free to trust another. Trust me. I promise I won't betray you."

It was like being reborn, without any guilt, any fears, or haunting memories from the past, and she clung to Michael, relishing the feeling of security she found in his arms. She wanted to trust him, wanted to begin anew—

"I'm not asking you to say the words, Kate. I can't even believe *I* said them. I'm just asking that you trust me not to hurt you. We can begin with that."

Shifting on the bed to gain access to his face, she felt something heavy in her pocket and reached down to investigate before kissing him. As she brought out the emerald, she lifted her eyes and smiled at the man she now knew she loved. It was too new, too fragile, and she was frightened of the emotion. She still feared telling him. Sniffling, her smile widened. She would first show him.

She held the jewel between them and watched as Michael's eyes examined it. "It's yours," she stated simply and laughed at his astonished expression.

"You won it. It was always yours."

She shook her head. "You're forgetting our partnership. I promised you the emerald in exchange for your help."

"But I didn't help you. It was your own skill that got the emerald back. I seem to recall my promising to help you regain the treasure. I haven't done that."

She placed the stone in his palm and closed his fingers over it. "Compared to what you've done for me tonight, Michael, the treasure is insignificant. What you've helped me regain in this room is much more valuable."

She watched as his features tightened, as if he were trying to control himself. "Do you think, Kate," he asked in a hoarse voice, "that the legend is real?" He searched her face and bathed it with love. "Look what it brought me . . ." he stated with wonder. Absently placing the jewel on a bedside table, he gathered her into his arms. Once more he laid her head back against the pillows while brushing her face with soft, adoring kisses.

364

"I'm going to make love to you," he stated in an emotion-filled voice. "And it's going to be slow and leisurely. I'm going to discover every inch of you," he promised while opening her robe and feasting his eyes on her exposed skin. She was beautiful—and finally his.

"I'm starved for you, Kate," he muttered thickly as he watched her breasts react to his words. "No one will ever take this night away from us."

It was the hardest decision he'd ever had to make. Buttoning his shirt, he looked down at the lovely vision asleep in bed. She was part of him now. What had started as a fascination with a beautiful woman and a sensual mermaid became love—something he had never thought to experience. She was his future, his whole world, and he refused to waste his life on revenge. He wanted to openly claim her, to walk into his home and introduce her to his mother. Lydia Sheridan might have denied him a lifetime of love, but Kate would give of it freely. And he vowed not to waste any more time in foolish plans of revenge. Ryan had been right. The way to vindicate his father wasn't here in Charleston. It was with the proper authorities. If he could find no help in Washington, then he was done with it. In the quiet of the night, he'd made up his mind that he would leave the city that held so many painful memories. He would take Kate back to New Jersey and start over again there. The only thing that mattered was that she was with him, standing next to him. But a truth, so clear in its wisdom, had also invaded his thoughts. He would never be free to begin a future with

Kate unless he finished with his past. It was then he'd made the decision to go with Ryan.

Exhaling, he picked up the small piece of paper while reaching for the emerald. He straightened the pillow next to her dark, shining hair and placed the heavy jewel on top of his note.

His message to Kate was only two words: Trust me.

Chapter 23

Rose Pringle observed Kate as she stretched in front of the window. The young woman's movements were slow and graceful, and when she turned back toward the room her face held a look of happiness.

"It's a beautiful day, Rose," Kate joyfully announced as she came to the small table that held their breakfast. Seating herself, she ignored the silver trays of food and instead reached for a crystal bowl of flowers. Picking up a pale-blue clematis, Kate inhaled its delicate fragrance. "What shall we do today, Rose? It's too pretty to stay inside."

Spreading peach marmalade on a thick slice of bread, Rose softly remarked, "You and I need to have a little talk, Kathleen. Michael woke me early this morning."

She slowly placed the flower back into the bowl and stared at the woman seated across from her. Not now, Kate thought as she took a deep breath. She didn't want anything to ruin this morning, especially a lecture. Why in the world had Michael gone to Rose's room? He might as well have announced that he'd spent the night. Kate mentally shook herself. She would not allow anything, even Rose, to take away her memories of last night, nor the warm, tender feelings of this morning when she'd awakened and had seen his note under the emerald. Trust me, it had read . . . and she would.

"Aren't you even curious to know what he said?" Rose asked.

Watching the older woman wipe a speck of marmalade from the corner of her mouth, Kate shrugged her shoulders. "I have a feeling you're going to tell me," she said with a smile.

Rose poured her a cup of coffee and lifted the lid from a tray of fluffy eggs. "Maybe you should eat something first. All this lovely food goin' to waste . . ."

Shaking her head, Kate laughed. "Now you've got me curious. What *did* Michael have to say?"

Rose sat back in her chair and gave Kate a look of pity. "He's gone, Kathleen," she said in a sympathetic voice.

For a fraction of a second her empty stomach rebelled as it lurched upward. "Of course he's gone," Kate said calmly as her stomach relaxed. "He couldn't be seen here in the daytime."

Rose shook her head. "No. I mean he's gone . . . to Washington."

The muscles in her body acted as one as they automatically tensed. "Washington?" The word was forced out of her throat and she felt as if she were struggling. Swallowing several times, she grabbed the arm of her chair. "You're wrong. He would . . . he would have told me last night. He wouldn't just leave without telling me . . . He wouldn't!"

Looking embarrassed, Rose placed a teaspoon of sugar in Kate's coffee. "You go ahead and be angry, child," she said in a harsh voice as she pushed the cup closer to Kate. "I'm not too pleased myself that he leaves it up to me to tell you like this."

Ignoring the coffee, Kate demanded, "He's really gone?"

Rose nodded while nervously twisting her napkin between her fingers. "This isn't the way I'd planned it. Who'd have thought he'd up and take off for Washington with that politician friend of his—"

"What are you talking about?" Kate struggled to overcome the returning nausea. "What politician friend? What did you plan?"

Rose deliberately placed her napkin onto the table and lifted sheepish eyes toward Kate. "I thought absence would make the heart grow fonder. It worked with my Willis. That's why I moved us to this hotel. And it was working too, Kathleen! Why Kevin told me that Michael was as ornery as a trussed-up—"

Kate raised her hand to stop her. "What politician friend?" she impatiently demanded.

Rose rearranged the cutlery on the table. "He's from Louisiana, I think. Ryan Barrington. Michael said he was a blockade runner durin' the war, too."

Confused, Kate shook her head. Michael wouldn't do this to her, not after last night. He couldn't have just left! "Wait a minute, Rose. Start at the beginning. What did Michael say to you this morning?"

The smaller woman straightened her shoulders. "I knew he was here, Kathleen. I heard the two of you talkin' last night, but I took off for my bedroom and

369

minded my own business. Besides, I was hoping all along he would lose that stubborn streak and—"

Too upset to be embarrassed, Kate forced a smile and again interrupted Rose. "I'm sorry I raised my voice," she apologized. "I'm not upset with you and I know you've been playing matchmaker. I appreciate everything you've done and I'm sorry you've been put in the middle like this." She leaned into the table. "Rose, you have to tell me what Michael said this morning," she implored. "You're the only one who knows why he's left."

Nodding, Rose said in a careful voice, "He came at dawn. Told me he had to go to Washington with his friend to try and get some help in clearin' his daddy's name. Said he was going to see if the government was interested in a southerner's troubles . . . whether he could finish this thing with his uncle the right way, through the law and all."

Kate's mouth opened in surprise. "Why couldn't he tell me this? Why did he have to leave without telling me? Didn't he think I could be trusted?"

Rose shook her head. "He didn't want you to know because he said you'd insist on going with him. And he didn't have the time to talk you out of it. He said he had to leave right away to catch his friend before he left the city."

Her shoulders sagged in defeat and Kate sat back in her chair. "He's really gone," she stated with disbelief.

Standing up, Rose walked behind Kate's chair and gently pulled the younger woman's dark hair over her shoulders. As she leaned down, she whispered near Kate's ear, "He also asked me to take care of you until he comes back. He said he's coming back for you,

Kathleen. And that you'd understand after reading his note. You did find a note, didn't you?"

Kate stared at her distorted reflection in the silver coffee pot and nodded. *Trust me.* Two small words that asked so much. Yet if she believed in last night, in the beauty of their union, in the emotional binding of their hearts, then she had no other choice. Taking a deep breath, she reached up to pat Rose's hand and slowly smiled.

"I trust Michael," she stated in a small voice and sat up straighter. "I *do* trust him," she reaffirmed with more strength and almost laughed with relief when she realized that she wasn't just mouthing the words. That dark void of mistrust she had carried around for years had been lifted and replaced with the warmth and security of Michael's love. She had come so far, so very far, to find it.

Smiling broadly, she placed her napkin on her lap and announced in a happy voice, "You were right, Rose. It would be a shame to let all this food go to waste." She lifted a silver lid and asked, "Now, tell me what would you like to do today?"

Surprised and pleased with Kate's change of mood, Rose Pringle gave her a quick hug and returned to her chair. "I wasn't sure which to tell you about first," she said in an excited voice. "Michael's trip to Washington . . . or this."

Kate watched as Rose pulled out a small envelope from her skirt pocket. "It was delivered while you were dressing this morning. My guess is your little escapade to Dunnemores last night with Kevin burned a path to her ears."

Handing over the envelope, Rose added happily, "It

371

finally came, Kathleen. Lydia Sheridan has invited you to high tea!"

At precisely quarter to four that afternoon, Kate arrived at Michael's home. She didn't know if she was more nervous at the thought of meeting his mother or the chance of another confrontation with Martin Masterson. Smoothing the material of her dark-green watered silk, she silently blessed Mamie Legare's talent and straightened her shoulders. Thanks to Mamie she was dressed in the height of fashion, although she could have done without the large matching hat with its netted veil and huge satin bow that rustled annoyingly against her ear. Taking a deep breath, she pulled on the house bell.

"Afternoon, ma'am," the old Negro servant greeted her. As she walked into the marbled foyer, the man quietly announced, "Miz Lydia asked if you'd wait in the drawin' room."

Nodding, Kate followed the gray-haired servant to a side room that took her breath away with its opulence. As she stared at the white and gold appointments, the servant excused himself. She tried to acknowledge his words, yet her eyes continued to explore the beautiful room. It was decorated with period pieces of furniture: a large upholstered couch of pale peach was the single piece not of white. Its rolled arms matched the wood of the three chairs that surrounded a high table already set for tea with fine bone china and gleaming silver. The twelve-foot walls were painted in a soft white with the most exquisite cornices meeting the ceiling. The same carved molding was duplicated on the huge mantel over the fireplace, where two large urns were separated by a domed gold clock. And above it all hung an oversized painting of a man who obviously was related to Michael and Kevin.

"The portrait is of Gabriel Sheridan, painted in 1757 by Charleston's court painter Jeremiah Theus."

At the sound of the cultured southern voice, Kate spun around. Michael's mother slowly walked into the room, giving Kate time to compose herself. Dark-haired, with only distinguished streaks of gray at her temples, Lydia Sheridan was still a lovely woman. For Michael's sake Kate wanted to like her, and smiled as she remarked, "I can see the resemblance to your son in his eyes."

Lydia glanced up at the painting. "Really? I always thought Kevin had the Masterson eyes."

Had Kate only imagined the slight hardening sound of her voice? Wanting to make a better impression, she walked in Lydia's direction and extended her hand. "Thank you for inviting me, Mrs. Sheridan. Your home is lovely. I was admiring the intricate carvings—"

Weakly shaking Kate's hand, the woman interrupted in an almost bored voice. "The furnishings have been in the family for years. This set of chairs and sofa reputedly was used by Thomas Pinckney when he served in the Court of St. James from 1792 to 1796." Gliding farther into the room, she stopped in front of the tea table. "Please be seated, Miss Bonaparte. I've been very anxious to meet with you."

Sensing the lack of warmth in the woman's voice, Kate mentally steeled herself for the coming interview. She tried to appear casual as she sat down on the edge of a museum piece of furniture. That was it, Kate thought. She couldn't imagine Michael or Kevin as young boys in this room. She couldn't imagine *anyone* relaxing in this elegant room filled with priceless antiques. Even Lydia seemed distracted by it. Her recitation sounded bored, as though she'd memorized her lines over the years, and her voice held a note of impatience. Kate decided to remain silent and let Michael's mother set the tone.

"I must apologize, Miss Bonaparte. When I sent my invitation this morning I was unaware that I would have unexpected guests this afternoon." Lydia's eyes searched Kate's. "I do have an important matter to discuss with you, so perhaps it would be better if I called at your hotel later in the week."

Kate glanced at the silver tea service. "I'm afraid I don't understand, Mrs. Sheridan. You wish to discuss something important with me?"

Lifting her chin, Lydia's eyes narrowed slightly. "This was not a social invitation. To be blunt, unlike the rest of Charleston, I seriously doubt whether you have any relationship with the Bonapartes." Seeing Kate's astonished expression, Lydia pressed further. Waving her hand in dismissal, she stated, "Your lineage is of little importance to me. What is, is your relationship with my son."

For a second Kate thought she was talking about Michael. Pulling herself together, she quietly asked, "Your son?"

Lydia Sheridan sat stiffly on the edge of an opposite chair and, as Kate took in her perfect posture, her black dress with only the relief of a cameo at the collar, she thought Michael's mother resembled a waiting crow with her dark, piercing eyes. She wondered if Lydia ever allowed herself to laugh.

"I would have preferred to do this when I didn't have house guests," the woman impatiently noted. "However, since you are here . . . It has come to my attention that you're spending a great deal of time in my son's company. From my brother I've learned that you've frequented establishments that no decent woman would enter. I would like to know, madam, exactly what your intentions are."

Feeling the hostility reach across and envelope her, Kate stiffened against it and allowed a small smile. "My intentions?" she asked innocently.

Kate had to admire the woman's composure. Not a muscle moved, yet her glare was near regal. "I can see I'll have to be more direct. Last night you won a great deal of money and a certain valuable object from my brother. If you are seeking to obtain anything else from the Sheridan family, you will be disappointed. Kevin's future wife has arrived just this afternoon and I'm sure his engagement will be announced within days."

Kate could only stare at the woman. Helene! Here? For a few moments her brain refused to function as she fought down panic. Dear God, why did Michael have to leave her to face this? She forced herself to rely on her training and treat this insane situation like a poker hand. With a surge of willpower, she kept her face impassive. Relaxing her facial muscles, she met Lydia's triumphant stare. Was it possible that this cold, scheming woman was her mother-in-law? She searched the still beautiful face for some sign of underlying warmth, but the lines around the older woman's mouth were not put there by laughter or easy smiles. She could just imagine the look that Lydia was giving her bestowed on Michael. Although Kate had yet to experience motherhood, something innately maternal surged up within her. In that moment she hated Lydia Sheridan and what she had done to Michael by denying him love. Picturing him always searching for this woman's approval stirred up such a dislike for Lydia that it counterbalanced any news of Helene's arrival.

"I only wish Kevin happiness," Kate said smoothly. "I enjoy your son's company, Mrs. Sheridan. We've had many discussions, some of them very enlightening. For instance, he talks a great deal of your other son . . . ?"

Lydia's mouth tightened as she provided the name. "Michael."

Kate again smiled. "Yes. Michael. He was a war hero, wasn't he?"

The woman nodded.

Kate pressed on. "Kevin also said his brother was a near genius at investments. I believe he said that before the war Michael had increased Sheridan Shipping . . ."

"That has nothing to do with our discussion," Lydia interrupted.

Kate noted that the woman's composure had finally cracked, for she was pulling on the cameo at her throat. "I just wanted you to know that Kevin and I are good friends," she said smoothly. "Your son is a grown man, Mrs. Sheridan. I believe he's mature enough to choose his own friendships." Kate straightened and smiled tightly. "If Kevin wishes to continue that friendship, I'll certainly welcome his company." Motioning to the tea service, she stood up. "Since it's obvious that neither one of us wishes to share tea with the other, I think it would be best if I leave."

Not waiting for Lydia to rise, Kate merely nodded to her and turned toward the foyer.

"I can ruin you," she heard from behind. "I still have connections in the North and sufficient funds to investigate your claims of royal lineage. Right now you're enjoying yourself with the city's leading families. I don't care who you deceive, but if you continue your association with my son, I promise to expose you for the fraud you are."

Kate stopped walking and slowly turned around. How she disliked this cold woman who had manipulated both Michael and Kevin's lives, and it took every ounce of willpower to remain calm and not strike back. "Which one of us is the fraud, Mrs. Sheridan?" she asked dispassionately. "In the North, southern hospitality is legendary, along with the graciousness of a southern lady. Since coming to Charleston, you're my first disappointment. I have not found hospitality in this home, nor graciousness . . . nor, I'm afraid, have I found a lady."

Noting Lydia's pale, outraged expression, Kate made the wise decision to continue her departure. As the old servant hurried to open the front door, she heard a small, familiar voice coming from the circular staircase.

"Wiley, would you know where Mrs. Sheridan is?"

Common sense told her to keep walking, to leave the house before Helene recognized her, yet since braving Lydia Sheridan she felt it might be wiser to warn Helene herself. Turning back to the foyer, Kate hurried to the stairs. Despite the veiling over her face, she could tell Helene recognized her and quickly reached for her hand.

In a voice loud enough for all to hear, Kate said, "How do you do? I'm Kathleen Bonaparte, and you must be Kevin's new friend." Watching Helene's startled expression, she promptly added, "I'm afraid I'm in a bit of a rush, but do ask Kevin to bring you to the hotel for dinner so we can all get acquainted."

Pumping Helene's hand to get movement back into the girl, Kate gave her a meaningful look and hastily returned to the door. Ignoring Lydia's appearance in the foyer, she somehow managed to thank Wiley for holding the door open and didn't expel her breath until it was shut behind her. Not trusting herself to stop, Kate forced herself to walk at a slow pace until she was outside the wrought-iron gate. She had only gotten a few feet up the street before she leaned against the high brick wall for support.

Staring at the cobbled street she waited until her heartbeat slowed and her breathing lessened. As perspiration broke out over her body, she tore the damned hat from her head and whispered in frustration, "Get back here, Michael Sheridan! Everything is about to blow sky high . . . and I'm not facing it alone!"

Frank Adams was not in Washington, and Michael's disappointment was lessened by Ryan's offer to accompany him to Baltimore. He appreciated his friend's concern and the fact that Ryan was willing to postpone his own business in the capital to travel with him to Maryland. It was a time of transition in Washington and even Michael found himself caught up in the political strategies taking place in the capital.

President Johnson's impeachment trial was finally over and the disappointed Democrats had overlooked Johnson's hopes for a second term and nominated Horatio Seymour to run against Grant. Michael's sympathies went to Johnson, for the man had truly attempted to stop the confiscation of Rebel property and the continued exclusion of many southern states from the Union. One didn't have to be a politician to realize that the problems facing the country were great . . . and that most southerners held very little hope of them being quickly resolved.

"I think it's that brownstone on the right," Ryan remarked while pointing to the last in a row of large three-storied homes.

Maneuvering their carriage through the early evening traffic, Michael pulled in behind two other vehicles by the curb. Securing the reins, he looked to the man at his side. "I really do appreciate this, Ryan. I know you have your own business to take care of."

Ryan Barrington looked at the younger man and smiled. Michael's appearance had undergone a dramatic change since he'd seen him in the casino owner's office. Clean-shaven and dressed in an expensive suit, Michael Sheridan now looked more like a wealthy businessman and less like a former blockade runner and defeated southerner. Leaving the carriage, he waited until Michael joined him on the sidewalk before saying, "You forget, my young friend, I, too, brought those spoiled supplies in for the Confederacy. I have an interest in seeing the guilty parties caught."

Michael nodded and looked toward the house. "I'm wondering how your friend, Mr. Adams, is going to feel about it. Especially since we're about to interrupt him on a personal matter."

Walking up the steps, Ryan said, "Leave that to me. His assistant said he could be reached at this address if it were urgent. And I consider this urgent." Ringing the bell, he patted Michael's shoulder. "You can't remain dead forever, can you?"

A heavyset man with suspicious eyes opened the door and asked, "Yes? What can I do for you?"

It was Ryan who spoke. "We're here to see Mr. Frank Adams."

"He's expecting you?" the man demanded.

"Please tell him that Congressman Ryan Barrington is calling."

Nodding to Michael, the man impatiently asked, "And who's this?"

Before Ryan could speak, Michael answered, "Michael Thomas Sheridan. Is Mr. Adams in?" He'd had just about enough of the man's rudeness.

Surprisingly, the door opened wider as the man stepped aside and allowed them to enter. "Wait here," he said and left them in a small foyer.

Michael and Ryan exchanged looks as they watched the ill-mannered northerner walk over to a set of double doors and quietly knock. They could only hear the whispers of conversation before the door widened and a man too young to be Frank Adams walked in their direction.

Holding out his hand to Ryan first, the man identified himself. "Morgan Trahern, sir. It's a pleasure to meet you. I was in the gallery last month when you spoke on state rights."

Ryan smiled warmly and introduced Michael. "We

were told Frank Adams could be found here."

Morgan had to tear his eyes away from the younger southerner. Strange that just a few years ago the two of them had been enemies, probably willing to kill each other. And now he was shaking the man's hand in the foyer of his home. More than ever, Morgan was convinced of the insanity of the war. "Welcome to my home, Mr. Sheridan," Morgan said in a low voice before turning to the congressman.

He indicated the double doors with his head. "If you'll give me a moment, I'll speak with Frank. We were in the midst of a heated after-dinner discussion and the two of you might just be what we need right now."

Smiling, he left them and reentered his study.

Ryan glanced at Michael and nodded. "These are good people here, Michael. We both may benefit, and possibly learn, from what takes place tonight."

In less than a minute the doors to Trahern's study were parted and their host motioned for them to enter. "Please join us for cigars and brandy," Morgan offered with a smile. "We're all in agreement that a fresh point of view would be most welcome." His grin widened. "I'll have to ask you to keep your voices low, though. I've had an unexpected guest tonight who seems to have just dozed off."

Both Michael and Ryan smiled their understanding as they entered the room. Passing Trahern, they quickly came to a stop when they saw who else was in the paneled study. Rising from a leather wing chair was a thin, fair-haired man who regarded their shocked expressions with amusement. Along with Frank

381

Adams, another man rose to his feet. He, too, was tall and quickly glanced behind him to a third man asleep on a leather couch. The sleeping man was shorter, heavier in build and sported a famous mustache and beard. He was also the Republican candidate for the presidency . . . Ulysses S. Grant.

Chapter 24

Ryan was the first to recover. As Michael watched his friend shake hands with the two men, he found his stomach tightening. What the hell was he doing here? He felt almost a traitor as he took the few steps forward and shook the hands of Frank Adams and James Wauburne, campaign manager of the man who'd defeated the south. He practically missed the introductions that were made, and the explanation that Grant had sought out a quiet, friendly place to rest after an exhausting campaign schedule in Baltimore. Stunned, it was only instinct that guided him to a chair as Morgan Trahern offered a snifter of brandy. Grasping the thin crystal in his hands, Michael made a supreme effort to concentrate on the conversation going on around him.

"Perhaps Ryan can settle this argument," Frank Adams offered. "Who, in your opinion, has had a greater effect on baseball? Abner Doubleday? Or Alexander Cartwright?"

Leaning back in his chair, Ryan chuckled. "I was

prepared for a political debate. This issue, I'm afraid, can prove to be just as controversial."

James Wauburne smiled. "Spoken like a true politician, Congressman. What is your opinion, Mr. Sheridan?"

Michael felt everyone's attention shift in his direction. Sitting up straighter, he cleared his throat. "I believe Doubleday claims to have invented the game. As far as I can see, baseball was developed from rounders. And the English were playing that game as early as the 1600's." He noted Frank Adams' grin of agreement and Wauburne's frown. Quickly, he added, "Of course, the main difference is the way the runners are put out at base. I believe it was called soaking, actually throwing the ball at a runner who was off base. In baseball, the runner is tagged out."

"Exactly!" Wauburne exclaimed in a hushed voice. "And it was Doubleday who set forth the rules."

Frank Adams looked to the ceiling in exasperation. "Nonsense! In 1845 Alexander Cartwright started the Knickerbocker Baseball Club of New York and wrote a set of rules."

Wauburne jabbed the air with his cigar, an action reminiscent of his candidate. "Doubleday did it in '39!"

Adams was not to be intimidated. "And Cartwright did it again in '48, and '54. In 1848 he ruled on tagging first base to put a runner out on a ground ball, and in '54 the force out rule was established."

"What do you think, Morgan?" Wauburne asked, obviously looking for support. "You've been pretty quiet over there."

Leaning against his desk, Morgan grinned as he pushed the side of his dark mustache down with his

384

thumb. "I think it was in '46 when my father and I traveled to New York. One day we took a ferry to a place called Elysian Fields in Hoboken, New Jersey. The Knickerbocker Club played the New York Nine, and I'll never forget it. The Nine's won 23 to 1." He smiled widely to the men in his study. "If Alexander Cartwright wrote down the rules, he should have gotten players that knew how to read."

Joining in the muffled laughter, Michael pondered on the powerful men in the room. He found it strange that they seemed so impassioned about a game of baseball. Of course, most southerners learned of the game during the war. Union soldiers who knew about it often played for recreation. Prisoners of war, or those in an occupied city, watched and started playing themselves. It was a popular sport that was quickly spreading throughout the country.

"I hear there's talk that the Cincinnati Red Stockings are thinking of paying their players," Ryan remarked.

"It'll ruin the game," Morgan pronounced.

James Wauburne again waved his cigar in the air. "It's not in Doubleday's rules. Can't be legal."

Frank Adams ran his hand through his thinning hair and issued a muffled curse. "You're prejudiced against Cartwright because Abner Doubleday went to West Point with both you and your candidate." He glanced to the exhausted man on the couch.

"He also fought with the general in the Mexican War," Wauburne added quietly.

Ryan lifted his chin. "He was also a major general in the Union Army during this country's war."

The words came out of Michael's mouth before he could stop them. "Abner Doubleday was also the commander of the troops at Fort Sumter that fired the first shots by the North."

Morgan lifted his weight from his desk and stood up. "He also fought heroically at the Battle of Gettysburg," he stated defensively.

Never intending for the conversation to get out of hand, and not liking where it was now leading, Frank Adams also stood and lifted his glass. "I don't think any of us can deny he's a remarkable man . . . but whether or not he invented the game of baseball is another story. I'm sure the controversy will go on for years." Taking his empty glass to the liquor cabinet, he added, "At any rate, it's something we can't settle tonight and Ryan and Michael have traveled quite a distance to talk about a different matter."

Reseating himself, he crossed his legs, sipped his drink, and smiled. "How can I help you gentlemen?"

Ryan broke the uncomfortable silence. "Michael has a problem, Frank, that I think you'll find interesting."

All eyes turned toward the young southerner. He was staring at the shelves of books on the opposite wall, and it would have surprised everyone in the room to know of the internal battle taking place inside him. His father had raised him to be a gentleman. He'd been hotheaded and strong-willed in his life, yet an innate sense of manners and honorable conduct had been bred into him. Michael was ashamed that he had let his emotions rule him only moments ago, for he'd committed a serious breach in the code by insulting his northern host and his guests in his home.

Looking toward the tall, dark-haired man, he squared his shoulders and said, "I'd first like to apologize to you, Morgan. It was insensitive, and in poor judgment, to bring up something that had no bearing on the conversation." He turned his head and nodded to the sleeping general. "And was unquestionably resolved three years ago."

James Wauburne surprised him by smiling. "Well said, Mr. Sheridan. I think all of us here will admit this is an unusual mix tonight. Yet I still believe such a gathering of those who fought on both sides can also prove beneficial. This country needs a healing right now, and it has to start with men like ourselves. The power and prestige of the presidency has received a blow from this impeachment mess. It might surprise you to know that the general's glad President Johnson was acquitted. This country has seen enough upheaval in the last seven years. He believes in the potential of the United States, sir. The *United* States . . . North, South, West— All of them." For the first time that evening, he brought his drink to his lips and sipped the smooth brandy. Looking back at the young southerner seated across from him, he said quietly, "Ulysses Grant happens to love this country . . . and I believe you share that sentiment. There's something troubling you about it, or you wouldn't be here to see Frank."

Michael stared at the sleeping man he now knew with a certainty would be sitting in the White House within half a year. "My father," he began in a low voice, "was Chief Supply Officer for the Confederate Army . . ." He told his story, relating the reports following the end of the war concerning spoiled food, clothing, defective artillery. His voice became angry when he spoke of his father's trial—first in the newspapers, then in a courtroom presided over by corrupt officials. His grasp on the fragile brandy snifter

387

became even tighter while recalling his uncle's betrayal in pointing an accusing finger at his father and at the same time taking over the family business.

Michael's throat constricted with anger, betrayal, and pain. Yet his outrage could not be contained as he related how he had traced a link between Martin Masterson and Winston Barnett; how Martin had tried to involve Kevin in his cover-up. He didn't spare himself, either. He told of his secret takeover plans, how Ryan had been acting as his agent in slowly acquiring Sheridan Shipping stock. He even confessed the fiasco in Bermuda, losing the dowry of shares and kidnapping the wrong woman. For Kate's sake, he left out her name . . . and anything pertaining to the treasure. The last thing he added was Denny's story when he'd brought the *Rebel* into Charleston Harbour.

Taking a deep, steadying breath, Michael sat back and let his gaze fall over the men in the room. "So you see, gentlemen, except for a certain few in Charleston who know otherwise, you're listening to a dead man. However, my problems didn't end with my demise."

They had listened patiently, without interruption, and, sensing the end of the story, they came alive as each shot forth with questions.

"The South wasn't alone in receiving damaged goods," Morgan stated. "Remember that story of the Fourth Infantry Regiment? How many were issued rifles that misfired? The story going around was that the shipment was tampered with—that it was a case of sabotage by the South." He looked at Frank Adams. "I never believed it. We had our own munitions factories . . ."

"A good number of unscrupulous people made a

388

great deal of money during the war," Frank interrupted. "It just so happens that the firing mechanisms for those rifles were imported from France." He looked at Michael. "They arrived here by way of Bermuda."

Ryan spoke up. "Then you're saying Winston Barnett might have been dealing on both sides? That he substituted damaged goods for those requisitioned? He had to have had connections, accomplices, in both the North and South."

Frank nodded. "It's been brought up before, but we've never had anything to go on, no positive leads . . . until now."

"Nothing's been done about this?" Morgan demanded, the military man coming out in him.

Frank shrugged. "He's an English citizen. Our relations with England are not the best right now."

Wauburne leaned forward in his chair, jammed his cigar into his mouth, and muttered, "If the general's elected, *that's* one area we're going to see to. Great Britain is going to be held accountable for the damages it caused during the war. Their affiliation with the South had nothing to do with the morality of right or wrong. It was pure greed."

Shaking his head, Frank Adams addressed the agitated man. "I've told you before, you'd do better to concentrate on the political machines right here, in the East. The Tweed Ring up in New York City seems to be cornering the market on graft. No one who knows 'Lyss will ever question his honesty—he just has to make sure his appointees are men of equal standards."

"I think Frank's right," Morgan commented. "You're going to have to deal with the corruption in the South and the low state of public morality because of the spoils system. This thing is bound to come to a head—successful candidates rewarding supporters by giving them government jobs. How many are incapable . . . or dishonest?"

"The general doesn't seem to think that he's much of a politician— I've been trying to stop him from including that statement in his campaign speech," Wauburne remarked with a wry grin. "But he's always believed in the merit system, saying it's the best way to get the best people to do the job." He glanced at Ryan. "Do you think we could get Congress to appropriate money for a civil service commission that would regulate government jobs?"

Ryan was quick with his answer. "You would have my support, James."

Michael couldn't stop looking at the sleeping man. How could it be possible that he was sitting in the same room with the most hated man of the South? Yet, if he believed these men, these concerned, honorable men, then perhaps Ulysses Grant stood for more than defeat. Perhaps, he could be the beginning of true reconstruction for the country. Choosing these men as his advisers would be a good beginning. He realized, as he watched the wide shoulders rise and fall with each deep breath, that he was seeing and hearing about the man, and not the legend. It took him a few seconds to acknowledge a startling fact: He liked the man. Two hours ago nothing on this earth would have made him believe such a thing could be possible.

Frank Adams cleared his throat. "I think we're getting a little ahead of ourselves. Coming back to Winston Barnett . . . until now we've had nothing to connect him with anyone in the States. I think you were

390

on the right track, Michael, with those shares of Barnett Importing. If he was using them as his daughter's dowry, then he wants to make a definite connection with your family. Maybe he's gotten wind of our inquiries into his business practices. My bet is he was using the shares to keep Masterson in line—to let him know that if he goes down, he's taking your uncle with him."

Michael swallowed several times. "And if my uncle falls then so does the name of Sheridan Shipping. *That's* why he insisted Kevin marry Helene Barnett! It was his countermove against Barnett. United by marriage, and the shares in each other's companies, they would both sink or swim together."

"The criminal mind cannot comprehend trust," Frank commented. "My suggestion to you is: I think it's time you resurrected yourself, so to speak. I'll send a few of my more trusted men down to Charleston to snoop around. And in the meantime, the more you can unnerve your uncle, the better our chances of discovering a slipup. Seeing his nephew come back to life will surely take his mind off his machinations."

James Wauburne spoke up. "I admire your tenacity, Mr. Sheridan. And, believe it or not, your honor in attempting to clear your father's good name. Perhaps if the general ever finds himself living in that white house in Washington, you'd consider coming to work for him. That town needs to hear what's really going on from loyal southerners like yourself."

"Now wait a minute here, Jim," Frank quickly interrupted. "I was about to make a similar offer myself. You see, Michael, for the last two years I've been putting together a small force of men to quietly investigate potentially dangerous problems facing the nation ... and diffuse them before they get out of hand. We could use someone like you. Couldn't we, Morgan?" He looked to their host.

Morgan Trahern shook his head and chuckled. "I keep telling you, Frank, I'm a businessman now—an importer. Not a spy ..."

Laughing, Frank Adams looked back to Michael and Ryan. "I'm here, tonight, to talk Morgan into joining my elite group. So far, I haven't been too successful. How about you, Michael? Are you interested?"

A picture of Kate entered his mind, and he tried to think of a polite way to refuse Adams and General Grant's aide. Smiling at both men, he said, "I'm afraid my life is uncertain right now. I haven't allowed myself to make any plans beyond solving the problems of my family."

Wauburne nodded. "We don't give up easily, you know."

Looking at the famous man still asleep, Michael lifted his drink in a salute and smiled. "I wouldn't expect anything else from a man whose initials stand for *Unconditional Surrender*."

Wauburne and Frank Adams glanced at each other and grinned. "Let me tell it, Frank?" Jim asked.

Frank Adams suggested they all sit back and listen.

As Morgan refilled everyone's glass, Grant's campaign manager began. "He never really objected when that business started about his initials—U.S. standing for unconditional surrender. It did a heap more for his reputation than if the truth of the matter were known."

Seeing he had everyone's attention, he continued.

"He's the first child of Jesse and Hannah Simpson Grant, and they wanted the best education for him. When his father heard in '39 that a neighbor's son had been dismissed from the Military Academy, he asked his congressman to appoint 'Lyss as a replacement. He was born Hiram Ulysses Grant, but everyone always called him Ulysses. His father's friend made a mistake with the first name and thought he'd taken his mother's maiden name for a middle one. He submitted the name as Ulysses Simpson Grant . . . from which came the initials U.S. 'Lyss never bothered to correct him and since then has had many an opportunity to be thankful. If it wasn't for his mistake, Unconditional Surrender Grant might be known by his real initials . . . H.U.G. Somehow I don't think the moniker 'Hug Grant' would've had the same effect on his military career."

Acknowledging the subdued laughter in the room, Wauburne turned to his friend, "For your good behavior in not interrupting me, Frank, I'll let you tell it next time."

Frank Adams permitted his eyes to wander over the younger men in the room. They were all tall, fine-looking men—strong men with honor and principles, men you could build a future with. So much depended on . . . He mentally chastened himself for daydreaming. He must be getting tired. Soon. Soon, he could take time off and return to his family . . . It had been far too long since he'd seen his wife and children. Thinking of those he'd left, he sipped his drink and looked at Louisiana's most powerful and influential resident.

"How is your lovely wife, Ryan?" Adams asked with interest.

Ryan Barrington relaxed against the high-cushioned back of his chair. "Brianne is as busy as ever. She and Rena Daniels have organized The New Orleans Trust, an organization to help with rebuilding and establishing temporary shelters to house the homeless."

"You'd better be careful, Congressman," Morgan warned. "It sounds as though your wife could challenge you on reelection."

Ryan laughed good-naturedly. "Please!" he asked, holding his hand up. "You should hear Brianne and Rena on the suffrage movement!"

Frank placed his drink on the edge of Morgan's desk and folded his arms over his chest. "And you, Michael? Are you married?"

"Yes," he immediately answered. "Her name is Kathleen."

Ryan turned and gave him a look of surprise. "Married?"

Michael smiled to his friend. "We were quietly married in Bermuda, after an exceptionally short courtship. For obvious reasons we haven't announced our marriage, but I think the time has come to do so." Again picturing Kate, he experienced an intense longing.

Very pleased with Michael's answer, Frank looked to his host. "Well, Morgan, it seems you're the only bachelor in the room. Doesn't marriage and family appeal to you?"

Although uncomfortable with the question, Morgan attempted to answer with some humor. "Some men are destined to lead a single life. I'm afraid I'm one. There's no woman yet to be born who could put up with me. At least not permanently."

Picking up his drink, Frank sipped the smooth brandy and mumbled, "Only time will tell, son . . ."

Michael Thomas Sheridan didn't know whether it was the excellent brandy, or the first-rate companionship he'd found in Baltimore, but he felt very pleased with the results of this meeting . . . and with himself. Tonight he'd found friendship, support, and good company. He'd also found that men, even former sworn enemies, had three things in common: sporting events, politics, and women. It had been that way since the Greeks . . . He supposed it would probably always be so.

How I miss you, Katie, he thought while again tasting Morgan's brandy. God, he couldn't wait to get back and claim her as his wife . . .

Just then a loud yawn was heard and the sleeping general unfurled his body like a giant bear awakening from hibernation. When he turned to the men in the study, the gleam in his eyes and the tilt of his grin showed he hadn't missed a single piece of conversation.

Trying very hard not to look astonished, Michael's only thought was that he'd give anything for Kate to be at his side to witness this night, for he was about to meet the next president of the United States.

Chapter 25

Opening the door to her hotel suite, Kate nearly attacked Kevin and, taking hold of his arm, she dragged him into the sitting room.

"Do you believe this?" she demanded. "What're we going to do?"

Kevin looked at her face, now flushed with excitement and near panic. "Calm down, Kate. I've already talked to Helene and she's willing to go along with our story."

"Which story?" Kate asked with trepidation. How were they ever supposed to keep all the lies straight?

Smoothing his jacket back into place, he acknowledged Rose, who was wringing her hands by the sofa, and motioned to the chairs. "Why don't we all sit down and discuss this? Some interesting developments have taken place."

Kate groaned as she moved toward the nearest chair. "Oh, God," she muttered with dread as she slowly sank down. "I'm afraid to ask."

Kevin looked at both women. Seeing Rose was nearly

cutting off the circulation in her hands with her handkerchief, he quickly said, "Martin's disappeared."

"Disappeared?" Kate's mouth dropped open in surprise as Rose asked the question.

Kevin nodded. "No one can find him. He was at the shipping offices this morning and then he just disappeared. He never came home. I went over to the office myself and checked. He had no appointments outside the city."

Kate leaned forward in the chair. "What do you think happened?"

Shaking his head, Kevin said, "I don't know, but I do think it's strange that he vanishes on the same afternoon Winston Barnett and his daughter show up in Charleston."

Kate looked at Rose. "Why would Martin do that if he and Barnett are partners? It doesn't make any sense."

"Where's Denny?" Rose asked Kevin.

"Don't worry. He's all right. My mother and Barnett sent for him early this evening. I was present when they interrogated him about the crossing from Bermuda. Since Helene was here in Charleston, they wanted to know who was the woman Michael had kidnapped and who then was washed overboard."

Kate tensed. "What did he say?"

"He said Helene Barnett. Then when they sent for Helene, both she and Denny swore they'd never seen each other. That was when Barnett got out of hand. He was relentless with Helene, demanding that she name the woman. No matter how her father terrorized her, she insisted that she didn't know. She claimed it was someone who wanted passage to the States and was willing to take her place at the wedding to obtain it." His fingers clenched into a fist as he brought his hand to the arm of the chair. "To think I've caused all this by trying to get out of marrying her!"

Kate was quick to speak up. She could see the guilt written over Kevin's face. "No! You're wrong, Kevin. Michael and I are to blame. It was madness to think we could get away with all our lies. I'm just sorry so many others are being dragged into it."

"I could have just met her, Kate. So much of this might have been avoided if I'd gone to Bermuda, instead of persuading Michael to go in my place."

"Ah, but then Michael never would've met Kathleen," Rose put in. "I just wish he was here now to help sort this out."

"When is he getting back, Rose? Denny said you were the last to speak with him."

"He said he'd return in less than a week. Sooner, if all works out . . ."

"It's the treasure!" Kate exclaimed.

Seeing the confused expressions in response to her statement, she explained, "Don't you see? Michael said his uncle was expecting shares of Barnett's company as the dowry. When Denny came in to Charleston, you said, Kevin, that Martin took Helene's trunk to send back to Bermuda. Only we know he didn't do it. The jewels were inside. He might not have gotten the shares, but he found something even more valuable. We know he's got the treasure . . . he lost part of it to me . . . and now he's afraid Barnett knows, too. Martin must think Winston Barnett's here to get back the jewels."

Kevin quickly rose to his feet. "My God, I think you're right, Kate." He started to pace the hotel room.

398

"And believing the jewels came from Barnett as part of the dowry, Martin's hiding somewhere until he can figure out what to do."

"He thinks he's double-crossed his partner," Rose cheerfully announced.

Kate looked at Rose, then Kevin. All three slowly smiled.

Three hours later, Kevin stood in front of Helene's bedroom door. He'd waited until the house was quiet before slipping down the hall. With Winston Barnett taking over Michael's room, he'd had to be extra careful as he approached the one next to it. Since returning from Kate's, he hadn't been able to speak with Helene in private . . . and he needed to fill her in on what they thought was taking place. In all honesty, he admitted as he brought up his hand, there was something about Helene that tugged at his heart. She was so young, so fragile, to withstand the brutality of her father. Feeling somewhat responsible for putting her in that situation, he softly knocked on her door.

Within seconds, she answered and her voice was a surprised whisper. "Kevin? What . . . ?"

Quickly, he placed his fingers to his lips and gently pushed the door open so he could enter. "We have to be careful," he whispered into her startled face. "I'm sorry to disturb you so late, but we have to talk, Helene."

Nodding, she more tightly wrapped her lacy white robe around her. "Has something else happened?" she asked in a small, frightened voice.

A totally unfamiliar emotion in Kevin made him want to place a protective arm around her tiny shoulders to guard her from any more harm. Seeing how the light from the single lamp highlighted her beautiful blond hair, Kevin mentally shook himself and cleared his throat. "I would first like to apologize to you, Helene. Sending my brother to Bermuda in my place was unforgivable." He jammed his hands into the pockets of his jacket. "I should have come and talked to you and your father."

It was the first time Helene Barnett had been alone with a man, and she was unnerved to find herself in a bedroom, no less, with a very attractive one. Excitement mixed with fear as she moved away from the bed and stood closer to the door. "You shouldn't blame yourself, Kevin," she said shyly. "You were not alone in opposing this marriage between our families. I, too, ran away to avoid it." She took a very deep breath. "I share the responsibility for creating this situation."

"No, Helene, not you," Kevin said quickly. "Your father and my uncle created this. We should have been given time together."

"It was a business arrangement," she whispered in a disillusioned voice. "I always thought marriage would be . . . would be . . . something else."

He could hear the embarrassment in her voice and quickly spoke. "It should be, Helene, but don't you see that you and I were pawns in whatever nasty business Martin has going on with your father? Don't hold yourself to blame for any of this."

She tightened her face to keep from crying. "It seemed like the easiest way out when Kathleen and I switched places. I should have just run away. If only he hadn't found me . . ."

Knowing she was close to tears, Kevin started to

move in her direction, but stopped himself from gathering her into his arms. Instead, he took her hand in his and gently squeezed it. "When this is all over, Helene, I promise to help you get back to your aunt, if that's what you wish. Just be brave for a little while longer."

Helene lifted her eyes and searched Kevin's face. His touch on her hand sent tiny shivers racing up her arm while a heavy warmth spread through her inexperienced body. A strange mix of fear and delight took hold of her and she couldn't help but wonder what it would feel like to be kissed by such a handsome, polite man.

The thoughts swirling inside Kevin's head were anything but polite as his eyes left her face and unwillingly traveled the length of her young form. The fullness of her breasts and curves of her hips were clearly defined by the thin robe. Why had he ever thought she was but a mere girl? What was she? Seventeen? Eighteen? Helene was no longer a girl . . . Standing before him was a lovely young woman.

Suddenly aware that his fingers continued to stroke Helene's, Kevin abruptly pulled his hand away and jammed his fists back into his pockets. Embarrassed, he turned away from her and studied the carved legs of the writing table. "I, ah . . . I wanted to tell you what Kate said this evening when I went to her hotel."

Shaken by the unexpected emotions rushing through her, Helene didn't trust herself to speak. She remained silent and waited for Kevin to continue.

"She came up with a pretty good reason for my uncle's disappearance. It's very possible Martin is hiding from your father."

Helene's eyes widened. "Why?"

Kevin glanced up and nearly groaned aloud when he saw she was standing in front of the lamp. The alluring silhouette of her body was plainly visible. Clearing his throat, he managed to say, "Martin thinks the treasure I told you about was part of your dowry. He must believe your father has come to get it back. Kate and Michael say it's worth a fortune."

Helene moved away from the light and smiled sadly. "My father doesn't place such a high value on his daughter. He would never offer what you've described as my dowry."

Hating to see the pain in her face, Kevin said softly, "Your father's a blind man."

She lifted her head and stared across the room before a shy smile appeared. She didn't say anything, yet her eyes held a look of gratitude and something else that stirred a flicker of excitement in him. Feeling more alive than he'd felt in years, Kevin suddenly asked, "Would you like to go to the hotel tomorrow for dinner?"

Seeing her pleased expression, he hurried to add, "Kate asked that we have dinner with her. She's very anxious to speak with you again."

Nodding, Helene moved closer to him. "I was hoping to see Kathleen, too. And I would very much like to have dinner with you, Kevin."

Running a hand through his hair, Kevin stepped to the door. As he placed his hand on the knob, he turned to Helene and whispered, "When this is over, I promise you . . . you won't ever have to be afraid again."

*   *   *

Kate walked ahead of Helene and Kevin as they left the dining room of the Charleston Hotel. Over dinner, she and Kevin had tried to explain everything that had happened since Bermuda, and it hadn't been easy. How could you justify all the lies? Rationalize the insanity of the last few weeks? In the end, she'd settled for Helene's quiet promise to remain silent and see as little of her father as possible.

Turning to her friends, Kate couldn't help but notice the interest that passed between them—Helene's shy, admiring glances and Kevin's bemused smiles. It was obvious they were discovering each other and Kate found it ironic that for all of their family's interference, it looked like Helene and Kevin were developing a relationship all their own.

Smiling at the couple as they stopped in the hotel's lobby, Kate said, "You two had better get back before Lydia sends the militia after you."

Kevin frowned. "That was something else I wanted to apologize for. I'm getting very tired of my mother's overprotective nature. She seems to forget I'm a grown man."

Kate smiled warmly at Michael's brother. "Please stop feeling you have to apologize for everyone's actions. All of us, including Lydia, have contributed to this mess. I just hope it's all straightened out before too long. Kathleen Anne Walker seems almost like a stranger to me now."

Helene clasped Kate's hand between her own. "You're so brave, Kathleen. I could never impersonate someone else and confront Mrs. Sheridan or Kevin's uncle . . . and I don't suppose I've been too strong in opposing my father."

Squeezing the younger woman's hand, Kate noted, "You're doing just fine, Helene. Try to avoid him as much as possible. Don't get into a confrontation with your father that you can't possibly win . . . not yet. This should all be resolved in a few days. A week, at the most. Then, I promise you Michael and I will take you back to Bermuda on the *Rebel*."

Seeing Helene quickly glance to the handsome man at her side, Kate added, "Whatever decision you make, all of us will stand behind you. Don't worry, I know it's all going to turn out for the best."

Kissing Kate's cheek, Helene whispered, "I do hope so, Kathleen. I will pray for all of us."

Remembering that Winston Barnett had found his daughter in a convent after she had fled the refuge of her aunt's home, Kate grinned at Helene's large, serious eyes. "Thank you. I think all of us can use some divine intervention right now."

After saying good-bye, she watched as they left the hotel before turning away. It was easy now to escape the stares from those who thought her to be a celebrity. If she didn't look at the curious strangers who followed her every movement, she could avoid eye contact and pretend they didn't exist. Besides, she was too preoccupied to play the part any longer. For the last few days, she'd been fighting the sickening feeling in her stomach, the nausea that tightened her muscles and filled her with dread. It felt almost like a premonition of something bad to come, something evil that was only waiting to surface.

Opening the door to her suite, she silently joined Helene in a prayer for guidance and protection. Something was going to break very soon, for the powerful people they'd been playing games with were surely going to retaliate. If only she were as strong as Helene thought!

Two hours later, she was attempting to relax with Rose as they sipped mint-flavored tea. They were both clad in their nightgowns and robes and the atmosphere had been warm and friendly . . . until Rose's last statement.

"I beg your pardon?" Kate asked, although she'd heard every low, muttered word.

"I said, Don't you think it's time the two of you got married proper? Denny told me about the weddin' in Bermuda and it doesn't seem right."

Kate sat up straighter. "We both used our real names when we signed the marriage certificate. Michael thinks it's legal."

Rose snorted. "Well, of course he would! It's hard enough gettin' a man to the altar once, let alone twice, to marry the same woman."

In spite of Rose's tone, Kate couldn't help laughing. "How you make it sound! As if I'd have to tie him up and drag him to the altar, if I decided to get remarried. Michael and I don't have to play any of those games . . ."

"Hah!" Rose rolled her eyes toward the ceiling. "You and that boy have been playin' games since the day you met. Any woman will tell you that you have to use some subterfuge to catch a man."

Grinning, Kate settled back in the comfortable chair. "Michael and I are adults, and any decision about remarrying will be made by both of us. Honestly, Rose, women don't have to go to all those extremes to develop a lasting relationship with a man."

Rose returned her cup to the high butler's table. "Oh, really? Are you saying you haven't schemed, just a little, to open Michael's eyes? To let him see that the two of you are meant to be together?"

Keeping a smile on her face, Kate took in Rose's wrinkled but cherubic face, the wiry strands of silver that escaped from her braid, and the merry twinkle in her aging blue eyes. "I will admit to a little scheming. But any . . . ah, maneuvering I did was for Michael's own good. When I met him, he was filled with such anger, such a burning need for revenge. Anything I did was to show him that his life could be so much more if he'd let go of it."

"Exactly! You're no different, Kathleen, than any other woman. Just less ready to admit . . ."

Both women jumped when they heard the loud knock. Staring at each other, Kate was the first to speak. "Who could it be at this hour?" she whispered in an alarmed voice.

"Stay here," Rose commanded. Getting to her feet, she smoothed the stray tendrils of hair back from her face and said, "Whoever it is, I'll get rid of them. No decent person would come callin' at this time of night."

When the door opened, both Rose and Kate were too shocked, too amazed, to speak as Michael immediately strode into the room, followed by Denny and a strange young man who wore the turned collar of a minister.

Coming to Kate's side, Michael placed a light kiss on her cheek. "I hope we didn't startle you, my dear, but time is of the essence. The Reverend Williams and I had a very interesting conversation on the trip from Baltimore." Seeing her shocked expression, he suppressed a chuckle and added, "He has very graciously agreed to solve our delicate dilemma by uniting us in holy matrimony—before he catches the connecting train to Atlanta."

Kate quickly turned to the man of God and almost screeched when he smiled in embarrassment and shot a curious look to her stomach. "What have you told him?" she demanded through clenched teeth as she spun back to Michael.

He patted her hand very dramatically. "Now, now, Kate. It's the proper solution to all our problems." Leaving her, he pried Rose's fingers from the doorknob and shut the heavy door.

"Rose, we have less than ten minutes to arrange this. I've promised Reverend Williams that he'd make his train, so you and Denny will be our witnesses. See if you can help Kate get ready. Maybe some flowers . . ."

"I am in my nightgown!" Kate cried in a near hysterical voice.

Michael turned back to her. "We don't have time for you to dress, my dear. I think we should have the ceremony before the fireplace. What do you think, Reverend?"

As Rose rushed to her side, Kate ignored her excited giggles. "Isn't this perfect? You and Michael will be married all legal and the reverend there will be out of town before anyone can ask questions. What a mind," Rose whispered with admiration as she glanced at Michael. "I was wonderin' how we're going to get out of this Bonaparte thing."

Feeling she couldn't possibly be fully awake, Kate watched in amazement as Michael took charge and rearranged furniture with Denny's help. It was a different Michael than the man who'd left her only a few days ago. In a dark-brown business suit, he looked successful, polished, almost modern. And he was in command. Was it only a few minutes ago that she'd told Rose if they would make the decision to remarry, it would be done *together?*

"Here," Rose offered, handing her a magnolia that was at least twelve inches across, "you can carry this."

Speechless, Kate held the huge blossom and walked on unsteady legs as Rose led her to the fireplace. Standing next to the handsomely dressed Michael, she looked down at her pale-yellow robe and, unconsciously, smoothed the silk material over her hip.

From behind her, she heard Denny's low voice as he whispered to Rose, "Isn't this grand? Who'd have thought Michael could arrange it all?"

Kate almost groaned aloud when she heard Rose's whispered remark. "We were just sittin' here talkin' about marriage when you came." Her pleasure-filled sigh was audible. "It's *so* romantic!"

Reverend Williams cleared his throat. "Are we all ready?" he asked kindly. "Michael? Kathleen?"

She watched Michael nod and found herself joining him. It was absolute madness . . . she was going to be married in her damn nightgown!

Within moments, as she faced Michael and looked into his eyes, Kate knew she wasn't making a mistake. And her attire meant little when compared to the expression on Michael's face. It revealed happiness, pride, and love. Smiling into his eyes, she tried to pay attention to the ceremony, for she never wanted to forget this moment.

She made the proper responses, but couldn't

suppress a gasp when Michael placed a thick gold ring on her finger. When he handed her a larger version for himself, she questioned him with her eyes. Interrupting to explain, he whispered, "It's from the chain we found in Bermuda."

Her fingers were shaking as she slipped the gold band onto his finger and her heart expanded as she listened to Michael declare his love, promising to honor and cherish her in a strong voice.

Before she could fully comprehend that it was really happening, Reverend Williams quickly declared them husband and wife. Taking her into his arms, Michael smiled down at her bewildered expression. "And that, Mrs. Sheridan," he said with finality, "is the *last* time you'll change your name."

Kate wasn't given the chance to reply as his lips slanted over hers in a deep, possessive kiss. Breathless, they broke away from each other as Denny and Rose congratulated them.

"It was just beautiful," Rose declared as tears welled up in her eyes. "I couldn't be more happy if you both were my children!"

Patting his sister's shoulder, Denny agreed. "I'm proud of you, Michael. And if your daddy was here, he'd be mighty proud, too."

Amid the hugs and kisses that followed, Kate heard the minister address them. "All that's left is the marriage certificate." Taking out a pocket watch, he glanced at the time and said, "Michael gave me the information on the train and I filled it out ahead of time. I'll just need your signatures."

Michael signed first and all watched as Kate bent over the paper. With a shaky hand she wrote *Kathleen*

Anne Walker for the last time. Satisfied, Reverend Williams affixed his signature and Michael blew on the dark ink until it dried. Folding the small paper in half, he slipped it inside his jacket pocket and announced, "This time I'll keep it."

As he shook hands with the minister, Michael thanked the man for his understanding and looked at Denny. Quickly, the wiry seaman stepped to the door. "If you'll still be plannin' to get that train for Atlanta, we'd better get movin'."

Nodding, Reverend Williams wished Kate and Michael a lifetime of happiness and hurried to join Denny. As the door was closed behind them, Michael turned to his wife. Grinning, he reached down and completely startled her by picking her up in his arms.

"Michael! What are you doing?" Kate demanded. The gigantic magnolia slipped from her fingers as she wrapped her arm around his shoulder for support.

Happiness lighting his face, he held her tightly and looked at Rose. The older woman was dabbing at the corner of her eye.

"Michael, my boy, you've made me a very happy woman," she sniffled.

Throwing back his head with laughter, he gazed at Rose and winked. "I would like to hear those words from another woman, too."

Rose was too happy to pretend shock. Instead, she joined his laughter and said, "Get on with you, Michael."

"That's exactly what I intend to do, Mrs. Pringle. Now, I don't want any nonsense from you. You, madam, will be packed and ready to return to your home when Denny gets back from the station. I've

410

instructed him to collect you." Squeezing Kate even tighter, he added, "I appreciate everything you've done for us, Rose—especially taking care of Kate—but now *I'm* going to take over."

Resting her head on Michael's shoulder, Kate smiled warmly. "Thank you for everything, Rose. We'll come to see you tomorrow and celebrate . . ."

"I'll have everything ready," the older woman announced, plans already starting to form in her head. "We can invite the crew, and—"

"Maybe," Michael interrupted as he turned and walked into the bedroom. "Right now I want Mrs. Sheridan all to myself."

Just before he kicked the bedroom door shut, they heard Rose's giggles. She sounded like a young girl.

He placed her gently on the bed and took her hand as he stood up. "You're not angry, are you, Katie?"

Lying back against the pillows, she didn't trust her voice and merely shook her head. They were married! Really married! Kate stared at the exceptionally handsome man before her. She didn't know if it was the ceremony they had just gone through, or the fact that Michael looked so different with his tailored clothes, but something about the moment was decidedly different.

They continued to silently stare at the other, each filled with love, with commitment and anticipation. Michael slowly let go of her hand and she was mesmerized as she watched him pull off his jacket. His eyes held hers as he ripped off his tie and shed his white shirt. Kate found she lacked the power to look away. It was as if she were under Michael's spell. She felt flushed, her heart beat frantically against her chest, and a wild need built inside her as his quick movements set off breathtaking thoughts.

Keeping her eyes locked with his, he removed each piece of clothing. He stood before her, his eyes already making love to her as they spoke of his hunger. He was so astonishingly male that Kate gasped as she felt her breasts, her body, already responding to him. The swirling emotions were overwhelming and she felt close to tears as she held out her hand.

"I . . . I love you, Michael," she whispered in a tiny voice. At that moment her emotions were so close to the surface that to deny it would have been impossible. "I think I have from the beginning."

Pulling her to her feet, he untied the belt of her robe and slipped the soft material down her arms. Hooking his fingers under the straps of her nightgown, he allowed it to fall to the floor. With a gentleness that touched her, Michael pulled her to him until their bodies were pressed together. As each inhaled with pleasure, Michael raised his hands to her face and entwined his fingers in the dark silk of her hair. Letting his thumbs graze her cheekbones, he searched her eyes and muttered thickly, "I've wasted so many years going down the wrong paths, always searching, waiting for the right one. I think, Katie, I've been waiting my whole life for you."

Letting the tears freely fall, Kate Sheridan clasped him to her and it was with joy that she welcomed her husband into her life.

Chapter 26

Kate brought her leg up over Michael's body, grazing her foot against the fine hairs on his calf. She couldn't help smiling with happiness, for she was honest enough to admit a very feminine surge of conquest. That she had attracted and captured the love of such a fine man made her feel special. As she lightly blew on the crisp hairs of his chest, Kate ran her hand over his muscled thigh. Michael was such a fine man ... and he was hers. Snuggling closer, she breathed deeply and sighed. "I don't think I've ever felt more relaxed in my life. Let's stay here forever."

"Not a bad idea," Michael murmured, while bending his head to place a kiss on her temple. "We could blockade the door and say to hell with the rest of the world."

Grinning, Kate asked, "What about food? We're going to need food."

"You're right," he admitted. "We are going to need food. Maybe we could go out just for supplies."

Kate shook her head. "First it will be supplies,

then . . ." Suddenly, she raised herself on her elbow and looked at him. "Michael, did anyone recognize you last night? It just occurred to me that you came in through the front door."

He smiled. "I certainly hope so. Even though I was in a hurry to get here, I can remember a few mouths dropping open with shock. I'm not totally unknown in this city, you know."

"Why? Why did you do it? It's going to get back to your family." She sat up and pulled the sheet over her body.

Michael's grin was wide. "That's what I'm counting on, Kate. I've officially risen from the ranks of deceased."

"Martin's disappeared." Now that the passion of their lovemaking had cooled, she was starting to think more clearly.

Michael's body tensed. "Denny told me. He also told me what you and Kevin believe is the reason for his sudden departure. I think you're right. It's to our benefit right now if he thinks Barnett is after the treasure."

"But what's going to happen when Martin finds out you're alive?"

He saw the look of concern on her face and smiled as he brought her back into his arms. "I would think it's going to make him react that much sooner. What we don't want is for Martin and Barnett to get together and talk. As long as they're apart, they're both suspicious of the other. My reappearance only adds to their confusion . . . and that's what we want." He hugged her and let his breath out. "We're not alone in

414

this any more, Kate. I've found help in Washington."

Hearing his heartbeat against her ear, she tightened her hold on him. "You should have told me you were leaving. I would have understood."

He heard the reproach in her voice and said quietly, "You know you would have insisted on going with me. I didn't have the time, Kate, to talk you out of it. I had to leave immediately."

He felt her nod and, glad that she wasn't going to argue, Michael quickly added, "There was one evening I wish you were with me. You'll never guess who I met."

Not waiting for her to question, he announced, "Ulysses S. Grant. Did you know his real initials are H.U.G.?"

Kate's head popped up. "You're kidding?"

"No. His real name is Hiram Ulysses Grant, but when he was appointed to the . . ."

She waved her hand in dismissal. "You *met* President Grant?"

"Well, he isn't president yet. Though I have every reason to believe he'll win the election." Michael was very pleased to see the astounded expression on Kate's face. He'd wanted to impress her.

"He does become president," she stated in a low voice. "For two terms, I think. But his administration is filled with scandal. I remember reading that he was a hard drinker . . ."

"That's not true," Michael said defensively. "I've heard those rumors, too, but I was with him all evening and he hardly touched his brandy. He seemed more like a quiet, family-type man."

She shrugged her shoulders. "I'm only telling you

what I've read."

Michael's eyes narrowed. "Where did you read these things?"

As she watched the suspicion gather in Michael's eyes, Kate wondered just how important it was for him to believe her. Should she try again to make him understand that she'd traveled a bizarre distance to find him? Just how important was it? Would it change his love for her? Her love for him? She'd already accepted that she wasn't going back to her own time. If that were going to happen, it would have taken place by now. Her heart, her life, belonged to Michael now. Hadn't their marriage last night reaffirmed that? Maybe someday the time would be right for him to understand, but instinctively she knew it wasn't now.

Smiling, she whispered, "I don't remember, Michael. Is it so important?"

He returned her smile. "You probably read some editorial by a northern Democrat. Even down here, they're always predicting disaster and corruption if a Republican sits in the White House."

Feeling it was a necessary deception, Kate nodded. "You're probably right." And wanting to change the subject she once more relaxed in his arms and pushed his hair back from his forehead. Spying the heavy gold band on her finger, she asked, "Are our rings really made from a link of that old chain we found?"

She could feel his chin move as he nodded. "I know you're going to think this was presumptuous on my part, but . . . before I left for Washington I gave mine to Rose with instructions for Denny to have it made into two rings."

Kate raised her face from his chest. "Rose knew what

you were planning? So that's why she was nagging me about a second marriage!" She grinned and shook her head. "But how did you have the rings made in such a short time?"

Michael laughed. "Over the years Denny has done business with a certain jeweler whose reputation is not, shall we say, above reproach. He owes Denny and, to be honest, Kate, I didn't ask any questions. Do you like them?"

Holding her hand up, she stared at the burnished gold. "I love them," she said positively. "But do you mean to tell me that old crusty chain is real gold?"

Laughing, Michael nodded. "It's real gold all right. Why do you think I was trying to get it up?"

Her mouth opened in shock. "Can you imagine how much that's worth? I thought the poor guy got wrapped in the ship's anchor and sunk to the bottom during a storm."

He again laughed and hugged her more tightly. "That's what I love about you, Katie. You're as greedy as I am! I can almost hear your brain trying to figure a way to raise the rest of the chain."

She playfully slapped his arm. "I am not greedy," she protested, then laughed. "Well, I'm not overly greedy. It's just sitting there in that cove. Somebody should bring it up!"

Michael chuckled. "And you think it should be us?"

Grinning, she murmured, "Why not? That's one heck of a necklace that guy was wearing . . ."

Kate could hear the rumble of his laughter as it escaped from his chest. "It wasn't a necklace, not exactly. The early Spanish explorers realized there wasn't any currency to use in the New World. They had

417

their gold made into a chain that they wore at all times, and when they needed money they would pry off a link."

"My God, it must have been heavy! No wonder he sunk straight to the bottom. Wearing that gold, he never had a chance."

Nodding, Michael lifted her left hand and stared at the thick wedding band. "Do you realize these are over three hundred years old? I kept that link as a memory of the beautiful mermaid who captured my imagination." He kissed her fingertips. "I had this made for the woman who captured my heart."

Lifting her head, she looked deeply into his eyes. "I think we've both turned into very superstitious people, Michael. We've made the legend come true. It was the treasure that helped us to find our hearts' desire."

He kept his eyes locked with hers and said, "It's almost dawn, Katie. We'd better get some sleep . . ."

Her lips moved closer to his waiting ones. "Later Mr. Sheridan. Right now I'm about to assert my wifely rights over you."

Panther-quick, Michael turned her onto her back. As he held himself over her, he grinned. "It will be my pleasure, madam."

Running her hands down his chest, she let her fingernails graze over him until she reached his hips. Allowing her hands to encircle him, she smiled when hearing his gasp of surprise. "It *will* be your pleasure, sir," she said confidently. "And mine."

They made a handsome couple as they walked toward the livery where Michael intended to rent a carriage. Several times people stopped and stared and Kate had to bite her bottom lip as Michael raised his hat in a polite acknowledgment. Never did they stop, though, and explain that Kathleen Bonaparte was now the wife of Michael Sheridan, a man believed by all of Charleston to have died.

Knowing the speed with which her own escapades had reached Lydia's ears, Kate asked, "Don't you think you should see your mother first? She shouldn't hear that you're alive from a stranger."

"Denny told me of your visit to my mother. I won't apologize for her lack of warmth, since I've never received it myself. We'll see her together this afternoon and announce our marriage."

Kate couldn't help groaning. "I can't wait for her reaction to that! If she disliked me for seeing Kevin, she's going to have a fit when she hears I've married you."

"Whatever happens, Kate, we'll face it together, all right?"

Before she could answer, a burly seaman walked into her and shoved her down the alley. She was too startled to do more than issue a muffled scream as Michael moved after them. Suddenly the man pushed Kate to the ground and spun back toward Michael. In his hand was a long knife, and he waved the blade in a small menacing arc in front of her husband.

"Should've stayed dead, Sheridan," he growled while moving closer.

Never taking his eyes off the man, Michael tore off his jacket and quickly wrapped it around his arm. "Stay down, Kate," he ordered harshly.

Clawing at the cobbled street, she fought with her

skirts as she attempted to rise.

"I said stay down!"

Immediately she sunk to the damp street and brought her fist to her mouth as Michael quickly jumped away from the sharp blade. She felt helpless. Part of her wanted to scream and run the few blocks back to the busier street, yet she was terrified to leave. Another part of her wanted to charge the man who threatened her husband with the deadly-looking knife. Instead, she was immobilized with fear as she watched the two of them engage in a silent dance of death.

It was over in less than thirty seconds as the man became desperate with Michael's ability to avoid each thrust. Kate watched in amazement as Michael side-stepped a charge and quickly turned to the seaman. With a grace born to a dancer, he rapidly brought his foot up and connected with the man's arm. The assailant looked momentarily stunned as the knife fell from his numb fingers. Within seconds, he yelled in pain and attempted to support his broken arm, but Michael's fist was quicker as he slammed the man's head back against the brick wall.

Both men were breathing heavily as Kate again tried to rise. Using the wall as a support, she watched as Michael first threw his jacket to the ground, then grabbed hold of the man's collar and dragged him to his feet.

"Who sent you?" Michael demanded in a ragged voice. "Who the hell sent you?"

Frightened, the man stared at Michael and didn't respond. Again, Michael thrust his head against the wall and Kate flinched as she heard a distinctive crack. "Who was it?!"

Unable to wipe at the steady trickle of blood streaming from his nose, the man gasped for breath and muttered, "Masterson . . . ! It was Masterson."

As if burned, Michael's fingers immediately released him and the man quickly sunk to the ground. Taking a step back, Michael stared at the bloodied seaman in disbelief. Slowly, he picked up the knife at the same time as his jacket and walked toward Kate.

She rushed into his arms and held him tightly. "Are you hurt?" she demanded, trying to stop the tears that were building in her eyes.

Leaning slightly against her, Michael shook his head and steered her past the moaning, injured man. He stopped for a moment and looked down. "You go back . . ." he said through clenched teeth, "and tell Masterson to face me himself. Tell him . . . tell him the time has come to pay for what he's done to the Sheridans.

"C'mon, Kate." Michael pulled her with him as he walked away from the broken man. Holding on to her husband, she could feel the rage contained inside him and didn't speak as he led her back toward the busy street.

"We're going home," he said in a cold voice, and she was too shaken, too stunned, to question him.

Lydia Sheridan looked across her late husband's desk to the heavyset man who faced her. It took a supreme effort to hide the fury that was building inside her as she listened to Winston Barnett vent his anger.

"You've spoiled that son of yours to the point where he thinks he can do no wrong. Where was this influence you claimed to have over him when he was supposed to come to Bermuda? You promised there would be no problems and since listening to you, madam, I've had little else."

"I could ask the same question of you, Winston," she coldly remarked. "I seem to remember you saying your daughter would do as she was told and go through with the marriage. Obviously, we both overestimated our authority over our children." Lydia suddenly felt her age. It was only willpower and self-restraint that kept her seated in her husband's leather chair. But that was something she had learned over the years—the ability to subdue her inner feelings and act the role she had been born to play. *Forced* to play, she mentally corrected as she stood up and walked to the front of the desk. First she had to appear as a loving daughter, then a dutiful wife and mother, and, finally, a grieving widow. Her latest performance had been only this morning when Kevin cheerfully announced Michael's miraculous return to the city. And that news on top of Martin's sudden disappearance had almost undone her. How much more turmoil was she expected to endure? And why was she wasting her time trying to pacify Barnett when she had to prepare for Michael? Even though he had not come directly last night, she knew he would today.

"Winston, try and remain calm. You're not blind. Can't you see Kevin and Helene are attracted to each other? It may all work out yet."

"You seem to forget, madam, that I have the United States government breathing down my neck. The whole reason for this marriage was because I'd received word from England that inquiries are being made about me. I want my daughter married to an American. London is eager to reestablish friendly relations with Washington and I don't intend being used as a scapegoat. I want those shares of Sheridan Shipping that were promised to me. And I want your son to be a shareholder of my company. It was agreed, Lydia, that we stand together."

She appeared calm. "Of course, Winston. Nothing will come of this investigation you keep talking about. Martin will see to that."

Barnett came to his feet and pointed an accusing finger at her chest. "And where is your brother? Why is he hiding from me?"

Taking a deep breath, she said, "I have no idea what's become of Martin. He's . . ."

"He's incompetent!" Barnett hotly interrupted. "His entire bungling of this affair proves it. You'll have to take over."

Lydia touched her temples while applying pressure. The tension she had been holding in was building into a headache. Straightening her shoulders she said, "Right now I have to prepare to receive my son. He should be here some time today and—"

"And that's something else I want to find out about," Barnett declared, arresting anything further Lydia was about to say. "Together, your two sons have managed to ruin everything I've planned. They are your problem, madam, and I expect you to handle them." He preceded her to the door. Opening it, he half turned in her direction. "If I had my way, I'd horsewhip Kevin. And that other son of yours, Michael, he'd find out that drowning in the Atlantic would seem pleasant compared to what I do to a man that crosses me!"

423

Lydia raised her chin. "I'll handle them both," she said tightly. As Barnett slammed the study door, she didn't even flinch. She had more important matters to consider.

"Hello, Mother."

Holding Kate's hand, Michael walked into the drawing room of his home and greeted Lydia. Kate had to give the woman credit. After a brief pause of shock, she reacted as any mother overjoyed to see her son. Kate wasn't sure whether Lydia was more stunned at seeing Michael after hearing that he had drowned, or seeing him walk in holding her hand. Whichever, she was convinced Lydia Sheridan was a consummate actress, for the robust woman of a few days ago seemed to have trouble rising from her chair.

Holding her hand out to him, she said weakly, "Michael . . . thank God!"

Quickly Kate's husband released her hand and rushed to his mother's side. "Please, sit down," he insisted. Waiting until Lydia was again seated on the sofa, Michael bent his head and kissed his mother's cheek.

To Kate it looked as if both Michael and his mother were uncomfortable with the small show of affection and relieved that it was over. She smiled at Kevin who stood behind his mother and beamed with happiness as he viewed the reunion. Thinking of her own relationship with her mother, Kate couldn't help but wonder at the lack of warmth between Lydia and her son. They were so formal, so polite in this extravagant room of cold white. Kate knew if the situation were reversed,

Leslie Walker would have been crying tears of happiness.

"Are you feeling well, Mother?" Michael asked, while behind him Kate wondered why Lydia hadn't asked the same question of him. Wasn't Michael the one who had been washed overboard and then stranded on an island? Wasn't the woman even concerned?

"One of my headaches again," Lydia replied, as if they were a frequent occurrence. Looking directly at Kate for the first time, she turned and smiled to her younger son. "I didn't know you were going to bring a visitor, Michael."

How cool she is, Kate thought while forcing a smile. She acts as if we've never met.

Michael smiled at Kate and walked the few steps back to her. Reclaiming her hand, he brought her to stand by the sofa. "I know you've already met, but I'd like to introduce Kathleen again." He took a deep breath and said, "Mother, I would like you to meet my wife, Kathleen Sheridan."

Lydia suddenly gained energy as she straightened her shoulders and shot Kate a look of pure shock. *"Sheridan?* I thought her name was Bonaparte."

Michael grinned. "Her name is Sheridan now. We were married last night."

"Congratulations!" Kevin chimed in as he quickly came to his brother's side and shook his hand.

"How?" Hearing the shrill note to her voice, Lydia asked more quietly, "But how is that possible? I wasn't aware that the two of you even knew each other."

Squeezing Kate's fingers, Michael said, "Kathleen and I have known each other for some time. She came

425

to Charleston because of me."

"That's why I was Kate's escort, Mother," Kevin explained with a wide smile. "She contacted Michael's brother and asked that I keep their relationship a secret until he returned. Like me, she refused to believe he wouldn't," he lied smoothly and kissed Kate's cheek. "Welcome to the Sheridans."

Both brothers looked to their mother. She swallowed several times before saying, "Welcome to the . . . Sheridans." The last word seemed to bring a bitter taste to her mouth, for she screwed up her lips in an unattractive smile.

"Thank you," Kate replied with little warmth. Even if her sons refused to see it, both she and Lydia knew there was no hope of friendship, let alone love, between them. *Love?* Kate didn't even like the woman.

Clearing her throat, Lydia tried to smile. "I'm sure we'll have to arrange some sort of celebration," she said with a forced tone of sincerity, gazing up at Michael. "Would you be terribly disappointed if we postponed it until I'm a little stronger?"

Michael shook his head, "Not at all. Kate and I intend to be married for a very long time. I've already ordered an announcement of our marriage to appear in tomorrow morning's paper."

Hearing Michael's words, Lydia truly looked ill. "If you don't mind, Michael, I think I should retire to my room now. All this excitement . . ." She let the word trail off as she reached for Kevin's hand.

Rising to her feet, she patted Michael's shoulder. "You gave us all a terrible scare, you know. We'll talk later, you and your . . . your bride. I want to hear everything."

"Of course." Michael smiled at his mother as she leaned on Kevin's arm and glided past him.

"Perhaps dinner tomorrow?" she asked with disinterest. "If I'm up to it. I'll be sure to send Wiley to the hotel with the time."

Michael stared at his mother's back as she walked toward the foyer. His gaze slid to Kate, then back to Lydia. "Kathleen and I plan to be staying here," he stated in a rough voice.

Lydia Sheridan stopped walking and slowly turned around. "Oh?" Her voice had miraculously gained strength.

"Yes. I've come home, Mother. My wife and I have come home," he amended. "I realize we have house guests and my room is occupied. However, I've also heard your brother seems to have taken up residence elsewhere. I plan for us to use Father's room while we're here."

Lydia and Michael stared at each other and Kate felt as if she were seeing exactly what Michael had once described to her. Lydia Sheridan did not like her younger son. Perhaps, Kate thought, because she knows he is as strong as she pretends not to be. Coming to a decision, Michael's mother looked at Kate and then back again at her son. "As you wish," she said quietly. "Then I shall see you both at dinner."

Nodding, Michael's face held a look of sadness as he watched his mother turn away from him . . . again.

Chapter 27

"I know it's strange, Kate. But somehow I find it very satisfying that we'll be using my father's room."

She tried to smile her understanding, but everything was more confusing than before. She hated being here, in Lydia's house. She didn't care how much Michael talked of this being his home, Kate knew it really belonged to only one person—Lydia Sheridan. And she felt less than an uninvited guest; she felt like an intruder.

"I just wish we could have talked about it first. I don't know who was more surprised . . . your mother, or me."

Coming to her side, Michael wrapped his arms about her waist. "We're not going to be here forever," he teased. "Just until everything is straightened out. Besides, this is the perfect place to start looking for the treasure."

She shrugged her shoulders. For some strange reason, even the prospect of finding the treasure held little satisfaction. "It's this place," she said in a small

428

voice. "I don't feel comfortable here."

He kissed her shoulder. "You'll get over it. Once my mother gets to know you, she won't be able to help loving you, too."

Spinning around, Kate faced him. "Open your eyes, Michael. Your mother and I are never going to be friends." Seeing how his face clouded with disappointment, she took a deep breath and added, "But I will try and get along with her. I just hate the way she treats you. She is so . . ."

He placed a finger to her lips and stopped any further words. "I wish I'd never told you all those things about her. You should have been given the opportunity to form your own opinions." Squeezing her hands, he said, "Give her a chance, Kate. She's been through so much since the war. And she isn't as well as she tries to pretend."

Clenching her back teeth to keep the angry words in, Kate nodded and returned to her unpacking. As she opened an empty drawer to place her underwear inside, her mind screamed the answer she'd been too afraid to say aloud. Lydia Sheridan's illnesses were nothing more than conveniences. She had been the picture of health only a few days ago, and it was obvious to Kate that the woman used her headaches to further manipulate her sons.

"My father used to sit in that chair and read for hours. He loved the classics."

Kate looked about the handsome bedroom. The dark, masculine furniture was offset by a red Oriental rug and varying hues of brown that were carried onto the upholstery and drapes. Seeing how much it meant to Michael to be here, she smiled. "It's a very nice room," she said truthfully. Once more she glanced about the bedroom. "I take it your mother has her own room?" she asked shyly. Kate couldn't picture Lydia in this obviously male room.

Michael nodded. "It isn't unusual for a married couple not to share a bedroom." Smiling, he added, "Just don't expect the same, Mrs. Sheridan. I found out this morning how satisfying it is to wake up and find you next to me."

Kate left the dresser and came up to her husband. Wrapping her arms around his shoulders, she said, "I hope you'll still say that in ten years."

"I'll say it fifty years from now."

"What about when I'm sick? I make a terrible patient, even when I just have a cold. I get miserable and want to be left alone. Do you think you can live through fifty years of that?"

He kissed the tip of her nose. "Then I'll just have to spoil you until you're better."

"I love you, Michael," she breathed and placed her head against his chest. As she felt his arms tighten about her, Kate couldn't help thinking that she had just described Lydia's life and Michael had responded as his father might have done. Was Michael used to spoiling a sick woman? Had he seen his father do so on so many occasions that it seemed normal? She had the strangest sensation that Lydia might use her weapon of illness to again trap Michael. It was a very sick game she was playing with her son's life. The woman would have to be blind not to see the devotion in Michael's face every time he looked at her. And why, when he showed signs of strength, did she revert to weakness to again ensnare him? What hold did she have over him, other than motherhood?

Kate returned Michael's hug. How do you fight a man's mother for his love, she thought in anguish, especially when it's all one-sided? Sighing, she closed her eyes and vowed to protect her husband from the destructive game Lydia was playing.

"So we meet again. Only it's Michael, isn't it?" Winston Barnett asked, his voice devoid of even the pretense of warmth.

Accepting a glass of wine from Kevin, Michael didn't bother to extend his hand. "That's correct. May I present my wife, Kathleen."

Kate returned Barnett's impatient nod with one of her own. After all this time she finally could attach a face to the cruel voice she'd heard while hiding in Helene's closet. His heavy features were set in a florid complexion with furrows of anger lining the sides of his mouth. Kate even managed to produce a small smile when she remembered that this man's treatment of his daughter in Bermuda had been the reason she'd traded places with Helene. It was Winston Barnett she had to thank for meeting Michael.

"You really a Bonaparte?" Barnett asked with a trace of sarcasm, as Helene and Lydia walked into the drawing room.

Smiling at Helene, she turned back to the girl's father. "I just became a Sheridan yesterday." And feeling Michael's hand slip around her waist, she added, "That's all that matters now."

"And you must be Helene," Michael said warmly, smiling at the nervous young girl. "I must say it's a sincere pleasure to finally meet you."

Helene's lips formed an embarrassed smile, for the implication was clear. Here was the man who had helped deceive her father. "How do you do, Michael?" she asked in a quiet voice. "I'm glad you've returned."

Lydia cleared her throat. "Wiley has informed me that we should proceed to the dining room." She glanced at the men in the room as if in evaluation. "Michael," she said finally, "could I ask you to escort your mother into dinner?"

Kate watched in amazement as Michael's eyes showed his pleasure. He briefly looked at Kate in a silent communication, as though asking for her understanding, before walking to his mother's side. As Kate watched her husband's back, she looked over his shoulder and took notice of Lydia's small smile. Was it only suspicion that made her think Lydia's expression held a note of triumph? Seeing Kevin move to Helene's side, she watched as the two of them fell in behind Lydia and Michael. Inwardly groaning, Kate tried to appear polite as Winston Barnett acted as her escort. She forced a tight smile as they followed the others into the dining room.

Kate felt like she was entering the lion's den.

Although everyone commented on the wild rice and delicately seasoned fish, Kate found the food to be tasteless. She could no more appreciate the cuisine than the beautifully appointed dining room. Several times she found herself daydreaming as she became lost in thought while staring at the huge chandelier over the table. She had to force herself to concentrate on the conversation going on around her. As eldest son, Kevin sat at the head of the table with Lydia at the opposite end. Somehow Lydia had arranged that both of them would be surrounded by guests of the opposite gender. Kate was seated on Kevin's left while Helene had been placed at his right, leaving Michael next to his mother, but on the opposite side of the table from his wife. Kate's dinner partner was Winston Barnett. Several times she had glanced toward the end of the table and observed Lydia almost flirting with her son, and a tremendous rush of jealousy surged up in Kate.

"So, Michael," Barnett interrupted her thoughts, "are you prepared to explain your actions when you were last in my home?"

All other conversation ceased as everyone directed their attention to the men seated across from each other. Tearing his eyes away from his mother, Michael wiped his mouth and slowly placed his napkin on the table.

"And what is it you would like explained?" he asked quietly.

As Barnett leaned into the table, Kate sat back and held her breath. "I want to know what you hoped to accomplish by your little charade. Have you any idea the trouble your interference has caused?"

Michael sat back in his chair and smiled. "I had no wish for my brother to be forced into a marriage for merely business reasons. And I understand now that your daughter shared that sentiment."

"You impudent whelp! You had no right to interfere or deceive me!" Barnett snapped. "It's time you learned to respect the decisions of your elders."

"You're addressing the wrong person," Kevin stated

433

in a cold voice. "I was the one who sent Michael in my place. He only went through with the marriage to protect me. If you've seen the marriage certificate, you'll have read that he signed his own name, instead of mine. If anyone is to be held responsible for this, then it should be I."

Helene looked ready to cry as she bit her bottom lip and Kate tried to reassure her with a strained smile. With her eyes she tried to convey a message to remain silent. The very last thing they needed right now was for Helene's conscience to start bothering her and for the girl to make a full confession.

"Since my daughter's memory seems to have been wiped away on that particular day, then perhaps one of you might tell us who that woman was?" Barnett demanded as he looked from Michael to his brother, and then back again.

"Would you believe," Michael asked with a grin, "that she was a mermaid?" Seeing Barnett's complexion flush even darker, Michael held up his hand and motioned that it had been a small joke. "Truthfully, I had thought the woman who was washed overboard was Helene Barnett." He looked down the table and smiled at the young blond-haired girl who was clutching her water goblet. "I'm very happy to know I was mistaken."

Good, Kate mentally applauded. So far he hasn't told any blatant lies. Now if they could just finish this dinner and get back upstairs.

"I should have had you arrested for kidnapping the minute you showed up in Charleston," Barnett snarled. "It isn't too late to have charges of manslaughter brought against you."

434

Michael actually laughed. "And whom did I kidnap? Your daughter happens to be sitting at this table."

Barnett's large fingers resembled a fist as they wrapped around his fork. "What about that woman who drowned? You can't prove it was an accident."

Michael's lips tightened. "And you can't prove it wasn't. In fact, Barnett, you can't even prove she existed." He crossed his arms over his chest and eyed the angry man opposite him. "Why don't we talk about why you want your family affiliated with the Sheridans. It puzzles me. Is the importing business off since the war?"

Barnett quickly came to his feet, causing his chair to fall to the floor. "Why, you insolent son of a—"

"Gentlemen!" Lydia rose, along with Michael and Kevin. "I think this has gone far enough. Your discussion is distressing the ladies at this table."

The angry males looked to Kate and Helene before Lydia drew their attention back to her. "Michael, you were wrong to impersonate your brother," she stated in a flat voice. "You've caused immeasurable stress for this family. And, Kevin—" She looked to her eldest son. "I am bitterly disappointed that you wouldn't have come to me before arranging this with Michael."

Taking a deep breath, she addressed Winston Barnett. "You have insulted the male members in this family. I would ask you, sir, to remember you are a guest in this house and to act accordingly. Any further discussion of this matter will take place at another time and behind closed doors."

Without looking behind her, she said to the ever-present servant who stood against the wall. "Wiley, would you help me to my room? I have no appetite

435

for dessert."

Keeping his face impassive, the elderly man stepped forward and presented his arm. Giving everyone a withering stare, Lydia Sheridan placed her hand on the man's sleeve and withdrew from the room.

"Wasn't she magnificent?" Michael asked as he unhooked Kate's blue gown. "She really put Barnett in his place."

Slipping out of the sleeves, Kate murmured, "She also put you and Kevin in your place."

Michael ignored her remark. "I don't think Barnett's going to remain here much longer. Tonight he found out that the Sheridans stick together."

Kate stepped out of the gown and threw it onto the large overstuffed chair. "Do you realize that if he leaves, he takes Helene with him? And both Kevin and I promised her our protection!"

"I didn't start it, Kate. The man nearly jumped across the table to get at my throat!" He pulled on his tie until it was free, then flung it on the bed. "Why are you angry with me?" he demanded.

Kate knew it would sound too much like whining if she told Michael that she couldn't stand his mother, or her house, so she smiled and picked up her gown. Walking toward the closet, she said, "I'm not angry with you. I suppose I'm just worried. You can cut the undercurrent in this house with a knife." As she hung up her dress, she turned back to her husband. "Do you know since I've walked into this house this morning, your mother hasn't uttered a single word in my direction? She hasn't spoken to me."

436

Michael looked confused. "Maybe you should initiate a conversation with her yourself. She's had a lot on her mind, Kate. I'm sure she hasn't meant to snub you. Why, at dinner tonight, she was almost as animated as when Father sat at that table."

Seeing the look of love cross his face when he spoke of his mother, Kate's stomach lurched. In that moment, she knew she had a mother-in-law problem. All Lydia had to do was pay Michael a small amount of attention and he was ready to forget the years of pain she had caused. Something intuitive made Kate realize that Lydia was playing with her son's affections. She pictured in her mind Lydia's smiles of triumph that had been directed toward her. Lydia wanted her to know which one of them had the most power over Michael. Tonight, Kate had to admit Lydia had been the winner. This first full day of marriage seemed destined to end with her husband's thoughts filled with images of his mother. Almost growling with outrage, she ran across the carpet and threw herself into Michael's arms.

Catching her, Michael laughed as he fell with Kate onto the large bed. As he pushed the hair away from her forehead and wrapped it behind her ear, he grinned. "Is there some reason, madam, why you have attacked me?"

She gazed into his eyes and returned his smile. "Yes, there is. I want to know when you intend to take me on a honeymoon!"

"A honeymoon?"

She nodded. "That's right. A honeymoon!" Hearing the word said over again, she realized for the first time how silly it sounded. *Honeymoon*. Whoever made up such words? "A wedding trip," she quickly amended, not sure if the other was a more modern term.

Michael's eyes lit with understanding. "Ah . . . a wedding trip! I have it all planned."

Kate's eyebrows rose in surprise. "You do?" she asked. "Do you think I might be included in these plans of yours? You're getting very commanding, Michael. First you arrange for a wedding while I'm in my nightgown—"

"It was a beautiful nightgown."

Kate ignored his interruption. "Then you tell me you've decided where we'll go on our honeymoon. I would appreciate—"

He silenced her with a quick kiss. "We're going back to Bermuda, Kate."

"We are?"

His grin widened and he nodded. "Now guess why."

Kate's expression became soft and tender. "Because that's where we met. How romantic you are, Michael, when you put your mind to it."

He shook his head.

"What do you mean, no?"

Seeing he had offended her, he quickly said, "Well, yes. Of course that's one of the reasons I want us to go back. But there's another. Try again."

"Because of Helene? You want to take Helene back? I do, too, but that's not exactly a romantic reason for a honeymoon." She watched as he chuckled and again shook his head.

"It has nothing to do with romance, Kate. If I'd chosen a place that was romantic, I'd have made plans for that island on the coast where we were stranded. What were we talking about early this morning?"

It suddenly came to her and she giggled with delight.

"The chain! We're going to bring up the chain?"

Nodding, Michael kissed her, nibbling at her bottom lip as he broke away. "You were right when you said it's just lying there, waiting for someone to bring up. Why shouldn't it be us?"

Kate hugged him. "How I love you, Michael," she exclaimed. "You're starting to think like me."

Kissing her neck, he laughed. "Now that's enough to frighten any man!" As he lifted his head, he asked, "Will you help me roll up the rug? I still say the treasure is hidden in this room."

Kate grinned and sat up. "I already started looking while you went back to the hotel for my things, but I never thought to look under the rug. What do you think Martin did? Pry up one of the floorboards?"

Standing up, Michael shrugged as he held out his hand to her. "Who knows the way his mind works? I only know if I had to hide it, I'd conceal it in something that was in view at all times."

Kate straightened the bodice of her chemise. "I say we start with the bed. He could have hidden it in the mattress."

Nodding, Michael rolled his sleeves up as they both prepared to tear the room apart.

It was past midnight when Kate started to give up. They'd checked every seam in the feather mattress and all were intact. They'd moved the bed and, on hands and knees, had examined the wooden flooring. All the nails were still tightly joined. Together they had moved furniture, checked drawers, inspected moldings, cornices, anything that might have been pried away and used as a hiding place. After scrutinizing the closet, they'd even tried the passageway with the possibility

439

that Martin had discovered it. Each time they came up empty-handed.

"Michael," Kate said in a tired voice as she collapsed on the edge of the bed, "maybe he didn't hide it here. Did you ever think he might have it with him, wherever he is?"

Using his shirt-sleeve, Michael wiped the perspiration from his forehead and shook his head. "Martin didn't have a chance to get to the treasure. Remember, he disappeared from the office after hearing that Barnett was in the city. We know he didn't come back here."

Kate sighed with defeat. "Wherever it is, he did a good job hiding it." She looked about the room. "Why don't we put this place back in order and get some rest? If it is in here, it's not going anywhere until tomorrow."

He didn't say anything as he quietly closed a desk drawer that he'd already checked at least twice before. Together they worked on the room in silence, each dealing with their own frustration. When they finally fell into bed, Michael held her close, yet neither made a more intimate move. Kate could almost feel the disappointment inside Michael and, in truth, she wasn't in the mood to make love, either. Michael's mother played heavily on her mind.

After some thought, she realized that by remaining quiet, by permitting them to intrude on her marriage, she was allowing Lydia and Martin a small victory. Determined to foil them whenever possible, she leaned up on her elbow and stared at her husband's profile.

"It's not what's really important, Michael," she whispered. "You know that, don't you?"

He turned his head and stared at her through the

dark. "The treasure," she said. "It isn't as important to me as you think."

"But it's yours, Kate. Martin has no right to it."

"You're mine," she stated emphatically. "And *that's* what's important to me."

Leaning down, she softly kissed his lips. "I want children," she breathed into his mouth. "I want your children."

"Children?"

She nodded.

"I never thought about children."

"Then start," she whispered, running the tip of her finger over his bottom lip. "I want lots of little Sheridans running around all over the place. And I want at least half of them to look like you."

She felt him deeply inhale as his hands swept over her body.

"Katie . . ."

Chapter 28

"May I join you?" Kate asked as she entered the sun room toward the back of the first floor.

Lydia placed the flower she'd been cutting into a basket and nodded once. "We missed both you and Michael at breakfast. Have you had anything to eat?"

Trying to be friendly, Kate smiled. "Wiley brought a tray to our room. It was very thoughtful."

Motioning to the porcelain tea service on a low table, Lydia remarked, "It was thoughtful of Wiley. Please don't expect it every morning. He's no longer young, and I'd rather he didn't climb the stairs if it isn't necessary."

"Certainly," Kate answered, not bothering to inform her that neither she nor Michael had requested breakfast in bed. Instead, she looked around the lovely room. It was almost a hothouse with its many plants and flowers. Softly cushioned wicker furniture was placed strategically to complement the nursery, rather than the other way around. Surrounded by so much greenery and color, Kate felt far more comfortable in this oasis than in the stark, formal drawing room.

"It's beautiful here," she observed while sitting down in a wide chair. "Did you grow all these yourself?"

Returning to her gardening chores, Lydia remarked, "It's my one avocation, a diversion, you might say, from running this house. This room belongs to me, not the generations of Sheridans that still occupy Hidden Haven. I'm sure you've noticed all the portraits. I had this room built on after my marriage."

"Hidden Haven?" Kate asked with confusion.

Lydia removed her gardening gloves and smoothed the material of her blue dress. "The unofficial name the Sheridan men have given to this house," she explained. "I have no idea which one came up with it, but after so many years it's become permanent."

Kate had to suppress a grin when she thought of the hidden passageway from the bedroom to the study. Somehow, she didn't think Lydia would find it humorous if she told how the name came about.

Sitting down opposite Kate, Lydia poured herself a cup of tea. As she settled back on the cushion, the older woman stared at Kate while stirring the added sugar.

"Are you . . . are you feeling better today?" Kate asked politely, wanting to fill the silence.

She watched the corners of Lydia's mouth slightly lift to resemble a tight smile. "Are you uncomfortable, dear? Your voice sounds strained."

Inhaling deeply, Kate sat up straighter and prepared for battle. At least she could say she'd tried to be pleasant. "Am I uncomfortable here?" Kate asked quietly, determined to control her voice. "The answer is yes. I certainly don't feel welcome."

There was a measurable silence.

"Like you, I haven't forgotten our last meeting, so I shall dispense with any pretense of friendliness. I don't welcome you," Lydia stated matter-of-factly. "Not into my home, nor into my family. I consider you to be an opportunist, looking for security after the war has taken away your chances for it. You should be forewarned, my dear, that I contacted my attorney this morning. I did tell you that I planned to have you investigated." She sipped her tea. "I should have something by the end of the week to present to Michael. We'll see then, dear, which one of us he believes."

Smiling tightly to control the anger within her that threatened to explode, Kate said, "I am not your dear. My name is Kate . . . Kathleen. Or," she added, "if that's too familiar for your taste, you may call me Mrs. Sheridan—a name I intend to have for a very long time."

Lydia appeared to flinch at Kate's last statement. Recovering quickly, her lips pulled back in a grim smile. "You're very good . . . Kathleen. Most would have become hysterical, or thrown a temper tantrum by now. You're very controlled. Perhaps that's something that comes with age. You aren't the young bride I had expected my son to wed. In fact, I'm sure once the blush of this union fades, Michael will see that you're actually quite common, and recognize you for the calculating woman you are."

"I don't think you ever expected your sons to wed," Kate blurted out. "You enjoy being the center of their attention. Isn't that what all these headaches are about? You like having young, handsome men fawn all over you . . . even if they're your own sons."

"How dare you speak to me like that? I am not the one who needs to explain herself." Feeling she was losing control, Lydia slowly placed her cup on the table and looked up. "Or is it that you're jealous of a son's love for his mother?"

Kate's stomach tightened and she clenched her back teeth. "From everything I've heard, Lydia, a cat is a better mother than what you've been to Michael."

"I don't believe my son would ever imply such a thing! Michael loves me."

"I've heard it from several sources. What I'd like to know is why you've done this to him." Kate was close to tears. "I have no idea why, but he does love you, Lydia. And because I love him, I'm going to protect him from you. You can't play with people's lives anymore. At least not Michael's."

Rising to her feet, Lydia walked to a plant and examined its leaves. "You're becoming very dramatic. Michael was a difficult child, always into trouble. Judging by his last escapade in Bermuda, he hasn't changed much. He needs a firm hand."

"He needed your love!" Kate stated angrily. "Now he has mine."

Lydia spun around and faced her. Her smile was almost evil. "As I said earlier, you're very good, Kathleen . . . but I'm better. Michael will listen to his mother. You won't be a Sheridan for long."

Kate refused to look away, though her mind screamed for her husband. Where was he? After Wiley had stopped him in the foyer, he'd said he would follow her. My God, Michael, she silently begged, get in here!

* * *

"Repeat it again, Wiley. And tell me what he looked like."

The old servant rubbed his ear. "This here man comes to the back door, with a face that looks like a mashed-in melon, it does. And he says, 'You tell Michael it would be in his interest to come to Sheridan Warehouse this mornin' at eleven-thirty. All the answers is there.' And then he says, 'You be sure to tell him that there's no setup. It's safe to come and get what you wants.' This make any sense to you, Mista' Michael?"

Michael stared at the old, familiar face—a face that had, through his own lifetime, shown concern, kindness, amusement, and friendship. Placing a hand on Wiley's bent shoulder, he said, "Old friend, it looks like I'm about to have a showdown. I've waited years for this day."

"I don't understand," Wiley muttered. "Show down with who? What'cha gettin' into now, Mickey Sheridan?"

Feeling like he was thirteen again, Michael chuckled. "You know you sounded just like B.D. just then? I haven't had the chance to talk to you, Wiley, but I saw him while I was out at Haphazard. He said you told him there was trouble here. What's happened?"

Looking uncomfortable, Wiley scratched his gray hair and searched the nearby rooms for any eavesdroppers. "Ever since your daddy died in that prison, Miz Lydia been actin' real strange. Then Mista' Masterson, he come here actin' like this a Masterson home, 'stead of Sheridan. Then you leaves . . . her own boy she put out. I tell you, since your daddy's gone, bad times come to this house. Miz Lydia and Mista'

446

Masterson, they's always talkin' together or shoutin' at each other. Mista' Kevin, he don't pay any mind to 'em. Jus' pretend they's ain't there. You back to stay, Mickey? My old bones tell me somethin' bad's acomin'.'"

Moving closer, Michael rubbed Wiley's upper arm. "Don't you worry anymore," he said in a rough voice. "You've been worrying long enough, Wiley. I'll take over. Everything's going to be settled in a few days." He looked at the man who had chastised him, taught him to fish and hunt, put him on a horse and then taught him how to ride. It was Wiley who had hid him when he was in trouble, laughed at his jokes, and made him understand he had to answer for his pranks. Never doubting his loyalty, Michael added, "Don't mention to anyone this conversation, or that visitor to the back door—especially to my wife. If she asks where I am, say that I had to check on the *Rebel*. That's what I'm going to tell her. All right?"

Biting on his bottom lip, Wiley nodded. "You in trouble, Mickey? Maybe you should get your brother to go with you."

Michael shook his head. "This is something I have to do alone. I'm going to find my wife now and tell her about the *Rebel*. If you're questioned by anyone you say that's where I am."

"You best be careful, you hear?"

Michael smiled at his old friend. "I told you not to worry anymore, Wiley. This time I plan to be very careful."

Wiley watched Michael walk toward the back of the house and sighed. Here it was Sunday mornin', he thought in disgust, and nobody in this house makin' a

447

move to go to church. Shaking his head, he looked up to the foyer ceiling and addressed his former master. "Joseph Sheridan, I been keeping your secrets for too many years," he muttered. "You best whisper to the Lord and tell him to start watchin' over your son. He got a might heap of trouble comin' his way."

Feeling his age, Wiley headed toward the kitchen to check on lunch. Before he reached the cook, he made up his mind that when Michael left this house, he, too, was through. He'd live out the rest of his life on B.D.'s farm and have some peace before the Lord called him. It was almost time. He'd kept his promise to Joseph, as best he could.

Facing the doorway, Lydia was the first to see him. "Michael!" she exclaimed. "Come over here and give your mother a kiss."

Startled by the unusual request, he glanced at Kate before quickly coming to his mother's side. Softly kissing her cheek, his face couldn't conceal his pleasure at his mother's new attitude toward him.

"Sit here next to me," she invited. "Kathleen and I were just having the most interesting discussion. Weren't we, dear?"

Both Lydia and Michael looked to Kate. Her only answer was a grim smile.

"Actually, Mother, I came in to tell you I wouldn't be joining you for lunch." Hearing Kate's tiny gasp, he quickly added, "I've just been called down to the *Rebel*. Some trouble with the hawser—the mooring ropes."

"I'll go with you," Kate hurried to offer. The very last thing she wanted was to be left with Lydia.

Michael smiled. "I wouldn't be able to spend any time with you, Kate. Stay here and keep Mother company. I'll be back for dinner this evening."

"Yes, stay, Kathleen. If there's one thing I've learned, it's that a Sheridan wife should never interfere with business." She patted her son's hand. "You run along, Michael. I'll take care of your wife."

The expression on Michael's face showed that he was pleased with his mother's words. Standing up, he came to Kate and kissed her hand. "Enjoy yourself," he said softly. "I'll be back before you know it."

Inwardly, Kate groaned, thoroughly annoyed with the way she had been manipulated. Forcing a smile, she could only nod, for she couldn't rely on her voice to sound normal. Was Michael blind? What would it take to wipe away that film of trust across his eyes? Every time he looked at Lydia, he was a blind man, groping for her approval.

As he left the room, Lydia's voice called out to him, "Michael?"

He turned around and faced her with a questioning smile.

Kate watched as Lydia continued to stare at her son. Finally, she murmured, "You really do have your father's eyes."

His grin widened with her compliment. "Thank you, Mother. And I promise not to delay your dinner tonight."

She watched him walk away before saying in a quietly reflective voice, "Good-bye, Michael."

He was in a strange mood as he left his home. He couldn't quite get over the dramatic change in his mother. She was almost warm and affectionate this morning. Maybe, he thought, the old saying of everything happens for a reason was true in this case. Perhaps if he hadn't been swept overboard and thought to be dead, his mother never would have come around. And he had waited so many years for it . . .

As he left the residential area of the city, he thought of Kate. All she needed was a little time with his mother. They were the two most important people in his life, and he wanted them to get along. He knew Kate didn't understand the relationship between him and his mother. Hell, he didn't even understand it. He only knew Lydia Sheridan had, with a single glance, the power to make him feel lacking. He wasn't a fool, though. He'd felt the tension between his mother and Kate as soon as he'd walked into the room. He also knew Kate thought he was deserting her this morning. He would just have to explain later that he'd made the decision for her to remain at home. She was far safer with his mother than accompanying him. And he saw that as much as he desired his mother's approval, his marriage to Kate was not up for debate. He realized he'd have to make that clear tonight, for he never wanted Kate to doubt his love. From personal experience, he knew how destructive that could be . . . and he also knew which of the two women had earned his devotion. He just hoped Kate wouldn't spend the afternoon wondering, for he could see now that he hadn't handled the situation properly. Away from his mother, he could think more clearly. Lydia Sheridan had given him a lifetime of rejection. Kate had given him her love . . . and the promise of a future.

Flicking the reins over the horse's back, he steered the carriage toward the waterfront and tried to overcome the queer sensation of being watched. Ever since he'd left home, the old instinctive warnings he'd developed as a blockade runner had come rushing back. He certainly didn't take Martin's word about the safety of this meeting and carried his old revolver inside his jacket for insurance. As the warehouse came into view, he slowed the carriage and proceeded on foot.

"He's fifteen minutes late. You sure that old nigra got the message right?"

Touching his injured arm, a man grunted. "I told you I made him repeat it. Ain't my fault if he got it messed up."

Martin Masterson paced the cleared area of the Sheridan warehouse. Michael was his only hope. He had to get back into that house and retrieve the treasure. From behind, he heard a voice that made his blood run cold.

"You wanted to see me, Masterson?"

Spinning around, Martin stared at his nephew. Recovering quickly, he swallowed several times and said, "You don't need that gun. I sent word that this was no setup."

Keeping the barrel pointed at Martin's chest, Michael flicked his head toward the man who had accosted him yesterday. "Then what was that supposed to be? A greeting for my return from the dead?"

Martin shook his head. "That was a mistake, Michael. I promise, you have my word as a gentleman, that I won't try it again." Running his arthritic fingers through his hair, he admitted, "You see, I find I need your help."

Despite the danger he was in, Michael issued a hard laugh. "A gentleman! You must be joking! And why would I ever help you, of all people?"

Masterson lifted his chin and said, "Because I have the information you want about Sheridan Shipping and Barnett's operations."

"What information? And why tell me? Why not Kevin?"

Martin shook his gray head. "You're the one who wants to clear your father's name. Isn't that why you've hated me all these years?"

Michael clenched his back teeth together. An almost blinding anger rose up in him when Martin mentioned his father. "Send them away," he ordered, looking at the two rough-looking men by his uncle's side.

Masterson smiled. "But they're for my protection ... against you. You're not going to like what you'll be hearing."

Michael's grin was cold. "I could have killed you while you were waiting for me. If I did decide to kill you, they wouldn't be any protection. One of them can't even raise his arm, and the other'd be dead before he could reach his gun. Even if he managed to shoot me, I'd still be able to take you with me. Rest easy, old man, I'm not going to take your life today."

Martin's aging eyes widened. Pointing a finger, he exclaimed, "That was you on the road to Dunnemores! Wasn't it? You said the same thing that night. You're the one who robbed me!"

Smiling, Michael inclined his head slightly. "So you see, I've had the opportunity before. Now send them away."

He watched as Masterson nodded to the men.

Glaring at Michael, both of the guards walked toward the warehouse opening. He waited until he could see the men standing in the distance before addressing his uncle. "Now what the hell is it you have to say?"

"I want to make a deal with you."

"A deal? For what?"

Martin picked up his cane and leaned his weight on it as he walked closer to Michael. "I can clear your father's name. And . . . give you back Sheridan Shipping. That's what you want, isn't it?"

Not relaxing his guard, Michael raised his chin. "How?"

Excited by Michael's question, Martin slapped at his own chest. "I kept records, boy! Records that show how they been stealing from the governments. They never thought I would, but I did in case I'd have to protect myself someday. Barnett already has trouble with investigations. He told me so himself six months ago."

Michael's eyes narrowed. "Who are *they?* Barnett's working with someone else besides you?"

Backing away from Michael, Masterson said, "You put that gun away and I'll tell you. I'm not saying another word while that's pointed at me."

Michael spent less than ten seconds debating whether to do as Martin requested. In the end, he figured this new information was worth the chance. Slipping the gun back behind his jacket, he said, "Now tell me. Who is this third partner?"

Masterson took a long, shuddering breath before he uttered the name. "Lydia."

His heart stopped beating for an instant before sanity returned. "You lying son of a bitch! What kind of man are you to shift the blame to your sister? God Almighty, you aren't worthy of her . . . If it wasn't for my mother, you'd be nothing more than a sharecropper on your father's old plantation right now!"

Holding up his hands to ward off Michael's anger, Martin persisted, "I'm telling you the truth. If you want proof, you'll have to help me tonight."

Shaking with a barely controlled rage, he glared at the small, pathetic man before him. "What the hell are you talking about now? Jesus Christ! I never believed you'd stoop this low. What happened, Martin? You heard the Federal Government is down here to help me get you out of the company?"

He reeled back with shock. "They're investigating me already? But I tell you, Michael, I was nothing but a front man. It was Lydia and Barnett who are the brains behind this. I told you. I have proof!"

Although he wanted to strangle the man, had dreamed of doing so many times, something in Michael made him ask, "What proof? Where is it?"

Martin took a few steps closer. "You get me in that house tonight and I'll give it to you."

"It's in the house?"

Masterson shook his head. "I'd never keep it there. She could find it. I need to get into your father's room for a few minutes, that's all. After tonight, I'm getting out of the country. You arrange for a meeting of Lydia and Barnett, say at nine o'clock, and I'll give you the information you want . . . in exchange for letting me back into your father's room."

"What are you looking for, Martin? The treasure?"

He looked frightened as his complexion turned to ash. "You know about that?"

454

Michael laughed. "Whose ship was it on?"

Breathing deeply, Martin leaned against a wooden crate for support. "Then we negotiate a new deal. You can have half. There's enough for both of us."

"And what do I have to do for it?" Michael asked out of curiosity.

"You make arrangements for a meeting between you, me, Lydia, and Barnett. No matter what you find out tonight, you've got to promise to protect me from them. And after it's over, you get the books I been keeping and I get half the treasure. I'm the only one who knows where it is."

"I don't want my mother involved in this. We'll leave her out."

Martin's voice showed his frustration. "She can't be left out! She never wanted you to have the company, but she could see before the war how your father took notice of you over Kevin. You had a natural flair for it, while her favorite would always be mediocre, at best. Either she's at that meeting, or the deal's off."

The truth of his mother's betrayal hit him squarely between the eyes and for a moment he felt physically ill. "Nine o'clock. In the drawing room," he managed to get out. "And God help you if you're lying this time."

Nodding, Masterson slowly offered his hand. "It's a deal, then? I have your word?"

Michael looked at the old, gnarled fingers and almost shuddered with revulsion. Ignoring the gesture, he brushed past the man he had spent three years hating and walked out of the warehouse.

He was like a blind man as he sensed, rather than saw, his carriage. As he walked up to it, he had to continuously blink in order to see straight, for the rage inside of him was blurring his vision. Only ten more feet and then he would be able to . . .

Suddenly, gunfire exploded all around him and he instinctively sank to the ground as a bullet whizzed past his ear. Pulling out his gun, his vision quickly cleared as his eyes searched the rooftops of the surrounding warehouses. It was over in seconds as he watched a man's body fall from the roof of one building. A rifle followed the body and crashed not ten feet away from it, breaking up as it met the cobbles. And Michael hadn't fired a single shot! Glancing up to Sheridan Warehouse, he saw the two stunned guards slowly move toward the body while Martin came rushing out of the interior.

Seeing his nephew, Masterson started shouting, "I swear I had nothing to do with it! It wasn't me that ordered it. Damn it, I need you alive!"

Michael stood up and explored the deserted street. It appeared he either had a guardian angel or someone else wanted him to make that meeting tonight, too.

"Michael!"

After slamming the front door, he looked up at his mother as she paused on the stairs. Clutching her chest, Lydia looked ready to collapse back onto them. "What . . . what's wrong?" she stammered, her face as white as the walls behind her.

Clenching his jaw, Michael climbed the stairs. When he was two steps below her, he stopped and searched her face. Taking a calming breath he said, "I would like to meet with you and Barnett tonight in the drawing room. Nine o'clock."

Lydia tried to smile. "Why? We'll see you at dinner before that."

"I'm having dinner upstairs," he remarked coldly as he walked past her.

Looking at his back, she demanded, "Michael, what's wrong with you? What happened? Come back here and explain yourself!"

"I'm going to see my wife," he said in a dull voice. "I'll speak with you later tonight." He never turned around.

Chapter 29

Shutting the bedroom door behind him, Michael glanced at Kate's shocked expression before closing his eyes and leaning against the wooden frame for support.

"What happened to you?" Kate asked in a frightened voice as she came to stand in front of him. His face was pale, his hair out of place, and his clothing was soiled. "Michael?"

Opening his eyes, he stared down at his wife. Seeing her concern, he quickly wrapped his arms around her. As he buried his face in her hair, he whispered, "What would you think of starting our wedding trip tonight? The *Rebel* is ready and I've told Denny to come for our luggage at nine-thirty."

She lifted her head. "We're leaving tonight?"

Nodding, Michael tightened his hold on her. "You were right about coming here. It was a poor decision."

As she relaxed against the front of his body, she felt something hard and opened his jacket. Seeing the handle of a gun, she pulled back. "What do you have that for?" she demanded. "Michael, tell me the truth.

What's going on?"

He took a deep breath and walked away from the doorway, leaving her to stare after him. "C'mon, I'll help you repack. I'd like everything to be ready . . ."

"Tell me!"

Michael turned around and recognized the determination in her voice. Sighing with defeat, he said slowly, "I met with Masterson this afternoon."

"*You what?* Why didn't you tell me? You said you were going to the *Rebel!*"

He reached out and took her hand. "Kate, please don't argue with me . . . Not now. Can't you understand that I'm trying to protect you? I wouldn't have been able to do that and deal with Martin at the same time. I couldn't afford that distraction."

"God, Michael, what's happening? Ever since we came into this house yesterday, everything's gone wrong!"

Pushing his hair back from his forehead, he nodded. "Believe me, Kate. It'll be all over by tonight."

"What did your uncle say?" she asked with a feeling of dread.

"He wants me to arrange a meeting with Barnett and my mother."

"Your mother?"

Michael looked away and nodded. "He claims she's been involved all along."

Kate's mouth dropped open. "Listen, Michael, I'm not a great fan of Lydia's, but even I can't believe she'd do this to her son."

His face showed his pain. "Martin said she was protecting Kevin's interest in the company. He said she thought my father was going to appoint me over Kevin

459

to head Sheridan Shipping." He looked toward the window. "My God, I never even wanted the company until Martin started running it."

Not knowing how to comfort him, Kate touched his shoulder. "When is the meeting?"

"Tonight," he said in a flat voice.

Kate's body tensed. "Here?"

Quickly, he turned his head. "Listen to me, Kate. At nine o'clock tonight I'm going to be meeting with them in the drawing room . . . *alone!*"

"Please, Michael! You can't go in there alone. You don't know what they're planning. You could be . . ."

He sat in the overstuffed chair and pulled her with him. When she was seated on his lap, he held her chin so she was forced to meet his gaze. "What I need from you tonight, Katie, is support. Promise me I can have that."

She pursed her lips in anger. "You can't trust any of them. How can you walk in there by yourself? It's sheer madness! I wouldn't interfere with . . ."

"Promise me!"

She searched his face and found concern written across it. The mouth that could drive her to the brink of sanity with its exquisite tenderness, was held in a stern line. The blue eyes that would darken with a passion and ignite a fire deep within her were now exacting compliance. Grudgingly, she nodded.

Satisfied that Kate had yielded to his wishes, Michael shifted in the chair and squeezed her. "Now, we'd better start packing up. Besides, I think this chair needs to be restrung. With the two of us in it, I can feel a coil boring its way into me."

Smiling, in spite of the danger she knew the night

would bring, Kate rose to her feet and helped Michael up. "One more day in this house and *I'd* have to be restrung," she muttered while watching as Michael hastily massaged his abused posterior.

He stared at her for a few seconds before whispering her name, "Kate . . . ?" Abruptly looking back to the chair, he asked, "Did we check it? I mean, did we *really* check it last night?"

"I looked under it, but . . ." Quickly, they knelt before Joseph Sheridan's favorite chair.

Throwing the cushion seat to the floor, Michael's hands delved into the sides of the chair while Kate checked the welting and seams for any signs of tampering.

"Oh my God! I don't believe it!"

Hearing Michael's exclamation, Kate popped her head up and watched her husband's arm maneuver something from the chair's interior. "What? What is it?" she demanded as excitement built inside her.

Struggling, he shook his head as he continued to fight with whatever he'd found. "The stuffing from the chair's been removed and . . ." He never finished his sentence as his arm came free. His fingers were grasping a small but heavy-looking leather pouch.

Kate and Michael's eyes locked with expectation and she held her breath as he turned his attention to the leather bag. Bringing it to the bed, he drew open the pouch and turned it over.

Both of them watched in amazement as chunks of fiery emeralds, pale amethysts, glittering diamonds, and a gold cross studded with emeralds fell to the mattress . . . all followed by the large gold stone that had served as their resting place.

461

"Michael!"

At Kate's excited squeal, he quickly dropped the pouch and placed his hand over her mouth. Shaking his head, he tried to control his own laughter as he whispered, "Don't! We can't let anyone know we've found it!"

Nodding, Kate removed his hand and threw her arms around his neck. "But we have found it!" she exclaimed. "Isn't it beautiful?"

They broke away and stared down to the mattress. Almost reverently, Michael picked up the cross and held it before them. "This is unbelievable!" he said in a hushed, shocked voice. "It must be worth a fortune!"

Kate giggled. "It is! And now it's ours!"

Quickly, he scooped up the jewels and carefully placed them back in the sack. "We've got to hide it," he warned. "Martin thinks he's coming back here to get them."

"Tonight?"

Nodding, Michael looked about the room, searching for a place to conceal the treasure. As he spied the closet, he said, "What about the passageway? We know he hasn't found that yet."

Kate grinned. "Perfect." Hurrying to the closet door, she said, "You put it in the passageway, and I'll fix the chair. Just make sure you don't let him back into this room until we've left for the ship."

Watching as her husband moved clothes and found the panel, Kate returned to the bedroom. As she hastily crossed the room, she couldn't suppress an elated giggle. By ten o'clock tonight she would be back on the *Rebel* . . . with the man she loved, and the treasure. She could hardly wait to leave this house, she thought,

462

as she picked up the chair cushion. Only a few more hours . . .

"Wait here for me," Michael instructed as he stood in the doorway of their bedroom. "I've already talked to Kevin and Helene. I didn't have time to explain everything, but I did tell them if they planned on going with us to start preparing. They're discussing it now."

"Michael, please . . ." Kate watched as he shook his head. "You can't go in there alone. I don't trust any of them. Just let me come with you. I won't interfere."

"You'll stay here until I return. Be prepared to leave. As soon as this meeting is over, we're getting out." He kissed her forehead and smiled. "Stop worrying, Kate. I don't trust them, either."

Her mouth tightened with concern. "Just make sure your uncle doesn't come for the jewels until we leave. That's one confrontation I don't want to witness."

Nodding, Michael turned away and walked down the hallway. As Kate closed the door, she waited no more than ten seconds before slowly reopening it. Bringing her eye to the crack, she watched her husband head for the stairs. When he was no longer in sight, she opened the door and followed him. In her mind she felt no guilt for disobeying his wishes as she stealthily made her way to the stairs. There wasn't any way she was letting Michael go through with this meeting alone. He never had to find out about her presence, but she knew she couldn't spend the next half hour in that bedroom. She'd go out of her mind with worry.

Only a little while longer, she told herself, and they'd be free to get on with their lives. As she leaned over the railing and looked down to the stair landing, she tried to dismiss the sick feeling in the pit of her stomach. Only a little while longer, her brain kept repeating . . . as if in a promise.

Winston Barnett and Lydia were already in the drawing room as Michael entered. Acknowledging them with a nod, he said, "I'd appreciate your patience. We're waiting for a fourth person to arrive before we start."

Lydia lifted the hem of her gray gown and walked toward Michael. "What's going on? I don't care for being summoned like this so late at night. And who is this fourth person? I think you should explain yourself."

"That's right!" Barnett agreed. "Someone down the line should have taught you some manners. Why, if you were my son, I'd have . . ."

"But I'm not your son," Michael coolly interrupted. "Joseph Sheridan was my father—an honorable, caring man. Very respected, at one time, for his genius in business. Isn't that right, Mother?"

Lydia straightened her shoulders. "Well, yes. Of course," she said defensively. "All that scandal after the war was . . . it was appalling."

Hearing a knock at the door that joined the foyer, Michael nodded to his mother. "I agree. It was appalling," he said as he turned the knob and admitted the person who would complete the gathering. Martin Masterson used his cane as he walked into the elegant white drawing room.

"*Martin!*" Lydia clutched at her throat, as though she were having trouble swallowing.

Barnett recovered more quickly. "Masterson! Where

464

the hell have you been? And what's this about?"

Michael felt as if someone had kicked him in the stomach. Seeing the horror in his mother's eyes when her brother walked into the room had made him ill. Forcing himself to remain calm, he sat on the edge of the desk and said, "Didn't you say, Mother, that any further discussion concerning the family should take place behind closed doors?"

Tearing her eyes away from her brother, she glanced in Michael's direction. "Well, yes, but I don't see what Martin can contribute . . ."

"It seems to me that Martin is an integral part of our family's troubles," Michael interrupted. "As a matter of fact, it was his idea to call this meeting."

His mother and Barnett exchanged worried looks.

Kate pressed her ear against the door and listened. So far, it sounded as though Michael was in command. She just wished she could hear better through the heavy wood. Taking a deep breath, she tried to regain her composure, for she'd practically fainted when she had almost come face to face with Martin. It was only quick reflexes that had made her jump back to the landing before Masterson had been able to look up from the foyer and spot her.

"Kate . . ."

Spinning around, she nearly jumped out of her skin at the sound of her whispered name. Seeing Kevin and Helene coming from Lydia's garden room at the rear of the house, she held her finger to her lips and motioned toward the drawing room. When she was sure of their silence, Kate's hand reached out for the brass knob and slowly opened the door a fraction of an inch, just enough to really hear what was going on.

465

"I'm telling you it's over," Martin said in an impassioned voice. "It's no use anymore."

"Have you lost your mind?" Lydia shrilly demanded. "Martin, think about what you're doing." She quickly looked to Michael, who still remained seated on the edge of the desk. "He's mad!" she exclaimed. "The stress of the last few weeks . . ."

"I'm as sane as you are," Masterson declared. "Probably more so, because I can see when it's useless to continue." He looked to Michael and a tight coil of apprehension gathered in his chest. He had never been drawn to acts of bravery. In his life, when the going got rough, he'd had his father to shield him. Then, later, his younger sister had delivered him from certain failure with the loss of their family's plantation. Now he had to face her and Barnett with his defection. But greed brings its own form of fearlessness and the mental picture of the treasure played across his mind until he could almost see it again . . . It was waiting upstairs for him, and with it he could make a new life. He would finally be a success, without anyone's help. All he had to do was tell the truth. And hope Michael could put aside his years of hate to fulfill his part of it.

Taking a deep breath, he stood in front of the desk and began. "For the last seven years, Lydia, Winston Barnett and I have been defrauding the governments of three countries: England, the United States, and France . . . four, if you count the Confederacy."

"You are insane!" Barnett took a few menacing steps in Masterson's direction, but Michael stepped in front of Martin and blocked him, while pulling out his gun.

"You can't believe him?" Lydia pleaded. "He doesn't know what he's saying!"

466

"I intend to hear the rest," Michael said coldly. "Martin?"

Clearing his throat, Masterson continued. "It started right after the war began. All those supplies and munitions—"

"Shut the hell up!" Barnett yelled, then pointed an accusing finger at Lydia. "I blame you for this! You said he could handle any pressure. *This* is how he handles it?" His eyes mirrored pure rage and his voice was filled with disgust as he added, "I should have known nothing but disaster would come from listening to a woman."

Watching Lydia slump down onto one of the matching white chairs, Martin tightened his hold on his cane until his arthritic fingers ached. "You knew this was coming, Winston. You're the one who told us about the inquiries Great Britain was making at least six months ago. Now I hear Washington's sent investigators down here. We're like a house of cards, waiting to crash . . . But I also know the two of you, and I don't intend to be the one it falls on."

Michael kept glancing toward his mother. She was staring at a huge portrait over the fireplace. "What I want to know is why," he stated in a hoarse voice. "I want to know why you did this to my father. He loved you!"

She let her vision slowly drift to Michael. Her face was pale, making her eyes seem large and luminous. They also held a look of mockery. "Is that what you think?" she asked, her voice sounding like a challenge.

Forgetting the others, Michael tried to control his own emotions. He had never felt so angry in his life. "He adored you! You had the perfect marriage . . .

467

everyone always said so."

Lydia's sudden caustic laughter interrupted anything further he might say. "Everyone saw what I wanted them to see. Joseph Sheridan was a hypocrite. All his talk of honor and integrity. He lost that thirty-one years ago. Nothing he could do would make up for that."

Michael started sweating. Shifting his eyes to make sure Barnett hadn't moved, he looked back at his mother and harshly asked, "What are you talking about?"

Lydia seemed to focus her eyes as she continued to stare at him. "He actually talked to me once about making you head of Sheridan Shipping. Can you imagine that? He sounded so proud when he talked about your ability to run the company. I wanted to know about Kevin, his firstborn, and he said you were better suited. *You!* I couldn't let him do that. Not to Kevin."

"What did he do thirty-one years ago?" Michael demanded, feeling the sweat run down his back. God Almighty, he could barely keep the gun in his hand for the perspiration.

Lydia looked at him with an odd mixture of pity and scorn. "Poor Michael!" she taunted. "You were always looking for love and acceptance and now you think you've found it with that cheap impostor upstairs . . ."

"What did my father do thirty-one years ago?" He had to make her say it, although his mind was already denying the possibility. She looked him straight in the eye and he swore it was hatred that he saw reflected there.

"He brought you into my home," she spat out.

"His bastard!"

Michael reeled back as if physically struck by her words. "You . . . You're lying! He didn't . . ."

She glanced at the gun and saw he had let it drop to the desk. Not fearing harm, she gathered strength and released decades of held-in resentment. "How I hated the role he forced me to play! *My* son, my Kevin, was little more than a year old when he brought you into our lives. How he deceived me, my perfect husband! He actually made me go to Cuba and pretend I'd delivered you myself. And you wonder why I've hated you all these years, why I couldn't look at you without revulsion? You have been the thorn in my side for thirty-one long years . . . Why didn't you die this afternoon?" she rasped out, a sneer disfiguring her mouth.

"Lydia! You hired that gun?" Masterson felt older than his advanced years, for he realized he didn't know his sister at all. Although he had tried to have Michael killed, he never would have believed Lydia capable of such an act.

She glanced to her brother. "Why don't you ask Martin for the truth about your birth? He'll tell you."

Michael tried to swallow down the bile that threatened to choke him. Turning his head, he saw Masterson look away, unable to meet his eyes.

Lydia laughed derisively at her brother. "Don't even have the courage for that, do you?" She looked back at Michael and smiled. "Then ask Denny Moran. He was witness to all of it . . ."

She stopped speaking and her eyes filled with horror when she saw Kate, Helene, and Kevin standing at the open doorway.

469

Kevin Sheridan stared at the stranger, the woman who had claimed him for her son. His eyes were locked with hers as he slowly entered the room. He felt hollow, as though everything he had loved, had believed in, had been taken from him. Only a few feet into the room, and he stopped—not wanting to go closer. "You . . ." His voice was accusing. "You've done all this . . . !"

Lydia's face crumbled and she held out her hand to him. "It was for you, Kevin. Anything I've done was for you!"

"It was for yourself!" he spat out. "I heard everything. *Everything!* My God, I don't even know who you are."

"I'm your mother," Lydia cried. "Please," she begged. "Please, Kevin . . . I only wanted to protect you."

"How? By lying to us? By manipulating our lives to suit your grand scheme? You're a traitor . . . and you let our father die alone in that prison!" His voice was filled with disgust. "I can never forgive that. *Never!*"

Lydia's face was covered with tears and she clutched at her skirt. "You're my son! I'd have done anything for you. Michael was . . ."

"Michael was the innocent!" Kate practically growled as she walked past Kevin and stood in front of the near-hysterical woman. "How could you have done that to a child? What kind of person are you?" So great was her anger, Kate had to hold her hands together to keep from hitting her. "You made the child pay for the mistake of the father. All those years, a lifetime, without love . . ."

"Kate!" From behind her she heard Michael's hoarse command to stop.

Winston Barnett took a deep breath and cleared his

470

throat. "Why don't we just put these skeletons back into the closet. Every family has them. What needs to be discussed here is what all of you intend to do with the information you've just heard." He looked at Michael and sneered. "You have no proof, only the ramblings of an old man."

Thinking once more of the treasure, Martin attempted to straighten his shoulders and stand taller. "I have proof, Winston. I kept records of all our transactions."

"You *what?*" Barnett's complexion became flushed with anger.

"I kept records," Martin repeated, glad now that it was out, for it meant this meeting was almost over. "I'm giving them to Michael and he can do—"

"You fool!" Without warning, Barnett lunged for Martin and flung him against the fireplace.

All watched in disbelief as Martin's head connected with the mantelpiece and produced a sickening crack. The ever-present cane dropped from his fingers and, slowly, as if drunk, he sunk to the carpet.

No more than seconds could have passed as they watched the bizarre scene unfold. No one immediately moved; they were frozen with shock. Suddenly, Michael came alive and rushed to Masterson's side. Everyone held their breath as they watched him check for a pulse.

"He's dead."

Winston Barnett shook his head and frantically looked about the room as Helene and Lydia cried out. Spying Michael's gun, he quickly raced to the desk and picked it up.

Holding the pistol on them, he demanded, "Get over here, Helene! We're leaving."

Kevin pushed the young, frightened girl behind him. "You're not taking her," he stated in a strong voice.

"Helene!"

Trying to shut out her father's command, Helene grabbed ahold of the material of Kevin's jacket and placed her forehead against his back. Her body was shaking with fear.

Kate was too stunned to move. She watched Barnett's eyes scan the room, as if his mind were spinning with possible escape routes. Abruptly, without any warning, he reached out and, grabbing her arm, pulled her to him. A tiny scream escaped her throat as she found herself in front of Barnett with Michael's gun pushed against the side of her breast.

"Anyone tries to stop me and I'll kill her," he threatened while pulling Kate back toward the door.

She could hear her heart hammering away in her ears, and her breath came in short gasps as she stumbled against Barnett. Tightening his hold on her waist, she nearly fainted with fear. All she could do was stare into Michael's horror-filled eyes.

She watched as he slowly rose to his feet. "Let her go, Barnett," he said calmly. "You don't want her."

Kate could feel Barnett's breath against her cheek as his lungs heaved for air. She could actually feel the fear coming from him, and it matched her own. She didn't know how much longer her legs would support her.

"And who do I want, Sheridan? You?"

Michael nodded as he took a step closer to them. "That's right. I'm the one who started all this. If it wasn't for me, all your plans would've worked out. Take me, Barnett. She doesn't make a good shield; she looks about ready to faint as it is."

Kate stared into her husband's face. It had to be a

nightmare! Surely they couldn't be standing here like this! Could Martin really be dead? And why was Lydia moaning and rocking in the chair like a madwoman? These kinds of things didn't happen in real life! If only she'd wake up in the room upstairs and find out she'd fallen asleep while waiting for Michael . . . Or, maybe she'd wake up in Bermuda and find everything had been a dream. But not Michael. Michael couldn't be a dream . . . Suddenly, she felt an arm tighten about her waist, and she gasped for air.

"That's right," Barnett jeered. "You're the one who's to blame for all this."

"*I'm* the one," Michael agreed while slowly taking another step. "So why don't you let her go and . . ."

"Because you want her, right? She's the one, isn't she? She's the Kathleen who signed the wedding certificate. You two have been working together since Bermuda." Barnett laughed and again jerked back on Kate's waist. She moaned and her weight started to sag against him.

"Michael." Kate begged him with her eyes not to endanger himself like this. She could feel the wild, panic-filled tremors in Barnett's muscles. Michael was going to get himself killed if he didn't stop. "Please," she again whispered, "don't do this, Michael!"

As if she hadn't spoken, as though he hadn't heard, Michael abruptly dived forward, thrusting himself at her and Barnett. Her mouth opened in shock, yet before she could even utter a sound, Barnett released her—pushing her to the floor so he could have a clear shot at Michael.

Falling, Kate heard the sound, the sudden explosion of gunpowder.

It was deafening.

Chapter 30

Immediately, she heard Helene's screams and Kevin's shout of, "Oh my God!" Afraid, but desperate to know, Kate pushed herself off the rug and turned back. She saw the look of astonishment on Michael's face as Barnett dropped to his knees and pitched forward onto the white carpet.

Michael stared down at the blood soaking into the rug underneath Barnett. As if waking from a dream, he shook his head and lifted his face to the French doors leading to the terrace. A tall man stood there, his gun still trained on Barnett's unmoving form. Coming a few feet into the room, he lifted his head to Michael and touched the brim of his wide hat.

"Frank Adams sends his regards," the man said in a gruff voice. "Sorry about the warehouse today. I should have taken that gun out before he had a chance to get off a shot."

"Who are you?" Michael asked, still not comprehending what had happened.

The man looked about the room as if sizing up

everyone. Turning back to Michael, he holstered his gun and said, "Mike Hogan. I was sent down here to observe . . . and lend a hand if need be."

Swallowing revulsion, Kate walked around Barnett's body and ran the few feet to her husband. Feeling his arms quickly wrap around her, she clung to him as he buried his face in her hair.

Looking at the Sheridan brothers as they comforted the women, Hogan cleared his throat. "Look, I've got two bodies here and one hell of a mess to explain. Sheridan, you were down at your ship this afternoon. You getting ready to sail?"

Michael lifted his head and nodded. "We . . . we're going back to Bermuda." He looked at Kevin and breathed a sigh of relief when his brother nodded in agreement.

"Now would be a good time to start," Hogan suggested. "I've been ordered to clean up any problems. I'll take care of reporting this to the Federal authorities." He looked behind Kevin and Helene and said, "Randy, you can let them in now."

Everyone turned and saw a thin man standing in the foyer. Nodding, the man placed his gun back into a leather holster and walked toward the front door. They heard Hogan's partner ordering Denny and the crew upstairs to get any luggage. They could also detect the frightened weeping of the servants.

"Tell Wiley to come in here," Lydia said in a strange, almost girlish voice. "This rug's been here over a hundred years and we have to get the stains out right away." She smoothed her hair back and sighed. "So foolish to decorate in white. And so hard to keep clean . . ."

475

Michael looked at Kevin, then met Hogan's gaze. "What's going to happen to her?" he asked in a cold voice.

Shaking his head, Hogan shrugged. "It's not my decision. Nor yours. That'll be up to the authorities." He glanced over at the body by the fireplace. "I take it Masterson never gave you those records."

"How did you know he was supposed to do that?" Michael shook his head in amazement.

"When we're told to observe, we observe," Hogan stated matter-of-factly. "Don't worry. If they really exist, we'll find them. Now you'd better get going. Randy kept your men outside until we were sure it was safe. Anything you don't have packed we can send on to Bermuda, in care of Barnett Importing. You are taking his daughter back, aren't you?"

Michael nodded and tightened his arm around Kate. Extending his other hand, he said, "Thank Frank for me. I owe him for this. And thank you, I owe you my life."

Shaking his hand, Hogan inclined his head. "I knew what you were doing, trying to distract Barnett. I just didn't want to take any chances. You seem to have some pretty important friends in Washington. And I didn't want to answer to them if it had turned out differently."

Kate sniffled and tried to smile. "Thank you, Mr. Hogan," she said sincerely. "I'll never forget what you did tonight."

Looking embarrassed, Mike Hogan again shrugged. "I was doing my job, Mrs. Sheridan. That's all."

Michael steered Kate toward Kevin and Helene and stared at his brother. "You're coming?" he asked.

476

Kevin looked down at Helene as she whimpered against his chest. "I'm coming," Kevin stated and brought Helene through the doorway.

As they walked into the foyer, they noticed the confusion as the crew of the *Rebel* hurried past the bewildered house servants. Michael spotted Wiley sitting on the chair under the picture of a Sheridan ancestor and he looked down at Kate. "Will you be all right?" he asked gently. When she nodded, he added, "Try and hurry Helene. The carriage is waiting."

She knew now was not the time to question him and, feeling incapable of any intelligent speech, she merely nodded again. Kate watched as Michael walked over to the old servant and bent down beside him. Sensing everyone was holding back their reactions until they were safely on the ship, she tightened the muscles in her face to stop the gathering of tears and bit her bottom lip. As she brushed past a seaman, Kate turned quickly to Helene and accompanied her upstairs. Consolations would come later.

"Wiley, you want to come with us to Bermuda?" Michael asked softly. "You'd like it there."

The old man raised his head, and the creases of age seemed to have deepened since this morning. "I'm too tired to start again, Mickey. Been thinkin' about sittin' on B.D.'s front porch and rememberin' the old days." His eyes were questioning. "We had some good times, up at Haphazard, didn't we?"

Michael smiled and patted his shoulder. "We sure did, Wiley. You were a good friend—still are. Listen, why don't you stay there? I'll draw up a paper for you to take to . . ." Suddenly, he stopped speaking and realized he had no right to deed a property away.

Shaken by the discovery of his illegitimacy, he looked to Kevin.

As if understanding what his brother was going through, Kevin came up behind him and said, "You go write it up, Michael. We'll both sign it."

Needing to get away, Michael quickly nodded and turned to his father's study while hearing Kevin instructing Wiley to see the family lawyer in the morning and have everything recorded.

Ten minutes later, Denny helped Helene into the carriage and turned to Kate. "You forget somethin', Miss Kathleen?"

By the moonlight, Kate looked back at the house and watched as Michael walked up to his brother. Standing at the front door, Kevin stared into the foyer.

"Are you having second thoughts?" Michael asked thickly. It was taking every ounce of willpower he possessed to control himself until he reached the *Rebel*.

"I can't stay here," Kevin said in a disillusioned voice. "I don't know if I ever want to return." He turned to his brother and his eyes were glazed over with shock. "Were we really that blind, Michael, not to have seen what she was?"

Picturing Lydia, the hard knot in Michael's stomach tightened. He took a deep, steadying breath and put his arm around Kevin's shoulder and led him away from the house. As they passed through the garden and out the wrought iron gate, he said in a faroff voice, "I suppose she was right about one thing. People only see what they want to see. I guess we're all afraid of what we'll find if we look too close."

The last to step into the carriage, Michael didn't

bother looking back at the house where he had grown up. He didn't want to memorize it. He didn't even want to remember it. He desperately wanted to wipe it from his mind.

Kate helped Denny with the cabin arrangements. Denny gave up his quarters for Helene and he and Kevin would bunk in with the crew. Michael remained on deck, taking charge as he maneuvered the *Rebel* into the open sea.

"Drink it, Helene," Kate urged as she handed a glass of brandy to her. Helene's hands were still shaking and Kate brought her own up to help steady them. Watching as the young girl sipped the alcohol, then coughed at its strength, Kate sat down next to her on the narrow mattress.

"It might help you to sleep," she offered, handing Helene a towel to wipe her mouth.

The girl's eyes were tortured as she lifted her head. "I . . . I'll never be able to sleep," she muttered, her lips quivering with fright. "I keep seeing Martin falling and . . . and the look on my father's face when he was shot." On her own, she brought the brandy to her mouth and slowly sipped. "He looked so surprised before . . . before he fell over." She shuddered and moaned with horror.

Bringing her arm around Helene's shoulders, Kate gently pulled her closer. "Try not to think about it," she whispered.

"I can't think of anything else!" Helene cried. "I hated him," she admitted between sobs, "but I never wanted him dead. It's all my fault. If we didn't change places . . . If I'd gone with him when he called to me . . ."

"Stop it!" Kate quietly ordered. "You're not to blame for any of this. Your father brought about his own death. You're just in shock right now." She tightened her hold on the girl. "Drink the rest of the brandy," she gruffly ordered, afraid her own tears would soon return.

A half hour later, she gently eased Helene's head back onto the mattress. Between the brandy and the rolling of the ship, the girl had finally fallen into a fitful sleep. Kevin had appeared at the cabin door and she motioned for him to hand her a blanket. They both glanced back at the sleeping girl before leaving the cabin.

"She'll be all right," Kate said wearily as they stood outside the door. "She just needs time."

"And what of you, Kathleen? You look exhausted." Kevin tried to smile. "You, too, should get some rest."

Kate patted his arm. "I will," she promised. "But right now, I have to see Michael."

"Leave him alone, Kathleen. It's what he wants right now. He also needs time to sort out what he's heard tonight. I tried talking to him when we left the harbor."

Shaking her head, Kate brushed past her brother-in-law to get a shawl. As she left her cabin she saw Kevin still standing in the corridor. "Then I've got to try again. I won't let him handle that kind of pain alone."

Nodding, Kevin watched her fight the rolling of the ship as she headed up the companionway.

It was much colder on the open sea and Kate brought the shawl tighter around her shoulders. Using the moonlight, she picked her way over coiled ropes and equipment until she could approach Michael at the ship's helm. He looked so alone, gripping the huge wheel while staring ahead into the night. When he noticed her, his head seemed to snap up in defense.

"Go back below, Kate," he ordered, returning his gaze to the sea.

She stood next to him and held on to the housing of the wheel to keep her balance. "Come with me, Michael?" she asked. "Let someone else take over."

Not looking at her, he shook his head. "Get some rest, Kate. This is where I want to be right now."

She touched his arm and could feel his muscles tighten against her fingers. "I want you to come with me. We both need to rest . . . to talk."

"Don't you understand?" he asked in a hard voice. "I don't want to rest. And I especially don't want to talk!"

She pulled her hand back, not knowing how to break through to him, and her heart ached with the pain, the mental anguish, he must be experiencing.

"Go below, Kate," he whispered hoarsely while making an adjustment with the wheel.

Defeated, she stood on tiptoe to kiss his cold cheek. "I love you, Michael," she stated in a strong voice. "I'll wait up for you."

Although she could make out the clenching of his jaw, Kate didn't say anything as she left him. On the way back to her cabin, she met Denny and asked him to join her. When the two of them were alone, she poured them both a drink.

"He's going to need you now, Denny," she said while handing him the brandy.

Nodding, the old man accepted the cup from Kate

and sat down in one of the chairs by the table. "He won't talk to me about it. I tell you, Miss Kathleen, it's like he's lookin' right through me." He sipped the warming alcohol and met her gaze. "She finally told him, didn't she?"

Kate sat in the opposite chair. "Lydia? That she's not his real mother?"

Looking wearied, Denny again nodded.

"Yes, she did, Denny. She also told him that you've known about it."

He let his breath out sharply. "I was hopin' this day would never come. Michael's daddy, Joseph, was a good man, not what you're thinkin'. He had a real fondness for Christine."

Kate leaned her arms on the table and ran her fingers through her hair. "Denny, I'm not thinking anything right now, except how to help Michael. That was his mother? Christine?"

"Aye. Beautiful she was, with long hair like spun gold—"

Kate reached out and grasped Denny's arm. "You have to tell him! He's up there with a thousand questions running through his head. You're the only one with the answers . . . and he needs to hear them, Denny. He needs to know about his parents."

He stared into the cup, as if looking for an answer inside it. Suddenly, he brought it to his lips and drained the brandy. Letting out his breath, he rose to his feet. "I'll try," he promised. "I suppose I owe that to Joseph."

Denny looked up at the stars and took a deep breath. Michael hadn't spoken to him since he'd come up five

482

minutes ago. Knowing Kathleen was right, he broke the silence.

"Her name was Christine Layton."

Michael's head turned sharply, yet he didn't say a word. When he looked back ahead, Denny continued. "Your mother was beautiful, Michael. A real lady. She lived up there in New York City and Joseph had been sweet on her for years. Met her in a library, of all places, when we were in port. He was young then, maybe twenty-two when it all started. Every time we came to New York, she was waitin' for him. When his daddy arranged for the marriage to the Mastersons, it nearly broke his heart. Joseph took us clear to England, France, Spain . . . taking on cargo in one country, only to pick up more business in the next. He wanted to ship anywhere to get away from the responsibilities his daddy put on him."

Seeing Michael was listening, Denny took heart. Now, if he could only get the words right . . . say it the way Joseph would want his son to hear it. "He knew he couldn't run from his family forever and . . . well, he married Lydia and tried to be a good husband. Took more of an interest in settlin' down and runnin' the business, he did. Gave up the sea and ran everythin' in Charleston with his father. When Kevin came we all thought he would finally be happy, but Lydia put great store in that boy, right from the beginnin'. He was all she could see. I never asked your father about those details of his married life, and he never told me. I just know the next run we had to New York, your daddy decided to come. He saw Christine whenever he could. I didn't even know she was carryin' you, but I guess that's the reason Joseph kept schedulin' more and more

483

trips up there."

Denny stopped and tried to recollect his thoughts, wanting to get everything right. "Then one day right before we was ready to leave with the mornin' tide, he comes back to the ship lookin' like he went through hell. He was carryin' this bundle of blankets and followed by this skinny woman who was cryin'. He comes up to me and puts you in my arms and says, 'She's gone, Denny. It's my fault,' he says. 'I wasn't here for her.' I asked him what he was talkin' about, and he tells me Christine died from some fever after she gave birth. Then, lookin' like he's held together by spit and determination, he says to me and this woman who was wet-nursin' you, 'Take care of my son,' and he takes off for three days. Tried to drink away the pain, but he never did. He came back, lookin' worse than when he left, but he also had a plan. He said you were his son and he would claim you. He said if Lydia wouldn't go along, he would leave her before leavin' you."

Seeing Michael had trouble controlling the wheel, he patted his arm and took over.

Grabbing ahold of Denny's shoulder, Michael's face was filled with emotion when he demanded, "Why didn't he tell me? Why didn't any of you tell me! I had a right to know . . ."

Denny allowed Michael his anger. "I made a promise to your daddy. He said when the time was right, he'd tell you."

"When the time was right?! He died without telling me!"

"Don't you hate him, Michael," Denny said sternly. "Every time he looked at you I could see his eyes light up with pride. He loved you, boy. And not just 'cause you look like your mother. It was 'cause you were a son he could be proud of."

Taking deep, calming breaths, Michael looked up at the bright stars. His vision was blurred from the moisture at his eyes, and he tightened his eyelids to clear them. Raking his fingers through his hair, he again looked to the sky. He felt barren, everything familiar stripped away from him. Knowing he couldn't live with such emptiness, his voice was a raspy whisper when he slowly asked, "What did she look like, Denny? My . . . my mother. Christine . . . what did she look like?"

He sat on the edge of the bunk and stared at the wooden flooring. He looked exhausted, like a defeated man. Waking from an uneasy sleep, she saw him sitting there. Kate's heart went out to him and she sat up in bed, bringing her arm around his waist. She rested her head against his back and whispered, "Are you all right?"

He didn't answer her, just continued to stare at the floor. Wanting to reach him, she asked softly, "Did Denny talk to you?"

She felt his breath leave his lungs as he nodded. "I don't know who I am anymore, Kate," he said in a tortured voice.

"You're Michael Sheridan. My husband. That's who you are." She kissed his back. "And I love you."

"Am I? Am I a Sheridan? My parents weren't married."

"That doesn't make any difference," she protested. "Your father loved you and gave you that name."

"Don't you see? I have no claim to it . . . I have no claim to anything of his. Not his name, not his business, not even this ship!"

Hearing the pain in his voice, she sat up straighter. "Don't be ridiculous! Your father wanted you and he brought you to Charleston to be with him. Not many men would have done that. He wanted everyone to know you were his. It couldn't have been easy for him, yet he did it because he loved you. *You,* Michael. Because you were his son . . . and he loved you."

He turned to her and buried his face in her hair. Kate held him tightly and brought him fully onto the bed, trying to soothe the pain and fill the void. "I have nothing," he murmured. "Nothing to offer you anymore."

She brought his face away from her shoulder and searched his eyes. "Are you blind, Michael Sheridan! Haven't you known the only security I've wanted from you could be found in your love? I'm your family now, Michael . . . along with Kevin. Sheridans, all of us. We can all start over together. Just don't shut me out."

He looked into her aquamarine eyes and saw the love reflected there. Quickly, he brought his mouth over hers and kissed her with a fierce possessiveness. Here was his reality. With Kate he could negate the terrible discovery of his heritage. Michael erupted in a blaze of passion as he sought to claim her again as his. His mind wanted confirmation that she would not be taken away from him, and he strove to brand her with his love.

She accepted him with such tenderness that his throat felt raw with new emotion. Their lovemaking was frantic and wild with their need for each other.

Michael wanted to lose himself in the woman, to forget everything and concentrate on her softness, her scent, her incredible gift of giving.

He did lose himself in her, yet somewhere, as he slowly allowed reality to come back into his mind, he also realized he had renewed himself through her ... and through her love.

Feeling whole again, he pushed the hair back from her damp forehead and lightly kissed her mouth. "I do love you, Katie," he whispered against her lips. "You are my life."

At some point during the night, they were awakened by a shrill, anguished scream. Bolting out of bed, Michael handed Kate her robe as the two of them rushed to Helene's cabin. There they found Kevin soothing her. Holding Helene in his arms, he sat on the bed and rocked her back and forth. It was only when Kate and Michael appeared at the doorway that he looked away from the small woman who buried her face against his chest.

"She had a nightmare," he explained while gently stroking Helene's long hair. "You two go back to sleep. I'll ... I'll stay with her."

Something about his tone of voice told them that he would not leave her side, and Michael nodded before taking Kate's hand. They didn't speak as he led her back into their cabin and into their bed.

As he held her close under the covers, Kate snuggled against him and whispered, "Do you remember me talking about family earlier?"

Feeling him nod, she smiled in the dark and added, "Well, if I'm not mistaken, we're going to be expanding."

"You mean Helene?" he asked while running his hand up and down her arm. "You think they're that serious?"

Kate's grin widened. "What I think, Mr. Sheridan, is that I'm pregnant."

After a moment's silence, Michael's shout of happiness filled the cabin.

Chapter 31

They'd made the right decision in coming to Bermuda, Kate thought, as she made her way back from the beach. Helene's home was in the distance and she again experienced a sensation of déjà vu. Was it only two months ago that she'd made this same journey, only to find that by some incredible circumstance she'd been taken into the last century? She shook her head as she walked the street of crushed shells. Had she been singled out for this travel through time, she wondered while listening to the sounds of birds through the lush foliage. Or had others come before her?

Picking an exotic blossom from a bush, she brought the flower to her nose and inhaled while continuing to slowly make her way back to the stately white-bricked house. Two months ago she would have snickered at the thought of time travel. That someone or something, besides ourselves, had control of our lives was ludicrous. No wonder Michael refused to accept her explanations. But what of all those sightings of UFO's?

And why was the government always interested in them? And what of all that publicity some years back about the Bermuda Triangle? She remembered discussing it with friends and laughing at the gullibility of some people.

Well, here she was in Bermuda . . . and she had definitely been taken from her own time. But now, even the concept of time confused her. She remembered reading that most scientists agreed we hadn't used a fraction of our brain's capability. Was our conception of time that narrow, that different, from a more advanced race?

Alone on the road, she threw back her head and laughed at herself. She certainly had changed! Here she was contemplating the universe and higher life forms. Surely if it were possible that such a thing exists, any intelligent force would be eager to contact someone like Carl Sagan, rather than bothering with her!

Realizing that she would never find the answers, Kate smiled and continued up the narrow road until she was walking across the lawns of Edge Hill Manor. She noticed the burned stables that were in the process of being rebuilt. How much had happened since that day when she'd taken Helene's place at a marriage. She'd only wanted passage back to the States, but she'd found so much more . . . Quickening her steps, she hurried to the house.

Today Michael had promised that they would look for the gold chain. What a stroke of luck that Denny had kept her scuba gear, after trying to lift Helene's trunk. Wanting to know what had made it so heavy, he'd said he'd looked inside and saw her equipment.

Having no idea what it was, he told them that he'd thought Michael had put it in for safekeeping during the storm and he hadn't sent it along to Masterson.

As she entered the house, Kate was filled with contentment. Everything was going to work out after all. Helene's aunt Madeline had come to EdgeHill Manor and Kevin had decided to stay on and help them with organizing Barnett's affairs. Michael had said he would take her to New Jersey, or wherever she wanted, after they spent some time in Bermuda. Kate didn't think she wanted to go back to Jersey, for there was nothing there for her anymore. Besides, since Michael had brought the treasure with them, once they had the chain they could live anywhere they wanted. Maybe Europe . . . It would be nice to spend her pregnancy in Paris.

"Kate . . . is that you?"

Walking by the library, she peeked her head in and saw Michael and Kevin sorting through Barnett's papers. "I just got back," she announced with a smile. "I'm going to go upstairs and get ready for our little boatride." She winked at Michael.

Handing Kevin a folder, Michael stood up and crossed over to her. "I think we should discuss this further. Give me a few minutes and then I'll be up."

She made a face. "Michael, you haven't changed your mind again?"

Looking at the two of them, Kevin couldn't help smiling. "You look very pretty today, Kathleen. Did you enjoy your walk on the beach?"

Giving her husband a meaningful glance, she looked at his brother. "Thank you, Kevin. And yes, I did. The water is so beautiful here, so clear. And the beach is like pink powdered sugar under your feet."

"Then we can count on you staying for a little while longer? I know it would please Helene if you remained."

She looked at Michael. "I don't know what our plans are just yet. As of now we don't have anything definite."

"We'll probably stay for a few more weeks," Michael said while brushing particles of sand off her cheek. "Right now, I think you should go upstairs and rest. I'll finish here and then we'll talk about this afternoon."

She gave her husband a look of exasperation. "You're a nag, Michael," she said affectionately, and glanced at Kevin. "Who would have thought *I'd* be henpecked?"

Kevin chuckled. "He's attentive," he said in his brother's defense.

"He's impossible!" Kate retorted with a laugh. "Talk to him, will you, Kevin? Tell him I'm not the first woman to be having a baby."

Nodding, Kevin said, "I'll talk to him, but it won't do any good. We all want to watch over you, Kate."

She hurried to her brother-in-law and kissed his cheek. Seeing his pleased expression, she said softly, "Why don't all of us have a special dinner tonight and celebrate life? I know we've all been through a lot, but it's a time for new beginnings, don't you think?"

Looking up at Michael, Kevin inclined his head. "I think that's a wonderful idea. I'll talk to Helene and Madeline and we'll make all the arrangements."

Excited, Kate again placed a quick kiss on his cheek. "Terrific! I'll see you tonight then, Kevin." As she brushed past Michael, she lifted her chin and mouthed the words, "I'm going!"

"Oh, no you don't, Sheridan! You're not leaving me behind, just because I happen to be pregnant!"

Amused by her use of his last name, he said, "I see we're back to Sheridan. And what do I call you, now that it's your name, too? This can get very confusing."

Kate stood in front of him and crossed her arms. Defiantly raising her chin, she said, "You can call me the diver, because that's what I'll be doing!"

"Kate, I'm not going to let you put on that heavy equipment and go back down. Just put it out of your head."

Her mouth opened with outrage. "Now you listen to me, Michael Sheridan. You may be this child's father, but *I'm* carrying it, and I know what I'm capable of—or not!" She lifted her hand and jabbed a finger into his chest with each word. "Do you actually think I'd endanger this baby? Do you? I know how to work the scuba gear . . . and I'm going!"

From somewhere in the back of his brain he remembered talk of strange behavior in pregnant women. Wishing he'd paid better attention, he tried to reason with her. "You can teach me how to use it. It wouldn't take long."

She couldn't believe his naïveté. "Michael, you can't learn everything in one afternoon. What if there was an emergency? You wouldn't know what to do. I checked the tank and there's six, maybe seven minutes of air left. Enough for one dive . . . And I'm going to do it. With your help, or without."

He scowled at her and wondered what had happened to her sweet disposition. "I don't like it," he pronounced. "I don't like it one bit."

She smiled at his dark expression. "But you can see I'm right, can't you? One little dive, Michael. I promise, it can't hurt me."

"There's no hurry to get the chain, you know. We have the treasure. Why don't we wait a few more days and . . ."

"We're not waiting any longer. We've been here for a week and you keep putting it off."

Michael walked away and looked down to the polished wooden floor. The night they had arrived, Kate had insisted that they hide the treasure for safekeeping. After almost an hour of deliberations, he had come up with the idea of loosening a floorboard and depositing the jewels in the small space between the downstairs ceiling and this floor. Now, looking to where he had worked, he had to admit you couldn't tell the difference.

He raised his head and frowned at his wife. She was waiting for his answer. "You promise? One dive? If you don't get it the first time, we'll leave it until later?"

Kate ran across the room and threw herself against his chest. Wrapping her arms around his neck, she reached up and kissed him. "I promise! And after this I'll listen to every word you say . . . no arguments."

Michael looked to the ceiling and shook his head. "I'll believe that, madam, when it happens."

Although excited, Kate had to admire Michael's prowess with the small, open sailing vessel. Holding on

494

to the side of the skiff, she smiled with pleasure. How she loved him, she thought as they came into the cove. In a little over a week, he'd come to terms with his birth and she had Kevin to thank for that. The two brothers had taken many long walks, and each time, when they'd returned, Michael had seemed more content. It was only occasionally now that she could detect a faraway look in his eyes . . . and then she knew what he was thinking.

Wearing her wet suit, Kate took off her blouse and let the sun warm her shoulders and the wind lift her hair. She held her face up to the source of heat and closed her eyes, feeling almost as one with nature.

"I think we're there, Kate," Michael announced as he lowered the single sail. "What do you think? Does it look familiar?"

Opening her lids, she allowed her eyes to scan the light-blue water before nodding. "That coral reef looks the same, and so does the shoreline," she said while pointing to the deserted beach.

Carefully, she stood up in the fifteen-foot boat and unbuttoned her skirt. When Michael saw the material drop around her feet in a soft circle, he involuntarily moaned. His mermaid had returned, only without the breathing apparatus. Her black suit clung to her like a second skin, outlining every curve of her luscious body. Her dark hair was loose, hanging down her back, and in that moment, when she smiled at him, he could well believe she was a goddess, sent to him from the sea.

"I'll have to remember to wear this more often," Kate teased as she saw the look on his face.

Michael grinned as he pulled the canvas back to reveal her scuba equipment. "I don't think such attire is proper even in the bedroom."

As he helped her with her gear, she remarked, "Oh, Michael, you're such a prude. Why, this is modest, wait till we get back and I show you the bathing suit underneath it."

Handing her the mask, he watched as she put it on and left it atop her head. With an expertise that he admired, she fixed the black flippers onto her feet, then checked the mouth apparatus and let it hang onto her chest. Looking up at him, she offered a short, curved black tube. "If you want to watch from the surface, you can use this."

"What is it?" he asked, taking the thing in his hands.

"It's called a snorkel. As long as you keep the tip of it above water, you'll be able to breathe." She laughed at his confusion. "C'mon," she said while standing up. "Take off your boots and your shirt and come in with me. I'll show you how to use it in the water."

After several tries, Michael was confident. Removing the snorkel from his mouth, he said, "I think I've got it. It's amazing, Kate! I can see the reef, everything, while staying at the surface."

Holding on to the side of the boat, Kate laughed. "I told you," she pronounced, "that it would work." Her eyes widened. "Now it's my turn!"

As she brought the regulator to her mouth, Michael yelled, "Wait!" as if suddenly remembering something.

He held the snorkel in the same hand with which he held on to the boat. With his other, he reached under the water and tried to bring something out of his pants pocket. "I forgot," he muttered while struggling with the wet material at his hip. "Seeing you in full regalia again reminded me of this . . ."

From under the water that matched her eyes, he brought up a small chain. Hanging from it was the gold medallion that she'd discovered on her first dive.

"Denny found it with the gear. I was going to wait until I brought up the chain, but since you're going to do it, you might as well have it now. The completion of your mermaid costume," he said with a grin.

As he held it between them, the sun caught the gold and Kate had to blink several times at the glare. Treading water, she smiled and asked, "The legend's complete now, isn't it? We have the fortune and the desires of our hearts. I think Doña Marina would be happy."

Nodding, Michael stared at her. "You made one hell of a Messenger, Kate."

She laughed and grabbed the side of the boat to stay afloat. "How many times do I have to tell you? I'm not the Messenger . . . he's down there."

Suddenly her eyes widened. "Michael, let's put it back."

Spitting water out of his mouth, he raised his chin. "What? The treasure? You can't be serious!"

She shook her head and watched as they both rose and fell with the rolling of the small boat. "The medallion. We've taken everything from him . . . that man down there . . . and we've received so much. Let's give something back."

He stared at her for a few seconds before nodding. "Here," he said, offering the chain to her. "Give him back his medallion."

Kate grinned. "I love you, Michael," she affirmed while fixing her mask.

"I love you, too, Katie," he said quickly. "Now let's

get this over with and go home."

Putting the regulator in her mouth, she took the medallion, wrapped the chain around her wrist, and gave him the thumbs-up signal before submerging.

The only sound was her breathing and the flush of bubbles from her expelled breath. She had descended into a place of quiet beauty. Schools of brightly colored fish darted away from her path as she swam toward the reef.

Within minutes, she found him . . . just as she'd left him. Kate looked up to the surface, saw the bottom of the small boat, and waved her arm in a wide arc, to show Michael she was all right. She could see him return her signal before she turned her attention to the chain.

It surprised her that she didn't feel any distaste as she worked the encrusted metal away from the skeleton's rib cage. After all this time, she felt as if she knew him. Her mind pictured a dark, handsome Spaniard dressed in heavy robes and sporting a small beard . . . Doña Marina's messenger to Cortez. Within less than a minute, she had tugged the chain free. Amid the spray of sand that rose with it, Kate gathered the end links in her hand and prepared to surface.

Just then the glint of gold at her wrist drew her attention and she stopped to unwind the medallion's chain. Almost reverently, she laid the gold disk in the center of the rib cage and mentally expressed her gratitude. Whoever he'd been, he had finally completed his mission of love. Were it not for him, she and Michael would never have . . .

Suddenly, a sharp ringing in her ears began. It got louder and louder, making her drop the encrusted links and hold the sides of her head to stop the pain. She drew her head back and forth, as if she could shake the pain out. Looking up to Michael, she saw him gesturing to her, yet the image of him wasn't clear. In one moment she could see the small boat, and in the next it was gone from the water. Frightened, she looked back to the skeleton and saw the medallion sinking to the sand beneath it. Not knowing why, she reached down and grabbed the disk. Keeping her head back, she pushed off the reef and quickly swam to the clearing image of her husband. She had to reach him! It was happening again . . . just like before! Dear God, she begged, give me this time. Don't take him from me! Her mind screamed out his name. *Michael!*

When she reached the surface, Kate popped the regulator out of her mouth and gasped for fresh air as she frantically clung to Michael's shoulders.

"What happened?" he demanded, holding her close despite her equipment. "What went wrong down there? Were you in trouble?" He pulled her mask away from her face and slipped it to the top of her head.

Crying, Kate was desperate to pull him against her body. "It . . . it's happening again! Don't let me go! Promise me! Promise me, Michael!"

"I promise," he nearly yelled while trying to hold them both above water. "What's wrong with you?"

She kept her face against his shoulder. "It's the medallion," she sobbed out. "I . . . I put it back and . . . and you were gone."

He tried to comfort her. "I'm here, Kate. It's all right . . ." He stopped speaking and his whole body tensed as he looked beyond her. *"Kate . . . ?"*

Hearing the frightened call of her name, she raised her head to see his face. His mouth was open with shock and his eyes were wide with disbelief. Slowly, she turned her head to follow his vision.

No! It couldn't be . . . The shoreline changed like the appearance of a mirage. The deserted beach became dotted with people and the dense foliage disappeared to make way for huge hotels. As suddenly as it came, it started to fade away.

"What is it?" Michael whispered in shock.

Kate tightened her hold on her husband. "The future," she muttered in fear. "My God, Michael, what are we going to do?"

They clung to each other, trying to stay afloat. They were bound by the panic of indecision. Suddenly Michael said in a hoarse voice, "Throw it back."

She raised her head. "What are you saying? If I do I'll go back with it. I won't leave you, Michael!" She was almost choking with her tears.

"Throw it back, Kate," he said in a stronger voice. "If it happens, I'll be with you."

She shook her head. "I'm afraid. What if I lose you? How can you leave everything? What if it doesn't work?" Her fingers dug into his shoulder. "Michael, let's just get back in the boat? Please?"

"Give it to me," he said while taking the medallion from her clenched fingers. "I never believed you, Kate, but you're all I have now. There's nothing left for me in my time; maybe we can make a future in yours."

She screamed his name as he flung the medallion across the water. The sun caught the bright metal of gold once, before the disk slowly disappeared and returned to its home.

He kept his eyes focused on the astonishing sight as

500

his feet touched the sandy bottom. Gasping for breath, he let the waves roll over his back as he tried to stand. Not believing what was before his eyes, he quickly held out his hand as he walked through the surf.

She placed her fingers inside his and held tightly as they fought the undercurrent and emerged from the sea. Collapsing onto the beach, they tried to regain their breath amid the crowd of people that surrounded them.

"Are you two all right?" a male voice asked. "I didn't know whether to call a lifeguard!"

Panting, Kate slipped the tank off her back and tried to smile at the concerned stranger. "We're okay," she told him while gulping for air.

The excitement over, the crowd quickly went back to their towels and chairs.

Breathing deeply, she looked to Michael.

"We made it!" he gasped, pushing his hair back out of his eyes. "Can you believe this?"

Laughing, Kate reached for his hand and dropped back onto the sand. She closed her eyes and whispered a sincere, "Thank God."

Not caring that there were others on the beach, Michael leaned down next to her. "We're together, Kate. That's what matters."

She opened her eyes and gazed at his face. Seeing the happiness written there, she smiled and touched his lips. "I was so frightened that I would lose you."

He brushed the dark, wet tendrils of hair off her cheeks and kissed her fingers. "You'll never lose me. Not ever."

She sensed the excitement and wonder in him. Perhaps being an adventurer came easy, since he'd spent so many years on the sea. Taking a deep breath, she looked into his eyes and said, "It's not going to be easy, Michael. You left everything behind, everything that was familiar. It's a different world here. And what about Kevin?"

His eyes briefly closed over with pain. Swallowing, he said, "He'll always be a part of me. But Kevin's coming in to his own time now. And I guess . . . so am I."

He raised his head and looked across the beach to the tall buildings that reached into the sky. "What year is it?" he asked in a low voice.

"I think it's still 1987," she said, following his line of vision.

"Nineteen eighty-seven!" he repeated, laughing with amazement. "What wonders are in this century!"

Kate saw he was no longer looking at the hotels, but staring at the women in their scanty bikinis.

"They're practically naked!" he stated with shock.

She couldn't help herself. Giggling, she stood up and held out her hand. "Let's go, Sheridan," she said in a falsely stern voice. "I can see I'm going to have to begin your education quickly."

Grinning, Michael rose to his feet. "Well, they are!" he said defensively. "Can I help if it I've never seen so many nude women before?"

She bit her bottom lip to keep from laughing again. "They are not nude, just semi . . . And their attire is perfectly normal for the beach. Will you stop staring?" She picked up her face mask and said, "I'd better get you off this beach before we're thrown off. We're going to have enough trouble getting you back into the

502

States without drawing attention to ourselves now."

He rolled the legs of his pants up to his calves before standing. Picking up her tank, he threw an arm over her shoulder. "Why will I have trouble getting back into the United States? I'm a citizen," he stated while trying very hard not to notice the women. Yet, he couldn't help but stare at the wondrous sights around him.

"But can you prove it?" she asked as they walked through the sunbathers. Passing by the shelters for those who desired the shade, she added, "We're going to have to think about that one once we get back to the hotel. You don't even have a birth certificate."

"But I'm here. Why do I need a paper stating that I was born?"

Sighing, Kate let out her breath and raised her head. Seeing Michael's fascination with the hotels, she whispered, "You have a lot to learn, Michael Sheridan."

Staring at the tall, exotic dwellings, Michael asked curiously, "Which one of them is yours? I have never seen such extraordinary buildings!"

Kate shook her head. "You can't see it from here. I'm staying at EdgeHill Manor, a small . . ."

They both stopped walking and stared at each other.

"EdgeHill Manor?" Michael searched her face.

"It's . . . it's turned into a small hotel," she said in a strange voice. "Michael . . . ? Do you think the treasure . . . ?"

"Is still there?" he finished, excitement creeping back into his own voice. "There's only one way to find out. C'mon."

Their pace quickened until Kate pulled back and stopped dead in her tracks. Michael turned to her. "What? What's wrong?"

Slowly, she moved forward until she was standing next to him. "What if it's not there?" she asked, her eyes wide with the possibility. "We hid it over a hundred years ago!"

Michael dropped the air tank to the sand. Reaching for Kate's hand, he brought her to his chest and held her tightly. "Then we'll start over again, Mrs. Sheridan . . . just you, me, and our child. We're a family, right?"

Kate never expected to find such a love. All those years of not being able to trust, of fearing to give her heart to another. She knew now, looking at the deep love reflected in Michael's eyes that she'd just been waiting . . . waiting for him to come into her life.

"We're a family," she reaffirmed, sliding her arm around his waist. "The Sheridans."

He reached into his pants pocket and held out his hand. "And a Sheridan is resourceful." Opening his fingers, he revealed an emerald the size of an egg. "This should keep us in comfort," he pronounced with a grin.

Kate was stunned. "Where did you get it? I thought . . ."

"You gave it to me," he said softly. "It was part of our bargain. Remember?"

"But you didn't take it. You left it when you went to Washington."

"And I kept it when we moved out of the hotel and into the house." Very pleased with himself, he shrugged

504

his shoulders, "I was holding it, and the medallion, to give back to you as a wedding present. This was sort of my lucky charm, something of yours to keep close."

She smiled. "Maybe you're not going to have such a tough time adjusting here."

"Of course I'm not," he stated emphatically. "And if I don't find work immediately . . . well, there's always the chain. It's got to be worth a fortune—"

"Now, hold on there," she interrupted, seeing he was becoming too optimistic. He was like a young boy in his enthusiasm. "I don't think it's such a good idea to touch that chain. What if something happens . . ."

"I want you to teach me to use this thing, this scuba gear," he insisted, a look on his face that told her he wouldn't take no for an answer. He was determined to prove himself.

Catching her bottom lip between her teeth, she decided now was not the time to tell him his old-world ideas of male superiority were not going to work here. "All right," she said meekly. "I'll teach you."

Happy with her answer, he walked a few feet away, then turned back to her. "And I want a pair of those swimming pants! Did you see everyone looking at my longer ones?"

She threw back her head and laughed. "I think that can be arranged," she said between giggles. "Anything else?"

He reached out, caught her wrist, and crushed her to his chest. "I want you to promise you'll always love me, that you'll stay with me, Katie Sheridan. We can do this!"

She inhaled the clean scent of him mixed with the sea

and stared into his eyes. Brushing his golden hair back from his forehead, she whispered, "I traveled too far to find you, Michael Sheridan, to ever let you go. Don't worry, as long as we're together we can beat anything . . . even time."

And they did . . . as a family.

They were the Sheridans.

Epilogue

A single man, dressed in a white linen suit and Panama hat, sat under the thatched roof that sheltered him from the sun. He watched with interest as the couple made their way up the beach, oblivious to his presence.

Smiling, Frank Adams sipped his piña colada and flicked an ash from his cigar onto the sand beneath his chair. He'd probably have to be purged, he thought with a grimace, when he returned to his own time. Holding the cigar up to admire, he grinned and muttered aloud, "But there's certainly something to be said for the old vices."

Blowing a long line of smoke toward the ocean, he sat back and relaxed. The cycle was complete and everything was in place, he thought with satisfaction. Though his methods were sure to be questioned. He'd already gone over in his head the report he'd have to make. The biggest problem he could foresee was explaining why he'd brought the couples to this time out of sequence. His reasoning was simple: Kate and

Michael were the only ones to have a choice and they would be the most difficult. So he'd saved them for last.

Waiting for his replacement, Frank Adams thought of the children ... the reason for this important mission. They would all be great leaders. Brianne Barrington from Louisiana, child of two worlds. Daniel Trahern, infant son of Jenna and Morgan. Thomas Sheridan, yet to be born to Kate and Michael. It was Thomas who would give his replacement the most trouble, for the legendary warrior would have his mother's spirit of adventure and his father's rebellious nature. They were all destined for greatness, and revered in his own time.

The Guardian found it strange to admit that he would miss this period of history. He would especially miss the friends he had made—Ryan Barrington, Morgan Trahern, and Michael Sheridan. He had been sent back here, so very long ago, expecting to find barbarians in the nineteenth and twentieth centuries. What he had found was that humankind was no different, save for technologies, from his own time. Perhaps that was why the race had survived, because bred into each of us was the innate hope for a better future. And it belonged to the children ...

Filled with a sense of accomplishment, Frank Adams smiled and turned around for one final glimpse of the couple. Witnessing the love between Michael and Kate as they left the beach, his throat burned with a raw emotion.

It was time to go home ...

Author's Note

Timeless Passion, my first novel, was written for myself. It came as a complete surprise that a publisher would be interested in publishing it. What came as an even bigger surprise was that I was asked to write two more . . . the thought had never occurred to me. In each of the three time travels, I have acknowledged my editor for her contributions. Now, at the completion of my third book, that doesn't seem adequate.

For her foresight, for her belief in an unknown writer, and especially for her friendship, I dedicate this series of time travels to Hilari Cohen.

Taylor—made Romance From Zebra Books

WHISPERED KISSES   (2912, $4.95/5.95)
Beautiful Texas heiress Laura Leigh Webster never imagined that her biggest worry on her African safari would be the handsome Jace Elliot, her tour guide. Laura's guardian, Lord Chadwick Hamilton, warns her of Jace's dangerous past; she simply cannot resist the lure of his strong arms and the passion of his *Whispered Kisses*.

KISS OF THE NIGHT WIND   (2699, $4.50/$5.50)
Carrie Sue Strover thought she was leaving trouble behind her when she deserted her brother's outlaw gang to live her life as schoolmarm Carolyn Starns. On her journey, her stagecoach was attacked and she was rescued by handsome T.J. Rogue. T.J. plots to have Carrie lead him to her brother's cohorts who murdered his family. T.J., however, soon succumbs to the beautiful runaway's charms and loving caresses.

FORTUNE'S FLAMES   (2944, $4.50/$5.50)
Impatient to begin her journey back home to New Orleans, beautiful Maren James was furious when Captain Hawk delayed the voyage by searching for stowaways. Impatience gave way to uncontrollable desire once the handsome captain searched *her* cabin. He was looking for illegal passengers; what he found was wild passion with a woman he knew was unlike all those he had known before!

PASSIONS WILD AND FREE   (3017, $4.50/$5.50)
After seeing her family and home destroyed by the cruel and hateful Epson gang, Randee Hollis swore revenge. She knew she found the perfect man to help her—gunslinger Marsh Logan. Not only strong and brave, Marsh had the ebony hair and light blue eyes to make Randee forget her hate and seek the love and passion that only he could give her.

Available wherever paperbacks are sold, or order direct from the Publisher. Send cover price plus 50¢ per copy for mailing and handling to Zebra Books, Dept. 3304, 475 Park Avenue South, New York, N.Y. 10016. Residents of New York, New Jersey and Pennsylvania must include sales tax. DO NOT SEND CASH.